LOADED BLESSINGS

A Novel

FAITH QUINTERO

This is a work of fiction. Names, characters, businesses, places, events and incidents are either fictitious or used in a fictitious manner.

Loaded Blessings
Written by Faith Quintero
Published by Chaiwright, LLC – Marblehead, MA

Cover Design and Formatting: *the*BookDesigners
Image in back of book, page 341: by Sophia Smith

Printed in the United States of America

First Printing 2019

Paperback ISBN: 978-0-9980289-1-0
eBook ISBN: 978-0-9980289-0-3

Library of Congress Control Number: 2019901618

chai⌐wright

Chaiwright, LLC
info@chaiwright.com

Dedicated to all who advocate for democracy...
the quintessential loaded blessing.

Heading East

This time, I will outwit jet lag. Eleven-hour flight. Sleep for six. Touchdown at 5:00. I'm on it. But first, I need to unload my carry-on into this already full overhead compartment.

"Let me do that for you." A middle-aged man adjusts the luggage so mine can fit in as well.

"Thank you."

"You are welcome." He moves into my row. "Is this your first time going to Israel?"

I don't want to be stuck next to a chatty passenger. "No. And I can tell this isn't your first time, either."

"My English is not good?"

"That's not what I said. You have a lovely accent. I can just hear that English isn't your first language." *And that Hebrew is, and that you are a bit overly sensitive.*

Or perhaps *I'm* being overly sensitive. I'm exhausted. I've been in high gear the entire week to make sure that my husband and children will be all set during my month-long absence. My thirty-eight-year-old bones aren't designed for such efficiency. I don't intend to let anyone, however helpful, interfere with my perfectly calculated siesta. I cut him off as he begins to speak. "Again, thank you for your help in the aisle. I'm grateful for what you did. But look, I've calculated the precise time I need to fall asleep so I won't be jet-lagged. That time is about now."

"I see." He then unwinds the headset that comes with the seat and sticks the earbuds into his ears. He stares straight ahead at the instructional channel that's the only viewing option prior to liftoff. No one needs a headset to hear the instructions being broadcast through the loud intercom system. Point taken.

With that awkwardness out of the way, I hunker down in my cozy seat—and I do mean cozy, because with very little energy left, even the cramped accommodation of economy feels comfortable. I close my eyes as soon as the attendant finishes his safety spiel and revel in the bliss of hypnagogia, that pre-sleep state where I control my dreams.

I'm below the sea. The rumble of the jet engine is the sound of the current pushing against my ears. *I spy the medieval wreck and dive deeper to get a closer look at an irregularity in an otherwise uniformly decaying piece of wood. I carefully remove the object nestled between the ship's broken planks. I don't need to clean it to know exactly how it'll look and how it'll feel.* My eyes have already examined its every curve, and my fingers have already traced its every line.

A Lie Encoded Into Law

"We forbid any Jew to dare to leave his house or his quarter on Good Friday ... and if they violate this regulation, we decree that they shall not be entitled to reparation for any injury or dishonor inflicted on them by Christians."

—EXCERPT FROM THE *Siete Partidas of Alfonso X of Castile*

— 1478 —

Sancia inhales the citrus air as she strolls past the blossom-covered trees speckled with little oranges. She recalls the thrill when she became strong enough to climb up and grab a small fruit from the lowest branch. Her mother and father didn't stop her from peeling her prize. They laughed in delight as she puckered her lips from the startling taste of its bitter flesh. At nine years of age, Sancia now knows better. Those fruits are not to be eaten. Yet she cannot resist their fragrance.

She moves her long, golden-brown hair to the side. The hem of her undyed cotton dress is much higher now than it was when she folded it away at the end of fall. Her father made it over a year ago. No wonder it felt tighter after she pulled it over her shoulders. It's a little snugger than she'd like it to be, yet, a shorter dress is more practical. She looks at the tree. Then she looks over her shoulder and confirms that the others are far enough behind so that she won't interfere with anyone else's pace. She walks up to the tree and stretches to reach the lowest branch. She steadies an orange with one hand, taking care so that it remains attached to its stem. She uses her other hand to scratch off a barely noticeable layer of peel. She rolls it between her fingertips, and then she brings it to her nose and inhales pleasurably. She then pulls her hand away to look at the sticky residue on her fingers. She separates her fingers, just to seal them again. Fingers apart, together, apart, together.

"This is not a good time to pause," her father, Isaac, shouts impatiently. "It's almost the Sabbath."

He is far enough away that his gray strands are invisible, hidden by his otherwise dark-brown hair and a yarmulke. *Of course it is a good time to pause, Papa. We are ahead of everyone else. Why have you suddenly become so serious?* She has recently noticed how his disposition has aged beyond his three decades. Beyond his youthful and lanky appearance, his dark-brown eyes betray an aged sadness that he seems to try to hide. *Maybe he is working too much. He needs to have some fun.* She yells back. "Papa, we are many steps ahead of Rabbi Sol. We will get to the synagogue before he does." Then she looks past her father and past the rabbi to the small group of women from the Judería. They're strolling casually. She hopes that when she becomes an adult, she'll look as beautiful as her thirty-year-old mother walking among them. She has the same light-brown eyes and the same elegant poise. Sancia's hair is slightly lighter from the hours she spends outside with her cousins. *Papa is the only one in a hurry this evening.* She is glad everyone is walking slowly. Maybe her cousins will catch up with them. Her uncle's family is always late. *They probably haven't left their home yet.*

Sancia gestures to her father to join her by the tree. He shakes his head and motions for her to return to him on the path. She looks at Rabbi Sol, who averts his wise, watery, gray eyes from his discussion with their neighbor Jacinto, to nod his approval to her with a smile—a smile that is difficult to see between the hair on his lip and chin, but she sees it, and it fills her with warmth.

She smiles back, appreciating how she can always count on the elders in her life to balance each other.

She rejoins her father and turns her gaze to the sky. The sun is moments from setting. The moon is almost as full as it was a couple evenings ago on the first night of Passover. "Oh, Papa, the evening is so beautiful. Everyone else seems to be enjoying it. We do not need to hurry."

"You are right, my little one." Isaac accepts the gentle touch from his daughter's sticky hand. Then he asks, "But why are they hurrying?"

Feeling tension in his grip and detecting alarm in his

voice, Sancia quickly looks up. Before her eyes have a chance to adjust, two men pass by, nearly knocking her over. She and her father stop and turn. Sancia doesn't know why her stomach tightens into a knot but senses something is terribly wrong.

The men block the path of the rabbi and Jacinto, preventing them from passing. One man extends his arm in front of them. "Did you make this for your blood sacrifice of our children?"

Sancia strains to see what he is holding. It's an upright stick the length of his arm, with another stick, about half its size, lying flat near the top. She doesn't understand the meaning behind the accusation but is frightened by his tone. She looks up at her father.

"Shh!" He preempts.

Papa is afraid. Everyone is afraid.

Rabbi Sol quivers despite what seems to be his best effort to remain calm. "I am not looking for any children. I did not make—"

The man, less than twice her age and more than twice her size, refuses to allow the rabbi to finish his sentence. "You are a Jew!"

"Yes. I am a Jew. But what you say about children and blood is nonsense. We are prohibited from making any human sacrifices. As are you. That is the lesson from our prophet Abraham, as it is in your First Testament."

"You deny making this?" The man shakes the curiously arranged sticks. Sancia notices a sort of human-looking figure made from wax and twine in the center. She doesn't believe the rabbi could have made it. She knows he didn't.

The whole community has been busy all week preparing for Passover.

The rabbi swats the sticks away. "You just carried that here. I did not make—"

The other man slams his heel down on the rabbi's foot. "You did make it! Do not lie! You shall torment our children no longer!"

Sancia is terrified. She has never before seen a person bring such pain to another. Her stomach tightens as she strains to listen, in disbelief, to the accusation. But the man holding the sticks speaks so that everyone can hear him. "You made this crucifix! And, I know why you made it."

Crucifix? The craft has a name? What is its meaning?

His voice gets louder. "Year after year you hunt our children to drain their blood to bake into your ceremonial bread. The blood of a Christian is the main ingredient. We all know it. And today is Good Friday. Today is the day you perform your ritual. On our holy day. On the anniversary of when you killed our Lord. You tied this doll onto the cross, perhaps because you could not find a living and breathing child to steal. That does not make you less guilty."

Sancia is outraged. Rabbi Sol would never hurt anyone. He is as gentle as Papa. No one in their neighborhood would. And how could a person kill a Lord? That doesn't even make sense.

As the rabbi stands with his weight off his injured foot, the man grabs his arm, pries open his fingers, and then squeezes his hand around the crucifix. Rabbi Sol grimaces in pain.

Stop touching him! What can she do? She knows she is no match for the two men. She looks around at the others, wondering why no one is doing anything to stop them.

The man refuses to loosen his grip around the rabbi's hand. "I found your crucifix in the forest. That is where you go at night to kill our children."

The rabbi tries to free his hand. "Please let go of me. I have never even thought about doing such a—"

"You disgust me! My mother and father warned me when I would misbehave that the Jews would come and get me next. I will make sure that no other child will grow up being afraid of you people, for you shall be no more." He then punches the rabbi in the stomach.

Sancia can take this no more. She lunges forward. "Leave him alone!"

Her father quickly pulls her close and wraps his arms around her, as if to stop her from doing what she just did.

The man looks at her, as if noticing her for the first time. And beaming with fierce hatred, he holds her gaze as he removes the crucifix from the rabbi's injured hand. He pushes him down and then lifts the pointed object over his body.

Jacinto, who is about ten years older than her father, and ten years younger than the rabbi, pushes the man. But he becomes overpowered by the other one. Once the man with the crucifix regains his balance, he holds it up high over his head as he stands astride the rabbi on the ground. He looks straight ahead to make sure he has an audience in the young girl.

Sancia can do nothing but watch as he plunges the

crucifix into her beloved rabbi's chest. She becomes para-lyzed, unable to scream.

The man doesn't even look at the result of his attack before he takes a step toward her. He shouts an order to his companion. "Almerique, bring the crucifix here. We have more justice to serve."

The irony of his words fills her with rage.

Almerique shakes his head. "No, Sebastian. I am not going near that dead rabbi. I might have some form of curse put upon me if I do."

Dead. The word echoes through Sancia's ears. *Can it be?* She concentrates on his chest, hoping to get a glimpse of it rising. Nothing. Just stillness. And blood. She just stares at him. She does not notice the murderer push her father until it's too late.

Isaac yells, "Sancia, run!"

Sebastian is too quick. He grabs her arm. She wants to break free but is forced to rise awkwardly on her toes and move with him just to keep her arm from being torn from her shoulder.

"Sebastian, let go of her!"

Did she just imagine the protective order from the familiar voice?

"Baltasar." Her father's whisper confirms who she suspected.

Baltasar walks into Sancia's view. "Sebastian, let go of that child, or you will soon feel the sharp end of my latest commission."

Sancia spies the decorative handle of the sword secured

to his belt. She knows Baltasar doesn't need a weapon to command respect. His muscular body, toned from the hard work he does in his shop, emphasizes his lingering youth despite his graying hair and wrinkled skin. He is respected and beloved in her community as well as his own.

Sebastian maintains his painful grip on Sancia. "She is not a child. She is a Jew! She will one day make more Jews if we do not get rid of her."

Baltasar somberly looks toward the lifeless rabbi on the ground. "Sol." He then turns to Sebastian and Almerique. "Return to your homes now! I shall talk to your fathers about this. I will make sure they know what you have done, and I will see to it that you are both punished."

"I am going to talk to my father about what *you* are doing, Baltasar." Sebastian switches the hand he has been using to keep hold of Sancia. Then he shakes with relief the hand that previously clung to the grip. "You are interfering. I will not get punished by my father or by anyone. These Jews are out walking today, on Good Friday. This is our holy day! It is *they* who broke the law, not me. It is 1478 in the year of our Lord, and we still have to worry about these menaces roaming our land. It is you, Baltasar, who is making our community less safe."

"You think you made this community safe? You killed a peaceful man. And the girl, she is a danger to you? You are a stupid boy. You are both stupid boys. You disgust me. Go!"

They are not boys. They are murderers!

Sebastian pushes Sancia to the ground. "No bread for you this year." He then spits on her and walks away.

Bread? Matzah. That must be what he is talking about. There is no blood in matzah. They are prohibited from eating blood. Just days ago, her family and her uncle's family went to Jacinto and Bonafilia's house to bake matzah for the neighbors. Sancia helped. It's a favorite yearly tradition filled with joy and laughter and bakers with flour all over their faces. And every year they mix and flatten the dough. And every year they use just two ingredients: flour and water. *Those murderers killed the rabbi over a lie.*

She wants to thank Baltasar but is overtaken by her grief and her search for truth. "Why did those horrible men say such things, Baltasar? Why did they say I am not a child? Why do they think we use blood to bake, when we never do? If it is not legal to kill people, why will Sebastian not get punished for killing Rabbi Sol? I heard him say he would not get punished, but that *we* were breaking the law."

Baltasar kneels and wraps his arms around the only child of his dear friend, Isaac. "I cannot give you the answers to your questions right now, little one."

She hugs him back and notices her father place his hand on Baltasar's shoulder.

He whispers, "Thank you."

Did Papa just thank Baltasar for saving us, or for not answering my questions? Sancia looks to the crowd of neighbors surrounding the body of the rabbi. She then looks down the path to see the two murderers walking away, carefree specks under the moonlight.

SOMEWHERE
OVER THE ATLANTIC

———————◆◆◆◆◆———————

*Y*ou *might want to hold off on your sleep. Dinner carts are coming.*

Snatched from REM! Or have I been? I keep my eyes closed as I beam myself back to dreamland.

"Or maybe they are breakfast carts, or lunch carts. Who can tell when we enter such a time-warp machine as an airplane - taking us through time zone, after time zone, after time zone?"

I wish he'd stop.

He taps my wrist. "What did you take to sleep so soundly, so quickly?"

I finally got to sleep after a whirlwind week and now this guy is going to make it so that I suffer every moment on this flight. *I should have stowed away my suitcase myself.* I manage an unfriendly look in his direction, move my arm to my lap from our shared armrest, and face forward again. I close my eyes and touch my locket. It's there and closed.

Undeterred by my less-than-friendly body language, the passenger I was grateful to when boarding, is now, officially, the most annoying person on Earth. Well, above Earth. "I'm just wondering what it is that you took, because If you have any more of those magic sleeping pills, I could use one after we eat."

I take a closer look at the man attempting conversation. He is gorgeous—well, for an old guy. He compensates in looks for what he lacks in social etiquette. Shabby-chic clothing resting perfectly on a fit physique. A confident, warm smile. Mesmerizing brown-bronze eyes framed by thick, pretty lashes. Really. Pretty eyelashes. Topped off by exceptionally manicured dark-brown hair with strands fashionably out of place. He has the looks of an actor. He probably is an actor. Yes! That would make sense. He has been planted in this seat next to me by one of those television shows that pranks unsuspecting people.

I look around for a hidden camera. But all I see are tiny reading lights and attendant call buttons. I'm not going to be the butt of a joke on a prank show, but just an exhausted traveler.

I can't move away—the flight is full. All I can do is entertain myself by giving a little grief back to him. "I didn't take a sleeping pill. I avoid taking drugs unless I have to. Like, for motion sickness . . . Oh crap! My Meclizine!" I reach into my bag and pull out a small blister pack of anti-nausea pills. The truth is I intended to take them closer to when we touch down. That's when I typically get sick. My uninvited conversationalist doesn't need to know that. "And these pills work beautifully—well, when I remember to take them. I hope I don't get sick while flying today, or tonight, or whatever it is in this time warp."

He is quiet. I didn't know that was possible. I'm not stopping now. I'm on a roll. And I'm wide awake. I feign panic and hastily search the seat pocket in front of me. I find the airsickness bag and ease it up enough to be visible to him. "Thank goodness I have one. Sometimes these beauties get used without being replaced." This is fun. "Do you have an extra one in your seat pocket? I might need it if this one gets full." I then nod in the direction of the flight attendants a few rows away as they push the dinner cart toward us. "Excellent. I'm starving." I lower the tray table to welcome the meal.

"Are you trying to—how do you Americans say it? — fuck with me?" His smile turns smug. "Well, you can't."

I brace myself. He is going to slam me with defeat. I can feel it.

"I suffer from anosmia."

Boy, did I overestimate that blow. Unimpressed, I simply moan. "Seems I suffer from insomnia too."

"I do not suffer from insomnia. I was only joking when I said I might want the pill that put you to sleep. I have *anosmia*." He slowly enunciates the unfamiliar word. "Most people have never heard of it. It means that I do not have an ability to detect smells. While some people have difficulty seeing or hearing, I have difficulty smelling. It's a sensory disorder."

"You don't have to tell me you have a disorder — I can see you're full of them." Rude, I know, but I put so much effort into getting this guy back for waking me up, I need to hold on to a crumb of victory. But guilt takes the reins and forces me to quickly mellow. "Actually, I have never heard of anosmia before. What a curious thing."

He takes a deep breath as if he is trying to inhale an aroma. "Anosmia deprives me of the smell of warm fresh bread or of freshly brewed coffee. But it also allows me to have a stomach that is as sensitive as a rock. Sorry to disappoint you. You can fill your bag and you can fill my bag too. It won't bother me. Why don't you save your pills for another flight?"

Unmoved by his suggestion, I take two pills. I hate vomiting on planes.

"Anosmia is good for my job. I'm returning home after six months of working in a Haitian clinic that treats cholera patients. I was in the first group Israel sent to help Haitians after the earthquake of 2010, and I have returned several times since. Do you have any idea what it smells like to work in a cholera clinic?" He then taps my tray table and chuckles. "Well, I do not either." He then points to his nose. "Anosmia. But I do know that there is nothing you could fill your bag with, nor my bag, that I have not already seen or cleaned up every day for the past six months. Actually, it would be quite nostalgic for me. It is good that you sat next to me. I can help you recover from your sickness."

"Not if you're the cause of it." Okay, that was unnecessary.

"I thought we got past all this hostility." He lowers his tray table. "Look, I did not know whether or not I should have woken you. They started dinner service so soon after takeoff. I thought that maybe your anti-jet-lag calculation might not have taken that into consideration."

"I suppose you're right." Waking midflight hungry would have been miserable.

After the flight attendant brings our meals, I lift my water-filled plastic cup. *"Bon appétit."*

He lifts his cup. *"Bete'avon."*

Bete'avon. Indeed. We're heading toward Israel. "Before I reach for your barf bag, I think it's only fair I introduce myself. Hi. I'm Abi."

He holds out his hand for a shake. "Ari. Ariel, but my friends call me Ari."

I shake his hand. "It's nice to meet you, Ari."

Our conversation quiets. I take select bites but mostly use my fork to move the food around my tray. I try not to watch as Ari polishes off his meal.

He then pulls out a paper bag and places it in the middle of his tray. He moves his hand over it as if he is completing a magic trick. He must have been watching me not eat. "I always supply my own food on a long flight, just in case I do not like what is being offered, or in case I get extra hungry. I am not hungry enough to eat this whole sandwich, and whatever I do not eat will just go in the bin."

"Thanks, but I'm a vegetarian."

"What a perfect coincidence!"

"You're a vegetarian too?"

"No. But I happened to get a mozzarella, tomato and pesto sandwich. There is no meat in it. Please, take half. I see that you are not enjoying what you have."

"I forgot to order a vegetarian meal. That's why I've only been eating the potatoes."

He pulls the wrapped sandwich out of the bag. "If you do not eat the other half of this, it'll just go bad. Remember, my nose can handle most anything, including the smell of rotting cheese. But can yours?"

I shake my head and shyly smile. "Thank you." I take a bite. "This is really good."

"I am glad you are enjoying it. That means that you will have to buy half of a sandwich for me when we get off the plane."

I laugh at his attempt to prolong our interaction. "How about I just buy a drink for you now?"

He shakes his head. "I think it is only fair that you give dinner to me. Or at least half a dinner, like I gave to you."

Why is he trying to get me to dinner? I look down — and realize. He must have noticed that I'm not wearing a wedding band. I was wearing a wedding band until a month ago when I broke that finger while playing basketball with my kids. The ball jammed it back when I tried to catch it. It swelled so much that my ring had to be removed by cutters at the hospital. I look at my hand and see the swelling has gone down. *Why didn't I put the ring back on after I stopped wearing the splint?* I rub my finger and think of Daniel. And the kids. I tell Ari that I'm married. "I'm simply here to do a job."

Was that too presumptuous? What else could I say? I look at what's left of the sandwich he gave to me. "Do you want it back?" Of course I'm kidding.

He laughs and then he keeps the moment from becoming awkward. "A job. So, you will be working in Israel?"

"Yes." I welcome the opportunity to change the subject. "Have you read about the oil and gas fields discovered off the coast?"

"Yes, off the coast of Haifa." And then he snaps his fingers and points at me with certainty. "I knew it. That accounts for your snootiness. You are an investor type."

I admit to being insufferable, but not snooty. There's a big difference. "I'm not snooty! I just prefer, well, not talking to people so much. I'm an archaeologist. I'm much better at talking to things, or rather listening as they talk to me. There is an oil field off the coast of Haifa. But I'm specifically interested in a much larger one south of the one you mentioned. It has great potential for all the citizens of Israel. It'll boost your energy independence and economy. It's very exciting."

"And this particular oil-harvesting project brings an archaeologist on a ten-thousand-kilometer journey because . . ."

"I'll be a *conservator* for a developing project at the Eretz Israel Museum, in Tel Aviv. While divers were surveying the area to establish a system to transport the natural resources from the seafloor to the land, they came across a sunken ship from hundreds of years ago."

"A sunken ship. How unusual."

"Not really. Think about how roads would look if broken-down cars never got towed away. Millions of boats and ships have sunk since sea travel began over ten thousand years ago. Even nowadays, an estimated two ships sink a month. You don't hear about them because they often don't get reported."

He gathers his empty dishes on his tray. "So, you work for ha Eretz Israel Museum?"

I take his tray and hand it over with mine to the flight attendant collecting them. "Technically, I'm an independent contractor. Years ago, during my graduate studies, I was an assistant to one of my professors, Ben Irelander, who was the collections manager at that time. Now he is the chief curator. The Israel Antiquities Authority recently reached out to him regarding this most recent discovery. He called me. I specialize in the time period of the wreck, which is still being determined, but early signs point to the Middle Ages. And for personal reasons, this is of particular interest to me."

"Why? What reasons?"

I lift my shoulders. "It's personal."

He sighs. "You know, it is very annoying when people say things like that."

"Like what?"

"'For personal reasons . . .' and then they don't say what those reasons are. Like you just did."

"Well, it's personal. I don't want to tell anyone." But I told Ben, years ago, when we were taking a break while on a dig. Telling Ben wasn't to unload a secret. It had professional value. I know that's why he contacted me for this assignment. He is confident in my work, and he also knows that I have a special interest. I will find the match to my medieval Shabbat candlestick holder. But even Ben doesn't know everything about that family heirloom. I told him just enough so that he would keep me in mind for jobs that might unearth it. Or unocean it. Ha. *Unocean it.* I smile.

Ari pouts. "Then don't say anything. You could have stopped before that. Now you have me wondering."

What could be the harm in giving more detail to someone I'll never see again? "I think there might be something on the ship, something that I've been looking for, for quite some time. Something that belongs to me."

"You want to find something specific that has been buried at sea for hundreds of years? How will you know what it is if you see it?"

"It's mine. I'll know what it is *when* I see it. I've held it. I know what it weighs — its every angle and curve."

He has unease in his voice. "Are you talking about some kind of reincarnation or sci-fi time-travel thing?"

Wow, I didn't think of that. I could say yes, and that would make the rest of this flight much more interesting. "No. It's just — that's all I want to reveal—which is really more than most people know. You see, at home in the States we have a tradition. Let's say it's your birthday. You look at the candles on your birthday cake and make a wish. You then close your eyes, and if you blow out all of the candles with one breath, your wish would come true."

"I love that tradition!" Ari brings his hands together with a clap.

"Oh. You're familiar with that. You must know there's a caveat. Telling someone else what you wish for takes away the wish's power." I realize how silly this all must sound. For heaven's sake, I'm a scientist. I rush to explain myself. "I'm not superstitious, it's just that—"

"It's okay. I understand. I would not want to be the person that takes your wish's power away. I hope that you do find what you are looking for. I admire anyone who has a dream and drive."

Wow. That was so nice. "And, I admire anyone who's willing to clean throw-up to help sick people. Thank you for helping me with my luggage earlier — and the sandwich. And thank you for waking me when you did." I think I can sleep now. I slip my eye mask over my head.

"My pleasure." He looks awfully content with himself.

I sink in my chair, look at him and smile warmly. "Just don't do it again." And then I pull the mask down over my eyes.

Warning from the Late Bereaved

— 1478 —

Still terrified by her harrowing experience from earlier in the evening, Sancia inches her chair a little closer to her mother. Its legs scrape the floor, piercing through the silence.

In near darkness, from across the table, her father utters the first words since the three of them have returned home. "It is time. We must convert. We must become Christian."

Sancia is stunned.

"You will not and I will not!" Her mother then reaches for her hand. "And Sancia most certainly will not!"

Isaac brings his fist down on the table. "She could have been killed!"

Startled, Sancia looks at her mother and then past her to the lit Sabbath candles that miraculously haven't fallen to the floor. They supplement the moonlight, allowing her to see the outline of her mother and father.

"You do not need to tell me!" Esther rises from her chair and leans forward. "I was there! I am *still* there! Part of me will always be there seeing over and over again our beloved rabbi killed before our eyes. I was terrified over what would happen next."

"Esther!" Isaac motions toward Sancia.

"She was there! Isaac, you cannot protect her from knowing what she saw. And you certainly will not protect her by becoming one of them."

Sancia can no longer remain silent. "Papa, I do not understand. Why should we become Christian? Did those men attack us tonight because we are Jewish?"

Her mother answers before her father says another word. "Those men attacked us tonight, not because we are Jewish, but because they are Christian. You heard the lies they were saying. It is the way Christians are taught. They are madmen."

"Baltasar is Christian. He is a very good man. He saved us." Isaac doesn't need to remind Sancia.

She touches the necklace he crafted. She has worn it every Sabbath since her mother and father gave it to her after she first started helping at the shop.

"He is an exception." Esther sits back down and folds her arms across her chest.

"And Litiosa?" Isaac asks.

"His wife is also a good woman. Another exception."

"What exception? Many of them are good. Many give

me work." Isaac looks down and slides his hand over the red disc that Sancia sewed on his shirt. Before his fingers finish passing over it, it becomes the blood on Rabbi Sol's chest. She closes her eyes, but she can't make the blood disappear.

"They give you work because you charge less," her mother snaps. "You have to charge less because you are a Jew!"

Is mother right?

"Esther, please. I speak with them, they speak with me. We do not discuss G-d with one another. They are good people."

"Good people? Some, perhaps, but they do not believe in G-d the same way we do. They do not think like we do. What we think and how we believe is not acceptable to them."

Isaac lifts his shoulders and opens his arms with his palms facing up. "Well, how they think and how they believe is not acceptable to us."

"We do not make life difficult for anyone. They set forth unjust laws to strictly regulate our people. 'Grow your beard, wear the disc, tolerate murder!'"

"We will not be accused of breaking their absurd laws when they no longer apply to us," Isaac says. "We shall convert, I will shave my beard, we will discard the discs, we will move out of the Judería—"

"No! It is not the way. Our neighbors are our people. We go through this together. We stay strong together."

"Some have already converted and left. You know this."

That is what's been happening?

"They needed proper jobs. We do not need that. We have

our own business." Esther gently squeezes her daughter's hand. "Sancia has been learning how to work with clothes. You have been teaching her well."

Her father waves his hand dismissively. "She knows very well how to sew red discs on shirts."

When she once felt pride in being able to sew the red discs worn by all the people in her neighborhood, Sancia now feels embarrassed that is all she does. "I'll do more, Papa."

"It is not you, my little one." Her father reaches across the table to touch her cheek. They all fall silent and motionless. Sancia is exhausted but cannot sleep. The thought of even trying, terrifies her. *Maybe Mother and Father are scared to sleep too.* So, they sit.

Sancia hears a slight tap on the door before she watches it creak open. "Uncle Abraham!" She runs to him.

He hugs her. "You are still awake."

"I cannot sleep. I do not want to."

"It is so late. How about you come home with me now? You can crawl into bed with Astruga and Ana. Your cousins will be so happy seeing you when the sun comes up."

Sancia recognizes this to be an offer aimed at removing her from the discussion. She doesn't want to leave and is grateful when her father suggests that she stay.

Her uncle gently squeezes her hand. "If we were not running late, like we do almost every Sabbath, we would have all been there too. Your cousins would have seen what you saw. I am so sorry it happened and that you had to witness it."

"Do they know what happened?" Sancia strains to see her uncle's eyes in the darkness.

He shakes his head. "Once the word got to me, I hid it from them. I do not want them knowing. Not now. I am sorry for what you know, and sorry for what is. Do you understand?"

She nods. He doesn't want the children to know. She wonders how she might be able to tell her oldest cousin, Iuceph, without his young sisters finding out. Her ruminations are halted with another knock on the door.

Her father opens it.

Jacinto steps inside. "Sancia, you are still awake?" He sits on a chair by the table.

She makes out the shadow of the yarmulke that covers the back of his head where he is balding. She tells him she cannot sleep.

Jacinto nods. "I cannot sleep, either. Bonafilia and the children are sleeping. But I cannot sleep. I do not want to be alone. Imagine. I am a grown man and I am afraid to be alone." He then begins to sob. "I was right near him. Why did I not stop them? It is my fault the rabbi is gone."

"That is not true," Isaac says. "I saw you try to stop them."

"I saw too." *You pushed that horrible man.* Sancia takes his hand. "You were very brave, and I was scared for you."

"But, where was my strength? I was scared for you too. They could have hurt you." He then slouches over the table and buries his face in his arm. "I was closest to them, and I could not stop them."

"None of us can stop them! And they will keep coming after us. That is why I say we convert." Her father's tone is rigid.

Esther throws her hands in the air. "That is your answer? We should become like them? So those who kill and behave despicably should decide for us how we live?"

Isaac turns to his wife. "They decide *if* we live!"

Uncle Abraham interjects. "We live. We get harassed, but we thrive as much as they allow. We keep our little ones safe."

"We have been lied about, belittled, and mistreated." Isaac looks down and touches the patch on his shirt. "Singled out for humiliation with these red discs."

So that is why Papa was unhappy about my sewing the discs. They are a form of punishment, for no crime. Sancia didn't realize the extent to which they had been suffering.

"Tonight they have added murder to that list!" Isaac didn't need to tell anyone that.

Uncle Abraham takes a seat near Jacinto. "What good is being alive if we all just become captive to some rulers' ambitions? They will control our minds if we accept their faith."

Isaac seems to be the only one willing to convert. "I am not saying that becoming Christian is a *good* option. But they will keep bringing harm to us as Jews. We are stuck with horrible options."

Esther holds up a finger in the air. "We can move."

"Where shall we move to?" Isaac asks. "Out of Christendom? Just south, the citizens of Granada who are not Muhammadans are no better off than the citizens of Seville who are not Christians. Do not forget it was Emir Ismael Abu-I Walid, of Granada, who forced Jews to wear yellow badges there long before Isabella forced us to wear red discs here. The Muhammadans killed many Jews of

Granada hundreds of years before the Christians killed many Jews in Seville."

The image strikes Sancia with new fear. "Killed *many* Jews — here?"

Esther brings her daughter onto her lap and wraps her arms around her.

Jacinto lifts his head from the table and wipes his tears away. "It was not even a hundred years ago. Here. They destroyed everyone and everything." He holds up a folded paper. "My grandfather collected items in a box. I sorted through it after he passed. I found this note from Hasdai Crescas; may his memory be a blessing."

"Rabbi Crescas? How did your grandfather have a note from him?" Isaac asks with awe.

"I do not know. But it is a warning to us. Understanding our past is critical to surviving our future." Jacinto walks over to the window.

Sancia is surprised to see the sun rising. She knew the Sabbath candles had gone out some time ago, but she didn't realize they were gathered around the table for as long as they had been.

Using the light from the morning's first rays, Jacinto reviews the letter's contents. He looks up and gives an apologetic glance to Esther. "It has a horribly frightening message."

Sancia doesn't want him to stop reading on her account. She needs to know everything.

After her mother nods her approval, Jacinto reads aloud. ". . . On the day of the New Moon of the fateful month of Tammus in the year 5151, the Lord bent the bow of the enemies against the Jewish community of Seville . . . the Christians destroyed their gates by fire and killed in that very place a great number of people; the majority, however, changed their faith. Many of them, children as well as women, were sold to the Moslems, so that the streets occupied by Jews have become empty."

"That was just a few generations ago." Isaac interrupts him. "I do not want these streets to become empty again."

And I do not want to be sold.

Esther remains steadfast. "I'd rather empty streets than empty humans. We shall move, I say again. Further than Granada. Far away."

"Where shall we go?" Isaac stands up and backs away from the table. "Our people have been sent into exile from England and France. We cannot go to those places."

Sancia hadn't known this. But the others don't seem surprised.

Esther suggests Ratisbon.

"Germanic lands are not an option! It is worse there." Jacinto then tells them of word he received that Jews have been imprisoned in Ratisbon for torturing hardened bread.

"Torturing hardened bread, like matzah?" Sancia asks, not sure she has heard correctly.

Jacinto nods. "They call it a consecrated wafer. They believe it becomes the body of God, or the son of God or whichever, after they perform a ritual over it."

Esther sharpens her tone at Isaac. "And you are considering making believe that you are Christian — that you are among a people who place the well-being of hardened bread above the life of a human?"

Isaac exhales a deep breath. "That is my point, Esther. They will torture us for suspicion of breaking a wafer. We have no place to go!"

Esther sighs. "Lisbon. We can go to Lisbon. You know how to speak the language — I've heard you teaching it to Sancia. And we can find your family."

"Such travel would be too difficult. It is too far and dangerous a walk and we do not have enough money to hire a coach." Isaac shakes his head. "When there is more danger remaining here than traveling there, I will consider Lisbon. For now, this kingdom is still our home. This is our home! I will stay, even if I must make people believe I am someone else." As her father speaks with irreversible conviction, Sancia knows there is nothing she can say that would change his mind. She is not sure she would even want to. All the options are horrible. "I will no longer wear discs or grow a beard. That is the way I will handle this. Our family will remain in the Judería until you decide to join me in this decision. Then, as Christians, we shall all move from this neighborhood."

"That will never happen!" Esther snaps back with equal conviction. "I will never become one of them!"

Sancia silently agrees. *Nor will I.*

Approaching Tel Aviv

"**P**lease stow away your tray tables and move your seats to the upright position. The pilot has started our descent into Tel Aviv."

Ari reaches into the front pocket of my seat to remove my airsickness bag, and then does the same with his.

I drop my jaw. "This is the worst part of the flight for me! This is when I tend to get sick!" Very true.

"You took Meclizine. You won't need these." He flutters the bags in front of me. "But Steve will."

This guy is unbelievable! "Who?!"

"Steve. The curator of a museum. Certainly you could appreciate that. You could even call me one of his *collections managers*." What a riot this guy is. "I am going to send one of the bags to him so that he may add it to his museum's collection. And I will keep the other one."

"You collect barf bags?"

Ari shakes his head. "No. But Steve does. That is why I

will send one to him. I want to keep the other one to remind me of this flight."

"Does someone really collect unused puke bags and put them in a museum?"

"Absolutely. Used ones would smell horrible." He points to his nose.

"For those who can smell, of course. Fine. Take it. Knock yourself out. If I need to ditch my meal before touchdown, I know which direction I'll turn. I hope you aren't too attached to your jeans."

"I'm not concerned. Soon after I mail it, I will visit the museum to see it on display."

I touch my belt to make sure I'm buckled and then I touch my locket to make sure it's still there. "Is the museum in Israel?"

"It's anyplace there is Internet. It's a virtual museum."

"That's interesting. I'll check it out sometime." I really will, when I think of it.

Ari seems pleased that I'm interested in the museum. "We will be landing soon. Do you have a ride to where you need to go?"

I nod. "I do. Thank you. I'm going to be staying with my cousin, who is my best friend. She'll be picking me up."

I strain to see beyond the other side of immigration. Just a blur of people. Wait! I spot her! I couldn't miss that hallmark curly hair peering through an unmissable pink New England Patriots cap. I still think the pink cap is ridiculous, but during a time like this, I'm grateful she is wearing it. I run to hug her. I loosen my embrace and transfer her cap to my head.

"Hey!" She objects.

"Hey back. When are you going to trade in this cap for something that supports a local football team? You've been living here for six years. Why don't you start cheering on the Pioneers? You'll look good in blue."

"I'm not a fan of soccer."

"Not soccer. Football."

"Real football? Here? In Israel?"

Before I can respond, Ari approaches. "I just want to say that I enjoyed sitting next to you. And that I hope you find here what you are looking for."

"What are you looking for?" Annette asks.

"Artifacts." I then introduce her to Ari. "I told him about my job. We were sitting next to one another. He helped me with my luggage—on and off the plane." I smile at him with gratitude.

He then reminds me to find the barf bag museum. "Do not forget."

"If I do forget, I'll remember you as soon as I get sick." I smile, confident he knows I'm joking. I hope he agrees that it's nice to part on a fun note — even if it is at his expense. He kindly smiles, nods, and walks away.

I'm so used to shuttling my kids around, I didn't realize how much I like being the passenger, how much I get to see when not focusing on the mechanics of driving. The road leading from Ben Gurion Airport is dotted with a rather unusual assortment of what looks like palm trees and evergreens. "I never noticed that before."

Annette keeps her eyes on the road. "Botanical diversity, allegorical of Israel's diversity."

Poetic. "You really do love living here."

She nods. "I do."

In less than thirty minutes, she parks and helps me to carry my luggage to her apartment. This is the first time I've seen it decorated like this. I'm not sure I'm in Israel anymore. "The ride from the airport didn't seem that far. How did you get us to New Mexico so quickly?" I admire the Navajo carpet she shipped from our visit to Santa Fe last year. It's the focal point of the living room, which is where we enter her home. I scan the walls, full of Southwestern and Native American décor. "You decorated a lot since I last visited."

"Remember this?" She picks up the cute miniature adobe home I bought for her.

"Of course. I have its neighboring house on my nightstand." The one she bought for me.

I put down my laptop so that I can pick up Nunu, who is greeting me from the armrest of Annette's brown microfiber couch. I scratch behind her ears and nuzzle into her cheek. "Hello sweet girl. I can't believe it's been two years." I let her jump onto the couch and hug Annette again. "I can't believe it's been two years since I've been here."

"Remember when you first came to this apartment to help me move six years ago?"

"Oh my gosh was that a lot of work. This place was a mess."

Annette mistakes my observation for an insult. "Well, you helped me to move, but you didn't help me to unpack." I turn defensive after being reminded I left her when she still had much to do. "The whole family was waiting for me back at the hotel. I couldn't leave Daniel alone that much longer with Harry and the twins." I remember how rambunctious my toddlers and four-year-old were at that time. "In those days, I barely had time to breathe." On cue, Nunu nuzzles my ankle and I scoop her up again. "But I had time for you. You were just a homeless kitten meowing behind a bush. I was surprised that you were only one sweet kitten hiding behind that bush and not seven with that loud and constant meow."

I then bring my luggage into Annette's room, which will be my room too, and I unpack. I toss my pajamas on the cot that she set up for me. I smile at the Southwestern landscape on my nightshirt and at the pictures of miniature cactuses dotting my boxer shorts. Our trip to Santa Fe last year meant a lot to both of us.

We then walk a couple of blocks away to grab a quick bite to eat at Buddha Burgers. We catch up on some of the things we neglect to say when we FaceTime, which is a lot, since neither of us like talking on the phone much.

After we return home, I get comfortable in my Santa Fe themed pajamas and succumb to the sleep that interferes with our reunion.

My alarm goes off extra early. I set it so that I would have time to reacquaint myself with the bus system. Fortunately, Annette was already on top of that. On the kitchen counter near where I left my key, she left a detailed bus schedule with notes in the margin and a protein bar. I gratefully take it all and then head out the door to catch the bus that'll shuttle me to the past.

WHAT'S IN A NAME?

The summer that Ben was a visiting professor during my undergraduate studies, I submitted a winning application that secured my position, among five coveted spots, in his course that would end on a private dig in Maine. After a six-hour drive, I couldn't wait to get my hands on the tools and the tools on the ground. Ben arranged for each of us to excavate a specific area. *Abi, be especially delicate. Your area is of unique interest.* I was elated when I found an object relatively quickly. Once I drew Ben's attention to it—and consequently, everyone else's—my elation turned to devastation as I made the object crumble with the lightest touch. *What did I just destroy?* Ben's face went blank. I was mortified. Until he laughed and laughed and laughed. *Each year I play the same joke on a different student and it gets them every time.* I knew then that I would have to pursue my PhD at the graduate school in Israel where he was tenured.

I see Ben waiting for me as soon as I walk into the lobby of the Eretz Israel Museum. I hug him. "It's so nice to see you." I step back. "You have a new look."

He touches his gray mustache and nods. "Let's go."

We walk outside. The museum is a campus developed around an excavation site surrounded by buildings that house different themes. The education department, where I expect to go, is to the left. We go to the right.

"Is this the right way?" I ask.

"I thought it would be nice to walk the grounds first as I update you. It's such a beautiful morning. And, I remember how much you enjoy the gardens here."

"I do." They alone make this museum worth the price of admission.

He keeps a casual pace. "Abi, I wanted to get you here before they finish dressing the ship with a grid. I want us to approve it together."

"You mean they're still working on that?" I ask, referring to the time-consuming technique of setting up plastic pipe to map the sections of a sunken ship to record the precise location of its objects.

He nods. "We couldn't get that started until about two weeks after I contacted you. You emailed me your flight information the day after you accepted my offer. I didn't want to disappoint you. But, our team needed to work out the logistics with the oil company so as not to interfere with their progress. Our divers are excellent, very precise — some are students in my graduate course."

"You invited students to work on this project?" I'm

alarmed. "This is not some silly staged wreck. This is the real deal. We need to have exclusive access to all of the items removed from the ship, and they must be extracted with the utmost care." I would insist on that for any wreck, not just a medieval one with the potential of housing my other candlestick holder. Ben is one of the best in the field. I don't need to be telling him any of this. But I'm compelled to speak up. There's too much at stake! And I've seen, multiple times, how his soft heart wins out. No doubt it's why I'm here—I know I've been one of the biggest beneficiaries of his kindness.

He tilts his head with a smile. "Was it so long ago that you were a student yourself? Remember the hunger for that genuine experience? And who is more desperate to preserve their career than someone who doesn't exactly have one just yet? It'll be fine, Abi. I've been meeting with our team on a regular basis. I look forward to introducing you to them."

He is right. "I look forward to meeting them, Ben." After all, we are a team.

"Great. And once the grid is complete and we approve it in the next day or so, the excavation process will proceed relatively quickly—the first phase, anyway." His tone turns mischievous. "And not everything needed to wait for the grid."

I gasp. "You have something? Please tell me what you've got."

"Okay. Let's head to work."

We leave the gardens. I try to hasten our pace to the nondescript building beyond the Glass Pavilion and the

Migdal Gallery. We enter the room that Ben sectioned off for our current project.

He waves his arms, motioning a great presentation. "Abi . . . the items of . . . *El Carrillo*."

"You already know the ship's name?!" I can barely contain my excitement. "*El Carrillo*! Is that what it's called?"

Ben stands in front of the small tank filled with liquid and something brought up from the sea. "While the divers were applying the first set of pipes to mark the grid, they cleaned off a copper plaque attached to the hull. They could see that it was inscribed with the words 'El Carrillo.'"

"*El Carrillo*," I say as I exhale with a respectful sense of disbelief. "Did they remove the plaque?"

He shakes his head. "It's still on the ship."

"A photo?"

"Soon. After I show you how to use our new software so that you can see the photos when they get uploaded."

I want to see the workmanship on the plaque and the style used to form the letters, the depth of the embossing, the font, the size. The plaque alone could supply so many clues. "*El Carrillo* is Spanish. My Spanish is weak." I haven't spoken it since I lived in Seville during the summer of my junior year of college. "But I think a variation of the word would be *carrillito*, which I think means wheelbarrow. Maybe it transported wheelbarrows or was rather used like one. Do you think that's how it got its name?"

He answers, "I suppose it certainly is a possibility."

I search my phone to see if I'm correct. "My mistake. The word I was thinking of is *carretilla*. That's not close enough to be a clue. What is it that they've brought up?"

Ben points to the tank. "It's difficult to know exactly what we have here. I left these items in the seawater they were delivered in. I wanted your opinion before creating a solution to clean each of them." He then smiles and looks at me. "Plus, that's what I'm paying you to do. One item seems to be in the shape of a jug or pitcher. It could be made of metal or earthenware. The other seems to be a utensil, but due to all of the sea growth, it's difficult to tell for certain. Do you have any other thoughts?"

I snap my fingers and then point at him. "Alfonso Carrillo!"

"What?"

"During the early stages of the Spanish Inquisition, when many members of the clergy embraced it, others refused to. One such person was the Archbishop of Toledo who stopped the Inquisition from establishing roots in his territory. Alfonso Carrillo. He did his best to assure the safety of Toledo's Jewish subjects, until his death in 1485, after which his successor immediately established the Inquisition."

"You're suggesting that our wreck could have been named after this potential hero to the Jews?"

I nod. "This could be a Jewish ship!" I'm so excited.

"Well then, I'll have the divers check to see if its rudder has been circumcised – to confirm." He laughs. Ben always delights in his own jokes.

"Very funny, Ben." That was funny, actually. But I'm too excited by my hunch to get distracted. "If *El Carrillo* was named after the Archbishop of Toledo, it's possible that *conversos*, Jews forced into Catholicism, named it. They could have wanted to honor the ship in a way that wouldn't bring attention to its Jewish passengers or owners. Choosing a protector of the Jews with a Christian name would have been one way of remaining faithful to their mission without revealing who they were. They might have named the ship after such a protector so that they felt safer."

"Nautical superstitious behavior."

I nod. "This ship could have been funded by someone like the *converso* Luis de Santángel, the royal treasurer of Ferdinand and Isabella, the king and queen who established the Inquisition. He was compelled to convert to Catholicism publicly while clinging to Judaism privately. It was the most dangerous choice one could make."

"You are suggesting that it was more dangerous to be a Catholic than it was to be a Jew?"

"Not just any Catholic but a *converso*. Jews suffered from violence and restrictive laws. However, it wasn't until a Jew was baptized, by choice or by force, that the Inquisition would have had full reign over him."

"Or her," Ben says. "This doesn't necessarily get us closer to resolving the mystery of our ship — does it?"

I shake my head. He is right. Speculating without enough solid information is just speculating. We need to see the artifacts from the wreck.

Ben puts his notes in a folder and places it in the corner of his desk. "I wanted you to get acquainted with the project today. However, I also want you to adjust to the time difference, get some rest, and have some fun. You're in Israel."

"Are you saying we're done for the day?" *How disappointing.*

"Yes. Look, Abi, we discovered an interesting avenue to investigate. Let's grab some lunch and call it a day. Actually, let's call it a couple of days."

He is right. There's no point in lingering today. Our presence won't make the process faster when there aren't items ready to be handled, or data to be logged, or pieces to be investigated. I unfold the bus schedule to figure out my way back.

Ben puts his hand over it. "Forget the bus. I'll give you a ride back to your cousin's. That gives me a great excuse to take you to lunch at one of my favorite restaurants at HaTachana."

"HaTachana?"

"The old train station between Jaffa and Neve Tzedek. It was renovated long after you lived here, and now it houses shops, galleries, and restaurants."

I fold the bus schedule and put it in my bag. "Thank you Ben. That sounds so nice. I noticed it when I was here a couple of years ago. I didn't know what it was called, and I didn't have time to explore it because my children wanted to do nothing but pet the cats and go to the beach." I miss them.

Ben turns off the lights and walks to the door.

I follow, stopping short of crossing the threshold. "Do you think I'm going to find it, Ben? Could it really possibly be on this ship?"

With the warm touch of a father to a daughter, he brings my hands together and clasps them inside of his. "What matters is that you have something to search for, my dear Abi. What matters is that you are here."

ANUSIM

— 1480 —

Sancia brushes aside the thread she just removed from the seam she just sewed. *Too uneven.* She flattens the dress on the table and prepares another needle. She is grateful to have advanced beyond attaching red discs, but gets impatient with herself for making mistakes. Her father is never impatient with her, especially not in the shop where he can be himself, a rarity since tolerating baptism over two years ago. He no longer takes a day of rest on the Sabbath, so tomorrow he will be at work again. But, tonight, he will be by her side as she says the prayers to bring in the Sabbath. She has only been saying them since she turned twelve-years-old a couple of months ago, but with that, she never makes a mistake. And though her mother typically goes to sleep when the candles have burned half-way, her father stays awake to make sure they safely burn out. Sancia will stay awake with him tonight, as she has been doing, so that she can see his eyes sparkle when the Sabbath flames reflect in them. It's the only time, she can almost imagine, that he is happy.

After resewing the seam, Sancia rests for a moment to rub her sore hands. "I cannot believe how quickly time is passing this season. We are already a month into 5241. We have so many orders to fulfill."

Isaac keeps working. "We can do it. And actually, we are three-quarters into 1480 . . ." As if he means to be funny, or maybe to further accept his uncomfortable identity, he completes his sentence — "of the year of my Lord."

"Ugh." Sancia takes off her thimble and aims it at his arm. "Ow."

She giggles. "Sorry, Papa. May I please have it back?"

"Of course. How else could I get you to finish up?" He smiles. Her heart smiles back. He has to hide a lot of things, but he does not hide the love he feels for her.

She puts her thimble back on. As she searches the table for the needle, a regal man walks through the door. He's a large man, wearing scarlet tights and a velvet houppelande of the same color. Until that moment, Sancia hadn't realized how lifeless everything looked in the shop. Until that moment, the only color amid the beige cotton, undyed sackcloth, and gray burlap has been the red discs.

Sancia strains to listen as Friar Hernando de Talavera introduces himself. "I am in Seville to speak with all *conversos*."

Her father puts down the shirt he was sewing. "I am a *converso*. The only one here."

The friar takes a step closer. "What is your name?"

"Isaac Pareja."

"Well, Señor Pareja, Queen Isabella is deeply troubled by the way the righteous, those of pure Catholic upbringing, are speaking about New Christians."

"Oh?" Isaac remains seated.

"It is terribly unfortunate that they refer to you as *marranos*." Dirty pigs. The friar adjusts his houppelande. "I appreciate the struggle of adopting a new faith, for I, too, am a New Christian. I have told the queen that some of you violate the sanctity of the church, not because you are being intentionally disrespectful, but because you are ignorant of the path toward Christ. I understand that is not your fault. I implored her to understand too. You simply need education, not punishment."

What do you mean by punishment?" Sancia asks, unable to stop herself. "Why would he be punished? He has been doing nothing wrong."

The friar turns to Isaac, as if he is the one who asked the question. "Heresy is a crime. If you are caught committing it, you will be punished." He then points to Sancia. "You said you are the only Christian here. Why is she not a Christian?"

Isaac looks at his daughter, then back to the friar. "She and her mother are not ready."

"You should see to it that they will be. We are trying to make this kingdom a better place."

Then get rid of your stupid laws.

The friar clears his throat and straightens his posture.

"I am here to offer instruction to all of the New Christians of Seville — on not just how to behave like a Christian but also how to think like one."

Sancia refrains from gagging.

The friar continues. "I shall instruct you on how to love the One who died for you — for your sins. You will find value in the pain you see weekly, carved in the statue of Christ." He lifts his hands and faces upward. "God gave us his son to absorb the pain so that you would not have to." He then looks at Isaac. "A beautiful gift. All you need to do is accept Him with your heart and soul. Accept his glory and enjoy the beauty of God through his son, Jesus Christ."

Isaac stands and walks toward the door. "Thank you for your visit, Friar. I have already been doing those things since my baptism. There must have been a mistake in your suspecting otherwise. If you need an addition to your wardrobe, please do not hesitate to ask me."

"Very well. But I think your decision is a mistake. We all can learn more."

Yes. Sancia thinks. *You certainly can.*

Just as the chill of winter is beginning to set, Baltasar hurries into the shop. He is out of breath. "There are Inquisitors. They have been recruiting an army of soldiers from among us — ordinary citizens of Seville."

Sancia puts down the needle and thread and joins Baltasar and her father.

Baltasar is distressed. "They are aggressively working to

eliminate heretics and to force obedience among Catholics. Their keenest eye will be on you and any other New Christians. It is horrible. We have all been instructed to report anyone who attends church on Sunday but wears their finest clothes on Saturday, and to point out anyone who avoids eating meat from a pig."

"How will they know what people eat?" Isaac asks.

"They do not ask for proof. Just accusations."

Sancia thinks of a tailor who left the Judería long ago, a surly man who often seemed to feel threatened by her father's good work and low fees. "So, anyone with any grievance against Father could accuse him of anything, and they would need no proof to have him arrested? Can a New Christian inform against another New Christian?"

Baltasar solemnly nods. "Yes. They are looking for accusations about anyone from anyone. They will investigate as they hold each suspect in a cell."

Sancia is incensed that these people would arrest a man for how he might eat or dress. She tugs on her father's sleeve. "Switch back, Papa. It might be safer for you to be a Jew than a Christian."

Isaac shakes his head. "I cannot. Leaving Christianity is a crime."

Sancia recalls her mother's suggestion from long ago. "Maybe it is time we consider moving. My Portuguese is not bad, Father. We could do that."

Isaac turns to his daughter, taking both of her hands in his. "Nonsense, Sancia. You see, I go to church every Sunday. I pray the rosary, make confessions to the priest, and I kneel at that statue. I do not break Christian rules. I wear my best clothes on Sunday, and no one watches me eat except for you and your mother and sometimes our Jewish neighbors. Our ancestors reestablished roots here after being forced to flee the 1391 massacre. This is my home. This is *our* home. They worked hard to make it that way. I am not leaving."

Father is in danger. She needs to convince him to learn from Friar de Talavera. He might be her best hope, if only she knew how to contact him.

The sick feeling that unsettled Sancia a couple of days ago, upon hearing Baltasar's news, dissipates when she opens the door to welcome her aunt, uncle and cousins into her home for a Sabbath lunch.

"Did you cook our lunch yesterday?" Astruga's question warms Sancia's heart. She knows her younger cousins looks up to her the way she still looks up to Felipa, an older girl who used to help take care of her when she was younger.

"It is the Sabbath. I certainly didn't cook it *today.*" Sancia drags out the last word.

Iuceph makes a face as if he tasted something unpleasant. "Please do not tell me if *you* did the cooking again."

Sancia remembers how he asked for another serving the last time she cooked. She laughs at his pretend insult.

Sancia's mother walks into the room from the kitchen. "Is there a problem?"

Iuceph looks surprised. He shakes his head. "No, Aunt Esther. I was just thinking about how much I like *your* cooking and wouldn't want to miss out on it."

Sancia gives her cousin a look of playful disapproval. Astruga and Ana giggle.

"Next week *you* can do the cooking." Esther says to Iuceph while winking at the girls. She then smiles and walks back into the kitchen.

"I'll help set the table." Astruga says as she follows behind her aunt to get the plates.

Ana catches up with her sister. "I want to help too."

"And I'll see who is knocking." Iuceph then walks toward the door to open it.

Sancia watches, wondering who it might be. No one is expected, but she would be happy if David and his family stopped by.

Intruders push their way past Iuceph as soon as he opens the door. "We have been sent by royal authority to detain a heretic."

Uncle Abraham stands up from his discussion with Isaac to address them. "There are no heretics here."

Sancia dare not speak. Her body stiffens as one intruder takes several steps toward her father. "Are you Isaac Pareja, man of this household?"

Isaac nods. The man then turns to point toward the mezuzah on the doorframe.

"My family is Jewish. I am not," Isaac explains. "We are simply about to eat lunch together. I will go to church tomorrow like I do every week."

"I do not think you will be going to church tomorrow. Your house is cold. Where is your fire?"

Oh no. None of us would think of lighting the fire on the Sabbath. Sancia lies to help her father. Her heart pounds. "Fire makes me cough."

"Did it make you cough yesterday morning before it went out?"

Sancia nods, terrified by the realization that they must have been watching her family for some time. She is grateful when her mother intervenes.

"She was coughing terribly from the ashes. That is why we let it go out today, even though Isaac would have lit it to keep us warm."

"Nonsense. There is no fire because no one would light wood today, on the Jewish day of rest. You are all Jews — even the one who was baptized. Take the *marrano!*"

"No!" Sancia cries as the men force her father out the door.

The door slams. The men are gone. Her father is gone.

Her body becomes paralyzed by fear, dread and guilt. *Pikuach nefesh.* Rabbi Mosse told them just last week about how saving a life is always more important than observing Jewish law. *Baltasar warned us they would be looking at chimney tops. I should have lit the fire. Papa would be safe if only I had.*

Distorting Faith

—◆✦◆—

— 1481 —

Sancia is unable to think of anything but her father in
the hands of those evil people. She hates them. They
collect their victims with ease. When will they let her
father come back?

Unable to tolerate another moment in her house without
him, she walks out. She seeks her younger cousin, Iuceph,
and asks him to help her in the tailor shop. She wants it to
be in order for her father's return. She teaches him how to
sew the red discs. She was more than a year younger than
he is now, at the age of ten, when she first learned. Once he
demonstrates his competence, she moves to her own workspace to sew the more complex pieces.

A couple of hours into the afternoon, Iuceph complains
that his hands hurt. Sancia remembers how much her hands
hurt when she first learned to sew. She is grateful for how
much he has been helping her. "We'll come back tomorrow.

Let us go to the market now before returning home. I want to buy something there for you."

"I would like that. Thank you." Iuceph struggles with a few more stitches. "I'll finish up this last piece and then we will go."

Once he finishes, Sancia folds the shirt he was working on and places it on the pile of completed items. She then holds the door open for him. Iuceph reaches for his hat and steps outside. The shop didn't warm up enough for them to remove their coats. He rubs his hands back and forth to try to make warmth. Sancia blows hot air between her wrists. They walk.

Iuceph points to what looks like paper secured to a tree. "What is that?"

Sancia walks up to the tree and holds the paper flat so that she can read it. "It is a notice."

"What kind of notice?"

"I do not understand what this means." Sancia then points to a sentence that reads — *An auto de fé is to be held in the square on the sixth of February in the year of our Lord 1481.*

Iuceph steps closer to read it himself. "February 6th. That is in a little over a week."

"It has the seal of the Church on it. What do they mean that they are holding 'an act of faith?' And why is it outside, in the square, instead of in a church?" Sancia removes the notice from the tree, folds it, and places it in her pocket. "Let us show this to your father. We will go to the market tomorrow."

She is anxious to get to her uncle's house to escape from the unusually cold winter day. She follows Iuceph inside and then closes the door behind her. She basks in the warmth of the fire that both comforts her and burdens her with guilt. She thinks back to when the men took her father about a month ago. *I should have lit the fire.*

She then reaches into her pocket and pulls out the paper to hand it to her uncle sitting by the fire. He unfolds it and then reads it silently. He shakes his head and folds it back up. "We will not get mixed up in this."

Sancia grabs it from his hand. "I think it has something to do with my father! I'm going to find out!"

Her uncle jumps up off the chair. "What do you think you are going to do? We shall remain home and wait for this thing to finish. Word will reach us when it does. We will then talk to Baltasar."

Sancia is unable to hold back her tears. "I am tired of doing nothing! I already did nothing. I did nothing—" *I did nothing.* She wipes her eyes with her fingers and then her nose with the back of her hand. "And now he is in prison, like the people in Germanic lands who were accused of mistreating hardened bread, only he is no longer Jewish, and they were."

Her uncle wraps his arms around her. "Sancia, there is nothing you could have done. You understand what we are dealing with. Nothing is your fault."

She does understand what they are dealing with. *That is exactly why it is my fault. I should have insisted, really insisted, that Papa accept instruction from the royal friar.*

I should have lit the fire. I could have tried talking Mother into converting and then leaving the Judería together. That is what Papa was hoping for. I will not rest until he is home.

— FEBRUARY 6TH - 1481 —

Before sunrise, on the day of the *auto de fé*, Sancia heads to Iuceph's house as they previously planned. She hopes he is awake and ready to go before her aunt and uncle try to stop them. But when she gets there, she sees no sign of him waiting outside for her. She picks up a pebble, wet and cold from the frost, and wraps her fingers around it. She aims it at the window of the room where her cousins sleep. It taps the glass just loud enough to get Iuceph's attention. He peers out from behind the curtain - his black curly hair stuck to his forehead from a deep sleep. She motions for him to hurry, annoyed he is not already waiting outside for her. He soon appears at the door, walks out and gently locks it behind him so that he does not wake anyone else. She is grateful he hasn't changed his mind. She would not want to do this alone.

The children hurry to the town square and blend in among the peasants. Clergy and nobles scuffle about to take their seats. Men in elaborate attire address the crowd from the stage. They make religious references - some that Sancia is only familiar with from the stories her father has told her after he would come home from church. Several hours of repetitive monotony go by. Slowly.

Iuceph tugs at Sancia's coat. "How much longer is this going to be?"

She whispers, "I do not know."

"They just keep saying the same things. Can we leave now?"

Sancia shakes her head. She will not leave until this ends - or until she knows where her father is.

She suddenly rushes her hand to her mouth - gasps and points. "He is there!"

"Who?"

"My father."

Iuceph leans forward and squints. "I do not see him. But, is that Felipa?"

"Yes. How do you not see your own uncle? He is walking right in front of her." Sancia's eyes dart back and forth from the seventeen-year-old girl who used to watch her while her mother was busy, to her father, walking in front of her.

"*That* is Uncle Isaac?"

Sancia nods. The ghostly pallor of their faces scares her. Their bodies are practically withered away under humiliating black conical hats and robes. Her father is shivering. Of course he is shivering. It's freezing - and he has nothing on his feet. All six of them have nothing on their feet. They stand behind the Inquisitor, who is draped in warm velvet – a deep violet with golden trim. He inserts a key into a box decorated with a deep violet colored velvet and golden trim. The box appears to be an extension of the man about to open it.

He lifts the lid and pulls out a scroll, which he then unrolls. With an especially loud voice, he reads the dossier.

"... For not lighting a fire for warmth on a winter Saturday ... for wearing a clean and ornate dress on a Saturday ... for refusing to eat pork from a banquet ..." One by one, he reads an order for each heretic to be relaxed.

Felipa cries out. Her voice is severely strained. "Please do not kill me. I was wrong to forsake Christ."

He said relaxed. Why would she think he would kill her?

The expressionless Inquisitor acknowledges her repentance. Before proceeding, he asks if any others are so enlightened by the same truth.

Say something, Papa. Please, say something.

She looks to Iuceph, who is staring intensely at her father. She sees his lips move. "Uncle Isaac, just say it."

No one says anything else. The Inquisitor motions to another man - similarly dressed in deep violet but without golden trim. He prods the six men and women away from the center of the staging area. He instructs her father and the others. "You will step off the stage and then turn right and then you shall be transferred."

Exit the stage? Transferred? Why can they not just leave? Sancia tenses. "Felipa is crying. Something is not right."

"They probably made her lose her mind."

"Or she knows something we do not know." Sancia starts to leave the crowd of spectators to follow the frail group that her father is a part of.

Iuceph pulls her back. "Do not. No one else is leaving this ceremony. We are going to get caught if we try to follow Uncle and the others. These people are horrible. I am scared. I do not want to be seen by them. And the man said they would be 'relaxed.' Let us finish here and then go to your home and wait for your father there."

"No!" Sancia refuses to allow her father to leave her sight. She follows the group. Her toes are cold through her socks and shoes. She can't imagine how freezing cold her father's feet must be walking on the wintry cobblestones with nothing to protect them. She is grateful that Iuceph is staying by her side.

She doesn't know how long she has been walking when she hears a man's voice give instructions to the group. "Rise onto the *quemadero*."

Sancia and Iuceph stop a short distance away, just close enough to spy. A man, entirely hidden under a heavy black robe with black gloves, orders the six men and women to step onto the stage. He then orders them to stop in front of wooden stakes. Six stakes—one person per stake.

Then replicas of that same robe with the same gloves, presumably concealing men, tie ropes around each frail man and woman to each stake.

Sancia can barely breathe as she stares at the greatest evil she has ever seen. *This cannot be.*

"They are going to kill them!" Iuceph cries.

Sancia stares at her father - when a faceless figure, whose sleeve moves up just enough to reveal skin under his glove—just enough skin to show there might actually be a human underneath—strips him of the robe. Her father's naked body is covered in burn marks. *What did they do to him?*

"What do we do? What do we do?" Iuceph cries.

Sancia strains to hear Felipa. "But I confessed! Please. Show mercy. In front of all those people, I confessed. I will turn away from my evil ways and accept the one true way. I will never again observe the Sabbath of the Hebrews. I will no longer disgrace my Lord, Jesus Christ."

The Inquisitor—the one draped in deep violet velvet with golden trim—arrives from the other stage in time to hear Felipa. "Wait!" He orders the men in black. And then he walks up to the girl tied to the stake. "She will never observe her Sabbath, nor disgrace our Lord, Christ, again." He looks and takes a step closer to her. "Is that a promise?"

She pushes an answer through strained vocal cords. "Yes."

He pulls out a gold cross from his pocket and places it at her lips. "Show Christ how much you love him."

Felipa kisses the cross.

Sancia feels herself making a face. She feels nauseated.

The Inquisitor then turns to the black robe standing closest to him, standing closest to Felipa. "Show the others the compassion that this young lady has earned today, for they, too, could have been worthy of it."

Papa, quick. Save yourself. Do the same, do the same!

Sancia tenses as the man hidden under the black robe approaches to untie the ropes that secure the kind-hearted girl to the wooden stake. But, instead of watching him free her, Sancia watches as he squeezes her neck until he kills her.

A replica of Felipa's executioner lights the sticks, at Isaac's feet, on fire.

Sancia takes a deep breath. Before she can release her scream, arms restrain her – one wrapped around her waist, the other wedged into her mouth. *I am being suffocated. They have me Iuceph – run, run, run!* She tries to bite free, but cannot. She cannot bite, she cannot scream, she cannot breathe.

Run Iuceph, run! She cannot see if Iuceph has escaped. She wiggles and kicks as hard as she can. But, she is unable to get her captor to buckle. She exhausts her energy. She has no choice but to submit to her death. She collapses, pulling her captor down, too. She braces herself for a quick end.

Then, the arm around her waist loosens. The restricting grip suddenly becomes a tender embrace. She hears the comforting sound of a familiar voice telling her to remain quiet.

"You were about to scream. You must not or they will catch you." Her captor then gently removes his arm from her mouth. He dabs a cloth on her cheeks to wipe her tears.

Sancia involuntarily welcomes Baltasar's embrace. He cradles her, averting her eyes and covering her ears as the screams of agony get sparser. He cannot block her nose. To breathe is to inhale the ashes of her father and the others. She feels Iuceph trying to find safety in Baltasar's arms too. His hand reaches for hers. The three uninvited onlookers remain hidden, comforting one another a few streets away from the main ceremony, where a square full of people are being praised for their piousness.

Sancia squeezes her cousin's hand and returns Baltasar's embrace, appreciating that this is the second time he has saved her. And wondering if she wishes, this time, he hadn't.

EVEN THE LEAVES CAN HEAR

———✦◈✦———

I talk to Annette through the mirror in her bedroom as she fiddles with her hairclips. "Was that a knock at the door?"

She motions *yes* while holding one pin between her lips. "Can you get that?" She says, without opening her mouth.

It'll be Yoni, the man Annette started dating a little over a year ago. I let Nunu hop out of my arms and onto her bed. I walk out of her room and open the door to a tall, fair-skinned man with dirty-blond hair. He is wearing blue denim jeans, a beige collared shirt, and an ascot. Really, an ascot. I'm taken aback by the spitting image of Fred Jones. Though tempted to ask him if he knows where Shaggy and Scooby ran off to, I practice restraint.

"Hi. You must be Yoni. I'm Abi." I hold out my hand to shake his. "I've been looking forward to meeting you."

He returns the gesture. His English is consistent with a strong Hebrew accent.

Annette appears before I close the door behind him. "I'm glad you introduced yourselves."

I wink at her. "Had to. Didn't know how long you'd take."

As Annette steps out the door, she ties her sweater around her shoulders.

That reminds me it might be chilly this evening. "I'm going to grab a sweater. I'll lock up and meet you two outside in a minute."

I see Annette and Yoni waiting for me on the sidewalk. I join them, and then we stroll toward the beautiful, tree-lined street of Rothschild Boulevard. Annette points to a bland, boxy modern complex. "That's my favorite building in Tel Aviv!"

She can't be serious. I laugh. "It's ugly!"

Annette brings her hands to her chest and inhales dramatically. "I'm serious! The house is brilliant. I'm not the only one who appreciates it. This city was awarded UNESCO recognition as a heritage site because of the well-preserved houses built in this style. Bauhaus architecture."

Yoni kicks a small rock off the sidewalk. "Such double standards. They're worthless. UNESCO financially sponsors an academic chair at the Islamic University of Gaza." He then looks at me while continuing to walk. "Do you know the Islamic University of Gaza?"

"It's a school for Palestinians in Gaza?" I guess.

He stops and then he turns to me. "It is a school for *terrorists* in Gaza!"

"Oh, so people who attend university in Gaza must be terrorists?" That's a bigoted assumption. I try to move beyond him to continue walking. I want to eat before he makes me lose my appetite.

Yoni doesn't budge. His feet stay planted and he folds his arms. "The Islamic University of Gaza houses a bomb-making facility where militants are taught how to make explosives to use against Israelis. UNESCO claims that the money is for their 'astrophysics' department and not their bomb lab, as if killers honor such distinctions."

I repeat back to him what I hear him saying so that he can understand how ridiculous he sounds. "Yoni, you are saying that while UNESCO applauds Tel Aviv's architecture by naming it a heritage site, they financially support people determined to destroy it!"

"Yes!" He seems excited as if I actually buy into what he is saying. He totally misses the sarcasm in my voice. *Second language.* He then continues as if he thinks he is convincing me of any of this. "UNESCO is just a small example of what is wrong with the United Nations. They take measures to wipe out Jewish history —."

I've had enough of his nonsense. "Yoni, I know we just met but you are sounding a little too para—"

He cuts me off before I finish telling him how paranoid he sounds. "They officially refer to our holiest site, the Temple Mount, as Haram al-Sharif. By doing so, the United Nations lends more credibility to the Temple Mount's violent Islamic conquest than to its ancient Jewish origin. They enable Islam's invasive ways, even if not practicing them."

I look at Annette. How does she like this guy? He is an Islamophobe! And he just put a bit of a damper on our evening.

Yoni's eyes move from mine to Annette's. "Who cares that Tel Aviv is a UNESCO World Heritage site? You lend credibility to the UN's dangerous hypocrisy — to their self-destructive stupidity. Couldn't you have just said, simply, that you like the building?" He then turns and outpaces us.

Blowing off steam, I suppose. *And take your bigoted attitude with you!* He has made Annette sad. And he pissed me off. *What a jackass!*

I need to lift her spirits. "He is probably off looking for Shaggy and Scooby."

Three . . . two . . . one—there's the smile. She falls right into character. "Jinkies, I didn't notice that before."

I'm amazed. "How could you not have noticed? He is the spitting image of Fred Jones."

Annette and I were avid fans of *Scooby-Doo*, watching it regularly at our grandparents' house. We practically grew up in that house together while our parents worked. We played with a couple of friends in the neighborhood, taking turns plotting mysteries that the others would try to solve.

Yoni eventually stops to look in a window at a store in Neve Tzedek, giving us a chance to catch up so that we can finish walking to the restaurant together. By the time we arrive at Cafe Suzana, everything seems okay. We sit outside at a table below a branch of the large ficus tree that stretches over the patio. I open the menu and become instantly grateful that my appetite has not diminished. Not a single bit. I want one of everything. "Do you guys want to share plates?"

Annette hands the paper with the specials to me. "Sure. But what do you want to get?"

All I see are more options. "I don't know. I like just about everything."

"Without meat." Annette tells Yoni about my caveat. "Abi is a vegetarian."

I don't want my needs to restrict them. "You guys get whatever you want. I know I'll be totally fine."

Yoni folds his menu. "I already know what I want. Let's each pick two dishes. We will start with that, and if we are still hungry, we'll order more."

Not a bad idea. Maybe I can like this guy, after all. "Sounds good."

Soon after taking our order, the server brings wine, dinner rolls, and olive oil to our table.

Yoni reaches for a roll. "Annette tells me you have three children."

I nod and then I turn to Annette. "Harry loves the necklace you sent to her for her birthday."

"Her? Harry is a she?" Yoni asks.

"Yes. Harry is short for Harriet." Annette reaches for the olive oil, dips a ripped piece of bread into it and then she turns to me before indulging. "I'm so glad she likes it. I just wish I could've given it to her in person."

I snap my fingers. "That reminds me. Before I leave, I need to buy a Petah Tikva Troopers shirt for Sandy."

"Your daughter is an Israeli football fan?" Yoni asks.

Annette smiles — her mouth is full. She takes a moment and then answers. "Sandy is Abi's son. Not daughter. Sandy. Short for Sanford."

He holds up two fingers. "So, you have a daughter named

Harry and a son named Sandy." He then holds up a third finger. "—And one more?"

I nod. "Yes. Maya."

"What is his name short for?" His mistake does make
me smile.

I answer. "*Her* name is simply Maya."

Annette has always shared a special bond with my children. I was so grateful when she took them for an entire
day alone in Sante Fe so that Daniel and I could have some
vacation time to ourselves.

She reaches for my hand. "I can't wait to see them again."

I feel the same. It's been just a few days, but I already
miss them so much. And I feel guilt for enjoying myself without them. "I plan to return here in a few months, sometime
during the summer, because the job will take a while. I plan
to rent a place. I'll spend some time from work looking for
one in the next couple of weeks." I love living with Annette,
but I think we would drive each other nuts if it became too
regular. "Maybe I'll bring them this summer. I'll look into
one of the local camps for when I'll be working."

Annette clasps her hands together. "That's a fantastic
idea. Oh my gosh, they will love being here!"

They would. It's been too long. I'm afraid they don't
even remember this place. But I'm not sure Daniel could
leave work for that long. Before I think these things aloud,
the server approaches to top off our wineglasses. "Your dinner will be out in a minute."

I look up to thank him, and then I catch a glimpse of a
group of men standing up from their table, about to walk

out of the restaurant. I whisper to Annette, "I think that's the guy from the plane."

She turns her head to see.

He has to walk by us to reach the stairs. I'm conflicted between staring further to see if I'm right, or turning away so he doesn't catch me looking at him.

Too late. It's him. Ari.

He cocks his head. "Abi?"

His friends wait behind him. We make brief introductions before he says that the others need to be someplace else. "But I do not." He waves goodbye to them and then motions to ask if he can join us. It's a table for four. It's hard to say no. Yoni generously opens his palm to the unoccupied seat. Ari sits in it. He then refuses the extra empty plate the waiter brings over when he serves our food. "No thank you. I already ate." And then he reaches to take a braised carrot from my plate.

I snap a look at him.

"What? I shared my entire meal with you." He smiles as he chews. Then he explains himself to Annette and Yoni. "I gave half of my sandwich to Abi, otherwise, she would not have had enough to eat. She forgot to order a vegetarian meal before the flight." He looks at me. "I kept you from starving." And then he breaks off a piece of roll from the basket.

"How could I forget?" I sit back in my chair and wave my hand over my plate. "Help yourself."

Yoni invites Ari to order something else from the menu.

"No, thank you. I'm really not hungry." He then dips the piece of roll into the hummus on my plate.

I tilt my head at him.

Yoni asks about my job, I suspect, to distract me from the awkward dinner situation.

"I'm helping to investigate a sunken ship that was recently discovered off the coast of Tel Aviv. Divers came across it while plotting a way to connect a pipeline from an oil and gas field in the sea."

Yoni gasps with excitement. *Somewhat endearing.* "Does it have pirate treasure?"

Ari laughs off his suggestion.

I hand a napkin to him so he can wipe the hummus from the corner of his mouth. "Hey, don't knock it. Pirates are real and so are their treasures, which can tell us an enormous amount of information about the victims they stole from. In any case, we're just starting to learn about this ship. I've been told that the initial wood analysis dates it to the Middle Ages. Completing this project could take a long time. I'll probably be traveling back and forth quite a bit in the next year or so."

"Wow, the Middle Ages!" Annette then says, "that candlestick holder that you've been keeping on your dresser for years is from the Middle Ages, isn't it?"

"You have an item from the medieval era?" Yoni seems genuinely interested.

I nod. "It's a family heirloom."

Yoni then reaches for the plate with the grape leaves. He takes one and then offers the rest to Ari. "That is remarkable – to have an item survive within a family for so many generations. A candlestick holder?"

Annette snaps her fingers and points at me. "Maybe it's a Shabbat candlestick holder. Maybe it's one of a pair. Maybe there is another one just like it somewhere."

I shrug my shoulders. "Maybe." *Of course it's one of a pair!* I've known that since it came into my possession twenty-six years ago, when I became a bat mitzvah. I've been dreaming of finding its match ever since.

"That's it!" Ari then snaps his fingers. "That's what you hope to find! The artifact lost at sea. Now I understand. 'You've seen it and you've held it' because half of the set is already in your possession. My gosh you kept me wondering about that."

Fantastic. A table full of sleuths.

Annette seems hurt. "Why didn't you tell me that? Why did you tell him that?"

Because I didn't think I'd ever see him again! "Because it really isn't a big deal!"

Annette places the fork and knife on her plate to signal that she has finished eating. "But it is a big deal. That's what drove you to be an archaeologist."

"It's not." It really isn't. I touch my locket. *It's still there.*

Ari finally remembers the whole birthday superstition issue and my initial reluctance to be specific on the plane. He whispers quietly as he looks down at the table. "I'm sorry."

"It's okay." I just want to change the topic. "This is such a cute place. The food is awesome. Great tree, green leaves, nice building."

"We have lots of nice buildings." Ari points to the

direction we came from. "Have you walked up Rothschild Boulevard?"

"Of course. Many times. But earlier this evening I learned the name of the architecture. And that it is a UNESCO World Heritage Site." I probably shouldn't have mentioned that. I give an apologetic look to Annette for bringing up the topic that caused angst on our way here.

"Uh yes. The Bauhaus architecture is great. But UNESCO . . ." Ari shakes his head and then he reaches for an unused water glass from the set table next to ours. He empties the rest of our wine into it. "UNESCO and just about all of the United Nations has become garbage."

Yoni tilts his wineglass in a toast to Ari's comment. They both take a drink.

Oh brother. No organization is perfect. "So, UNESCO made an administrative mistake by giving money to some people who might aim to bring harm to one of their own heritage sites. I'm not even sure you're right about that, Yoni. If you are, they probably didn't know what they were doing."

"Oh - they know exactly what they're doing." Ari stares at his glass as he twirls the wine in it. Then his wrist stops moving and he looks up at me. "Abi, you've been spending too much time with artifacts and not enough time observing life."

How rude! I should be schooled by some guy who picks food off the plate of strangers? How do I respond to that?

Annette rushes to diffuse the situation. "I don't follow global politics either. I'm rather an anomaly in Israel."

"Indeed, you are. You should know the entire UN has

declined into a human rights disaster. It's disgraceful. You're a doctor, for heaven's sake. You should be outraged!"

She's a dentist! Her boyfriend should know what she does! I'm not sure if I'm full from eating or have simply lost my appetite from listening to these two men. "How can you say that? It must be its diversity that bothers you. The United Nations is an amazing global feat! Over a hundred nations work together to make this world a better place. It's cooperation at its finest. Does it have to be perfect to be great?"

"Apparently Israel does." Ari folds his arms. "You can't be serious, Abi, defending an entity that's so despicable."

You're despicable! "People from all ethnic and religious backgrounds gather civilly to collaborate. Just because you think it's despicable, doesn't mean I do."

He leans toward me. "Its greatest feat is the legitimization of the cruelest dictatorships."

Yoni adds, "And providing cover for the world to get together to condemn Israel."

Ah. Now I see where this is going. They don't like their "perfect country" being told to behave in the global arena. "I love it here, but it isn't perfect. Everyone around the world knows it. So, change."

Ari's tone becomes shy of condescending. "How to change, Abi? Should we conform to the will of the countries of the United Nations?"

Probably. "Maybe that would be a start."

Ari's tone remains combative, as if *I'm* some enemy. "Let's start with the UNHRC, The United Nations Human Rights Council. Saudi Arabia, where all women have been prohibited, by law, from driving, from visiting a doctor without permission from a male guardian —"

I cut him off. "I read that Saudi Arabia started letting women drive."

"Wow – you set the bar really high there. Did you also read about how that government created an app so that men can restrict and track the movement of their wives?"

"No. That's awful, if it's even true. But it's not up to me to decide on how people act upon what they believe is right."

"Seriously?" He moves his head as if he is shaking off water that splashed in his face. "You seem to act upon it when it's about condemning Israel."

"No, I don't. I stay out of politics. You two are bringing us into this." I motion to Annette.

"You just suggested that Israel should change to conform to the will of the United Nations, yet you are refusing to recognize whose will the UN bends to. Who serves on their Human Rights Council? In addition to Saudi Arabia, there is Iraq, Afghanistan, Pakistan." Ari pauses with a deep breath. "Do you know anything about the tortured lives of the people who live in those countries? Their misery has nothing to do with Israel. It has to do with the inhumane Islamic system that governs them. They have awful leaders who certainly should not be dictating to us about human rights."

Is he listening to himself? "Us! They!" And he says *Islamic* as if that's the cause of the problems. I make sure Ari hears me as I apologize to Annette for his presence. "I didn't know he was such a racist. And I didn't invite him to sit here with us." I'm not sure Yoni is much better. I need to get out of here. I motion to the waiter to bring the bill. "It's no wonder everyone hates this country. I used to think it was because they haven't been here, and they didn't know how accepting everyone was. But now I see it's I who didn't know how unaccepting you are. They hate this place because of people like you and your *Islamophobia!*"

Ari tilts his head and scrunches his face. "*Islamophobia?* We were talking about the United Nations Human Rights Council, Abi, and one of the chairs of one of their panels is Saudi Arabia – where the official religion is Islam and where official punishments include slicing off heads and publicly crucifying bodies – and we already talked a little bit about the inhumane treatment against Saudi women. I could go on."

"Really? I couldn't imagine that." I hope he gets my sarcasm. I need him to entertain a serious question. "Do you really think countries should be excluded from global decision making just because they behave in ways you don't like?" Rhetorical. I don't even want to hear his bullshit answer. I recall the comforting words of a college chaplain who said that separating Jewish identity, from Israel as a state, is very important. He was right. Fighting for Israel is not my responsibility. "It's people like you who make it difficult for me to defend Israel."

Yoni shakes his head. "Something tells me you don't defend Israel."

That isn't my job! "It's your job to make it so Israel doesn't need defending."

Yoni moves his plate to the side, as if clearing a path so that his words could better reach me. "What could we do to make the world happy? The countries that decide that we aren't behaving properly are countries in which gay people are severely punished, prison detention is a political tool, and torture is commonplace. Saudi Arabia, Egypt, Afghanistan. To be fair – not all the bad governments in that UN branch are Muslim. There is also Venezuela, Congo and Rwanda. Learn about them before you defend their 'right' to determine your rights."

Oh, other governments are bad, too. Bravo that you acknowledge that – how non-Islamophobic of you! I ask again, though not rhetorical this time – I want to hear an answer. "Do you really think countries should be excluded from global decision making just because they behave in ways you don't like?"

"Yes." Ari says without an ounce of doubt in his voice. So arrogant. "If I deem those laws barbaric, why would I want the people who implement such horrors, *against* their own citizens, to determine how *our* society should function?"

Yoni hands his phone to me after pulling up a video. "Don't listen to us. Listen to this guy, Hillel Neuer, the director of UN Watch."

"'Hillel Neuer.' I love him." Ari's mood lightens. He clasps his hands together then leans over. "Which video?"

"It's the 'Algeria, Where Are Your Jews?' one."

Ari motions his approval. "That's old, but it is a good one."

Annette moves closer to me as we watch the four minutes together. And then she presses pause to stop the next video from starting. "So many thousands of Jews used to live in each of those countries? What happened?"

Yoni touches his phone while I'm still holding it. It displays a map of Islamic countries shaded almost entirely green. There's a tiny speck of a different color in the center—Israel. "Well, the same thing that happened to the once majority Christians of what is now Turkey, or the once majority Buddhists in what is now Afghanistan. Indigenous identities gone with subsequent generations. They succumbed to Islamic conquest."

I'm still critical. "Those are big words." I hand him back his phone. But I must confess. "This is new to me. Maybe I should learn more."

Ari cups his ear with his hand and leans in my direction. "What was that you said?"

"I'll look up Hillel Neuer later." I need to keep a shred of dignity. "Because he is cute." And he is cute.

"He is cute!" Ari says as if he has a crush.

We laugh. Tension diffused.

The waiter brings the bill. I think he might have been too scared to approach our table before. I can feel the presence of the restaurant's grand tree. It's been listening to us. It's probably been losing a few leaves in the process.

I hand my credit card to the waiter while holding off anyone else from doing so. "This is my treat. It's to neutralize my indebtedness to the passenger who gave edible food to me on a very, very, long flight, and to thank you, my friend and favorite cuz, for allowing me free room and board. Considering this small token, I really get off easy, actually."

Annette objects. "Free room but not free board. I know how it is when you're in the kitchen. Abi cooks so well — you wouldn't even miss meat if she were your chef."

"That sounds like an invitation!" Ari hints as we all stand up.

"In your dreams!" Annette pushes in her chair.

Ari pushes in his. "Thank you for dinner. Sorry about any rough moments."

"At least this was shorter than the flight," I say with a smile. This was a less-than-pleasant dinner, but I learned something new, and I prefer to part amicably.

Yoni motions for Ari's phone. I think he is entering his contact information. Cute. Annette's boyfriend will have a new friend. This evening had its share of bumps, but at least it wasn't an entire loss.

Committing to Live,
Being Torn Apart

— 1484 —

Not a moment goes by in which the image of her father burning in the fire set by order of the Church, three years ago, does not share space with Sancia's current focus. Even the home of her cousins is heavy with her father's absence. Yet she is able to delight in their presence.

She brushes and twists Astruga's long hair into a fancy braid when younger Ana walks into the room. Both girls have thick, wavy, dark-brown hair, almost black, like their older brother. "Will you do mine next?"

"Of course." Sancia's hands welcome a task that is not sewing.

"I thought Iuceph was next," Astruga says, giggling.

Iuceph looks up from a piece of wood he is carving into a figure. "Very funny."

"When are Mother, Father, and Aunt Esther returning?" Astruga rubs her stomach. Sancia is hungry too.

"I hope they take a long time." Ana sits next to her sister in line for her hair to be styled. "Sancia will have to go home soon after they return."

"Not right away," Sancia says. "We will have dinner together."

"And the Buendias will be here too," Iuceph says.

"This evening? David will be here?" Sancia feels her cheeks redden. Fortunately, no one is looking at her as she hides behind Astruga's hair.

Iuceph nods while remaining focused on his project. "Soon. I asked him to come here when he is done with his chores."

No sooner does Iuceph finish saying that when David arrives.

He touches the mezuzah on the doorframe and brings his fingers to his lips before stepping inside. "This door was not locked."

Ana looks up. "We will be more careful next time."

"That is very grown-up of you. I see we have some beauties here today." David nods toward the younger girls, but Sancia can't help wondering if he is directing the comment at her as well. She tries not to blush, but remains partially tucked behind Astruga's head just to be sure.

She then finishes tying up the end of Astruga's hair. "My beautiful cousin, go and see if there is something you can eat for now, so you will feel better until the others get back." She signals to Ana to take the spot Astruga left.

"My turn!" Ana skootches so that Sancia can reach her hair.

Before Astruga walks to the kitchen, she shapes her hands around an imaginary dress. "Will you make a beautiful dress for me? I want to sparkle under the sun."

"I do too!" Ana turns to Sancia so quickly her face almost gets scratched by the hairbrush.

"Be careful," Sancia delights in her cousins' imaginations. "You both sparkle. You do not need a beautiful dress. Your smiles shine, and your eyes sparkle more than any piece of clothing ever could." Sancia holds Ana's hair in place to pin it up.

Iuceph puts his wooden project down. "Tell them why you really will not make dresses for them, Sancia. Go on." He doesn't give Sancia time to answer before turning to Astruga. "You are not allowed to wear pretty clothes outside. So why should our cousin waste her time sewing such a dress for you?"

Sancia looks up. "Iuceph, what has gotten into you?"

"I'm a bar mitzvah. That means that soon I will be fourteen years of age. Then the law will apply to me." Iuceph is cryptic.

"What law?" Sancia asks.

Iuceph looks up at David. She knows that David, at seventeen years of age, is like a big brother to her cousin. They have spent a lot of time together since their fathers are the closest of friends. David doesn't look confused but concerned. She realizes they've had this conversation before. "What is going on? What are you two up to?"

"Not me," David says. "Just Iuceph."

Sancia could not be prepared for what Iuceph says. "I'm going to convert."

"Have you gone mad?" Sancia stands up.

"I have told him not to!" David says.

"He did tell me not to. But the more I argued back, the more I realized that it is what I must do." Iuceph turns to his sisters. "And I want you two to do it with me."

"Now I *know* you have gone mad." Sancia steps toward Iuceph. "How could you even think of this? You watched them burn your uncle to death! You see how *conversos* disappear. You must have noticed the wound under the chin of Maymon and the awkward way he holds his head. They wedged a metal bar between his chin and his chest. He couldn't rest his head for days. And now his neck is damaged – maybe forever. Tomás de Torquemada, the Grand Inquisitor, has unlimited soldiers to send after anyone he wants. Why would you give them power over you like that?"

Iuceph answers. "Because we are still too young. The Holy Office cannot arrest us for some time. Being thirteen gives me almost a year, and my sisters even longer, to really understand their ways—the Christian ways—so we can blend in properly when it matters."

"Why would you want to blend in with them? I am fifteen years of age." Sancia points to herself. "But even if they extended the age to twenty I still would not do it."

Ana panics. "I do not want to, either. Mother and Father will kill us!"

"No." Iuceph slams his hands on the tabletop. "They will not. But the Inquisition will."

"That is not true," Astruga says. "I have cried with worry that they would take us away too. Mother and Father said they do not arrest Jews who have never been baptized. They killed Uncle Isaac because he was baptized - because he was a Catholic who did not behave the way they wanted him to, not because he was a Jew."

"I cannot stop thinking of the stories from a hundred years ago." Iuceph brings up a history that Sancia knows all too well. "Not even a hundred years ago, right here, Jews, just like us, were dragged into churches over the bodies of people already slain by the mobs instructed to kill Jews by . . ." Iuceph pauses, struggling to remember the name of the friar who sparked the massacre.

Sancia doesn't want to come to his aid but can't help herself. "Friar Ferrand Martinez."

"Right, Friar Martinez. Christians sprinkled water on the Jews they dragged into the churches and announced, 'This Jew is now Catholic.' If such a thing would happen today, we would not be able to escape the Inquisition. To them, we would be Catholic the moment they would sprinkle water on us. They would then tie us to a stake and set flames to our bodies." Iuceph's eyes widen in horror. He begins to breath deeply, quickly.

Sancia knows what he sees - the same image seared into his memory, too. She thinks back to the day after they killed her father. Three guards came to her home to demand payment for the cost of keeping him in prison. *Iuceph has a point. But Papa had a point, too, when he took the same path.* And it was a horrible path to take!

Iuceph regains control of his breathing. "We have to outwit them. We need to make sure they will not do that to us. I have almost a year to learn how to perfect becoming a Christian, and Ana and Astruga have a little more than that."

Sancia raises her voice. "Do you think these people are logical? Do you think they will need a legitimate reason to harm you?"

Iuceph raises his voice. "They harm us, anyway. While we are Jews, they tell us what we can and cannot wear, where we can live, what jobs we are prohibited from."

Sancia knows he is right. *Yet, my argument is just as strong.* "But the laws of the kingdom allow us to live as Jews. If you become a Christian, those laws will allow them to kill you like they killed my father." She looks at her youngest cousins. She doesn't want to burden them with this frightening information, but they need to know before they might get tangled in their brother's misguided plan. She then looks at David imploringly.

He responds to her prompt. "Iuceph, do you really think they killed Diego de Suson because they wanted to keep this kingdom pure for their god? Do you really think they wanted to 'save his soul'? Or is it more likely they killed him because he was among the richest of the converts and they simply wanted to take his wealth? They force people into a faith that they cannot believe so that they can label them as heretics, kill them and then steal their wealth while adhering to their laws. They kill. They steal. We bleed. They take." David takes a deep breath. "Iuceph, you are upset that now we are prohibited from jobs that could make us rich. That is the biggest blessing we could ask for in this life. The Crown, their greed—they are not interested in us, you and me. We are too poor. But as soon as you can be productive and have some money to your name, allowed to you as a Christian, they will come after you. They will charge you with wearing too nice a shirt on a Saturday or some other nonsense, then torture you and kill you. They will take your earnings."

"Then they will do that, anyway." Iuceph looks at his sisters. "Do this with me. They cannot control what we think— they can only control how we behave."

"But we will behave in ways that we do not like." Astruga makes a face. "We will have to eat pork, we will have to go to church, if not now, then as adults. We will not be able to observe our day of rest."

"We will observe their day of rest. HaShem will understand."

Sancia fears Iuceph might be reaching his sisters. "I will not let you!"

"I will also do whatever I can to stop you," David says.

Iuceph stands straight and touches his chest. "This is my choice."

Sancia becomes conflicted as she hears the adults right outside. *Should I tell them what is going on? Iuceph would never trust me again.* She knows that when she or Iuceph is determined to do something, they find a way. *He is determined to convert. I am determined to stop him.*

Her mother, aunt and uncle hold bags from the market as they walk through the door, each touching the mezuzah and bringing their fingers to their lips.

Her mother is cheerful. She hands a small package to Sancia. "Please, bring the salmon into the kitchen."

"Salmon? We have salmon?" Iuceph asks with excitement. They have all tired of eating sardines, the more affordable fish.

"Yes, my loves." Esther opens her bag to reveal vegetables. "We want to enjoy spring. The weather is beautiful, and the trees are blossoming."

Sancia's Aunt Regina puts sliced bread on the table and then kisses her on the cheek.

The mood inside the home has shifted. Sancia feels helpless, yet she goes along with the spirited atmosphere to keep her cousin's secret — for now.

On their walk home from dinner, Sancia looks behind, to see how far away David's parents and her mother are. She knows they won't be able to hear her. "They cannot do this, David."

David turns, seeming to confirm their parents' distance. "You know Iuceph has made up his mind."

"How long has he been talking to you about this?" Sancia senses David feeling trapped by her tone. She tries to soften it. "I know you are a big brother to him and you kept his confidence as such. I feel like I am in that same position now. But we need to work together to make sure he does nothing foolish."

David nods. "Almost a fortnight. He knows I have been against the idea since the moment he brought it up. He does have some valid points, but I think his plan is too dangerous. I did not hold back on telling him any news that I have heard. Those who are stolen but get released are tortured with an evil cleverness."

"They are *clever* when torturing people?"

"The Catholic clergy are not allowed to draw blood. That is why they brought your father to a different area. His death was supervised by the Church, while the secular authorities did the actual killing."

"That does not make sense," Sancia says. "Even if they design their system so they do not actually kill anyone, they torture people. People bleed when tortured."

David slows his pace. "Not when the Inquisitors do it. Think about it. You brought up Maymon earlier. The Heretic's Fork. It damaged his neck, but it did not draw blood. It forced his head back in a painfully awkward position. I have heard even worse. I told Iuceph even worse."

"What else have you heard?"

David looks at the ground. "Sancia, you understand my point. That is enough. And Iuceph understands too."

I demand to know! "I know things are happening. I know that everyone still treats me like a child because they are afraid I might break because I saw my father murdered. I saw my father murdered! I will not break. I need to know what everyone else knows. What else happens in the dungeon, David?"

"They trap their prisoners' feet into metal boots and

set them to fire. They do not draw blood. They do not draw blood when they tie men and women to the ceiling and then drop them with such speed so that the rope dislocates their limbs without them hitting the floor." Then David's voice trails off to a near cry. "The Church does not draw blood."

Sancia focuses on her breathing. *Keep breathing.* But that doesn't stop her from being haunted by the image of Ana suspended her from a ceiling before they drop her, Astruga screaming as they burn her feet in heated metal boots, or Iuceph in agony as they force his head back by a metal fork. She feels her father burning in the flames. She feels his ashes rise into her nose.

"Are you all right, Sancia?"

How can any of us ever be all right?

Options of Mortals

— 1484 —

Sancia walks out of the Judería — quick pace and trousers in hand. She passes taverns that have yet to start the day and orange trees with mature fruit. *Trees grow here just like in my neighborhood. People stroll, eat, and meet with one another just the same. We breathe the same way. Why must they make problems for us?* Six minutes later, she arrives at the metal worker's shop. She opens the door and steps inside.

Baltasar looks up from his workstation. "Nice to see you, Sancia. When I came to your shop yesterday, it was already locked up."

"I did close the shop early." *I couldn't focus on work, not after what Iuceph told me.* Of course, going home early and pretending that she didn't know anything, wasn't any easier. "And I suspected you might have tried to come by.

So, here I am." Sancia extends her arms with the trousers. "And here you go."

Baltasar unfolds the repaired clothing to have a closer look. "Again, you did wonderful work. Thank you. How much?"

"No charge." *A lifetime isn't long enough to repay you for what you've done for me.*

"I will have to stop asking you to repair my clothing if you do not let me pay you."

"I'm the best around. You would not bring your clothing to anyone else." She knows he would not anyway.

"Little one, you learned from the best." Baltasar honors her father whenever he can.

Sancia nods in appreciation. Her loss is his loss too.

Baltasar folds the trousers and puts them on the counter, away from his working area. "Well, it just so happens that our garden produced an early crop of vegetables. Litiosa is home making vegetable pies. I was already planning to bring one to your home and one to your uncle's home."

"Litiosa's cooking is marvelous! Now *that* you could all be charging for. And you would make quite a profit. But do not even think about closing this shop to pursue selling pies. I would miss your beautiful pieces. I always enjoy looking at my necklace when I wear it on special occasions — the one you created."

"Your father designed it. I only followed his instructions."

Sancia places her hand where the pendant of the absent necklace would fall. Her father hadn't told her that. "Just always be here, Baltasar."

"I do not plan on going anywhere. Not for a really long time, little one. What is on your mind? I see something is bothering you."

"Iuceph has been on my mind. A couple days ago, he confided in me that he plans to convert to Christianity. He wants his sisters to do it with him."

"Sancia, if your cousin wants to discover Christ, why should that be a concern? Finding Christ is not bad."

Sancia is taken aback. How could Baltasar say this after seeing what's happened to her family? "He isn't trying to find Christ, Baltasar. He is trying to avoid death. And he thinks the best way to live a satisfying life in this kingdom is to become baptized. It will only bring harm to him and my other cousins—to the whole family."

"Searching for Christ is not bad, no matter what motivates someone to do so. In fact, I wish that the Inquisitors would find Him, especially that demon, Torquemada."

"What do you mean? He is one with the Church. Does he not believe in Christ?"

"I do not know what he believes. But he and the others do not behave in ways that honor Him. They do not behave in ways that tell me they found Him."

Sancia is amazed that Baltasar actually seems pleased about Iuceph's decision. "I know you like Christ."

"I love Christ!"

"Okay. You love him. But we are Jews. He is no more than a man to us. We cannot believe what we cannot believe. We believe in G-d."

"But Jesus is—"

I cannot listen to another word. "Can I count on you to help me stop Iuceph from taking this step? Please, Baltasar. If he shows up near your church, would you please stop him?"

"What about his mother and father?"

"They do not know. My mother does not know. Only David, the son of Nina and Jacob, knows. And he is helping. Will you?"

Baltasar solemnly nods. "I will. He is too young to make such a decision without speaking with his mother and father. Christ is best found when the seeker has his heart in the search."

"Thank you." Sancia breathes a sigh of relief and then gives Baltasar a kiss on the cheek. "Please give my regards to Litiosa."

"Of course. Expect her at your shop before the end of closing tomorrow—with the pies."

Sancia smiles and touches her stomach. "I'm already hungry for tomorrow night's dinner." Then she walks out of his shop and closes the door behind her.

She arrives at her own shop just in time to unlock the door for Oro, a tailor who had been working with her father a couple mornings each week. Sancia surpassed her in height when she was ten years of age. She often complains about her unreliable knees, yet reliably greets Sancia with a smile.

"Good morning, Oro. I was going to apologize for being late, but I see you also took your time getting here this morning."

"I was here rather early today, actually, and saw that

you were not. It was such a lovely morning that I decided to take a walk." Oro points to the direction from which she came. "I happened to stroll by what was once our synagogue. I do not know if you would remember what it looks like inside. It was beautiful. As I was looking at that dastardly church that it has become, I was tricked by an illusion. I thought I saw your three little cousins near the steps, talking to each—"

"No!" Sancia drops her keys and runs as quickly as she can to the old synagogue. *This soon?! Oh no, oh no, oh no, please don't let me be too late.* She runs until she arrives at the newly appointed church.

"Stop!" she orders the three figures ascending the steps.

Astruga turns. "Sancia, how did you know?"

Iuceph does not turn. He keeps his back toward her. "I love you, Sancia, but do not stop me from protecting my sisters."

She takes a step closer, slowly, as if speed will scare them into running into the irreversible. "I want to protect all of you. Do you not see how this will tear apart our family?"

"Iuceph says that we will not stop being family." Ana looks at Sancia while taking her brother's hand. "We will see each other. We just will not be able to practice our traditions. But we will have new ones. If I convert, I can become a teacher. But if I stay a Jew, I cannot."

Sancia's heart plummets. "You can teach Jewish children. We will all need a great teacher like you."

"She is right." Astruga takes a step down one stair.

Iuceph turns in her direction.

Sancia looks at her three cousins, now each looking back at her with the same gray-green eyes. "Just come home with me now. How about that? We will talk more about this. We will talk more about the good points of converting and the good points of staying a Jew."

"We did that a few days ago," Iuceph says. "This is difficult for me. I do not *want* to do this. But I have one year to get this right. That is not much time. And I cannot do this alone. Please, stop. If you love us, you will let us reach our full potential. And the only way we can do that legally is by being the same as everyone else."

Sancia wants to laugh in his face. "You want to be like everybody else?"

Iuceph shakes his head. "No. But I want the same opportunities. I'll work harder and more than everybody else."

She takes a step closer. "You know what would happen if you would become more successful than others. We've already talked about Diego de Suson, who took the path you are about to take. He worked harder and more than almost anyone. He earned a fortune. That only motivated the Church to take what he earned by forcing him to inhale every last piece of his own flesh, like they did my father. Then they took his fortune. The most successful *conversos* are the most in danger. You were born a Jew. It will not matter how perfect a Christian you become."

Astruga trembles. "Is that true?"

"Yes." *If only they could know everything I know.* Sancia doesn't like scaring the children, but they need to be scared enough to reconsider the mistake they are about to make.

"Do not go through with giving the Church full rights over your body and mind."

Iuceph's feet remain planted on the step. "What Sancia says is true. One thing she is leaving out is that Diego was a scholar of the Talmud. He could not pretend to be Catholic enough." Once again, he cites the riots of 1391, which depleted Seville of its entire Jewish community through murder or forced conversion. "It is best for us to convert - to blend in."

"I am scared." Astruga looks pleadingly at Sancia.

"I am too," Ana says.

"And, I am too," Iuceph confesses. "But it is the most risky for me. You two have time before the Inquisition can legally go after you." Iuceph looks at his little sister whose hand he is still holding. "Especially you, Ana."

Sancia stretches her hand toward her cousins. *Please take my hand.* "Do not do this. We will talk more at home. I shall skip work today. Oro can work without me. She has the key. Let us go to my house and talk."

"No! Every day that goes by I have less time to learn." Iuceph turns to ascend the steps. Ana stays by his side. Astruga stares longer at Sancia but gives in to her brother's final plea.

Sancia cannot bear to let her cousins leave her sight. Suppressing the inner voice that warns her to stop, she runs up the steps and enters the church right behind them. Will they arrest her for trespassing? Will they force water on her? Will they let them leave? She tries to adjust her eyes, yet everything is a blur. Faces, statues, so many candles. The menorah is gone. Only faded and inconspicuously placed Hebrew inscriptions remain clear. She turns back to look at the open door and sees the indentation on the frame that once held the mezuzah before the Catholics converted her synagogue to this church. *I could just walk out right now.* No, she will not leave without her cousins.

The smell inside the large room is unfamiliar and awkward—sweet, burnt, and something else. She anticipates coming face-to-face with someone who has been taught to hate her, face-to-face with someone who erased the character of this synagogue. The thought sickens her. She whispers loudly. "Iuceph!"

Instead of turning to her, he approaches a man in a long woolen robe. "We are here to receive Christ."

No, Iuceph, no.

Astruga and Ana hold hands silently behind their brother.

"How wonderful!" The friar the clasps his hands together so that the wooden cross, dangling from a necklace to the center of his chest, sways.

Sancia finds him to be plain, and artificial. Dangerous. *Maybe the sweet, burnt smell is coming from him, not the candles.* The friar then lowers his voice and speaks with the same rhythm as the inquisitor who conducted the *auto de fé*. Sancia remains near the door as she struggles to hear what he says.

"In order for the conversion to begin, you must have a Christian adult to support you through the process and to make sure you remain on the path of Christ. I will be happy to perform the ceremony after we find you a proper Catholic sponsor."

Sancia is relieved. They will have to leave now and she will not let them return.

Iuceph wipes his palms against his trousers. "But we would like to become Christian today. We do not want to wait."

A petite woman steps forward from the pews. "Please excuse me, Friar Deza. But, I could not help but to hear your conversation. The spirit of Christ prompted me to interrupt. May I sponsor the children's transition into Christianity."

Iuceph turns to face her. "You would do that for us? You do not know us."

The woman looks as if she belongs to the upper class, though she is not dressed fancily. A beige kerchief covers the top of her long black braid. "What is your name? And, how old are you?"

"My name is Iuceph. I am thirteen years of age." He motions to his sisters. "This is Astruga—she is eleven—and Ana is ten."

The woman looks past Iuceph and nods toward the entrance. "The one with the golden-brown hair - standing by the door?"

Sancia's heart sinks when she realizes she's been noticed.

Iuceph turns his head to look at her and then back again. "She is my cousin, Sancia. She is fifteen years of age."

Friar Deza brings the palms of his hands together at his chest. "Jesus brought you into this house of worship while Doña Sarmiento was praying. This was all meant to happen. It is rare that such an event could take place with such little planning. Are you certain you have time now, Doña Sarmiento, to sponsor these four children looking to join the ranks of Christ?"

Doña Sarmiento clasps her hands together. "It would be my honor."

Sancia's nerves intensify. She didn't think it would happen so quickly.

The friar looks at her. He motions his hand for her to walk in his direction. "Come closer."

Sancia shakes her head. "I . . . I . . . I am not here for that." *Please do not grab me.*

He frowns. "Then you must leave."

Sancia's feet, desperate to run, remain planted. "They need to come with me!"

Iuceph shakes his head and then looks at the friar. "She does not understand our calling to receive Christ."

"Well then she is trespassing," Friar Deza says. He then takes a step toward her.

Her heart races. She turns and runs out the door. She squats on the platform step to catch her breath and slow her heartbeat. She can't believe she left her cousins in there. *I have failed them. What will become of them? I should have told Uncle Abraham.* She stares at the ground, trying to come to terms with this new disaster. Then two shoes come into view. Familiar, small shoes, with frayed laces. She looks up.

Astruga looks down at her. "I could not do it. I left them. I just left them."

Sancia feels a flicker of relief as she wraps her arms around her cousin. Her presence spared one. But her inaction compromised two. She takes Astruga's hand, and together they descend the steps of the church that was once their synagogue.

Forced Festivities

— 1484 —

Sancia looks down the long road and sighs while deliberately slowing her pace.

Her mother motions for her to keep up. "Hurry, we will be late!"

Sancia knows the consequences of being late. Yet, she stops, plants her feet, crosses her arms and frowns. "I do not want to go. I always hate going! And this year will be worse with Ana and Iuceph on the other side." She has been dreading this moment since people began stretching decorations across every balcony in preparation for this annual spectacle, the Corpus Christi parade.

Esther stops and turns to face Sancia. "Do you think I like this?" She raises her voice. "I also hate going. I also want to be close to all of your cousins. At least Astruga will be with us when we meet up with the others."

"But we will not see Iuceph and Ana."

"You know they will be safer attending alongside their sponsor. This is very difficult for all of us. Please do not make this more difficult."

How could I make suffering through hours of belittling and mindless revelry, just to avoid having to pay a fine we cannot afford, more difficult?

Sancia and her mother meet up with the rest of the family. They all make their way to the crowd. Across the path set for the parade route, Sancia spots the dreadful woman who enabled her cousins' baptism. Iuceph and Ana are standing next to her. They are wearing beautiful clothing that she has not seen before. She can't believe they are dressed up for this horrible obligation. She has had enough of this charade and is determined to bring them back with her. Without saying a word to the others, she crosses the road to fulfill her mission.

A boy, maybe a man, steps in front of her as she gets close to Iuceph. He looks down at him. "Juan, do you know these *marranos*?"

He just called me a pig! He reminds Sancia of the boys who killed the rabbi six years ago. *Could he be one of them?* No, he is about the same age now as those murderers were then. Calculating how to respond to his slur, she realizes she is not alone. *He said, 'marranos.'* She turns to see her mother is right behind her.

"Lorenzo, my dear son, where are your manners? No one here is a Jew pretending to be a Christian. Juan and his sister are proper Catholics, even though they are just learning." Doña Sarmiento looks at Sancia. "And you, you are the girl from the church who chose not to be baptized. Is that right?"

Sancia nods. *Why are they referring to Iuceph as Juan?*

Lorenzo's upper lip curls as he snickers. "Jews content being Jews. So, they are actually *lower* than pigs."

Esther steps in front of Sancia and directly addresses her nephew. "Iuceph, what have you done? How can you stand to be with these people? Both of you, come to the other side with us now! We shall take you home after this."

Sancia was thinking the same thing but is worried her mother's words might get them into trouble. Or get the children into trouble.

Lorenzo's lip remains curled. "Who is Iuceph?"

Iuceph pleads to his cousin and aunt with his eyes. *Please do not answer him.*

Sancia glares back at Iuceph accusingly. *Look what you have done.*

Doña Sarmiento answers Lorenzo. "Iuceph was Juan's name before he came to Jesus."

Lorenzo puts his wrists to either side of his waist and leans forward. "That is your pig name? Iuceph?"

Iuceph remains silent.

Lorenzo gets louder. And he enunciates his words more rigidly. "Answer me. I am asking you a question. Is Iuceph your pig name?"

Doña Sarmiento seems embarrassed by her son. "Lorenzo, please behave like a Christian. Juan and Ana are both good Christians, and they know it feels good to be so. Is that not right, children?"

Sancia watches in disgust as her cousins obediently nod.

Their sponsor responds in delight at their conformity. "Maybe their cousin and this woman will join us one day soon. But they will not seek to be saved if you say such distasteful things." She turns her head to Sancia and her mother. "You see, we want you to be saved."

Sancia is as sickened by Doña Sarmiento's misguided good intentions as she is by her son's blatant hatefulness. "We need to get back to the others." She tugs on her mother's dull burlap dress while motioning to Iuceph and Ana to follow.

"No!" Lorenzo says sharply. "You will stay with us. You will all stay with us."

Sancia ignores him, motioning again for her cousins to come with her. *He can't stop us. Let's go.*

Lorenzo announces, "The penalty for apostasy is death."

She stops.

"Lorenzo, enough of this! There is no apostasy here!" Doña Sarmiento says.

Lorenzo holds Iuceph's gaze. "I just want them to know that anyone who abandons Christ after finding Him shall be tried in a court of law. And killed."

He is right. Father said the same thing when I suggested he leave the Church. But they killed him anyway. Iuceph and Ana are at the mercy of these horrible people. Sancia focuses on her breath to make sure she is taking in air and releasing it, breathing in and out.

"What was Ana's name when she was still a pig?" Lorenzo feigns caring. When his mother frowns at him, he dramatically corrects himself. "I mean, what was Ana's name when she was a Jew?"

Doña Sarmiento responds as if her son asked out of

genuine curiosity, though she likely knows he did not. "Ana did not need to change her name. Only Juan did. His previous name, Iuceph, is not an appropriate Christian name." She gives Ana a soft smile while gently lifting the little girl's face by her chin. "Ana is a beautiful Christian name for a beautiful Christian girl."

Sancia's skin crawls at the sight of the woman touching her cousin. That woman put her cousins in danger. She did not save them as she seems to think. Sancia looks at Doña Sarmiento. *Mindless.* She looks at Lorenzo. *Evil.* Weakness of the mind, no matter the intention, becomes fertile ground for evil.

"Ana should have a new name so that she forgets the filth she came from."

"That is not necessary. Hush now, Lorenzo. The parade is coming." Doña Sarmiento clasps her hands in excitement and turns her head toward the end of the street.

In the distance, marching before the consecrated hosts and the nobles, are people dressed to look like dwarfs and giants, their bodies topped with disproportionally large heads. Sancia has had to tolerate this spectacle since she can remember. She knows the dwarfs and giants are supposed to look awkward — touched by evil. They walk alongside a figure of the devil. They are supposed to represent the spiritual opposite of the king and the consecrated host, the pure, the holy, the perfect. Sancia scans the crowd. They all accept the idea of good versus evil simplified by masks and costumes, kings and noblemen. So primitive. Yet Sancia understands the attraction of getting lost in this nonsensical bliss—the attraction of getting lost in a world in which everything is simple.

After pointing out and narrating the obvious, Doña Sarmiento notes with particular amazement the large groups of uniformly dressed men. "Look at all of those bodyguards. There are hundreds of them. Only a most precious person would be given so many bodyguards. Friar Torquemada must be coming soon. How exciting to be so close to a man so close to Jesus." Her face beams with pride when she turns to Iuceph and Ana. "Lorenzo will be a bodyguard for the Grand Inquisitor one day."

Iuceph looks confused. "I recall you mentioning that Lorenzo is already a bodyguard for the Inquisitors."

Lorenzo corrects him. "Yes, Inquisitors — those who work under the Grand Inquisitor. But Torquemada, himself, is who I will work for one day."

Sancia is surprised when her mother asserts herself again. Esther says, "Torquemada already has two hundred fifty bodyguards. Maybe you could be a bodyguard for the meek whom he arrests instead. I know of Old Christians who are afraid of him." Sancia wonders if she is referring to Baltasar and Litiosa. Esther continues, "He does not need the two hundred fifty bodyguards he already has. But his victims could use some to protect them from that disgusting man, who has no mercy."

Lorenzo's eyes inflame. "How dare you criticize him? He has mercy indeed! His mercy is for our Lord, Jesus Christ. Friar Torquemada does not arrest the meek as you dare suggest, but he arrests heretics, those who use their strength to disgrace Christ. Do not question any Inquisitor's need for protection. None will die on my watch."

"Lorenzo," Doña Sarmiento chides, "I am sure she means no harm. She made an ignorant comment. That is it."

This woman thinks she knows ignorance?

Lorenzo's cheeks flush and his eyes widen. "That is not it, Mother. The comment comes from the vermin who create the need for these servants of God to have protection."

"She is not vermin! She is my aunt!"

Iuceph, no! Sancia remains severely silent. She worries that Iuceph has put himself in more danger by attempting to defend her mother.

Lorenzo softens his tone, but not his language. "That is right. You share her blood, Juan. Juan. I know a Juan. He is sitting in jail right now awaiting execution."

"Juan de Esperandeu," Esther says solemnly.

Who is Juan de Esperandeu?

"Lots of people have that name, Lorenzo." Doña Sarmiento pulls Iuceph protectively close to her. "A lot of fine Christian boys, like our Juan here, have that name."

Sancia becomes ambivalent about Doña Sarmiento's protective affection. Since this dull-minded woman already put Iuceph and Ana at risk, *she might now be the only barrier that keeps her son from harming my cousins.*

"True, Mother. Our Juan here would never dare think of approaching an Inquisitor, a loyal servant of the Lord, to stab him in the neck while he is on his knees in prayer in a church."

Esther leans forward and holds her wrists slightly behind her back as a counter weight. "Juan de Esperandeu killed to stop more killing — to stop your murderous soldiers from further ruining this land of Andalusia, which, by the way, we built on long before Christians built on it, then reclaimed it from the Muhammadans who conquered it. And the way Christians reclaimed it was by killing our people and stealing our money to pay for your army. And you treat us like we are not even human. We, Jews, were here long before your Christ was ever born. And he, by the way, was a Jew like me. Do you think you please him by killing his brethren? Do you call Him pig?"

Lorenzo strikes Esther across the face.

"Mother!" Sancia cups her mother's face in her hands to get a closer look at her injury.

Lorenzo shakes his hand from the sting of contact. "Do not link yourself to Jesus, vermin. Jews killed Jesus like Jews killed Pedro Arbués, one of His innocent soldiers, and Juan de Esperandeu is paying for it now."

Esther lifts her face from Sancia's hands and rubs her cheek where Lorenzo struck her. "Pedro Arbués was not innocent! Perhaps Jesus was innocent before Romans, and not the Jews, killed him, but Pedro was not. Pedro killed innocent people." Sancia admires her mother's knowledge and bravery in teaching facts to such a forbidding presence. When did she learn all of this?

Lorenzo spits at her shoe. "No, vermin. He did not kill *people*, he killed Jews. Actually, he killed *marranos*. I will protect righteous soldiers like him who work tirelessly to cleanse our land of your filth. Pedro de Arbués's soul will live forever with the Father. His glory will be honored eternally in the Cathedral of La Seo, where the *marranos* ended his life of flesh. And do you know what will happen to this hero of yours, to Juan, the *marrano* who drove the blade into his flesh between his chain-mail vest and iron helmet while he was praying? Do you know what will happen to him?"

Esther is silent. Sancia isn't sure if her mother doesn't know or simply doesn't say.

Lorenzo is all too happy to answer his own question. "His hands will be cut at the wrist before he is dragged to the marketplace, where he will be quartered and then burned. But with a special touch. Before he is relieved of his miserable life, he will watch his father burn at the stake." Lorenzo lifts his shoulders and snickers. "He will only be too grateful when we take his life to end his suffering."

Sancia steadies her breath to deny Lorenzo any pleasure he might take in her pain. More than three years after they murdered her wonderful, gentle papa—their thirst for the blood of her people has not been quenched. Their theft of all the belongings of their victims has not yet satisfied the treasury of the Crown or Holy Office. They are all either as evil as Lorenzo or as stupid as his mother. She has no category to fit Baltasar and his wife into at this moment.

Doña Sarmiento seems exasperated by her son's behavior. "Lorenzo, I do not need to remind you of the holiness of this day. This is Corpus Christi. We just observed the very holy Trinity Sunday a few days ago. Have mercy the way Christ would."

Sancia wonders how this woman cannot see that her son is incapable of mercy. He does not try to hide this fact.

She lives in a delusion within a delusion. She knew who her son was that day in the church, that day she stepped in for her cousins. She must have known that bringing Jews close to him would be dangerous. Yet Sancia does not blame her. She blames herself. *I did not stop them.*

A Soccer Ball
Is Not an Artifact

I arrive in our nook at the museum, two coffees in hand.

Ben looks up from his computer. "Thank you. And just in time. I'm about to finish with my first cup. And I got one for you too. It's over there - on the counter. I thought it would be okay even though I knew I'd be here much earlier than you today. I know you don't always like your coffee hot."

"I like it iced, Ben. Iced coffee, not lukewarm." I chuckle, and then I take a sip. "Thanks. This will make a perfect second cup."

Ben motions for me to bring his coffee to him. He swaps the cup in my hand for a soccer ball that was in his.

I look at the ball I'm now balancing on my open palm. "New hobby of yours?"

"New? Not new. I've always loved football—greatest game on Earth. But the ball isn't mine. It's yours."

"Was it brought up from the ship?" A little artifact humor. "Ben, this isn't my ball."

"But it is your invitation."

"Are you deliberately being cryptic?"

"A nice man," Ben continues rather joyfully, "a good-looking man - found his way to this building. He asked me if I knew you. When I told him I did, he asked if I would have you return his ball, today, at 4:00. He said it was important. The address is already printed on it — probably in case it should get lost."

"Ben, you could have compromised my safety by being charmed by my stalker. Get a grip on yourself." I spin the ball and see the address. 132 Kedem Street, Tel Aviv, Jaffa. I don't know where that is. "Did you get his name?"

Ben shakes his head. "You don't look too concerned."

Not concerned about my safety - but my sanity. "Is he in his forties?"

He nods. "Do you know who the guy is?"

"Yes, I think so. I think it's Ari, a man I met on the airplane and bumped into during dinner last week. He knows where I work."

Ben takes the ball from my hand and spins it. "Well, Abi, it's a good thing you arrived a little early today so that you could leave on time to return the ball."

It is intriguing. But I do not know who this guy really is. "It's kind of creepy."

"He didn't seem creepy to me." Ben pulls out his smartphone and snaps a picture of the address. "Accept the invitation. If you go missing, I'll send a squad out to find you."

"Very funny." Though smart idea to record the address. I'll do it. I can't help but to feel curious. So, I'll return a ball to an address that I am not familiar with, to a man I don't know. I would ground any of my kids if they pulled such a stunt!

I text Annette to let her know that I'll be home late and not to worry. I don't tell her why. She would worry.

I look at the tank with the items that have been here, in this dark quarter of the museum, since right before I arrived. I check the notes on the computer to see what the field archaeologists last wrote and then I prepare vats with deionizing water to first tackle the jug. Earthenware. I put on gloves and pick up the item that was last exposed to air hundreds of years ago. I bring it to eye level. "Dressed for your date in calcium carbonate."

Ben laughs from across the room. "Talking to the artifacts again?"

I have a hard time keeping my mind from wandering. The soccer ball reminds me that I still need to buy a football shirt for Sandy.

On his way out for the day, Ben taps me on the arm. "Time for you to follow the bouncing ball."

"See you in the morning. Keep that address handy just in case." I'm only half joking.

The cabdriver is very friendly. We chat a little until he pulls up and stops alongside an unusually contemporary building in an otherwise-old location. Definitely not a house.

"132 Kedem Street?" I take off my seat belt.

He looks at me through his rearview mirror. "Yes. Is this okay?"

"I guess so." I thank him, tip him, and get out of the car. I do wonder if there is some kind of mistake.

With ball in hands, I approach the building. I'm relieved when I see Ari standing in the entryway. He is holding some clothing. I pile the ball on his already full arms.

He smiles. "Great, you're returning my ball. I wasn't sure you'd know what to do with a football."

Is that athletic arrogance I detect in his voice? "I might not know what to do with a football. But I do know what to do with a soccer ball, which, by the way, is what you now have in your hands."

He tosses the clothing to me. "Great, because now what you have in your hands are a pair of soccer shorts with a team shirt. There is a bathroom to the left. Go change and meet me out front—I'll pull the car up." He places the ball on the ground near the exit. "Oh — and bring the ball." He walks away before I have a chance to object.

I look at the clothing in my arms. *Shorts! Hmph. Well, I'm glad I shaved my legs this morning.*

When I walk out, I see Ari standing by the open passenger door. He closes it after I get inside.

I look at him once he gets into the driver's seat. "Polite. Wow, chivalry is in. Although, I believe it would be more polite to tell the lady what this is all about."

He secures his seat belt and points at me to do that too. "We're in a hurry. Buckle up."

I do. "Wait a minute. Why is your shirt different than mine?"

He starts driving. "Is it not obvious? You and I will be on opposing teams."

I drop my jaw. "You think I'm going to play soccer competitively against you?"

He smiles. "You aren't nervous, are you?"

"What? Me? Nervous? Playing against you? Just because I haven't played since I was a star—a *star*—in college, doesn't mean I'm nervous. In fact, I feel sorry for whatever team you're going to be on. I'll run you down, and I'm not even wearing sneakers." I am nervous. Very nervous. I was a star, but on an intermural team. And. I'm about to meet Ari's friends, who have probably been playing soccer continuously for some time. I'm nervous about feeling stupid like I did during dinner. What did he say about me? He must have asked if bringing a guest player is okay—or maybe that is what they do. Maybe that is how their membership grows. I'm leaving in about three weeks. He knows I can't join the league. Does he think this is a date?

"We are here." He parks the car, and then looks at my feet before getting out. "I didn't think about your shoes."

"Don't worry. I'll be fine." Frankly, I'm glad that I have the "bad shoes" excuse to take the blame for insufficient skill. I mask my insecurity with hollow trash talk. "You're the one I'm worried about." That was a little weak—too transparent.

He steps out of the car and closes the door.

I hop out before he has a chance to open mine. "So, how

long have you been in this league? Are you sure your friends won't mind a guest?"

"We aren't going to play with my friends. Well, I adore the players, but they are kids. Typically, I'm one of their coaches, but today, I'll be one of them. You'll be one of them too." He stops to look at me and laughs. "With an over twenty-five-year age gap."

He did not just say that. "So. That'd be a bigger age gap for you, then, grandpa." Nice comeback. The crowd stands and applauds.

Ari continues walking, toward a field. "My, my... I do hope you handle defeat well."

I keep up. "Actually, I'm not sure if I can handle defeat well. I've never had to before. But I'm a curious girl, so do tell me what it feels like later."

"Do you care to make a bet on the outcome?"

I should be offered a handicap. I have too much stupid pride to ask for one. "Bet? On the game? What do you want to bet?"

"What do you suggest?"

Come on, Abi, don't lose the bravado. Psyching him out is your last hope. Make it good. "Are you ready to lose your shirt?"

He gently shakes his head with a smile. "Your confidence is admirable."

"I'm betting you'll lose your shirt." Nice. Confident. Bold. And no risk of becoming broke.

He smiles and nods without a hint that he's taking me seriously. "I can't wait to introduce you to the kids. They make the Peres Center for Peace great. The building we left is just a part of what the center is. The main function of the organization is to bridge the social and political gap between Jews and Arabs. A football field is a great place to make that happen. It's great for me because I manage to fit in some exercise as I coach and bond with these great young people. I missed them while I was away. The amazing welcome I got a few days ago is enough to make me want to leave again just to return and repeat."

I rub my freshly healed finger, remembering what happened the last time I was sporty with children. My children. How I long to feel their greeting when I return home. "So, while you aren't busy cleaning up puke or stealing airsickness bags, you spend your free time volunteering as a soccer coach?" I think about the moment he woke me on the flight. And when he aggravated me in the restaurant. Each time I was too irritated to even try to imagine what kind of life he leads.

"Believe me —I get so much more than I could possibly give. And I want you to see. At dinner, you said you were open to learning more. I get the impression that your knowledge about this country is obtained either from under oceans or in caves, or bombarded to you from loud and obnoxious voices—JVP, SJP, BDS."

"JV-what?" I stop and wait for clarification.

"JVP, an acronym for the erroneously named Jewish Voice for Peace. They are similar to SJP, an acronym for the erroneously named Students for Justice in Palestine – both founded by professors at otherwise elite universities in your country. And BDS, a movement led by some of the same Israel hating professors to rally people to boycott, divest and sanction just one country in the world. Come on – you know which single country they target for abuse and isolation . . ."

"Let me guess." I point to the ground we're standing on. I do not know much about global governments, but I do know enough to know that this one should not be singled out for such aggressive and ugly behavior.

We remain quiet for the rest of the walk.

As soon as we get to the field, we become surrounded by an enthusiastic group of preteen and teenage boys. Ari greets the kids with some impressively choreographed handshakes. He holds his hands up in the air to get everyone's attention. "Hello, everyone. I am looking forward to this scrimmage, and I brought along a new friend. Fortunately, the center had a perfectly sized uniform for her." He points to my feet. "Unfortunately, there were no shoes . . . A small detail in football." He pauses as the boys laugh. "Everyone, this is Abi." He then names every player on both teams. I can tell by some of the names whether the child is Jewish or Muslim, but their names are the only way I could distinguish between them except for a few of the Jewish boys wearing yarmulkes. Then Ari introduces me to the other coaches.

He speaks a few words in Hebrew and then Arabic. I was thrilled when I learned that I didn't need to be fluent in Hebrew to pursue a PhD here, but I do wish I spent more time learning it. I'm not able to catch all that he says. But, then he returns to English for my benefit. "Which team will take some pity on my American friend here and allow her to join them?" To my surprise, all of the players welcome me on their team. "Very well, then." He flips a coin without calling it. What a character. "You'll go with the players in yellow, and I will go with the players in red."

I clearly stand out as an old has-been. Yet, my teammates include me in passes and high fives. They make sure I feel like one of them — and I do. The final score is 3–1. My teammates must have put in an enormous effort to compensate for their rusty American newcomer. We kicked butt! The kids shake hands at the end of the game as they form a single-file line so that everyone on one team acknowledges everyone on the other. We have that tradition back home.

Ari and I are last. He graciously congratulates me. "It was a good game."

"Thank you. I saw some of your moves. Fancy. But 3–1, you still lost your shirt."

As the evening winds down and after all of the kids make their way home, Ari offers me a ride. "It's silly to grab a cab. Come on, I'll take you."

I accept.

The ride is quick.

"Here. This is it." I point to my building. I start to get out of the car, but then pause and turn to him. "I'm sorry for being obnoxious the other day."

"Forgiven. Well, you can make it up to me with lunch. How about noon the day after tomorrow?"

"I can't. I'll be having lunch with my boss."

"Excellent. I like him. We'll all go. Wednesday. Noon. See you then."

Despite my misgivings, I can't help but feel excited.

Once a Jew,
Forever a Marrano

———— ◆◆◆◆◆ ————

— 1485 —

Sancia catches up to David and greets him as together they walk toward her uncle's house. After a small awkward silence, he tries to make conversation. "I know that Iuceph has given you some problems lately. Well, given all of us some problems lately. But right now I am thankful to him for giving us something to celebrate so that we can soon forget the events of last week."

"I am too. But I fear that they will, from now on, watch his every move more closely. He is fourteen. You know what that means."

David nods. "I think that it might be safer for him to live with his sponsor."

"What?" How could he suggest Iuceph live with that dim woman and her horrible son?

David explains himself. "If Iuceph allows them to watch him and tell him what to do all the time, he will not be arrested for anything that he is not allowed to do."

Sancia is pained by the suggestion but doesn't think it to be unreasonable. "Do you think Ana should live with them too?"

"Let us not think about that now. Is your mother already at their house?"

Sancia nods. "How about your mother and father?"

"No. They are behind us."

Sancia looks behind her to see them. Then she waves a greeting and keeps walking. "I wanted to talk to you after the Corpus Christi spectacle but had to catch up on work at the shop."

"I know."

She is surprised by his answer. "You know?"

David explains. "Well, not that you wanted to talk to me. I knew you were at the shop trying to catch up. I did not want to bother you. I went to your house the day after the parade, and your mother told me."

He went to my house looking for me. Sancia touches her cheeks, to detect if they are as red as they feel. She wills herself to say something, anything, to change the subject. "My mother has been reading the Christian Bible. And she has been learning about Christianity from Litiosa."

"I know. She told me. Did you know that the man they pray to, Jesus, was Jewish?"

Sancia nods. "She told me that." *But she did not mention you came by to see me.*

"Do you think she is thinking about converting?" David asks.

"No. I think she just wants to learn." *She would never convert.*

Astruga and Ana hop outside to hug Sancia before she is ready to end her private time with David. Yet she is delighted to see the girls, and Iuceph, who is right behind them.

David hugs Iuceph. "I cannot believe a year has gone by since you became a bar mitzvah."

"I am not Jewish anymore," Iuceph reminds him.

"Of course you are not." What else could David say?

Sancia is sad she might not see Iuceph much now that he is fourteen. The potential danger has increased too much, especially during the Holy Days. The Inquisitors would accuse him of observing Judaism even if he was not. It would be three more years until the same would happen to Ana. Her heart aches.

As David's parents approach, Uncle Abraham comes to the door and enthusiastically invites everyone inside. It's time for Sancia to enjoy her family. They can still spend birthdays together. And she intends to enjoy this celebration.

She walks into the home and casts her earlier doubts aside. She can no longer resist the tempting smells and visual appeal of the feast awaiting. "I recognize one of Litiosa's famous vegetable pies."

"Yes, you do." Aunt Regina confirms while greeting her with a loving hug. "We invited her and Baltasar to join us, but they both said they needed to rest after a busy week."

"I saw them at church this morning," Iuceph says. "They wished me a happy birthday then."

Aunt Regina cuts into the pie and serves the first piece to Iuceph. "We also asked Iuceph's sponsor and her son. She already committed to helping out at the church for today, and he had to work."

Sancia will not miss them. She is eager to start eating. She waits patiently as the others get served.

The door flies open. The handle slams the wall. Napkins fly off the table.

Uniformed men barge in.

Sancia recognizes one. *Lorenzo.*

He grabs Iuceph by the arm, lifting the boy's gangly body off his seat.

Her heart clenches.

"Stop!" Uncle Abraham demands. "Unhand him!"

"He is now fourteen years of age." Lorenzo then turns to Iuceph. "Happy birthday, Juan. You are now accountable for your actions."

The Inquisitor, standing near Lorenzo, makes an announcement. "Juan, who was born as Iuceph Lebanaza, is under arrest."

"No. Why?" Uncle Abraham shouts.

Another guard walks right up to him. "We do not need to tell you. We are not accountable to you."

Lorenzo eagerly volunteers an explanation. "Juan, a Christian, was observing the Jewish Sabbath and hence disgracing Christ."

With alarm, Sancia realizes they did not account for the difference in the dates. Iuceph turned fourteen, several days before, according to their calendar.

David stands and leans forward with the palm of his hands on the table. "Your Christ was a Jew! He honored the Sabbath. You believe he has risen. Maybe he is in Seville. Go find him and arrest him."

Sancia is awed by David's courage and frightened by his boldness.

The Inquisitor walks right up to David. "You stupid Jewish boy. You filthy pig. I can hand you over to the civil authorities. What is your name?"

"Get out of my home now!" Uncle Abraham points to the door.

"We will leave." Lorenzo's knuckles are white from gripping Iuceph. "And we are taking this *marrano*."

No! Sancia prays that G-d will quickly intervene.

Ana runs to block the door. "You know we are Christians, Lorenzo. How will your mother feel? Please. This is a mistake. She has been teaching us well. We have been practicing all of her lessons. Both of us have. Iuceph and me."

"You are Christian? Another *marrano*?" The Inquisitor, seeming to notice the child for the first time, orders her arrest as well. His cold glare toward Ana penetrates Sancia's bones.

Lorenzo shakes his head. "She is too young. It is not allowed—yet."

"Please do not take my son. There must be a misunderstanding. He would not honor the Sabbath. I wanted him to, but he refused. He told me I should call him Juan and not Iuceph. He stopped responding to the name we gave him. He has been refusing to join us for the candle lighting on Friday nights when we bring in the Sabbath. Anyone who would have seen candles through the window would not have known it was just for my wife, Astruga, and me, — not for my other children, who are faithful Christians. They go together to the church every Sunday, and then they dine at your house. We leave them behind every Saturday."

Sancia knows her uncle is telling the truth but also knows that they don't care.

Lorenzo scrunches his face in anger. "Your children are nothing but *marranos*. They behave like dirty Jews, though they have the indelible seal of Christ on their souls. And if you know what is good for Ana, you will also become baptized. Learn the way to properly serve the Lord, and no longer lead your children astray with Judaizing. Then there might be fewer 'misunderstandings.'" As quick as they came - they left.

Overwhelmed by guilt for her negligence in overlooking the calendar discrepancy, Sancia is filled with despair. Her cousin is now in the hands of these awful people. *How do I bring him home?*

SEARCHING FOR LIFE

―◆◆◆◆◆◆―

― 1488 ―

Sancia searches for apples in the bag her mother just brought home from the market. She'll serve them at the start of Rosh Hashanah dinner this evening — the first time they'll formally welcome the Jewish New Year since Iuceph was taken from them over three years ago. The Church still has her seventeen-year-old cousin locked away. Maybe this will be the year he'll return home.

She hears a knock as she sorts through utensils to set the table. "Mother, could you please get the door?"

Esther's voice reaches the dining room. "I am still finishing up in the kitchen, but sure. I am happy to, actually." She walks past Sancia as she wipes her hands on her apron before opening the door.

Sancia looks up to see everyone is here — Jacinto's family and David with his mother and father, Nina and Jacob.

Esther greets each of them. "This all looks lovely. Had I

known you were going to bring so much food, I would have slept in late today."

It's the first time Sancia has heard happiness in her mother's voice since she can remember. She looks up to see each guest touch the mezuzah and bring their fingers to their lips.

Jacinto gives Esther a kiss on the cheek before greeting Sancia. *"Chag sameach."*

A choir of voices wish each other *Shanah Tovah*, a good year.

We need this to be a very good year. Sancia adds, *"L'shana tovah tikatev v'tichatem."* A greeting she also sends from her heart to Iuceph, *may you be written and sealed for a good year, my dear cousin.* And then to G-d, *please HaShem, please make it so.*

As she watches what seems like joy among her guests, knowing that each is suffering through this life in their own way, while loving and contributing to this life, in their own way, she somberly reflects back to the autumn after the Church took Iuceph, after the rest of her family converted and moved out of the Judería. Sancia invited her aunt, uncle and cousins to come to her home on erev Rosh Hashanah. She hoped to maintain normalcy for when Iuceph would return.

Aunt Regina answered so bitterly. *Think about your offer! We cannot return to the Judería ever again! None of us can. It is no longer our home. The people within it can no longer be our friends. Christians are not our friends. We have no friends. Our family is broken. Rosh Hashanah is not for us anymore. Your Uncle Abraham no longer exists. The man you see standing in front of you is Anton. And all we want is to have our Iuceph back.*

Juan, Sancia's uncle corrected.

Please excuse us, Sancia, Aunt Regina spewed at her with contempt, *if we do not accept your invitation to dinner for Rosh Hashanah. Regards to your mother.*

Sancia shakes off the trance as her mother offers the honor of lighting the candles to David's mother, Nina. Then Jacob says the prayer over the wine that he already poured into cups from the flask he brought to the dinner. Sancia enjoys the warmth of the wine in her mouth. She is grateful for the affection emitted from everyone.

Her mood dips as Jacinto says the Shehecheyanu. "Blessed are You, L-rd our G-d, King of the Universe, who has granted us life, sustained us and enabled us to reach this occasion."

What about those who did not make it?

After the brief ceremony, the nine friends feast and celebrate together. Sancia can't remember the last time they enjoyed so much company since . . . She can't complete her own thought. For now, she is simply trying to adjust to the empty feeling of a full house.

It is the start of a new year. I am going to stand here and stare at that church until they walk out. I just want to see them, Aunt Regina, Uncle Abraham, Astruga and Ana. No, seeing them will not be enough. I need to touch them and talk to them, too. Sancia misses her family so much. As they approach, her body tingles with anticipation. Yet, not one of them offers any warmth.

Uncle Abraham is the first to speak. "The date is set for another *auto de fé.*"

Sancia shakes her head in disbelief. "How do you know?"

Aunt Regina steps in with an abrupt reply. "The friar said so. He said the entire congregation must attend."

Astruga, unable to hide her resentment of having to be a Christian, mimics the friar with a deep voice, folded arms, nodding head, and mocking tone. "Not attending is not an option. In order to fulfill your duties as faithful and pious, you must join your community in celebrating the good and condemning the bad and perhaps encouraging the reachable to repent."

Fourteen-year-old Ana looks at her older sister with alarm. "Shh, Astruga. You are going to get us into trouble."

Sancia notices her aunt and uncle survey who is near and who might have caught their daughter mocking the friar.

Her uncle lowers his gaze. "I have no doubt that Iuceph will be there."

Sancia tries an assuring tone, but it falls flat. She knows she cannot offer any of them any sense of genuine comfort.

Her aunt cuts her off. "Enough, Sancia!"

Sancia can no longer tolerate her aunt's coldness. Does she solely blame her for the children's actions? Does she love her anymore?

Uncle Abraham bursts into tears. "I just want my boy back."

I want him back, too. Sancia stares helplessly at her family. *I want all of you back.*

On the morning of the *auto de fé*, Sancia sneaks out of her home. She is a mature woman at the age of nineteen, yet does not want to worry her mother who still thinks of her as a child. She will always be her child.

Sancia climbs up to a midway branch of a tall tree just off the path of the procession, close enough to the square, to watch for her family. She glances down to see so many people with vacuous cheer. She spies Baltasar and Litiosa solemnly walking near their grown children and grandchildren. She knows they hate this too. She looks up to the sky to see any sign of HaShem. *Where are You?* The sound of a branch snapping off the tree alarms her. She keeps her balance. It's David. He climbed the tree to protect her. *I do love him.* In this moment she wishes she could still experience the joy she once felt. She yearns to rekindle a sense of hopefulness for the future. Her body won't allow it. It keeps her from being vulnerable to her dormant grief. Being numb has enabled her to cling to life. She nods an acknowledgement of presence to the beautiful young man on the tree limb next to her, and for a brief moment wonders what could have been.

Her reflection shaken by the noise of the procession below. She looks down and sees the Grand Inquisitor. She points him out to David. "He does not attend every *auto de fé*. Why is he here now?" Then she sees the local Inquisitor.

They parade one after another, each surrounded by hundreds of guards, one of whom holds the white cross that will set fire to the pyre. It's identical to the cross they used to light the fire that killed her father. She does not see Lorenzo, but she knows he is there. The guards flow as a sea of identical beasts full of hate, happy to obey orders. All of these people are. Or are they? She glances in Baltasar's direction, certain that he feels disgust toward the proceedings.

After the guards, march the clergy. Then the caskets containing exhumed bodies of *conversos* who have been accused, after death, of heresy. The Church will order their remains to be burned and the inheritance of their children be taken.

Sancia hates these people. They convince their easily manipulated followers that all of the destruction that they usher, all of this theft of property, theft of life, is done in service to G-d.

Sancia cranes her neck to look at the sea of barefoot victims in the humiliating uniforms the prisoners of the Church are forced to wear. But it's impossible to spot Iuceph among them. Then she sees a patch of fabric sewn onto the yellow sanbenitos. It's an image of an upside-down flame. She realizes these people will be spared from the flames. *Thank G-d.* She sighs. *But where is Iuceph? Where is he?!* Sancia looks down to see her uncle, who is unaware of her presence. He is standing on his toes to look for his child in the swarm of yellow.

There he is. *Iuceph.* She does not need to see the embroidered image of a demon consuming flames to know that these monsters marked her seventeen-year-old cousin for death after keeping him locked in darkness for over three years. Sancia gasps and loses her balance.

David's arms steady her on the limb. "I know. I see him." She stares at Iuceph draped in black. She cannot do anything else.

Numbness keeps her breathing. Numbness keeps her alive.

Iuceph is no longer alive. They kill us, not because we do anything wrong, but because it suits their ambitions. The Church fosters hatred against us to mask their own short-comings. The more people they force to become Christian, the more minds they control. How do we survive this wretch-edness against humanity? They have no incentive to stop. Their most devout subjects are conditioned to believe that stopping would be a sin. Is there anything that can be done against so great a machine?

Sancia struggles with her thoughts as she walks with her mother, to her aunt and uncle's home the day after the Church killed their son. *Will they allow me to enter?* She hasn't visited them since they moved from the Judería.

There's no trace of Jewishness in this Catholic neigh-borhood. She steps inside their home and sees no trace of Jewishness in their home, not even hidden beneath the thick veil of sadness. She sees her uncle sitting. She imag-ines he is praying, but she knows he has entered the vacu-ous isolation of a dark abyss.

Her aunt is also unreachable. Iuceph will never come back. No one wants to live with that. Unable to shake the guilt she feels for not doing enough to stop Iuceph's conversion, unable to shake the feeling of her aunt's resentment, Sancia concludes there is no room for her here.

After barely walking through the door of the place her aunt, uncle and cousins have made home, without a word to any of her family, she walks out of the house that Iuceph never knew—the house heavy with his absence. She can no longer tolerate the despair of others when she can barely manage her own. She needs air.

Sancia aches to have a discussion with her father. She aches to have him in her presence. *Look at what happened to Iuceph, Papa. Look at what happened to you. How did you do it, Papa? How did you succumb to their plan? They abandon their mind and heart within the vessels G-d gave us to enjoy our lives. How could you think you could do that? I remember clearly your wisdom. "Where you see little love of life, where you see merely scraps of joy, you will see no Divine spark. And without passion, life is nothing but stale challah." Ah. Stale challah.* Sancia places her fingers to her lips. Did she just smile? She misses her father incredibly. *Oh, Papa. I love life, I love joy, but they have taken it all from me. I feel nothing.*

She cannot return to the inside of what should be Iuceph's home. No. What should be Iuceph's home is actually in the Judería. She sits on a step outside the *shiva* home.

"There is an ant," says a familiar voice.

Sancia looks up to see Nina, David's mother.

Jacob, his father, points to the ant. "On the trim of your dress."

Sancia moves to let them pass so they may enter the home of mourning. "Is David not with you?"

"He is full of torment, he cannot leave our house." Nina places her hand on the door handle, seemingly unready to push it open and walk inside.

When she does, Sancia's eyes begin to tear.

Jacob follows right behind, but stops and turns to Sancia before crossing the threshold. "Maybe he will come here next week. We thought it best not to overwhelm your aunt and uncle with too many visitors. And to give David more time."

Sancia nods as he walks inside. She reaches down to the ant that's still on her dress and extends her finger for him to crawl on. His feet tickle her wrist. She recalls when she used to find ants and walk the path that hundreds of them made. She would follow them to their home, to investigate their mound. As the ant climbs up her arm, she leans over a small patch of dirt by the steps and blows him off to safety.

She turns to look at the door behind her, the one blocking her view of the suffering of those she loves. She notices the indentation on the post of where a mezuzah was before the Jews were confined to the Judería.

She stands. She walks. She runs from the emptiness of the home full of mourners, a home where the one they mourn, never lived. She continues running. She reduces her speed to catch her breath, and then, still breathless, runs again. Her side aches, but she ignores the pain. Nothing hurts more than the numbness that replaces life. She runs to the Judería. She runs past where Iuceph once lived. She runs past her home.

By the time Sancia reaches David's house, she is no longer aware of the soreness in the soles of her feet, nor the ache of her lungs. She pushes her way through his unlocked door. Her trembling voice calls for him. "David!"

"Sancia, what is wrong?" He runs into the living area that opens from the entryway. The shutters are closed — the home is dark with grief. "What happened?"

She didn't mean to alarm him. She shakes her head to indicate there is nothing new to be concerned about. *Enough has happened.* "I want to live. I want *to want* to live." She tries holding back tears so that she can get the words out. "They have killed my father and my cousin. My aunt hates me. I love her so much, and she hates me. I am not sure how my uncle feels. If he could feel anything, he might hate me too. I have no more strength to live like this. Whether by flame or by despair, they will kill me." With her voice trailing off, she pleads to David. "Before they do, I want so very much to live." Sancia cannot stop her body from trembling.

David wraps his arms around her and holds her close with tenderness. She knows that he knows her grief. He cannot take her pain away. She does not expect him to. All he can do is hold her close until the demons settle. He steps back just a little to look at her. His finger gently traces a tear down her cheek. She closes her eyes. When did she stop wondering what it would feel like to be touched by him?

She imagines what he sees when he looks at her. Red puffy eyes, disheveled hair and cheeks sticky from tears and sweat. Another tear escapes. His fingertip meets it and travels until the wetness trails off. Sancia presses his hand close to her body. Her heart feels a fleeting moment of peace and acceleration. She wraps her arms around him and breathes him. She wants more. When Sancia ran to David, she was looking for more than survival. She was looking for life. Life, indeed, is what he gave to her.

THE LAST DAY OF ABRAHAM

———◆◆◆———

— 1492 —

L istening intently to their conversation, Sancia stares
at the table. She traces her fingers over the natural
lines and imperfections of its wooden surface. Chaos in the
grooves of the wood create character. Not the case for the
grooves in her family.

Her three-year-old son, Ruben, plays on the floor
nearby as she sits with David, her husband, at a dining
room table with her cousins. She is tormented by the vehe-
ment arguing between her mother and her uncle on the
other side of the room.

Esther holds her hands out toward her brother.
"Abraham, it is possible the date will come to pass, and
nothing will happen. They may not make us leave as they
threaten. The king and queen's most trusted advisor is
one of us."

"Luis did try to stop the madness!" Uncle Abraham's face reddens. "But, he is one of me, Esther! He is not one of you!"

Sancia is still unaccustomed to the absence of the yarmulke that was, until several years ago, dancing daily on her uncle's short, curly, black hair. She always preferred watching to see how long it would cling before slipping off, rather than fixing it for him and ruining the little entertainment she'd get from watching the dance. *Luis.* Sancia tries to place the somewhat familiar name. He must be referring to his old friend, Luis de Santángel.

Her uncle continues. "He accepted baptism to remain in service to Queen Isabella, as royal treasurer, hoping to be influential enough to stop the violence against us. He pleaded to His Majesties to dispose of this heinous law, the Alhambra Decree, before they announced it. He pointed out how it could bring harm to not only the Jews but the entire kingdom. Yet they would not budge. Why would they? They want our wealth and they confiscate it every time they banish, imprison, or kill one of us. Luis told me about this law before they announced it because he could see that he would be unable to stop it. He wanted to give the Jews as much time as possible to act before it would get enforced. He wanted me to warn you."

The Alhambra Decree. Such a dreadful law. *Convert, leave or face death. Convert, leave, or be killed.* Sancia reviews the options again and again. *Convert. Leave. Die.* She snaps out of her fog of despair when she hears a glimmer of hope.

Uncle Abraham offers it. "After recognizing the unrelenting nature of their determination and greed, Luis searched for another answer."

"Did he find one?" Sancia asks.

Her uncle nods in her direction. "He has invested in a sailor, Cristóbal Colón, who calls himself Colombo. He believes that this Cristoforo Colombo might find new land, perhaps a safe haven. Perhaps he could be the answer for those of you who choose not to find the path of freedom through Christ, our Savior."

Christ, our savior?!

"Don't sicken me, Abraham! 'Christ our Savior'? 'Those of you'?" Esther's voice rises as she echoes her brother's words. "'Those of *you*?' You mean 'those of *us*'! You were born a Jew and will always be considered a pig to them, a *marrano*! You might be able to flawlessly recite — what do you call it? The rosary. You move your arm across your chest and wear out the knees of your trousers from kneeling to that statue at church regularly. You might be able to fool the evil zealots who look to destroy us—and G-d willing you can—but you cannot fool me. You love and serve HaShem!"

Abraham raises his voice, exuding an anger so rare in the genteel man. "I should love HaShem? I no longer love or serve any such entity!" He then snaps his hand in the direction of the empty seat at the large family dining table where Sancia, David, and her cousins sit witnessing the torturous dynamic. "I was abandoned by your HaShem!" He struggles to hold back the tears that compete in a race to the surface of his tired eyes. "I do not need to fool you, my dear, dear

Esther. I just need to fool the fools, to fool those cruel beasts who are bent on destroying us and calling it service to G-d. I only need to fool those people who tortured and killed my son. They killed my beautiful son, Esther." His voice cracks and tears roll down his cheeks. "My Iuceph."

Sancia is struck by how thin and frail they look, how thin and frail all of them look. Hope is scarce, and so are appetites. Esther takes her brother's hand in hers.

He pulls away. "You know it is only for the sake of Regina and my girls. Yes. I go to church regularly, Esther, just as you say. I kneel and I pray. I look up. I see them hanging on the walls. They turn my stomach more than that statue of a god. They hang those robes on display as some form of per-verted artwork. Flattened. Empty. The red. The yellow..." His voice then trails off to a tearful whisper. "The black." He pauses to gain breath. "This is not easy for me, Esther. Every day they cut more and more into my soul. Every day I walk into that church and I see the robes. First, I see the reds and the yellows. I study the congregation, and my eyes fall on the men and the women, young and old, each who wore those very sanbenitos on that day. I saw them as they were forced through the streets. These once-Jews now go to church and physically blend into the congregation in the hopes that no more harm will come to them. They were capable of doing great things, of standing out. Now they aim to be invisible, unnoticed. Every day I see the sanbenito they forced my son to wear. I see the very fabric that last touched the skin of my boy before his body was stripped naked of the robe and then his soul stripped naked from his body. The beasts of the Church preserve the black robe as sacred yet saw fit to burn my son."

"But Abraham —"

"These people will not change. I do not need to remind you that what they did to my son they did to your Isaac." He looks at Sancia. "Your father."

Sancia can barely speak as she struggles to hold back her own tears. "I just want us to be together again."

"And *I* want us all to be together, my dear niece."

I am still dear to him. Sancia chokes from her uncle's sentiment. She wouldn't blame him for hating her for not telling him about Iuceph's plan to convert. She should have known she couldn't stop him. Maybe he could have.

Esther shakes her head. "This is madness. People cannot be so irrational and unjust toward us forever."

"Can't they?" Abraham exhales in disgust. "And even so, *now* is what matters. And *now* it is happening again. Do you not see how sweet our bitterness is for them? Even in death we are not safe. Look at what they did to Nina and Fagim, bless their souls." *Conversos.* Nina died from sickness of the heart a fortnight after illness took her husband. Days after her burial the Inquisitors exhumed both bodies. They burned their bodies during the *auto de fé*. And then they marched to what had been the couple's home to confiscate their possessions from their children. Sancia knows all that he is referring to by the mere mention of their names. They all know, but this doesn't stop her uncle from articulating it aloud. "The 'Holy' Inquisitors steal our belongings from our descendants. They tear apart our families and pull us away from G-d, and then they convince their followers that this destruction is in deference to G-d. People who are convinced that their horrible actions are in service to their God are rather unstoppable."

He is right. But he has become so hardened, so consumed by grief, so far removed from the man he once was — the man he is supposed to be. Sancia looks at her son, Ruben, almost four years old. *And who is the man you will become?* She looks for his hazel eyes hidden under his golden-brown hair as he animates dolls that belonged to her cousins.

Her mother refuses to concede the argument to her brother. "Think about what this law would do to Castile. Some of King Ferdinand and Queen Isabella's most trusted confidants would have to go into exile. Would they really kill men they rely upon?"

"Esther, do you really doubt that a monarchy that demands you mark your clothing, restrict you to the Judería and forbid you from pursuing your career, would follow through with its threat to kill any Jew left on this soil after July 31, 1492? They might change the date, but not their goal. If it does not happen in July, then August; if not this year, then next. Convert, Esther. You, David, Sancia, the baby. Just accept the Savior, Jesus Christ, and we can all be together again. You can live here, in this part of town. You could be our neighbors." Then Abraham tenderly adds, "I would like that very much."

Esther shakes her head. "I cannot do that. I cannot become one with those who steal from us — one with those who have murdered our loved ones."

Abraham's eyes fall on Ruben. "Do it to keep them from killing more of our loved ones. They will come for you if you leave. You are a Jew. They will always seek to harm you."

"They will always seek to harm you! The Holy Office, the Church, the Inquisition - they will not go away. They are here to monitor all of *you*. Being here is too risky. Perhaps it is best if we all move before this insane law will be enforced."

Sancia knows David senses her waning strength when he intervenes. "Abraham, Pesach begins in almost two weeks. We will come back here in three days, close the shutters, do part of a Seder and finish this discussion after we've all had time to think about it more. We should be safe. The Inquisitors' sharpest eyes will not be surveying as strictly as they will on the fourteenth of Nisan."

Sancia is satisfied with that suggestion. *Passover so soon.* She looks at Ruben. Soon she'll be teaching him how to make matzah. It'll be nice to have some fun as a reprieve from all the heartache. They wouldn't bring the matzah here—too risky—but they could be together.

Abraham shakes his head. "Two weeks before Passover or two weeks after Passover - it does not matter. Every time we meet, we bring danger to ourselves — to Regina, the girls, and to me. They are predators searching for easy and preferably wealthy prey. Our only defense is to be among them. Really among them. Regina and I are. The girls are. We are managing. And we do not have to flee. It is time for you, David, Sancia and the baby."

"Never, Abraham!" Esther picks up the dolls from Ruben and hands them to the girls.

"Do not call me Abraham!" His voice trembles. "It has been four years since my baptism. I was Abraham, now I am Anton. I had a son, and until now I had a sister, a niece, a nephew, and a most dear, beautiful grandnephew." He then grabs hold of a cutter and deliberately tears his shirt on the left side above his heart.

Sancia feels a pain in her chest. She performed the same ritual of Kriah a little over ten years ago, after the Church killed her father in the first *auto de fé*. And, rarely, she has seen others do it to symbolize the end of the life of a Jew who has abandoned Judaism. This is the first time she has ever witnessed it to mourn family who are living and dedicated to Judaism.

Ruben reaches for his uncle's shirt. "Do not cry, Uncle. Mother can fix that. She will bring it to the shop and sew it. Put on a different shirt and give your ripped shirt to Mother. I will bring it back with her tomorrow. It will be all better." Ruben looks at Sancia. "Is that right, Mother?"

How does she explain to her son what this means? How does she tell him that his uncle deliberately ripped his own shirt to mourn his death? How does she explain death and the reason their lives will soon be in chaos — in order to avoid it?

Abraham turns his watery eyes away from the little boy whom Sancia knows he loves, the one who breathed sweet life into his broken home. He then looks at Esther and whispers with painful determination. "Leave now. I need to mourn the family I once had."

"Abraham . . . no, no, no! Please do not do this. I am

alive." Esther breaks down and cries as she gently presses the flap of the torn shirt back into place. "What about Ruben? He needs you. What about your girls? I love my nieces. We are all strongest together."

"Not if any of us are imprisoned or dead." Abraham opens the door to the outside and motions for them to leave.

Esther walks out. David follows. And then Sancia gently touches her uncle's hand as she steps out the doorway.

While Ruben is being led away in his mother's arms, he reaches to touch his uncle. "Do not be sad, Uncle. Your shirt will be mended. Mother will fix everything."

I cannot, my love. I cannot fix this.

A Trusted Catholic

— 1492 —

Ruben sleeps in Sancia's arms as they walk from her uncle's home to the Judería of Barrio de Santa Cruz. No one speaks. She places him into the bed he shares with her mother. She pulls the blanket up to his shoulders and kisses him on the cheek. She hopes to make it through the night uninterrupted by nightmares.

When the sun rises, she gets out of bed, not knowing whether she really slept. She then dresses Ruben, gives him breakfast, and leaves him with her mother. David has already left for the shipyard. Changing their routine is not going to change the laws against them. They need to work until they have a plan. Sancia has become an expert at carrying on as if nothing is wrong.

On her way out the door, she reaches for a coat belonging to a man almost twice her size and more than twice her age. She holds it close to her chest as she kisses her mother and son goodbye. Her thoughts are muddled with exhaustion as she walks toward Baltasar's shop.

"Good morning, Baltasar." She holds out his folded winter coat.

"Good morning, Sancia." Baltasar smiles with his eyes. "My goodness, I just gave that old coat to you. Look at your speed. A perfect repair, not only before the weather cools again, but even before the heat of the summer arrives." He then slips it on and admires her work. "Sancia, I do not know how you do it. Your father taught you well. This old coat looks better now than on the day I bought it." He takes it off and hangs it on a hook. "But you know I do not need it back until the weather turns again."

"Baltasar, I won't be here when the weather turns again."

He lowers his eyes. "The Alhambra Decree." He then brings his fist down on the counter. "This is not Christian! These rules, this cruelty, what they did to your father, to your cousin, to all of you. It hurts me! Not just because I love your family, but I also love Christ, and this is not His way! The God I worship is full of love. Christ gave his life so all who worship him may do good for the world in which we live. This machinery of the Inquisition, the hurtful and hateful laws — I do not know what it is, but it is not of Christianity."

The clergy and the royals say it is. No point in arguing. Instead, Sancia leans over to kiss her friend goodbye on the cheek.

His fingers catch and release Sancia's gold necklace.

"You are wearing it today. It is so lovely on you. But I thought that it was just for special occasions."

Sancia touches the pendant. "It was. It is so precious to me. But the Crown's edict forbids us from taking any of our gold or silver from the kingdom. They are making us leave with almost nothing. I will not be allowed to take the necklace, nor the brooch that you designed for my mother—the gold brooch with the emerald. So we enjoy wearing them now."

"They are yours. Take those pieces out with you."

Her family worked hard to pay for these items. Baltasar made them. They mean so much to her, but they don't mean more than life. "I need to be there for my family. For Ruben. I cannot risk arrest or risk being prevented from crossing into Portugal."

"So, you will be going to Portugal?"

Sancia nods. "It is likely. That is where family from my father's side escaped to during the riots against us from a century ago. Many of his relatives chose not to return. I will look for them in Lisbon, if that is where we go. I sent a note and have been waiting to hear back. Even if I do not find them, I will be fine. I have my mother, David, his mother and father and Ruben. We will probably travel with Jacinto and his family, too." She takes a deep breath. "Baltasar, if you or Litiosa have other items that need repair, please do bring them to me as soon as you can so I may fix them before I leave. I shall make that a priority."

"I will, my dear." He hands her a delicious-smelling savory pie. "I planned to walk to your shop later this morning, but here you are. Litiosa made this one for you. She withheld the meat. The pie is full of vegetables and spices. Enjoy your day, my dear Sancia. I shall see you soon."

Why couldn't more people be like him and Litiosa? She says goodbye to her old friend as she walks out of the shop, knowing that at least for a little while longer, she has the small comfort of knowing he is nearby.

After a long day of work, Sancia is grateful she doesn't have to cook. At dinnertime, she pierces the center of Litiosa's pie. She then inhales the aroma, savors the scent, and passes the pie under the noses of the others. She cuts it up and serves it with eggs.

David takes his plate. "Thank you, Litiosa."

Esther suggests that she and Ruben make some pies from peaches and bring one to their home. "Will you help me to do that, Ruben?"

He nods. *Always so happy to help. How could anyone, anyone, ever dream of hurting him?* And yet there are so many who do.

"Peach pie!" *That is a fantastic idea! What a great way to indulge before the start of Passover.* "Will you make sure you save some pie for me?"

"I will, Mama."

She knew he would. She Remains quiet until she finishes her last bite. "I think we should give our jewelry to Baltasar." She has been mulling that over since leaving his shop earlier in the day.

Esther coughs as if she swallowed the wrong way and then regains control. "We could try to hide it in our belongings. Our wedding bands could fit under our feet between our shoes."

Sancia shakes her head. "If we get caught trying to take our valuables with us, they might lock us up. We cannot take that risk."

Esther stands and begins to wipe crumbs from the table as if this work will distract her from the difficult topic. "Then let us give everything to Abraham."

"No Mother. That is not a good idea."

"She is right, Esther." David collects the empty dinner plates. "Your brother has not spoken to us in weeks, and he will be too afraid to let that change. And for good reason. It is time for us to move on, away from the pain of this land, away from the dangers of the Inquisition and to not endanger anyone while doing so."

Esther expresses agreement about them acting quickly. "But I disagree regarding what to do with our jewelry. It is valuable, but it also means so much. It is from Isaac. Let us give our jewelry to Abraham. He will talk to us for that purpose — to help us put things in order."

David shakes his head. "No, he will not, and he should not. He does not even go by the name Abraham anymore. He has made it clear that he does not want to take the risk of associating with us. How would you be able to live with yourself if any one of them had been arrested after meeting with any one of us? You would forever be burdened with guilt, wondering if the Inquisition took them because of contact with one of us."

Sancia touches her necklace. She needs extra strength

when clashing with her mother. "Baltasar has always been a friend to us, Mother. He saved me — two times. He has not been swept into the lunacy created by the fear, hatred, and greed that has been driving his coreligionists into madness."

Esther sits back down. "But he is not family and he is not Jewish. He cannot be entirely trusted."

She is right about so much, but not this. "In what way can he not be trusted?"

Esther insists that the jewelry should be given to her brother. "If we somehow manage to sneak it to him, maybe in the middle of the night, I am certain he will give everything back to us when this is all over."

"This will never be over! Uncle Abraham will not give the jewels back to us, because we will not be seeing him again!" There. She said what needed to be said. Denial does not make them safer or make the facts less real. She hates this reality as much as her mother does. "Baltasar is a good man who has always been kind and generous to this family. He is an Old Christian, secure enough in his faith so that the Inquisition is not likely to harass him because of our communication. Whereas Uncle could get arrested because of our communication. We can sell everything else for the pittance allowed to us, but we give the jewels to Baltasar."

Esther withdraws from the argument and wipes the already cleaned table. "Just do what must be done. Parting from these silly objects is nothing compared to what has already been taken from us. We must count our blessings."

That night Sancia dreams she is working in her shop when Baltasar enters and gives her an armful of clothing to sew. She is confused as to why anything needs to be repaired. All of the clothing looks new. Then Baltasar hands a stack of red discs to her. They are to be sewn on the items to be worn by him and his wife. She does not understand. When she tries to speak - to ask -she cannot. She opens her mouth, but she has no voice. He places the pile of clothing and the red discs onto her work area, turns, and walks away. Sancia knows she needs to sew the discs onto the clothing right away. She does not know why, but she understands the task to be urgent. Piece by piece, she begins to thread the red discs. First she starts with a simple dress to be worn by Litiosa. Then she moves on to trousers for Baltasar, then another item and another item. She grabs the last red disc and the last piece of clothing. After she completes her task, the pile instantly changes into two piles—the same two piles Baltasar brought into the shop. Untouched. As if she did nothing even though she completed everything. She is disheartened and confused but diligently grabs the dress and sews the disc onto it. Next, the trousers. Sancia works on this endless job through the night. She often gets no rest, even when she sleeps.

Sancia is especially exhausted this morning, and oddly, her hands ache as if she already endured a full week of work. Before leaving, she eats a quick breakfast with her mother and Ruben. And then she goes into her bedroom to collect the items to be given to Baltasar. She isn't able to bring herself to ask for her mother's wedding band, but she slips off her own. She thinks it best to part with their valuables quickly in the hopes that she will lose her attachment to the objects, to these things that she grew to love—among them, the necklace that was designed and touched by her father. She removes the necklace and places it in her hand when her mother walks into the room. Esther then removes her brooch and bracelet. She hands them to Sancia. And, without prompting—her wedding band. All made from gold, all made my Baltasar, all designed by Isaac. She places her jewelry into her daughter's hand, which Sancia reluctantly opens. Sancia then places the valuables in the pocket of an apron tied to her waist. She kisses her mother on her cheek and, without saying a word, leaves.

The walk to Baltasar's shop seems to take longer than usual, as if her feet aim to delay what her head knows must be done. Before she opens the door to the metalworker's shop, she practices her expression so that her appearance will look less glum than her reality. She wants to give her jewelry to him without giving him guilt along with it. *He will refuse. I will insist.*

She enters. She conjures the cheeriest voice possible. After thanking Baltasar for the pie, she takes a couple of steps toward his corner countertop to investigate an unfamiliar object cooling on it. "What is this?"

"Do not touch it! That piece is still very hot. I am waiting for those parts to cool so that I can combine them to make —"

"To make what?"

His evasiveness is odd. "What is the other purpose for your visit?"

"What makes you think—?"

He tilts his head. "You walked in here with a look of purpose, and you started off by saying that first you would like to say thank you for the pie. That means there must be a second."

Sancia takes a deep breath then gently exhales. "You are right, but not yet. Please tell me about your work on this item. I have never seen pieces like it before." Sancia has a genuine curiosity *and* a will to delay her chore.

"Of course you have not." He looks down as he fiddles with a tool. "It only has meaning to those of the Catholic faith. It is a ciborium. During a ceremony within the church, members approach the friar to receive a piece of the body of Christ, the Eucharist. The friar will take the Eucharist, which was a wafer before it transformed into Jesus's body, from the ciborium, and place it in the mouth of the believer so he or she may be filled with the spirit of God."

Do I understand this correctly? "A Catholic person fills his body with the spirit of God by eating a wafer that is somehow converted into the body of a dead man?"

"Sancia, he was not just a man. It is more than a symbolic gesture. Wafers are placed in the ciborium. During the Mass, the wafers become the body of Christ, and the wine becomes the blood of Christ."

Sancia sees why he was hesitant to explain this to her. And now she is closer to understanding the insanity surrounding her. "Jews in Germanic lands are in prison under accusations of torturing bread! So, this wafer, that you speak of, is the bread. And what makes the lies against us so ridiculous is that we are forbidden from eating even the blood of animals - we remove it during the kashering process. But, this practice of yours . . ."

Baltasar looks at the cooling pieces and then back at Sancia. "My dear little one—and you will always be my dear little one—but before you further insult my beliefs, you must understand how grateful I am when I see the image of Christ, at death, and how He allowed himself to suffer so that I would be saved. Unless you listen to Mass every Sunday, and understand the catechism, you do not know enough to have a valid opinion on what I believe and practice."

If G-d had a body, and if the body of G-d truly entered all who consumed the contents from this ciborium, to bring His good spirit into them, they would not be torturing and killing others of His creation. "I do not mean for my opinion to insult you. You are one of the most decent men in this kingdom, probably in this world. This belief, Baltasar, I just do not see it. How much of Christ's blood did the executioners swallow, and how much of his body did the executioners eat and digest before they lit the flames that ate the body and blood of my father and cousin and all the others?"

Baltasar frowns. "Christ would not do such horrible deeds! This beast that is consuming the Church and the Crown is masquerading as Catholic. It is not. Christ speaks through those of us who are compassionate and just. He spoke through Toledo's archbishop when he refused to allow the Inquisition in his district. Have you heard of him?"

"No."

Baltasar seems relieved that he can present an angle that Sancia hasn't considered before. "Toledo's Archbishop Carrillo prohibited the Inquisition from being established in his region. Christ worked through him and through King John, who over a hundred years ago prohibited Friar Ferrand Martínez from continuing his hateful preaching against your people."

"I did not know about King John either. How was it that Friar Martínez sparked the riots against the Jews here in 1391?"

"Martínez was unstoppable after King John died."

Sancia smiles with her eyes. "So, you are telling me, Baltasar, that you are not the only terrific man who is Christian?"

He blushes. "God's work is mysterious."

She attempts to be sincere. "I hope that you enjoy working on this latest piece of yours for the Church." But as the words come out, she realizes that it's impossible to mask her disdain.

"I am a metalworker, and this is a job that I've been commissioned to do. I am Catholic, and so I am happy to do it."

"You are talented. I admire your work." Sancia then pulls the brooch, bracelet, rings and the necklace from her pocket. "I must return these to you. And you must accept them."

Baltasar steps back. He shakes his head and his hands no. "Sancia, I cannot buy these back from you. Even if I had enough money to make a fair trade, these are yours."

Sancia places them on his workspace. "I am not asking you to take them. I am leaving them here with you."

"Give them to your uncle; he is staying here. He might even return them to you one day."

Sancia tells him about the risk of leaving them with her uncle. "Maybe Litiosa will wear this." Sancia touches her necklace, resting on the counter. "I would be honored to imagine her wearing it. I wore my necklace all week— the memory of your work and your kindness will live in my heart always, where the pendant rested. That is what matters most. I cannot bring these things with me. But I will bring you with me — always and everywhere."

Before sunset, on the 15th of Nisan, 5252, Sancia lights the candles to welcome Passover. While her mother leads the Shehecheyanu, the prayer thanking G-d for bringing them to this season, Sancia's heart desperately misses those who did not make it. She is grateful for her family, David's mother and father, and Jacinto's family, all gathered around the table.

David looks at the children while pointing to the book he is reading. "The history in this Haggadah is to prevent us, the Jewish people, from forgetting our bondage and from forgetting our freedom. We must never forget our quest to reestablish our home in Jerusalem."

Esther asks, "Why does each of us dip a finger into cups of grape juice, and pull drops out one by one?" The children fall silent. She answers her own question. "We pull out one drop each time we name a plague that G-d sent upon the Egyptians after warning them it is what He would do if he would not free the Israelites, our ancestors, from slavery. When the plagues killed Egyptians, G-d was sad even though Pharaoh and the Egyptians brought so much harm to the Jewish people. Drip by drip, we read each plague - one by one. The loss of liquid from the glass symbolizes the loss of Egyptian life."

"Why are we sad when bad people die?" Ruben asks. *It is a good question.*

David answers. "Our people's joy in freedom must always be tempered with the knowledge of the suffering of enemies who try to inhibit that freedom. We have joy in a good life for all, but where that conflicts, we must protect ourselves." He leads the rest of the traditional Seder.

Sancia intermixes the story of the exodus her family made from Seville to Portugal one hundred years ago, and how they are doomed to repeat it. "Matzah reminds us of the speed our ancestors needed to escape when Pharaoh agreed to letting them go before he would change his mind again." *Matzah is the excuse those boys used to murder Rabbi Sol a decade ago.*

"Will we be taking matzah with us when we leave our home?" Ruben asks.

It is lightweight, easy to make, and lasts long. "That is a good question, Ruben. You did such a wonderful job making it. Will you help me to make some when it is time to leave?"

"Yes, Mama. We will be just like the ancient Israelites!"

"Could we help too?" Jacinto's children ask.

The children sound excited, as if this is a game. Sancia considers explaining how serious this situation is for them but holds back. People have created plenty of sorrow for all of them to experience; how wonderful if they are blessed to interpret obstacles as challenges. Can she do that? Can she see the good in being forced to live a present-day exodus?

A Frayed People

<hr />

— 1492 —

Sancia hosts the same people, on this third night of Passover, so they can talk about a plan. Everyone is here except for her mother, David and Ruben who will be returning from the market at any moment.

Esther walks in, rather breathless. "We found out more. We heard stories. This is horrible." She clings to the bag from the market, holding it to her chest as if it is a shield.

David takes it from her and walks toward the kitchen. "You can explain while Ruben and I unpack the vegetables and fruits and prepare food for our hungry guests."

Esther looks vulnerable without her shield. "We will be escaping the venom of snakes only to run into the jaws of a lion. We cannot even be sure that King João will allow us to remain in Portugal. He will only allow six hundred new families to remain in his kingdom. And they will have no money to survive after they pay the exit fee from here and the entrance fee there. He is not a good man."

"Who told you this?" David's mother asks.

"Nina, I overheard conversations that were overheard from his former subjects. David heard them, too. The king mistreated nobility so terribly that many of them have settled here, in exile. He killed Diogo, Duke of Viseu, his own brother-in-law! As soon as this king took over his father's throne, he humiliated the nobility who flourished under his father's rule. He did to them what Ferdinand and Isabella are doing to us."

Sancia had previously considered the difficulty of the journey and already knew that not all families could stay in the Portuguese kingdom indefinitely, but she didn't know King João was such a horrible man. "So what do we do? If it is just a matter of time before King João's wealth dries up, no doubt he will look to our people as King Ferdinand and Queen Isabella have. And how can we be sure he will allow our families to live there permanently out of the tens of thousands who will try to stay?"

David returns from the kitchen, carrying some vegetables on a plate. "We will make it. We do not have better options right now."

"That is small comfort." Esther takes the plate of vegetables from his hands and sets it on the table. "We likely will not be there many days before we are faced with the same problem we have now."

"We will find your family as soon as we get there," David says.

Sancia still hasn't received a response from her relatives in Lisbon. They might have to begin their journey before she hears anything.

Jacinto says, "I do not want to keep hopping from land to land, but we might have to do that no matter where we go. Maybe Portugal is not the best place for us. I heard that the sultan of the Ottoman Empire seems to rule with a just mind and generous spirit."

His wife, Bonafilia, shakes her head. "But things can change quickly there, too. Certainly, the Moors are victims here, but that is just because the Catholics happen to be stronger here than they are. It is not because they would rule any better."

Esther says, "She is right. The Ottomans steal Christian boys from their families and force them to accept their Muhammadan faith before they force them to serve the sultan's army, the Janissaries." She then puts her hands up to her face, covers her eyes and moves her head side to side. "And the story of the sultan's harem, and how it is made up of Christian women taken from their lands, is just awful."

Jacinto's eyebrows furrow. "And what they do to the men they steal from Africa is awful. The Ottomans force them to undergo removal of their reproductive parts so that they will not have relations with the sultan's harem they must tend to."

This is news to Sancia. She learned long ago how the Muhammadans massacred Jews in Granada but hadn't realized that Muslim kingdoms consistently rival the Christian kingdoms in their cruelty. *Boys stolen to serve the army of the enemy? Women stolen to serve the king of the enemy? Men from the tribal nations stolen and* . . . Sancia cannot stop herself from gagging before completing the image in her mind of how the Ottomans treat the people they capture and force into slavery.

David says, "My understanding is that the sultan seems to treat Jews well, but we do not know if one day he will do such a thing to us too."

Esther says, "Better to go where most of our people are going and where family is likely to greet us."

"What about having our own land?" Ruben asks. *Of course - he has been listening - and wondering.*

David lifts Ruben onto his lap and puts his arms around him. "We do have our own land. People forced us out of it a long time ago, but some of us never left and have family going back to over two thousand years ago. Some of our friends will be going there now. The long journey will be very difficult for them, much more difficult than for us. For now we will be going to Portugal - but as we continue to say, every year, after the Seder—"

Ruben finishes David's sentence. "—next year in Jerusalem."

"That is right, my son. Next year in Jerusalem."

But next month in Portugal.

Sancia stands outside of the synagogue with her family after the service on the last day of Passover. Jacinto walks up to them. He takes a deep breath. "We are not going to Portugal."

We are not going to Portugal. His words echo in her head. She doesn't want to ask for clarification — not now. They can't fray before they even try to journey together. She looks around at the other neighbors who've been lingering outside of the synagogue. She catches words here and there signaling to her that everyone is talking about where to go and what to do. She hears names of countries, dates, modes of travel.

Jacinto continues. "The news that came to us a few days ago is too much for us to overcome."

Sancia takes his hand. "Please, Jacinto. It is best if we stay together."

He says, "I have received word that, despite what we discussed, some Jews are leaving Ratisbon to live in the Ottoman Empire. They are fleeing from Germanic lands to escape compulsory baptism. We can no longer be at the mercy of Christians anymore. We will be going to Salonika."

"Where is Salonika?" David's mother, Nina, asks.

"It is far. We would not meet again unless your journeys would bring you." Jacinto looks pleadingly at his friends. "Maybe you could consider building a home there with us."

David asks Jacinto if he has really made up his mind.

Jacinto nods.

David's mother looks at her husband and then at David. "We were not going to say anything now, but since this is the discussion we are having . . ."

Sancia braces herself.

After a brief pause that feels like an eternity, Nina reveals her news. "We also will not be going to Portugal."

My son will not lose more grandparents! I could not have heard correctly.

"What do you mean? Why did you not say anything sooner?" David asks.

"Your father and I needed to figure this out first. You know his health has not been so good. His knees hurt too much to travel. And from the news you and Esther brought to us from the market, we knew we could not take a risk of such difficult travel to potentially be turned away or forced to leave."

David's voice trembles. "Where will you go?"

Where in the world could they go when Jacob has so much difficulty walking and Portugal is the closest option?

She squeezes David's hands. "We are not going anywhere."

Sancia's stomach plummets. *They are staying here and leaving Judaism.*

Sancia needs to process all she just heard. "I need to walk more. I do not want to go home yet."

Ruben frowns and holds his stomach. "I want to go home. I am hungry."

Sancia is relieved when her mother says she will bring Ruben home. *Does Mother, like Nina and Jacob, also feel too old and tired to go to Portugal?* She is too scared to ask. She doesn't know what she would do without her.

As if Esther could read her daughter's thoughts, she volunteers her own. "I'm going wherever you go."

Sancia holds back tears of relief. But she can't imagine

how heartbroken David must be. She turns to him. "Will you walk with me?"

He nods and then he takes her hand. Her heart still flutters from his touch. They do not talk. They do not need to. The air is comfortable, flowers have blossomed, and the sun is high in the sky. *How do these elements remain normal amidst so much chaos?* Sancia's attention becomes drawn to a small object that rolls in their direction after slipping out of a boy's hands.

David bends down to pick it up, and then he hands it to the child who is chasing after it. "Here you go."

The boy, who seems to be both spirited and reserved, is about Ruben's age. "Thank you." He examines his toy to see if it has any damage.

Sancia takes a closer look. "Is that a yoyo?"

"No, it is not." The boy's brown eyes light up. "It is a compass."

Both Sancia and David kneel to listen.

The boy points at parts of his compass. "This is the orienting arrow. It tells me where I am." He moves his finger. "And this tells me how to get to where I want to go."

Sancia is impressed. "Thank you for teaching us about something so complicated. And I already thought a yo-yo was difficult enough." She lets out a small laugh.

The boy smiles wide, revealing teeth too large for his small mouth. "I am happy to. My father taught me."

A man of medium stature, white hair, and the age of Sancia's mother, calls out from a distance with a strong voice. "Fernando, we must go."

"Okay, Papa. I was just explaining about my compass."

The man walks up to them. "At the rate you are going, you shall lose it or break it before you get to Lisbon."

Sancia's ears perk up. "We will be going to Portugal, too." How is it that she hasn't seen this family before? "Do you live in the Judería?"

Old enough to be the boy's grandfather, the man gently smiles and shakes his head. "No. No. I am bringing my son, Fernando, and his mother, to stay with my brother in his home in Lisbon while I will be taking to the sea."

David straightens his legs from kneeling. "You are a sailor?"

"Somewhat. Thank you for saving my boy's compass before it would get crushed under someone's foot." The man looks at his son. "You need to keep this safe if you plan to chart out my travels one day."

"I know, Papa. I will."

Sancia smiles softly. "Safe travels."

The man's face betrays a hint of regret. "You too." Then he and Fernando walk away.

David shakes his head in wonder. "I have worked with wood to make so many things, but I have never seen something like that before."

That compass is very interesting. Yet, she has always been impressed with everything David has made. "He seems to be a smart boy. And about Ruben's age." Sancia's imagination takes her to a less forbidding place. "If things were different . . ." Not only could the boys have been friends, but David, who has helped to build ships, would probably have enjoyed learning more from an experienced sailor. He could have focused on charting a path across sea and not land. But things are not different. They are what they are. "David, if your mother and father will not change their mind to join us in Lisbon, do you want to remain here as well?" Sancia holds her breath.

He shakes his head. "No. But leaving them behind will be difficult. I actually think it might be the best decision for them. But it is not for us."

Sancia exhales with relief. "Uncle Abraham, no doubt, will appreciate it. I think he and my aunt were feeling too lonely."

As they walk toward home, David reaches for Sancia's hand, again. "I suppose that if any good can come out of pushing all Jews to convert or leave now, is that those who've given in to conversion a long time ago, will have more company from those forced to convert now."

He is right. Yet, Sancia knows that future generations will never know their heritage once their ancestors become entirely consumed by a culture they've been forced to adopt.

THE GIFT

$$\diamond\!\!\!\rightarrow\!\!\!\times\!\!\!\leftarrow\!\!\!\diamond$$

— 1492 —

David returns home from the shipyard and hands Ruben a small deer that he carved from wood. "We are leaving in a couple of days. You must take good care of this as we pack and journey."

"I will, Papa." Ruben hugs him. "How did you make it?"

David motions for Ruben to put on his shoes. Then he looks at Sancia. "Ruben and I are going for a walk so that we can collect some sticks and I can explain how to carve a shape."

Sancia reflects on the times when David taught Iuceph how to make shapes from wood. "Okay. But not too long. We have packing to do. And he is too young to hold a knife."

"I agree." David then gives Sancia a kiss on her cheek. "We are just going to collect sticks and talk."

"Maybe you will see my mother on your way. I think she is at your mother and father's house. She joined them for dinner." She watches the door as her husband and son leave. She hopes her mother returns soon. They all need to pack, and Sancia has only just started. How many shirts will she need? How many can she carry?

Her thoughts are interrupted by a knock at the door. She opens it. *Baltasar.* She knows the purpose for his visit. "I do not want to say goodbye, Baltasar." She tightens her lips hoping that doing so stops tears from escaping.

"I do not, either. I am going to miss you, dear, little one - your kindness, and your feisty arguments. I am going to miss seeing your son grow up with the same sense of generosity and curiosity that blesses his beautiful mother." He then reaches into his bag and pulls out a pie. "Litiosa could not handle the thought of saying goodbye. She made this for you, knowing that you would otherwise be too busy to eat properly."

Sancia breaks into tears. Baltasar puts the pie on the table, next to his bag, and then wraps his arms around her. She is a child in his arms. She cries into his newly tailored shirt. She cries into his shoulder, her father's shoulder and her uncle's shoulder. Baltasar supports her with a strength she didn't know he still had. She does not remember the last time she felt so safe.

When her trembling slows, Baltasar pulls a cloth from his pocket to wipe her cheeks. He places it back into his pocket and then reaches into his bag. One by one, he pulls out two artfully crafted candlestick holders.

Sancia's face softens. "They are precious." *Like the man who made them.*

"Only to you. I made them out of bronze - so you can take them with you when you leave the kingdom. They are heavy, but you *must* carry them."

She is drained from her tears, yet she knows she has enough strength to do as he asks. "I will use these to bring in the Sabbath wherever in the world I go."

He then holds out a small piece of folded paper. "When you are settled and safe in the land you will call home, then and only then, unfold this paper. It has a message to you, one you must not know, until you are safe. Until then, keep the paper hidden. You are not to look at it until you get to your destination. But you must look at it then."

Sancia wonders what the message could possibly be when Baltasar does not know how to write. She assures him she'll do as he asks. She takes the folded paper from him and places it in a pocket of a sweater to demonstrate that it will be tucked away safely. Then she folds the sweater and places it in the bottom of her travel bag. "I am going to use your candlestick holders this week, and then I will pack them after the candles go out."

"May God be with you, always, little one." Baltasar picks up his empty bag and gives Sancia one last warm look before walking to the door. As he steps away, she grabs him and hugs him tightly, not ready to let him go.

THREE IS DEFINITELY A CROWD

The hands of the antiquated clock on the wall point to five minutes before noon. I compare its accuracy with the time on my phone. *Crap – it's right. I didn't realize it's so late!* "Ben, I meant to tell you, Ari will be joining us for lunch. Is that okay?"

He looks up from his computer. "Hm. 'Is that okay?' It's a little late to ask me now. It seems that you've already invited him."

"Not exactly. I know I should've told you first thing this morning, but I got distracted and then forgot." I tell him how Ari invited himself.

"It'll be nice to see him again." Ben is a good sport.

I text Ari to let him know we'll be right there.

He hops out of his car to greet us. After formal introductions, I insist that Ben take the front seat. While he does, Ari opens the back door for me.

I smile as I hop in the car. "Nice. Chivalry is in . . . still. Thank you."

He closes the door and then gets behind the wheel. "With me, chivalry is always in. Where shall we go?"

I roll the window down. "Someplace quick. We have a lot of work to do."

"Nonsense, Abi." Ben then looks at Ari. "We only have a few items. We're waiting for others, and they seem to be arriving at a slow pace. Certainly, a leisurely lunch won't hurt anyone."

"I like your boss already." As Ari starts to drive, he tells Ben he seems familiar.

Ben looks at him, maybe wondering the same. "Well, we technically did meet a couple of days ago when you asked me to deliver the invitation to Abi."

Ari keeps his eyes on the road. "I wondered that then, too. I'm fairly certain we've met before."

"If you were an archaeologist, I would know you. So, it is not through profession."

Ari shakes his head. "I'm a doctor. That's how I met Abi, actually."

"It is?" That's not how I remember it.

"Sure. I told you. I went to Haiti right after the earthquake in 2010. I was sent by MASHAV. I still periodically go back and forth through IsraAID. I was returning home from my most recent trip when I met Abi on my connecting flight from New York." He glances at me through his rearview mirror. "Abi, do you not remember? I told you that I was returning from the Haitian cholera clinic." He then points to his nose.

No sense of smell. I didn't forget. "I knew you cleaned vomit. I didn't know that you were a doctor."

Ben boasts, "Israel always sends our finest overseas whenever there's a crisis."

"Israel's finest? Ari? Jeez. I didn't realize you were all in such dire straits here." I cringe at my own joke.

Ben is appalled. "Abi, what has gotten into you?"

"I'm only joking. But seriously, Ben, 'Israel's finest' here stole my barf bag on the flight. You've been with me on a dive on choppy waters. You know how sick I can get."

He looks at Ari. "You'll have to manage this on your own. You've crossed a monster."

Ari defends himself. "She took meclizine. Abi, I knew you were going to be fine. I was sitting next to you when you took the pills. And I am actually very good at cleaning up vomit. I'm the best cardiologist at it."

Now I'm confused. "A cardiologist working in a cholera clinic?"

Ari's tone quickly goes from upbeat to solemn. "Untreated, cholera victims will likely die. It's especially deadly to children. They can suffer from cardiac arrest when their salt balance is so greatly disturbed, which could've happened too easily within the already horrible conditions throughout Port-au-Prince, conditions that only worsened in the aftermath of the earthquake. As a pediatric cardiologist, I was sent there to prevent such imbalances from occurring and to try to reverse them when they did." He quiets, as if he is holding back tears. "I wasn't always successful."

I'm hoping Ben says something. But like me, he doesn't seem to know what to say. We all remain silent for the rest of the ride.

Before too long, Ari parks the car and lightens up. "We're here! This is a compromise to my workaholic friend and her laid-back boss. The food is good and quick, yet we can linger here until the boss says we have to go."

Ben steps out of the car. "Sounds terrific."

We step inside the restaurant and look at the menu board. I give my lunch order to Ari.

He turns to Ben. "Please allow me the honor of buying lunch for you, too."

Ben is hesitant to take him up on his offer.

So, I nudge him. "Don't hold back, Ben. Extra chips. You heard the man. He is paying."

Ben thanks Ari and gives him his order. He then turns to help me find a table. "Interesting man, no? Do you like him?"

"Ben, I'm married!"

He pulls out a chair from an empty table. "I didn't ask you if you were married. I asked you if you like him."

What's wrong with me? Why did I assume he meant romantically? *Just because I think he is incredibly sexy in a self-assured, mysterious and intelligent kind of way doesn't mean I think of him romantically.* "He is a nice guy. He is fun. Um . . . he is paying for lunch. What's not to like?" I'm relieved when Ari joins us before Ben can pursue his interrogation.

He gives us each a cup of water then sits next to Ben and across from me. "They'll bring our food to the table when it's ready."

We thank him and then Ben snaps his fingers. "That's

it! Pediatric cardiologist. We did meet once before. And now I remember where. A few years ago, SACH hosted an event—"

Ari smiles with satisfaction. "Yes. Now I remember. We sat at the same table. You were with Evelyn."

Ben is still glowing from his ability to recollect. "Yes. She is a good friend. I accompanied her. Amazing. Small world. So, you were a physician for SACH?"

"I was until the foreign ministry sent me to Haiti."

I'm lost. "What exactly is 'sack'?"

Ben answers. "*S-A-C-H*. It stands for Save A Child's Heart. It's an organization in which Israelis, whether Jewish, Muslim, Christian, or atheist, volunteer to repair heart disorders for children in the West Bank and in Gaza and in developing countries."

"I've never heard of this organization before." It sounds wonderful! How could I not have?

Ari does not seem surprised. "The loud stream of angry voices tends not to bring these kinds of things up. Remember – JVP, SJP, BDS? There are more like them. They just want you to think of Israel as 'an illegitimate Jewish occupation of Muslim land.'" He makes air quotes with his fingers. "They do not want you to see that people of all faiths and ethnicities enjoy coexistence here like no other place for thousands of kilometers." Then he turns to Ben. "Have you not noticed that your protégé leans American toxic-left?"

That was rude! "Colleague!" I clarify. "And, I don't lean."

"You were falling off the cliff until Yoni and I stopped you." He turns to Ben, "Yoni, Abi's cousin's boyfriend, introduced Abi and her cousin to UN Watch and its attempt to counter the damage created by the UN."

Ben's eyes light up. "Ah, yes. Hillel Neuer. He deserves an award. I love that guy. And that organization is one of the most important I contribute to."

I find that a little surprising. "Ben, you're gay. With so many liberal causes, why support one that focuses on protecting Israel?" Especially since Israel can protect itself.

Ben tilts his head and looks at me as if I have two heads. "Because Israel protects me, Abi. Not perfectly, but it is my home and one of the safest places in the world for me to be, in general and especially as a gay Jewish man."

Now Ari knows that Ben is gay. I hope he doesn't feel the same toward the gay community as he does toward the Muslim community. I'm ready to pounce on him if he makes any personal attack on Ben.

Ari looks at Ben. *Watch it, buddy!* Then he looks at me. "Many people from the LGBTQ communities surrounding us try to escape their Islamic governments – to be here, in Israel, where they know they will be safe."

That is not a response I would have expected from Ari. I wait, in vain, for Ben to intervene and correct him. But, he stays silent. *I'm so confused.* "That doesn't make any sense. At home, the very people who support causes for the LGBT community support the Palestinians and constantly shout about how horrible Israel is."

Ben sighs. "You'd think they'd shout about the country that forces gender reassignment surgery on gay people and publicly hangs suspected gay lovers from cranes."

That's disgusting! "Who does that?"

"The Iranian government does both of those things," Ben answers. "But it isn't just Iran. Yet there is a reason they are among the biggest supporters of Hamas even though they are ideological enemies of one another. Hamas has the biggest geographical advantage to cause us harm. The best way to support anyone is to be truthful about what causes them harm. Intersectionality in your country has become woefully toxic."

That's a big word for a non-native speaker. "Intersectionality?"

Ari leans toward me with his elbows on the table. "Yes. You are influenced by it without even realizing the destructive strategy behind it. 'If you support the gay community, then condemn Israel.' 'If you support women, then condemn Israel.' 'If you support Black Lives Matter, then condemn Israel.'" Again, with the air quotes. He continues, "I ask, do Black lives matter in Nigeria where Islamic militants have been slaughtering African Christians by the thousands?"

I had no idea that Islamic militants were slaughtering Christians in Africa today. Has that even been in the news?

Ben slams his hand against the table. "I say they do. But I don't hear about it from your country." He looks at me. "What I do hear too often is ugly distortions about Israel. And the irony is that Jews were and are among the most aggressive in taking action to assure equal rights for all. Martin Luther King Jr. recognized Israel as one of the great outposts of democracy. He said so. His bond to the Jewish people was strong. He was right then, and he would be right now. Sinister people are trying to hijack all these bonds, by turning the very people we have always been standing by, against us and quite frankly, against their own best interests." He pauses. "That's why I belong to A Wider Bridge. Equality—"

"—in Israel. Equality for Israel." Ari joins Ben in unison.

Ben smiles. "You know A Wider Bridge – the pro-Israel LGBTQ organization?"

"I'm a worldly man. I know a lot." Ari winks at me.

Oh brother.

The server places our order on the table. Perfect timing. Hmm. Maybe too perfect. I wonder if he had been listening and waiting for a break.

We lift our water cups and in unison and say, "*Bete'avon.*" Food does seem to have a way of neutralizing a mood.

My first bite is amazing. Wow! "This falafel is so good. Thank you, Ari."

Ben, with a full mouth, nods his head and gives the thumbs up. After a few minutes of quiet, while we all indulge, he picks up the conversation again. "Abi told me that you took her to play football. I understand her team beat yours."

Ari holds up a finger requesting Ben wait a minute for his answer while he chews. "What matters is that we had fun."

"That is what people who lose say." I wink at him. "Ben, it was the kids. They are fantastic! And they play really well."

"Of course they do," Ben says. "See, Israelis do ethnic diversity imperfectly well, but we could improve much on our ethnic non-diversities."

"Ethnic non-diversities?"

Ben brings a napkin to his mouth before answering. "Orthodox Jews versus secular Jews. And to a lesser extent, the Jews in between. Diverse in culture but not ethnicity."

Ari elaborates. "Often the tension between Israeli Orthodox and secular Jews is as great as the tension between Israeli Muslims and Jews. Orthodox Jews have too much influence in the Knesset. That is a threat to seculars and freethinkers."

"So, you don't like Muslims *and* you don't like Orthodox Jews?" I wait for an answer.

Ari purses his lips. "I have not said either of those things. I do not even feel either of those things. Could you please try to be as accurate with people as you are with objects?"

Clever. An insult that doesn't compromise my professional integrity. *Can you refrain from being a jackass for more than thirty minutes at any given time?* I can't believe I find this guy attractive. He is such an ass.

Ben rushes in to save Ari. "What we mean is - the Jewish people are a tree. The Orthodox are the roots that keep us grounded and nourish the tree from the earth. The seculars are the leaves who demystify us from the rest of the world and nourish the tree from the sun and air. Too many roots despise the leaves and too many leaves despise the roots."

I never heard Ben make such an analogy before. I find it funny. I laugh. I don't mean to. And now the awkwardness of my out-of-place laughter is making me unable to stop. I laugh more. *Ugh – I want to stop.*

I look away but can feel the eyes from my lunch companions staring at me. I fear if I look around, I will see the entire restaurant staring at me.

Finally, I catch my breath. "I'm sorry, Ben. That was so lovely. I just never heard you talk in a hippie kind of way before. I mean, I know you're saying something so much deeper than simply an earthy, crunchy, tree thing, but it just struck me as funny."

Ben clears his throat. "Maybe that's because you are used to me talking about objects from dead people and not about something living, like a really, really, really big plant."

Ari's expression of surprise is classic. "A tree is a plant?"

I nod.

He looks a little baffled as he processes this new bit of information.

We all burst out laughing.

Then Ari catches his breath. "Tree or not, I can manage some Orthodox, as long as their laws don't intrude on my life any more than they do now. For example, I do wish that someone would come up with another solution to the ever-maddening Shabbat elevator."

"Hear, hear!" Ben holds up his water cup.

"What's a Shabbat elevator?"

Ari puts his hands to his face and shakes his head. Then he moves his hands away. "Many large buildings have designated Shabbat elevators that function so that no observant Jew will dishonor the Sabbath by having to press a button to ride one. The elevators are set to stop and open at every floor."

Ben enunciates: *"Every* floor."

"Imagine living on the twentieth floor. You would need meclizine, or a barf bag, just to get home." Ari smiles at his own cleverness. Then he points his finger up, indicating he just remembered something. He pulls out his phone to do a search. "The barf bag museum."

"What better time to look at barf bags than while eating?" I smile and then I explain to Ben the story behind the whole barf bag fiasco.

Ari beams as he hands his phone to me. "See. Look here. I'm a Patron of Puke. And these are my bags." His pride is endearing.

I take his phone and glance at the page. "That is too funny." And then I look at him with exaggerated admiration. "They are lovely bags." It really is a cool idea and site. I then hand the phone to Ben. He smiles and scrolls to see other bags. Then he hands it back to Ari.

Ari puts his phone away. "I have not sent in the bag that I took from meeting you, yet. When I do, I will use your name. After all, it was your bag."

"I'm not sure I can handle such fame." I smile.

Ben looks at his watch. "I'm afraid we do need to get back."

I stand up and gather the wrappers and napkins. "It's about time. I was hoping we'd get back to the ship before the 100th anniversary of the annulment of the Alhambra Decree."

"The Alhambra Decree?" Ari wipes crumbs from the table and sprinkles them in the pile of trash that I'm holding and about to dump.

I try to keep the wrappers from falling to the floor as he does that. "Well, the *annulment* of the Alhambra Decree. In 1492 the Spanish monarchy set forth a law which forced every Jew to choose between conversion, exile or death. That edict was called the Alhambra Decree. It was illegal to be a Jew in Spain for almost five hundred years. After WWII even."

Ari furrows his eyebrows. "So is the 100th anniversary of its annulment coming up soon?"

"No, I was exaggerating. It's a testament to how slow our project is going. Last December, was just the 50th anniversary." Finally, a topic in which I have the upper hand. Too bad we need to leave now.

Ari places his hand on his chest. "Last December was the 50th anniversary of my birth. Are you telling me that the month I was born, was the precise month it became legal to be Jewish in Spain again?"

Anniversary of my birth? That's an awkward way to say birthday. Wait a minute! "You just turned 50? You were born in 1968?" I hope he doesn't think I'm saying he is old. I'm just surprised he is *that* old. But wow, he is one hot quinquagenarian.

"Yes. December 16th. Do you know the exact date that law got annulled? I'm Sephardic. I know about the expulsion of my ancestors, but not the details, like the name of it and such. How cool would it be if I were born when Spain annulled the Alhambra Decree?"

Holy cow! Yes. I do know the exact date. And you were born on it! What are the chances that a Sephardic Jew, whom I encountered on my way to Israel to investigate what is likely a medieval Spanish ship, is so intrinsically tied to a place and a people I specialize in?

He is looking at me, waiting for me to respond. I look back at him. *Sometimes silence is the most precise answer I've got.*

Old Family, New Life, More Horrors

— 1492 —

Sancia watches closely as the guard rifles through Ruben's travel bag. She can see the sailboat she embroidered, despite the dust embedded into it. She looks at each member of her family, wearily standing with her outside the fort of Marvão, after traveling more than a fortnight, mostly by foot and briefly by coach. The heat from the approaching summer is oppressive.

She forces herself to refrain from objecting as a guard pulls out a pair of Ruben's unworn shoes and shows them to one of the other guards. "Ruy, these look to be the right size for your son." He then tosses Ruben's shoes to Ruy, who responds by tossing a beautifully crafted cane in turn. Sancia uses the elementary Portuguese she learned from her father to order the guard to return the cane. "Look at her. She cannot walk without it." With newfound bravery, she continues. "And those shoes belong to my son. He wore out the soles of two pairs while walking from Seville. We've been walking nearly every day for more than two weeks. I just had those made for my son yesterday so that he would have something to wear on his feet in Lisbon."

The guard returns the shoeless bag to Ruben. He then sifts through Sancia's bag and finds one of Baltasar's candlestick holders. He pulls it out and holds it up to show Ruy, who shakes his head. "No. It was probably used for some Jewish ceremony. Throw it away or give it back. I do not want that junk."

The guard tosses the candlestick holder back into the bag. "Pay the hundred crusados, and then I will issue your papers to stay. Because of your disrespect, you are undeserving, but because of the quality shoes you gave to my friend here, I will allow it."

David whispers to Sancia in Ladino as he pulls money from his satchel. "He is allowing us to stay because we have the ability to pay. But now we have almost nothing left."

After counting the coins, the guard hands documents to each adult. "These permits and this receipt must be with each of you at all times. Should any of you be caught in public without the ability to produce these documents, you will be arrested, and your belongings will be claimed by the king."

Sancia tries to suppress her nerves and instead focuses on her relief that they have been accepted among the six hundred families allowed to stay. It's a good thing she and David continued working in Seville, even though they knew they would have to leave almost everything behind. She hears the other guard demand the same fee from another family who cannot pay the entire amount. The guard tells them they must leave within eight months or become slaves to the kingdom.

"How much money do we have left?" David asks Sancia and Esther.

Sancia wishes they could help the other family. She suspects that's why David asked. But they barely have enough to make it through the week.

Sancia is barefoot by the time her soles touch the cobblestone streets of the Alfama district of Lisbon. She stops two women walking in the direction of the market her family just passed by. "Excuse me. Do you happen to know the family Pareja?"

One woman smiles joyfully and clasps her hands together. "You must be the cousin from Seville." She then gives them directions. "I would bring you there, but I am already late. You will find it. You are almost there. They have a mezuzah on their door."

The other woman laughs. "That is not specific enough. We all do."

After getting more detail and thanking them, Sancia carries on with a new energy. She counts the doors they pass before ascending steps on the right. She then steps in front of a dark wooden door and points to the mezuzah. "Here is 'the middle door on the hill.'"

"Are you certain?" Esther asks.

"No. But, if this is not right, maybe they will help us." Sancia knocks and looks at the door as it creaks open. A woman, with soft brown eyes and with more years than her mother, peers through the crack.

"Carima?" *Could you be the wife of my father's distant cousin?*

The woman widens the opening of the door and of her smile. She calls into the home to a man, whose name is the same as Sancia's uncle. "Abraham, Isaac's family is here."

It's been so long since anyone referred to her father in life.

A man with thick eyebrows and a large smile appears at the door. "Please come in. I hoped you would come even though I was concerned I did not respond to your note on time.

Sancia brings her fingers to the mezuzah on the doorpost and then to her lips. She steps over the threshold into Carima and Abraham's home. Esther and David, while holding Ruben, do the same. They each collapse on chairs.

Carima looks at their feet. "You are bleeding." She then glances at Ruben's worn but intact shoes. Her eyes tear.

Sancia doesn't look at the damage to the bottom of her feet but knows she doesn't want to stand up again for at least a week. "Ruben walked some. But we each took turns carrying him. The guards stole his only unworn pair of shoes."

And with some effort to stand from her chair, Carima walks into one of the rooms off the dining room area. She then returns with a pair of lady's shoes and a pair of men's shoes. "These are extras. Please see if they fit you after you have been able to wash and rest."

Sancia immediately motions for the lady's pair to go to her mother. They have the same size feet, and she would rather her mother have them. She is grateful when Abraham carries a bucket full of water and some rags to the door and offers for them to freshen up outside.

After they have taken care of the wounds on their feet, Abraham shows them more of his home. It's bigger and nicer than what she has been used to. He opens a door to a room that's twice the size of their bedroom in Seville. Decorative blankets top the beds. He looks at Sancia and David. "This room used to belong to our daughters, who sometimes come to visit. Please make yourself comfortable." Then he walks to an empty space against a wall. "Sancia, we can help you to set up your sewing table here. Carima was thrilled when we got the notice that you make clothing. She has been looking for a new craft since the children moved out, although taking care of the grandchildren keeps her busy."

Sancia and David place their small satchels on the floor. And then Abraham leads them to another room. "Esther and Ruben, this is yours. This was our sons' room before they made families of their own."

Ruben walks over to the windowsill and picks up a wooden carving of a bird that was resting on it. "Papa, this is like yours, but yours is better. This one has a funny neck."

"Ruben!" David fumbles for words. "That looks like a crane, and a magnificent one."

Abraham smiles. "That is okay. We bought that at the market a long time ago."

Sancia is relieved that her son's bluntness wasn't as

hurtful as it could've been. "Abraham, these rooms are perfect. I do not know how we can thank you or repay you for
your kindness."

Abraham answers generously with no reservation in his
voice. "I am happy you are here. We are family." He then
points outside the bedroom door where there is the sound
of plates being set on the table. "Come, let us feast."

Sancia could probably eat straight for a year. Carima
invites them, in Ladino, to sit down. "Today you are our
guests, maybe tomorrow too. But, as soon as you have
strength, we will put you to work as our housemates." She
smiles warmly. Sancia can tell that she is a woman who
would be happy to serve them all as guests indefinitely. And
though she is grateful that they have a shared language, she
knows she will have to improve her Portuguese.

Sancia helps Ruben settle in a chair before sitting in
one herself. She looks at Carima. "Abraham told me that
you would like to learn how to make clothing. I shall teach
you when you are ready."

Carima smiles as she finishes pouring water into the
last cup on the table. "I like that idea. Thank you. We can
go to the market after your feet have had time to heal. We
will buy fabric, and we will announce that you can repair
clothing. You will start to earn money right away."

Sancia is not used to sitting while others work around
her, but she does not have enough energy to even offer to
help Carima serve dinner. "Thank you. The taxes to enter
your kingdom cost us almost everything we had left after
we paid the taxes to leave our kingdom."

Carima takes a seat at the table. "This is your kingdom now."

Sancia, Esther and David take turns describing everything that happened at the border.

Ruben pouts and folds his arms over his chest. "They took my new shoes."

Sancia shows them the documents. "We must carry them at all times, or they will take everything from us."

Abraham looks up from his plate. "They will take all that belongs to you if they catch you without papers? I hope that does not mean they would take *our* property." He then quickly addresses the panicked expression on Sancia's face. "It is best to be sure to always keep the papers with you. But, I did not mean to worry you. Our family has lived here safely for a hundred years."

Sancia enjoys a sense of peace that has too long eluded her. She looks at the pile of clothing she is about to deliver to her customers of ten months - people she has known since her arrival to this kingdom. She deeply inhales the fresh spring air, grateful that there are no red discs in sight. She no longer needs to sew them. She no longer needs to wear them. What she does see is a cloudless blue sky above her village in Lisbon. She delights in the flowers blooming, the bees gathering and the birds chirping – harmony shattered by a horrible scream. She turns the corner and sees a man mounted on a horse with a blank expression on his face. He is looking down at a woman who is buckled over in pain.

She must have been kicked by the horse, but why is he not helping her? Why is no one helping her? Why am I not running to help her? Sancia's gut tells her not to, despite the overwhelming objection of her conscience. She strains to hear the exchange - but cannot make out the words. The man, seemingly unfazed, backs up his horse and gallops by the woman he leaves behind in an agonized state. Sancia is frozen, gripped by the fear that she hoped to leave behind.

She musters up her best attempt to speak Portuguese to standers-by. "Did you see what happened?"

A short and slender woman turns to her, about to answer, but is urged to leave by the man standing by her side. "Mencia, the entertainment is over. We have much to do before noon." He tugs at a basket she is holding.

"Just a moment, Bernaldo." The woman shrugs him off. "Why deprive this woman of the excitement we just had? We have plenty of time to finish what we need to do. Let us relive the moment."

How could she possibly have enjoyed what she saw? "Was the woman not in pain?"

Mencia rolls her eyes. "Of course not. She howled like a dog, but she was not harmed at all. She was simply informed that she is now to be owned by the kingdom. She was duly warned this would happen. Isn't that right, Bernaldo?"

The man nods. "They all were."

"They?" Sancia asks.

"The Jews." Mencia rolls her eyes again. "Our kingdom could not absorb the tens of thousands of them living in the outskirts, in unkempt shelters. They were fortunate to have transit through here. It is not the fault of our king if they could not pay to leave. That woman who you saw crying will be lucky to be a slave. Her lot will improve if she cares for Christian children in a clean home rather than for her litter in a dirty home. They have been here for months. What would she expect? To keep living here with her urchins?"

Sancia can no longer string a complete sentence together. "'Litter?'. . . 'Urchins?'"

"Yes. A litter of urchins, actually." Mencia shakes her head in disbelief that Sancia seems lost. "Urchins. Jewish children. She brought with her six of them. Of course she could not work properly while caring for the beasts, so the king has taken care of that."

"What do you mean?"

"The king collected them as payment, of course." And then Mencia places the palm of her hand on her chest. "But really it is such an expense for him. It will cost him a fortune to ship her vermin, and the thousands of others just like them, to our kingdom's island off the coast of Guinea."

Just keep breathing. "The King is going to ship her children to an island? How do you know all of this?" *This must be incorrect.*

Mencia assures Sancia that she is giving her an accurate report. She looks at the sky. "The friar of our congregation told us last sermon. He led us in prayer for the souls of the Jews including the piglets being shipped to the island. There will be about two thousand of them— to São Tomé." She then lowers her eyes to look at Sancia. "I do not even know if they have souls. What do you think?"

Sancia stares blankly.

Bernaldo speaks. "If only the families of those children would have been able to pay the exit tax, then none of us would have to be going through this. Instead, we need to stay away from the outskirts - away from their unclean and sickly bodies that litter our land. I hope this woman didn't bring the plague with her into our city."

Sancia is horrified. "Who will take care of the children on the island if he is enslaving their mothers here?"

Mencia snickers. "How charming. You refer to piglets as 'children.'" Then she looks at Bernaldo. "She refers to the piglets as 'children.'"

Bernaldo shakes his head. "You should learn otherwise if you want to be respected. But you are young. São Tomé is the island of lizards. The crocodiles and the snakes will take care of them and do whatever else reptiles do when they encounter fellow vermin."

Can it be true? Sancia wonders. *Jewish adults enslaved? Their children shipped to an abandoned island? Can the cruelty of King João rival that of King Ferdinand? Can he really turn tens of thousands of Jews, escaping persecution, into slaves, and steal their children, leaving them to die on an uninhabited island?* She knows the answer.

She hurries home with the undelivered clothing. She can't stop hearing the mother's scream, nor imagining her pain. A horse's kick to the stomach would have been lot easier for her to survive. Ruben greets her as soon as she walks through the door. "Mother, you are home so soon. Did you leave something behind?"

Esther and Carima look up from preparing vegetables for dinner. Ruben knows so much, but this she does not want him to hear. Esther stands up from her chair. "Ruben, please come and sit here and snap each of these beans in two with Carima and place them in the bowl. That would help me very much."

Sancia is grateful her mother could read her expression. Ruben diligently fulfills his grandmother's request. Esther then takes the undelivered clothing from Sancia's arms and brings her into the room she shares with her grandson. She places the clothing on the bed, closes the door, and then gently squeezes her daughter's hand.

Sancia tries to muffle her cries by nuzzling in to her mother's shoulder. She doesn't want Ruben to hear her. She then wipes the tears from her eyes with the back of her hands. "She was in so much pain. I keep hearing her scream. He took her children!"

Esther pulls her close and holds her tightly. "Who took whose children?"

"The king took a mother's children. They are enslaving our people again and stealing our children - banishing them to death on a desolate island with dangerous creatures."

Esther steps back to look into Sancia's eyes. "Are you sure?"

Sancia knows she knows the answer. "I do not know how we can help them. Even if we could afford to commission a ship to the island, São Tomé, we could be met with death or enslavement. We cannot break any laws. But we also cannot watch more horrors against our people."

"All we can do right now is stay safe, stay alive, and not do anything that would draw attention to us. We need to keep Ruben with us at all times."

Sancia's heart races. "It will only be a matter of time before they come for us. It will only be a matter of time before they take Ruben."

Esther takes both of Sancia's hands into hers. "I do not think that is the case. Nothing like this should be happening to the people who could not pay. But we did pay. At dinnertime, when David and Abraham return from work, we will discuss the next steps we should take."

Sancia pulls her hands away. "There are no next steps, Mother! We do not have enough money to leave. We barely have enough to live. We have been surviving off the generosity and kindness of our cousins. I do not want to leave them. And this is the best option that I can imagine. As you said, we just need to make sure we keep Ruben near one of us at all times. Even though we are one of the 'lucky six hundred families,' I am not sure when that 'luck' will run out."

Sancia lights the Sabbath candles and then says the blessing. Abraham offers the blessing over the wine - and Carima, over the challah. They eat. No one speaks. When Sancia sees that everyone has finished, she signals to David that they all need to talk. She glances toward Ruben. David then reaches for his workbag and pulls out an object to give to his son.

Ruben examines it. "Thank you, Father. What is it?"

"It is called cork. Do you remember when I told you how

before we moved here that I cut trees for wood in the winter, when they are clean from sap?"

Ruben nods.

"Instead of cutting trees here, I harvest cork from special cork trees. This is much nicer. The trees do not need to come down. And it is actually good for them when we do that."

Ruben scratches off a little piece and rolls it between his fingers. "Did you pick this from a high branch? Do they all grow in this funny shape?"

David laughs and then he answers his son. "Those are great questions. Cork is part of the cork tree's bark that wraps around each tree trunk. In the spring and in the summer, I help to carefully remove the bark without harming the trees. The rest of the year, I work to make ship parts with it."

Sancia is pleased to see Ruben's curiosity. She excuses him from the table and encourages him to go and try to make a shape with the cork. Ruben hugs his father before going to his room with his new toy. Sancia then recounts the scene she witnessed earlier in the day.

David slams his hand on the table. "Can you believe it? There are laws in this kingdom that protect the trees. Jews, on the other hand – we are left to die of thirst and hunger, disease, or on an island with predators. You would think that well over a hundred years ago, when the rulers thought fit to protect the trees in law, they would have developed some compassion and decency toward all human beings."

Esther says what is already on Sancia's mind. "We are not human to them!"

Sancia falls silent at the sound of this truth, and then rises to clear the table. The others insist they will clean up instead. They urge her to rest. She doesn't even try to protest. Instead, she sits alone and stares at the glow of the Sabbath candles. She sees the ghost of her father looking at her from the other side of them.

She reflects on how the evil misuse the flame, and how her people have mastered it in goodness. She stares at the blue center — the scorching air that dances within the yellowish glow. The wick is always the same size, no matter how long the candles burn. It is steady and reliable, even in the face of adversity - just like her people.

She moves her eyes from the candles, a little lower, to the candlestick holders. *They are beautiful.* A warm memory of Baltasar overwhelms her. She misses him and hopes he and Litiosa are doing well. She suddenly remembers the paper he gave to her. She wore that sweater several times but didn't place her hands in the pockets. A panic rushes through her as she fears the note might have slipped away. She gets up from the chair and searches through the drawer in her bedroom until she finds the sweater. She is overcome with relief when she hears a crinkling sound coming from the pocket that contains the paper. She wonders what the private message could have been from a man whose writing ability was limited to his signature on his artwork.

She brings the paper to a nearby lantern in the room and unfolds it. *Drawings.* Three distinct drawings. The first is of the candlestick holder with a circle drawn around the top. An arrow indicates she twist the top. The second and third image is of the candlestick holder in two parts. The bottom is tilted at an angle, almost upside-down, with an object sticking out of it. If she understands this correctly, they open. These are not just candlestick holders but capsules. She looks at the paper again to confirm her assessment. She folds it and puts it into the pocket of her sweater and brings it back to the drawer in her room. She returns to the table where the flames still have time left. Though her hands are eager to examine the pieces, she won't dare extinguish the candles prematurely. She stares at them with a will to hurry them to darkness.

Finally. She uses the light of the lantern lit before sunset. She picks up the candlestick holder and tests the rim with her finger. It's still too hot. She blows on the metal. When it's cool enough, she twists off the top. She turns the bottom upside down — her palm ready to catch the contents. Nothing. She taps it and then hears a ping on the table, and then on the floor. She then looks inside the bottom of the candlestick holder and sees that it's been hollowed out.

In near darkness, she looks on the floor for whatever fell. She sees a cylindrical object, similar in color to the capsule it came from. She holds it to the light. Whereas the candlestick holder is bronze, the piece between her fingers — is gold.

My jewelry. Melted, secured, and returned. She sees the sparkle of her mother's emerald amidst the gold. How can she ever thank him? Sancia sends thoughts to Baltasar, hoping he can feel her love — hoping he never stopped feeling it. She reaches for the other candlestick holder and carefully repeats the process so as not to drop its contents. More gold. Now she sees how everything he did made sense. He was even more remarkable than she knew.

She puts each gold piece back into each capsule and twists the covers back on. She then puts the candlestick holders away. She needs to think. If they sell the gold right away, they might have enough money to leave the kingdom. A comforting idea but for a moment. She knows that horror is waiting for her people wherever they go, and that right now Portugal is no worse a hell than the other lands are, or are doomed to become.

New King, Old Horror

1495

Sancia welcomes David home from work. He greets her and then walks to the basin to wash his hands. "Did you hear the news? King Manuel has released the enslaved Jews."

Sancia holds out a towel. She has been hoping that King João's successor would rule justly. This is a good sign that he will. "I did not hear that. But what about the children on the island? Will he bring them back?"

David lowers his eyes. "I think it is too late. King João's deed cannot be undone. If only he died two years ago — before he did what he did. Rumor is that most of the children did not even survive the journey. Those who did survive the journey—" David doesn't complete his sentence.

Esther was sitting quietly until then. "The best justice we can do for those children now is to make sure we live, to make sure future generations live. And to always remember them."

Sancia is startled when David returns from work early. She barely had time to sew one item.

He is distraught. "I did not even reach the wooded area when I overheard some men from the village mentioning a sermon they heard in which the friar relayed a message from King Manuel ordering all of the Jews —," He then glances at Abraham and Carima, "*all* of us must leave. We are to be in exile again."

Abraham falls back on a chair. The color fades from his face. "But our family has been here for generations. Why, in less than two years, would this king behave as cruelly as his predecessor? This does not make sense. He freed those of us taken as slaves. Maybe he also would have saved the children from the island if it were not too late."

David brings a glass of water to Abraham before sitting next to him. "He freed the captives because he was financially motivated to. He knows we are more valuable left to our own devices to be productive. He knows that his kingdom loses when restraining us as slaves."

Abraham takes a sip of water and then speaks slowly. "*Now* this makes sense. I heard rumors that King Manuel plans to marry the vile spawn of the royals whose kingdom you left. The rumors must be true. King João's son left the Infanta Isabella widowed, and now she might remarry, into the family, to Manuel. I'm certain that these events are connected."

"Whether they are connected or not, it is certain, from what I have heard, that he will force us to convert. We have until October. We should —" David stops in response to loud but distant activity outside.

Sancia hears it too. She and the others run out the door and down the steps to see what the cause of the noise is. Without putting a foot onto the road, she sees a mob destroying her synagogue. People are surrounding a large fire right outside of it—a fire they are fueling with her holy books. She sees her father and cousin trapped in the flames. "We need to leave! I cannot take this. We need to leave! We need to leave now!"

David grabs both of her arms and restrains her with his eyes. "Where can we go? The world is getting more mad, but I cannot let you unravel on me now. You are insisting we need to go. But where do you think we can go?"

He is right. We have no place to go. But we cannot stay. I will not be baptized. I will not become one of them.

— 1497 —

The rhythm of kneading dough at the kitchen table helps Sancia temper her emotions. The execution of the new law of exile is looming. "Mother, we cannot avoid this discussion any longer."

Esther cracks an egg into a bowl and gives it a quick stir. "Let us finish preparing dinner. The others should be here soon. We will talk after we eat. Then we will decide where to go. I know the time is about up."

Sancia agrees. She looks at her son, almost nine years old. He is making an animal shape from cork. He's grown so much in the five years they've been in Lisbon.

Hands kneading dough, Sancia turns her attention from Ruben to the door as she hears David and the others approach. She wipes her hands on her apron to welcome them. Instead, she runs toward the door and throws herself against it. "Get out! Get out!"

Several of the king's soldiers burst in. One takes hold of Ruben. "This boy will be baptized, and his soul saved. He will be placed with a Christian family. When you are ready to be a suitable mother and accept Christ and learn the proper ways to keep a child, then you may be reunited. Until then, he no longer belongs to you."

"You are not leaving here with my son!"

The soldiers overpower her with ease. One push and she lands on the floor across the room. Ruben escapes his grasp to run to his mother but is quickly caught and carried away. Sancia is unable to move as she hears her son's cry. *Let go of me! Let go of me!* His voice fades away.

Sancia is on the floor curled into herself, in the same spot where she landed when the soldier pushed her. She hears David walk in.

He runs to her side. "What happened?"

Sancia can't get any words out. *My boy is gone. My heartbeat is coming to a halt.*

David stands up and walks to her mother. "Esther, what is wrong? Say something!" He opens the door to a room, "Ruben?" Then another room — "Where is Ruben?"

Sancia must listen helplessly to her husband's frantic

cries as he searches in vain for his son. *Your son is gone. He isn't here. They took him. They took my boy.* Then she hears the sudden absence of noise. The quiet sound of certainty. Despair. The footsteps. She feels David's arms wrap around her. *He knows.* His body cradles hers and he weeps into her shoulders.

The sun is about to set. How obscene that time continues passing. Everything should have stopped when they took her baby.

Sancia hears a knock at the door. *No, not again!* Another knock. She cannot commandeer her limbs to run. Where will she run? She feels David get up. *No! Do not open the door.* Her words do not leave her lips.

David looks out the window. "A boy is standing outside. He is the same height as Ruben. I think he is alone. I am going to open it."

Sancia then hears the door creak open. She can barely see.

A shadow speaks. "Is this Ruben's home? Are you his father?"

"Yes." David then invites the boy inside. "What do you know about my son?"

He answers. "I am not supposed to be here. We could all get in trouble. My mother thought it would be safer to send me than to come herself. But she had to reach you."

Sancia watches from the floor, unable to get up.

The boy looks up at David. "As you know, our king has taken all of the Jewish children from their mothers and fathers and will only return them after they accept baptism. Ruben is at my home. My mother wanted me to tell you that he is safe and will remain safe with her, and that she will not bring him to be baptized. She will lie to the authorities and say she did. She told me that lying is less of a sin than forcing anyone to do something against their will. She will teach Ruben how to behave like someone who is Catholic so that he will know how to stay safe. She finds the king's law to be repulsive, yet says that the best way to counter his damage, for the time being, is to make sure neighbors and priests believe she will abide by those laws. It breaks her heart to have someone else's boy under this condition. But she knows that she is better than any other prospective godmother would be."

Sancia stirs out of her curled position. She props herself up on the floor. She tries to process all that's been said. *Ruben is safe.* But she can't get any words out.

"Can we see him now?" David asks.

"No!" the boy states emphatically. "It is not safe! That would put us all in danger. If they suspect anything and then take him from us, we could get thrown into prison, too, and then all is lost."

David goes quiet.

"What can we do to get our boy back?" Sancia hears herself ask.

"One day soon we will find a way. It would be best if you could pretend that you are Catholic. To do this, since you have no credible Catholics here to lie for you like my mother will for Ruben, you must become baptized. I think there is no other way for you to get your son back without at least making a show of being baptized." The boy pauses. "If you bring attention to us, I could be taken away from my mother too. Please, she did not want you to worry. She felt sick hearing Ruben tell us how he was violently taken, how they pushed his mother to the floor, and how he could not get to her. She is home consoling him now."

Sancia looks at the boy and notices some familiar features. *I have seen him before.* But where? She struggles to hush her mind so that she can hear the boy speak.

"Mother is reassuring him I would find you. I have a way with directions. We are risking a lot for me to get this message to you. I know we will meet again, when the time is right, and the conditions are safe."

Is he an angel? Has she lost her mind?

"You have our word," David says.

The boy expresses sadness he cannot do more. "Whenever we can, we will get messages to you."

"Thank you. My name is David. This is Sancia." He then turns to where his mother-in-law has remained unmoved. "And she is Ruben's grandmother, Esther."

Sancia is touched by the boy's sincerity as he says that he is pleased to meet them and that he can understand why Ruben is so sad to be away from them.

He tells them that his name is different from his mother's name. "She is Beatriz Enríquez. We've been living at my uncle's house for five years now, even though he has not been home for some time. One day, I might also go to Hispaniola and become governor of Santo Domingo, like my Uncle Bartolomeo, even if that means being away from home, like him. My father says that I am too young to go on such trips right now. I disagree. But I am glad that I did not go on his last trip, because then I would not have met Ruben, and I would not have been able to give you this important message."

David says, "I am so grateful you did."

Sancia is too. She rubs her wrists, massaging out the soreness from holding herself up on the floor.

The boy says, "But, one day I'll go. And when I rule a land, I will make sure it is ruled with kindness, fairness, and justice."

David smiles at the boy. "I have no doubt you will. I already see that you are intelligent, brave and just."

"Thank you." He pulls a round object from his pocket and holds it in his closed palm. "I need to go now."

David opens the door and tells him to be safe and to please thank his mother for them. "And, please tell Ruben we will do everything we can to bring him home. We will not rest until we do."

The boy nods. "I will." He then focuses on the round object in his hand and steps outside the door.

David takes a step outside after the boy. "You told me your mother's name, but you did not tell me yours."

The boy turns to him. "Fernando. Fernando Colombo, son of Beatriz Enríquez and Cristoforo Colombo." He waves goodbye and then continues on his way.

David steps back inside and closes the door. He kneels by Sancia and then helps her off the floor. They both walk to her mother. Sancia takes her hand. "Did you hear that, Mother? Ruben will return to us. We did not lose him."

Esther remains silent.

Sancia is gripped with fear from the lack of color in her mother's face. "We have to get you to a doctor."

Esther places her hand on Sancia's arm and shakes her head with an unmistakable message. *No.* Sancia supports her on one side and David on the other. They help her walk to her bedroom. David assures Sancia that she looked like her mother does now, when he first walked through the door. "She will be okay."

Grudgingly, Sancia respects her mother's wishes to not fetch a doctor. "I am not going to leave you. I will spend the night in here with you." *And that way I will also be closer to Ruben.* She says good night to David and then lies next to her mother. She protectively drapes her arm around her. As soon as Esther falls asleep, Sancia does too.

Sancia wakes before the sun rises. Her sleep is always interrupted. She reaches for her mother. *Something is wrong.* She puts her hand on her mother's shoulder and gently rocks her. "Mother." Esther does not respond. Again, "Mother." Harder, "Mother." Louder, "Mother." *No, Mama. What am I going to do without you?* Sancia weeps in the moonlight as she caresses her mother's hair — golden brown and blended with salt-and-pepper gray. She looks at her face, her skin only slightly wrinkled, a sign of how much living she had left to do. *I cannot withstand this world without you.* Brokenhearted, she continues to weep. Her tears are of sadness and of envy. Sancia whispers tenderly in her mother's ear how she loves her and how she hopes the world to come is a much more welcoming place for them all.

Sancia catches a glimpse of her mother walking into the kitchen. *No, that is not her! She was buried hours ago.* She touches the flap of clothing she tore in grief. She lifts and presses it, as if holding it will make it mend, and as if mending it would bring her mother back. She moves her hand and lets the flap fall back down, to its new natural state. She recalls her uncle ripping his shirt and Ruben trying to patch it with his fingers. She recalls Seville. She recalls Litiosa and Baltasar. She then cries to David, "I never got to tell her!"

David moves to the seat near Sancia and leans closer. "Of course you told her. She always knew how much you loved her. I have heard you say it to her many times."

He is right. That she knows. "I still love her - so much. But I did not tell her . . ." She leans back and then looks into her husband's eyes. "I did not tell you, either." *How could I not have told you?* "I have been so distracted and did not find the right time —" She then fetches the candlestick holders. "David, Baltasar did not keep the jewelry. He melted it all and returned it to us." She fumbles with each holder as she shows David the hidden gold and emerald.

She watches David as he experiences the same amazement she had upon the discovery. He takes the gold from her hand and then holds it to the window. His eyes widen and then they connect with hers.

She holds his gaze. She then leaves the room and returns with the note. She gives it to David. "Baltasar gave this to me before we left Spain, but I forgot all about it, until I remembered. I kept the discovery to myself. Maybe this would have made her heart stronger."

"Maybe, but not strong enough to handle the theft of her grandson. Nothing could have made her heart strong enough for that." David puts the gold and the note on the table and takes Sancia's hands. "She has completed her life as a Jew, in deference to G-d and to herself. No one was able to take that away from her. We are mourning her as Jews."

"But . . . there is no way we can *stay* Jews." Sancia's statement is a question. She hopes David has a better solution.

His expression says he doesn't. "Not if we want to get our son back."

"All we did was buy time. Had we converted in Seville, we would all still be together with my uncle, aunt, and cousins. Ruben. My mother. Your mother and father. If we were going to lose to the Church, we could have given up before they took so much from us." She then cries into David's shoulder. "They have taken so much from us."

"They would have continued to take from us there, in Seville, even if we converted. The Inquisition is relentless. At least here, the king will grant us twenty years to get it right. He does not really want us to leave. He is just trying to satisfy the hateful demands of his bride and have more control over us."

She takes a step back and wipes her eyes. "This is disgusting. Humans wanting to control other humans. Abusing HaShem to validate cruelty. I hate being controlled by others." *But they have my boy!*

"At least there is no Inquisition here. In Spain we would not have been together for long. We could never have been 'good enough' Catholics. One by one, we would have been thrown into the dungeons and tortured before being burned at the stake. In five years, when Ruben becomes fourteen years old, they would have gotten him too."

Sancia aches for her father and cousin. "You are right." *At least in this hell, we will get our boy back.*

An Unjust Trade: One's
Faith for One's Child

─ ✦◈◈◈✦ ─

─ 1497 ─

Nine days after the theft of her son and eight days after the death of her mother, Sancia, along with David, converts. As the pair sit, trying to absorb the enormity of being forced to embrace a way of life they can't respect, Carima walks up to them. "We are going to move."

"Move?" The thought is too upsetting for Sancia to say more.

Abraham says, "Not move from the kingdom. But from this home. Carima and I want you to have it. We are going to live with Joya and her family. Our daughter has been asking us for some time to come live with them and to help her with the children."

Sancia can't imagine how much she will miss them. Visiting them will not be the same as coming home to them.

Sancia watches David remove the mezuzah from the door-post. *It's a good thing Carima and Abraham are no longer living here. They should not have had to see this.* David tries to etch a horizontal line in the stone post at the top of the vertical space left behind by the mezuzah. Sancia frowns. *A cross.* She tries to convince herself that it means noth-ing. *But will it mean something to Ruben one day? Or to his children? Will there be a day in which people become unaware they were once Jews? Will descendants of Jews learn to hate the people they are from? Will there even be any Jews left to hate?*

She knows David to carve wood with ease, yet he is struggling. *Is it the stone or the chore?* The chisel slips and cuts his hand.

He holds his wound. "I cannot do this."

Sancia takes the chisel from his hand. She bangs and scratches at the stone. The horrible sensation pene-trates her bones. She hates the feeling and the sound. She completes the task. She steps back to see the cross that has taken the place of the mezuzah. *Done.* She hates her accomplishment.

But the friar is pleased. He touches the cross on the doorframe post. "Nice work."

Sancia cannot thank him for what he thinks is a com-pliment. After he inspects their home, she follows him to the door.

He hands documents to her. "Congratulations! You are officially Christian. Well, you were at the church, but now I see that you have brought Christ to your home."

A knot tightens in Sancia's stomach as she holds out her hand to take the papers. Then the friar leaves. She closes the door behind him. *You and your church will never have permission to control my mind!* The knot in her stomach loosens. She turns to David. "Let us go get our son!"

"Just give me one moment to get the map."

Sancia steps outside and David follows right behind her to begin their journey. They walk along streets and around corners. They spin the map and turn themselves.

Finally! Sancia points to a home. She walks up to the door and sees the plaque next to it. *Bartolomeo Colombo.* "This is it! Ruben is here!"

David agrees. "Are you ready?"

Sancia answers his question by knocking.

A woman opens the door.

"Señora Enríquez?" David asks.

With a gentle nod, the woman standing in front of them, wearing an elegant soft-pink, ruffle-trimmed dress, invites them inside. Her dark, curly hair is tied by a ribbon of the same color as her dress. "Please call me Beatriz. You must be Sancia and David."

"Thank you." David shows Beatriz the papers.

She waves the documents away, as if they are unimportant. "Later."

Once the couple enters the foyer, she closes the door behind them. Sancia notices there is no cross on her doorpost. The unsightly tradition must just be reserved for the once-Jews who needed to destroy any semblance of the mezuzah. Sancia has never before been inside a home that has more than one level.

Beatriz cups her hands to her mouth and calls up the stairs. "Ruben, Fernando . . ."

Sancia's breath stops the moment she sees her son appear at the top of the stairs. He is in her arms before she sets foot on the first step. She fears she might never let him go. She loosens her grip only to allow David into the embrace. The three of them hold each other.

Ruben is the first to step back. "They told me about Grandmother."

Beatriz moves behind Ruben and places her hands on his shoulders. "When I learned what had happened, I thought it only fair that he know too. He was inconsolable. Fernando had to help me keep guard at the door to prevent him from running home to you."

Sancia tries to hold back her own tears as she looks into her son's watery eyes. "You gave her the strength to remain forever a Jew. You were her life and strength." She pulls him close. *You are my strength too.*

Beatriz gently states her question. "So, you have been baptized."

"We have been." David shows her the documents, again.

Ruben then says, "I have not been baptized. Señora did not insist."

Sancia is so grateful that he will not be forced to lose sight of who he is and who he is descended from. But she knows the façade will be a challenge to maintain.

Beatriz reminds Ruben to keep that secret.

"I will." He then turns to his mother and father. "Señora Enríquez and Fernando said they will teach you how to behave like a Catholic. They will show you the rituals and anything else you need to know."

I want to know as little as possible. Just enough so we can remain together, unbothered. "That is very kind of you, Beatriz. I am afraid we have a lot to learn. So, we will need your lessons and we kindly accept your time, though you have already done so much for us."

Beatriz smiles. "It has really been my pleasure. I am often alone with just Fernando, so we have greatly enjoyed Ruben's company. You have raised a wonderful boy."

David returns the compliment to Beatriz as he looks at her son. "As you have."

Ruben's voice becomes animated. "This whole family is wonderful. Fernando's father is at sea. Fernando may be able to go on one of his journeys soon. I want to go with him!"

A journey on the sea? This is not a dream Sancia wants for her son.

Ruben reaches to a windowsill behind them and grabs a small wood carving of a ship. Sancia recognizes the work of her son's inexperienced hand. "Did you make this?"

Ruben nods.

David takes hold of the little wooden ship and turns it while examining all of its parts. "Well, now that I have seen your talent, I will be expecting much more from you."

"It is beautiful, my son." *You are beautiful. They cannot destroy us all.*

— 1502 —

Sancia enjoys the shade offered between buildings on a particularly hot April afternoon, as she sits on a step outside her door and glances at the homes descending the hill. Her eyes meet each of the crosses where there once were mezuzahs. She cannot believe that four years have passed since her own door had a mezuzah. She wonders, knowing what she knows now, if she had it easier than the others on this hill. She imagines what that day in October of 1497, after her Ruben was stolen, was like for them. King Manuel, *the bastard*, told those who avoided baptism that he commissioned ships to help them safely get to other lands. *The liar.* It was the theft of Ruben that prevented her from being among that crowd who gathered to accept the king's offer. She would not leave the kingdom without her son. But her neighbors, who chose to leave, went to the Estaus Palace to board the ships that King Manuel promised. There were no ships. Instead, he locked the gates and deprived them of food and water. He forced conversion on them upon pain of death. Sancia's heart aches for the many who chose death and who even took their own lives. *Iuceph was right. It was all just a matter of time.*

She nods a hello as she scoots aside to allow a neighbor to pass. *Everyone is a Jew, and yet no one is a Jew.* Ruben begins ascending the stairs. He is fourteen years of age, the same as Iuceph was when Sancia saw him last, outside of Church custody. *I lost Iuceph when he was this age.* His return home signals she is behind in preparing dinner. She stands up to greet him. "Hello, my love. I hope you are not too hungry. I will set aside some carrots for you to eat now, before I cook the rest in the stew."

"I can help. But, Mother, I need to talk to you about something."

She opens the door. "Anything. Let us go inside and start. Your father will be home soon."

"Is he still working on the same ship?"

"I think so."

"That is what I want to talk to you about."

"Your father's ship?"

"No. Fernando's father's ship. I have met him - Admiral Cristoforo Colombo." Ruben puts his hand in his pocket and pulls out a round wooden object. "He gave me this."

Sancia looks closely. *Letters, numbers and arrows. A compass.* She has seen one before.

Ruben puts the compass back in his pocket. "He is a wonderful man. He gave that compass to me. He knows so much about the world and the sea. Fernando loves him dearly. He said that Fernando is old enough to help him on his fourth voyage."

"He has been on *three* others?" Sancia doesn't like where this conversation is going.

"Yes. His first was in 1492. He told me he had to delay his journey because the port of Palos, in Spain, was overcrowded with Jews forced to leave the kingdom."

Could Fernando's father be the sailor that Uncle Abraham mentioned, the one funded by Jews in the hopes he might find land?

Ruben continues. "He is very experienced on the sea. And land. He said that one day we might be able to make homes on the lands he discovers. He invited me to join him, as a cabin boy, with Fernando."

How can he even consider this? "Absolutely not!"

"Mother. Other cabin boys are *conversos,* they were once Jewish. *Conversos* make up much of the Admiral's crew. I can learn from them - doctors, translators, and an astronomer."

She purses her lips and focuses on cutting vegetables. She won't give him any opportunity to win this argument. No, no, and still no.

"I became a bar mitzvah last year! And it is because I was with Fernando, and his mother, that I am an adult who is still a Jew. Think about all of the children who were taken from their mothers and fathers that same year."

Sancia puts the knife down and turns to her son. "Do not tell me to think of those children! I think of *all* those children every day. Every day! I have collected the sadness of every person unjustly harmed." She fights to hold back tears. "It has accumulated in my heart and in my soul. It remains there only in competition with the blessings I count every moment." She touches her son's face. "I am not about to let my most precious blessing get lost to the sea."

"I will not, Mother. But, if I do not go, the opposite might happen, and I'll be lost here. The only chance we have of keeping our traditions, beliefs and freedom, is to look to how we might be able to live elsewhere - a land not conquered and controlled by Christians or Muhammadans."

Sancia looks past Ruben to see David open the door.

She hurriedly intercepts him to voice her objections before Ruben has a chance to speak. As soon as she pauses, he jumps in to plead with his father.

David closes the door, steps inside, and puts his satchel on the floor. He walks to the basin to rinse his hands. "Your mother and I will talk about this with Señora Enríquez. Whatever we decide, we know that you are mature and ready. But we might not be."

"But Father. I want to go! Nothing you will say will change my mind!"

"Enough about this — until after we talk to Fernando's mother."

And nothing she will say will change my mind!

With David by her side, Sancia knocks on Beatriz's door.

Her friend of four years opens it. She does not seem surprised to see them. "I know what this is about."

I cannot believe she kept this from me. Sancia folds her arms across her chest and frowns from outside the threshold. "How long have you known?"

Beatriz takes a deep breath. "I did not want to accept it myself. When Fernando was age four and we lived in Seville, Cristoforo gave him a compass and taught him how to use it. He then left for his journey. Fernando was heartbroken. I do not want my son to leave."

She is also heartbroken. Sancia takes her hand.

Beatriz motions for them to come inside. Sancia and David follow her through the house to the garden. They sit around a small table. Beatriz walks back into the house and returns with a pitcher of freshly brewed tamarind water. She pours. "I have known for some time that this would be a battle I would lose. After his second voyage, Cristoforo played a game with Fernando. He hid a treasure on a street some blocks away, from our home in Seville, and he told Fernando to use the compass and his directions to find it. If he did, Cristoforo would allow him to keep the treasure and would consider having him on the voyage after he returns."

Sancia picks up the cup. "He just returned from his third voyage." She takes a sip. "But are you not too afraid to let him go?"

"I am," Beatriz says. "However, I am more afraid for his loneliness and his comfort than I am worried about his safety. He will be in the company of skilled sailors. But, I want him to have a friend on the ship. Ruben is his closest friend."

How can she say no to this woman? She owes her practically everything. *But not my son.* She brings up the threat of pirates. Storms. Starvation.

Beatriz addresses each concern. She has clearly struggled with the same arguments. "The boys want this adventure. Everyone on this crew is skilled. They are good men. I have met many of them before they began other voyages. We have seen too many injustices by the kings on this peninsula. It is best that the boys see what else is out there. There are many places in this world that we do not know about." Beatriz pours more of the flavored water into her glass. "They will leave next month. Well, the ship will leave from Spain in May. They will leave Lisbon next week to journey to Spain."

Next week is so soon!

David looks at Sancia. "I am not saying yes, but I am asking—" He then looks at Beatriz. "When do you think they will return?"

"I think this voyage will last maybe a little over a year."

Sancia is alarmed. "That is a really long time!"

"I know it is. Please say yes."

David assures her they'll think about it.

He and Sancia continue the discussion as they walk toward home. David supports the idea. "Ruben will be helping the family who helped us, and he will see other lands with his own eyes." He says his concerns, but has confidence that in a year from then, when Ruben returns, they will be glad they let him go.

So, that just leaves Sancia to decide. She sees her joy, her Ruben, walking to meet them. He is eager to know how the conversation with Fernando's mother went, but Sancia is hesitant to discuss it. How is it that the people she loves the most are the most capable of destroying her? She reaches for her son. She pulls him close and holds him tightly, knowing she will only have a few more moments like this before he returns, in over a year from now.

New Land
and Native People

━━━◆◆◆━━━

— 1503 —

Fernando sleeps. Ruben cannot. Or maybe he's the one who's sleeping and this is all a bad dream. Ruben looks at other crew members – unmoving figures in the moonlight. He hears the water lap against the shore. The sound cools his body from the humidity of early summer. He isn't ready to tolerate the sun again. Maybe he won't have to. Maybe he will wake up in his comfortable home in the Alfama district of Lisbon, where he'll walk the cobblestone streets to the plush mansion of his friend, Fernando, who is somehow sleeping next to him. He touches his friend's face and then feels the disorganized stubble on his own young adult chin. *This has to be a dream*, because, if it's not, then he's been away from home for over eight months. *All those storms, all those islands, all the broken ship parts scattered.*

Damaged wood as shelter. *Some shelter.* Through the darkness, he looks to the horizon — toward the water he can hear more than he can see. He recalls the queasy feeling he had during the storms, when the sea was not as peaceful as it seems to be now. He acknowledges his intertwining aches of hunger, thirst, and exhaustion. He admits to himself what he knew moments ago. *I am awake. I am stranded on an island. This nightmare is real.*

He lets Fernando sleep and walks over to one of the crew members, four times his age, who has been stirring, as if he too is awake. Ruben has noticed that Lope declined any opportunity of beard trimming since setting out from Spain. He is a man with a small build, draped in clothing that was already too large before he had to endure so little to eat. Ruben is certain Lope has previously accompanied the admiral to this very place. He sits next to the elder crew member. "Everyone was so quick to rest after making the shelter. We did not see if there are people on this land. You have been here before, though, have you not?"

Lope's voice is as withered as his body. "Yes. And I plan not to return once we are able to make our way back home."

"Do you think that we will?" Ruben asks.

"The admiral is a clever man. We will make it back home — I just hope to live that long." Lope laughs at his joke. Ruben doesn't find it funny. Lope catches his breath. "Do not be so serious, boy. Sailor humor. Days are long and nights — even longer. We need to find high spirits whenever we can. To answer your first question, yes, I know there are people here. I have met them. The island once had many."

"You say that as if now there are not so many?"

"There are not. The Arawaks. Likeable people. Many died after we first arrived here almost a decade ago. Well, we killed them."

"If they were likeable, why would you have killed them?" Ruben struggles to see Lope's expression in the moonlight.

"We did not attack them," Lope says. "They were very peaceful. And not all died. Some were taken. The admiral forced some to go to Spain with the crew that headed back. Those who survived the voyage became slaves. Those we did not send on ships, we forced to collect gold for us. We worked them too hard. We did not attack them. We overworked them."

Ruben hears the regret in his voice. *Why did he do this if he did not want to?*

Lope scoops up a handful of sand and allows it to cascade through his fingers. "If they were able to find enough gold — the Arawak men we sent to look for it — they were awarded with a copper ornament to place around their neck. The ornament signaled to our men that they successfully served us and should be left unmolested. However, if an Arawak was spotted without the copper around his neck, that meant that he did not serve us well. We were ordered to slice off his hands." He shakes his head mournfully while continuing his interaction with the sand. "So many bled to death."

So, they did kill some native people. "Fernando's father, ordered that?" Ruben listens in disgust and wonders if this is true. *But why would he lie about something that implicates him?* He wonders if he should tell Fernando. Then again, the story might be false. His friend's father, as far as he knows, is an admirable man.

Lope's voice trails off. "He charged us to do other horrible things." He pauses. "The Arawaks — they referred to this island as Xaymaca. They were very kind to us when we first got here. They had villages right by the water. You might not have noticed signs of ruins from when we first wrecked, but if you look around when the sun comes up, you will see them. Now, I imagine, those who have survived find more safety further inland, away from anchoring ships."

Ruben tosses a rock in the ocean. "Away from people like us."

Lope nods. "It was so nice when they had homes here. They had these cooking things. Pepperpots. They continually tended to pepperpot meals, with small fires burning throughout the day, making a soup with the spices and vegetables they would collect. Clever people. When they ate from them, they would immediately replenish the pot with fresh ingredients for a future meal. The smell was inviting." Lope inhales deeply, as if the air is scented with food.

Ruben's hunger intensifies. "Why did you all turn against them?"

Lope lifts his shoulders and tilts his head. "Well, riches, I suppose. The admiral wanted to please His Majesty. I cannot imagine how much he would have gotten. More than half of the captured Arawaks died on the ships on the way to the kingdom. I suspect they all would have been quite profitable had they survived. We had the native women work in the fields for us." Lope's tone becomes a blend of regret and indifference. "It was just the way it was."

But it is not the way it should have been. Lope and the admiral are no better than the monsters of the Inquisition. Lope is too pained and too detailed to be lying. Ruben believes him. He expects to see the ruins at sunrise. Until then, he knows he won't sleep. He wonders if the admiral—the man whom he has looked up to after keeping him safe during such an arduous journey, the man his Uncle Abraham suspected of trying to keep Jews safe—is any different than Torquemada. Right now, it seems the only difference is that the admiral's victims were not Jews and not given the option of converting or leaving before they were exploited, tortured, and killed.

"Hey, dreamer." Lope taps Ruben's shoulder. "I am hungry. The sun is coming up. Get ready to get some fish."

Ruben notices Fernando stirring as the morning brightens. The arduous journey has brought them to several shores where they honed their catching skills. Since none of their boats can float, they will have to make do with just the nets they have. Ruben tosses one end to Fernando and then offers his hand to help him stand. The tide is low, the walk is long. The water is a refreshing. Ruben stays focused on the task of collecting fish though he is weighed down by what he has just learned about Fernando's father. Does Fernando know the cruelty his father is capable of? Ruben shakes off the question. *No. He would be horrified if he knew how his father abused people.* It's something he hasn't witnessed on this trip.

— 1504 —

Ruben knows the admiral sent word that they've been marooned to Nicolás de Ovando, the governor of Santo Domingo in Hispaniola. He also knows there's tension between the two men. He is concerned the governor will ignore the admiral's request for help to get off the island and that they'll remain stuck there forever.

"Do you think Nicolás de Ovando will help get us off this island?" Ruben asks his friend while they eat their midday meal by the water.

Fernando raises his shoulders but says that he believes so.

Ruben is confused by Fernando's optimism. "But, when we were at his mercy, he forced us to anchor in an estuary during a storm. He would not let us remain on his island. Why would he bother to get word that we are stranded here?"

Lope comes out of nowhere. He has been listening. "I have heard how wretchedly Ovando has treated the Natives of Hispaniola. He has unmatched cruelty."

Fernando offers a piece of fish to Lope. "I have heard that too."

Worse than his father? Ruben wonders. *Does he know about his father?*

Lope, seeming to consider the same thing, gives Ruben a glance. "Worse than . . ."

"Worse than whom?" Fernando asks.

"Never mind." Lope turns to leave. "Thank you for the fish."

Fernando shouts toward his back. "If you insist on interrupting the conversations of others, at least complete your sentence before walking away."

Lope waves — his back still toward them.

Fernando returns to the topic of rescue. "Ovando has not been good to us. However, he wants to be valued by the royals. He would not want to risk their knowledge of his treachery if he neglects seeking help for us. He might relish that we are withering away here, but he will send for help. Father assured me."

Ruben picks up a shell and tosses it into the sea. "We have been here for a year and have not heard anything."

"That does not mean that Father has not heard anything. I do not think he tells me everything."

Ruben certainly hopes not.

Winter has been difficult, and Ruben often goes hungry. His intense craving for something sweet prompts him to get Fernando's company to the inner island to search for blim blims.

They don't find much. But, they do encounter a familiar Native who hands them a small basket full of apples. Ruben nods a thank-you. He and Fernando then return to the area where they've set up makeshift homes. Basket in hand, Ruben surveys the hungry men, withering away, awaiting ships that may never come to rescue them. *We will not be able to sustain this winter much longer.*

The admiral's once impressive clothing has been reduced

to rags. He has visibly aged as the seasons have passed — his hair a whitish gray and his eyes — blueish gray. He approaches Ruben and Fernando and glances in the basket. "This is simply not enough. Come to my quarters in three nights, the last night of this month of February." He then turns and walks away.

"Do you know what that is about?" Ruben asks Fernando.

Fernando shakes his head. "But I will find out."

On the way to his father's quarters, Fernando explains to Ruben the purpose of the invitation. "My father has an almanac, a book that describes everything there is to know about days and nights, about the Earth, the sun, the moon, and the stars. It is very precise. It has helped him navigate our direction. He told me he is going to use it to help us to get food. He knew exactly what to do when he saw that there would be a total eclipse of the moon on the last day of the month of February of 1504. Tonight." He points to the sky and explains to Ruben about the celestial activity that will cause the eclipse. "The Arawaks do not know to expect such an event, but they will."

The admiral invites his guests inside. Though his walls are constructed from the best wood salvaged from the battered ships, even they do not seem long for this world. Fernando, Ruben, Chief Huero and members from his tribe, listen while sitting in a circle on the floor. The admiral speaks with the same strong voice he uses to command his crew. "My God is angry with your people. You slowed in helping us some time ago. My men are starving. Tonight, when you see the moon, notice how my God will take it away as a display of his anger toward you for letting my men go hungry. That will be a warning."

Once the admiral finishes his announcement, everyone in attendance steps outside. Ruben welcomes the cool winter air. The quarters were warming up too much from the gathering of men. He looks up at the sky and is awestruck when he sees the moon becoming increasingly tinged with red as it is being swallowed by the darkness.

Chief Huero is clearly convinced that the admiral's God is swallowing it. He instructs his tribe to provide the crew with whatever they need. The admiral tells the harried Natives that if they respond swiftly, their moon will return.

The chief and his tribe depart into the darkness of the inner island. They each return with a basket full of the past season's preserved harvest. After which, as the admiral assured, the moon indeed returns to the sky. Ruben understands that now, the entire crew, including himself, will be able to count on the cooperation of the frightened Natives.

Ruben doesn't like a lot about the admiral, the cruelty he has been told about, and the dishonesty he has witnessed. However, if it were not for the admiral's cleverness and willingness to deceive, Ruben and the crew would have likely starved to death. He struggles in coming to terms with the reality of benefiting from someone else's bad deeds.

Three months after the life-saving eclipse and two years after he left home, Ruben sees a vision on the horizon. *Spanish ships!* He surprises himself when he decides not to board either ship back to Spain. His revulsion toward Fernando's father is one reason. He resents having to feel gratitude to a man who does things he despises. He simply can't envisage himself on the sea for months, sharing a journey with a man who might have the same capacity for cruelty as his staunchest enemies. And he cannot imagine returning to a land where a king dictates how he should think.

So, Ruben stays behind with a few other men. He asks Fernando to look after his mother and father. "Please let them know I will see them one day. Encourage them to come here." *A safe haven from the persecution that continually haunts them.* If he had an instrument with which to write, he would explain to his mother and father how he prefers the nature of the Natives over that of the people back home. But he isn't inclined to share these thoughts with his closest friend. He simply hopes Fernando makes it back safely and shares his message.

— 1509 —

Ruben is twenty years old when he contends with his first hallucination. He spies a Spanish ship anchoring on the shores of Xaymaca. If he has kept track with accuracy, this year is 1509 by way of the Spanish King. He has been away from his family for seven years. He misses them. He misses his home. *This is my home.* He realizes that his yearning is intense and possibly the cause of his hallucination. After all, he has regularly seen people anchor here. Most, for just a brief stop on route to other destinations. He has seen pirates with criminal behavior and peasants who are genteel, but never before has he seen . . . a ghost.

He rubs his eyes. He steps closer to get a better look at the crowd of exhausted and disoriented people disembarking. They all have a ghostly appearance, worn and emaciated. But what shakes him to the core is the image of his late grandmother—the unmistakable ghost of Esther. He misses her and thinks of her often. Could that actually contribute to his hallucination? He just drank all the coconut water in a single coconut, so he is not suffering from dehydration. Did he eat something that has made him ill? *Can anyone else see her, or am I the only one?*

The eyes of the ghost of his grandmother meet his, and holds his gaze. She edges toward him. She then reaches to touch the hair under his chin. First with one hand and then with both.

Ruben is overwhelmed by this otherworldly experience. But it is not otherworldly. *Are you really here? "*Mother?"

Sancia pulls her son close and holds him tightly. He feels the tears on her cheek — or are they his own tears?

"My boy!" She confirms his hope.

They hold one another in silence. Then Ruben takes his mother's hands, steps back, and looks into her eyes. "I did not know if I would ever see you again. I did not know if I did right by staying. I was hoping you and Papa would come sooner. But you are here now, and that is all that matters." He is suddenly flooded by memories of his childhood. How his mother and father talked to him with kindness and wisdom. He still has the deer his father carved for him before they left Spain. *Father.* "Father." His arms ache to touch his father. He looks to the men now disembarking. He knows he might not recognize him. He loosens his grip from his mother and turns back to her. "I will be quick." He assures her, as he goes to hug and to help his father.

Sancia clings to him – unwilling to let him walk away.

He offers her a tender smile. "It is okay, Mother. I'll be right back."

Sancia won't let go.

"How about you come with me?"

Her feet stay planted. She doesn't say a word, but her lips quiver and her eyes water.

Father is not here! Worse — he knows his father is gone. Ruben buckles in pain. Sancia wraps her arms around her aching son, and holds him, as they both cry. Although Ruben had previously imagined that he might never see his father again, he was not prepared to face the knowledge of his death. He needs to hear everything, but little by little. His mother has been through so much. He can't ask her to explain it all now.

Instead, he leads her to his home, a simple structure, and he opens a coconut for her to drink and to eat. She then sleeps in the middle of the day, but just for a brief time. After she wakes, Ruben suggests they walk back to the shore. Before the sun begins to set, they find a log wedged in the sand and they sit on it. Ruben finds solace in the lapping of the waves. He hopes it brings solace to her too.

Sancia speaks a full sentence — her first since arriving. "You are the only reason I am grateful to have survived." She looks at Ruben with so much love. "And what a reason you are."

He tenderly squeezes her hand. "Please tell me what happened." He doesn't want to make his mother relive the pain, and yet he needs to know.

"He died a hero. Your father died a hero." Sancia pauses. She releases some tears. Ruben waits for her to regain her composure. "Vives, our neighbor. Do you remember him?"

Ruben shakes his head apologetically.

"That is okay. You were just a boy. I still cannot believe I let you go on that voyage. But had I not, you might not be alive, either. Vives, our neighbor, managed to survive the riots that day. Beaten and bruised, he told me what he saw. Some men were attacking a fragile, elderly man and his son. The man could not protect his father, or himself. Your father ran toward them and peeled the crazed attackers off. He managed to push some away and even injured some severely. But it was not long before more attackers came to the assistance of the defeated perpetrators. Your father used his strength, that fantastic strength that allowed him to fell great trees. But he became too outnumbered."

"Were you home when this happened?"

"No, but it would not have mattered. Home was not safe. The rioters were uncontrollable. They went into our homes and attacked all the Jews they could get their hands on . . ." She corrects herself. "All the New Christians they could get their hands on. Even babies." She stops, seeming to consider whether or not she should reveal more. "The babies." She begins to hyperventilate. She cries. "They grabbed a baby from her mother's arms and swung her with force against a wall. Crazed men cracked babies' bodies in front of their mothers." She cries more. "I am sorry. I am so sorry."

"It is okay." *No, it is not okay.* Ruben tenderly holds his mother as she catches her breath.

"My friend's grandson. A baby. A man grabbed the baby by his arm. Another man pushed my friend and took her grandbaby by his other arm." Sancia stares at the water that is too dark to see. Her eyes widen in terror. "They pulled his arms off and forced my friend to see."

Ruben cannot even imagine the horror. He pulls his mother close. "This all happened the day Father was killed?"

Sancia nods. "I was with Beatriz in her home. That visit saved me. I had no idea of the riot until it was too late."

"How did the riot start?"

Sancia wipes her eyes. "How do people go mad? First hate gets planted and then gets nourished. The mind becomes a fertile garden, unaware of the toxicity growing within. The seed of that riot was planted long before that Easter Sunday three years ago. But it was that day when people crowded into a church looking for hope. Lisbon was suffering from a plague. Many people were getting sick and dying. They looked for hope in their statue of Jesus. When they saw an unusual light coming from its face, the Catholics interpreted it as a sign, Divine proof they were in Jesus's direct care and would be spared from more pain. The glow was likely the reflection from a candle. A visitor suggested such. No one wanted to accept that the glowing face had nothing to do with a Messiah. The visitor was accused of being a *marrano*. The people in the church killed him. And then a friar promised Divine forgiveness for anyone who would kill any New Christian."

What kind of spiritual man blesses people to kill innocent people? Ruben knows the answer. He is overwhelmed with guilt. *If I were in Portugal, I could have saved Father.*

Sancia continues, "I moved back to Spain. I could not bear another moment in Lisbon. I saw my uncle, aunt, and cousins. Do you remember them?"

Could I remember? I was maybe four years of age when we were torn from them. How do I tell Mother that I do not remember my family?

She doesn't wait for an answer. "I just wanted to find you. I did not know I would have the strength to make this journey. But I knew I would not have the strength to be in any kingdom, any longer, without you."

"I am so happy to have you here with me. There will be no kings ruling this island."

"I know, Ruben. You are right. I am not sure if you know how right you are. But first I must tell you some more unfortunate news."

Ruben knows nothing could be worse than what he has already heard.

"Fernando's father died."

"The admiral? Cristoforo Colombo?"

Sancia nods. "He died in May — their year was 1506 — a month after the Lisbon Massacre. But his death had nothing to do with that. He simply became very ill."

"I noticed that his health was failing before he left this island. How are Beatriz and Fernando?"

"The loss has been difficult for them, but they are doing well. Fernando's older brother, Diego, has been fighting for his father's title of this land. He currently has authority over this region. He will not allow people to riot against us. He will not allow any Inquisition to come here. And as you said — there will be no king."

"That is great! At least we know where their heart and intentions are, even if their capabilities might fall otherwise." Ruben extends his hand to assist his mother off the log. As they walk, he warns her about some challenges they might face living on the island. He also tells her that the Natives have been nice to him despite the disasters the Spanish put upon them. He does not want to reveal everything. They both have their horrors to live and to relive. *It is best to retain some knowledge in solitude.*

After she has had some time to recover from her journey, Ruben brings his mother to the Arawaks' garden, which, with their permission, he has been helping to maintain in exchange for some of the harvest. "This has been a practical arrangement since I built my home too close to the sea for vegetables to thrive."

Sancia tells Ruben she is eager to help. On her first day, she pauses and inhales deeply. "What is that delicious smell?"

Ruben explains how the Arawaks keep stew in an ongoing pot. "They continually add fresh ingredients to their pepperpots as they take from it to eat." He enjoys bonding with them and knows his mother does too. But the sorrow and helplessness he feels when they fall ill upon the arrival of more newcomers is overwhelming. *Why are so many dying?* He sees that his mother becomes distraught, too. They can do little to stop the spread of the illness killing them. They give coconut water to their sick friends, and they press cool cloths to their feverish heads. Too many of the more recent arrivals seem to only care when the Arawaks fall ill if they happen to be a servant or slave. Loss of such life is merely a financial inconvenience.

JAMAICA

— 1517 —

At twenty-eight years old, Ruben has long ago adjusted to the island's rhythm. He wasn't prepared for the day that rhythm would be disrupted by new and unusual arrivals. He watches, from the sand, as muscular, yet emaciated, dark men—darker than the Arawaks—are led off a vessel into smaller boats that bring them to the land. They are shackled and they struggle to walk. Single file, long faces, weakened spirits. The Spanish men bark orders at them. Behind another small boat, at the edge of the shoreline, stands two people who must have come off the ship before the others.

As Ruben walks toward them, he passes by dark complected victims. He stops and stares.

A hearty Spaniard steps in front of him. "Move back! If you want to buy one, go to the market."

Ruben dismisses the vulgar suggestion and gets closer to the two people standing outside the small boat — an older man, richly clothed, and a beautiful young woman with fair skin, wearing an elegant light blue dress. They are arguing in Spanish. Neither looks emaciated.

He turns when he hears one of the shackled, dark men fall.

A well-nourished Spaniard strikes him with a whip. "Get up!"

How can he stand when you keep slamming him down? Ruben is stunned — lost in the vortex of this new insanity. He returns his focus to the arguing pair.

The young woman leans toward the man, clenched fists by her side, slightly behind her, like a counterweight. "You said you would let them walk freely! You said they were too weak to run, and yet you still bind them and torture them!"

"They are not your business! They are beasts, and you should pay no mind to them."

Pay no mind to the suffering of men?

"*You* are a beast!" She quips.

The man raises his arm and brings his fist down hard upon her face, knocking her to the ground.

Ruben runs to block the man from further harming the young woman.

The man shows no regret about his actions, or concern for the young woman. He looks into Ruben's eyes. "Get lost, savage!" He then raises his hand against Ruben.

"Savage?" Ruben is incensed. "Put your fist down."

"You will not interfere with me as I tame my daughter to be proper."

"You are taming her? I see that you make no distinction between human and beast, whether they are stolen men, or your own daughter. How can you be sure which you are?"

The man looks as if he is planning to strike Ruben, who has the strength to stop him with as little effort as he would need to move a light branch out of the way. He is built like his father—tall, muscular, and lean. Ruben stares into his eyes. The man puts his hand down. *That is right. You are no match for me.* "Go away. Walk back to the gutless men you control—and I am not referring to the captured men whom you restrain with whips and chains."

The man looks down on his daughter. "Get up!"

Ruben kneels by her side. *What will happen to her if she goes with him? What will happen to her if she does not?*

"I said get up and come with me!"

The young woman doesn't move from the position she fell into. "No!"

"What did you say!" her father asks — not as a question but as a threat.

Ruben hopes he is not about to deepen her troubles. He stands and says, "She said no!"

The young woman remains on the ground, unable or unwilling to stand. She looks up at her father and boldly addresses him. "You are a liar and a beast! I prefer dying of thirst here, over spending another minute with you."

The man snickers. "Do you think I care? You have a hero. You better hope he takes care of you." Then he raises his voice and snarls. "Because I will make sure that no one else does."

Ruben realizes that he will take care of her. *Mother and I will.*

The man turns, as if expecting to be followed.

Ruben sits by the young woman as they watch him walk away, alone. "Are you okay?"

She rubs her head as if to test how tender her bruise is, and then she nods. "Thank you. I will be. It usually just stings for a little while. That is all."

Usually? "He has struck you before?" *What kind of man strikes a woman?*

"Yes." She starts to stand, but before she can straighten her legs, she sits back down.

Ruben notices his mother in the distance and signals her over. He raises his voice as she gets near. "She was hit on the head. She cannot stand."

"I can stand. I just need a moment."

Sancia quickly walks to the shoreline where she lowers the bottom part of her skirt into the ocean. She wrings out the excess water and then walks back to kneel beside the girl. She presses her cold skirt to her head. "This should stop any swelling, but you must lie down for a few moments."

After resting a little more, the young woman slowly sits up. Ruben and Sancia support her on either side to help her to stand.

She looks at Ruben. "Thank you." Her beautiful dark-brown eyes are the same shade of brown as her long, wavy hair. She then turns to thank his mother. Grains of sand fall from her hair, reflecting the sparkle of the sun. She glimmers. *Is she an angel?* Though she doesn't look undernourished, she does look very thin, though shapely. He thinks he should probably get her something to eat.

The young woman looks at the ocean. The ship is no longer there. "Is he gone?"

Ruben is worried that she may have regrets. "I think so."

She breathes a sigh of relief. "Do you have any idea what it is like to be a prisoner in your own home? Do you have any idea what it is like to want to be free?"

Sancia nods. She introduces herself and her son, though she doesn't explain their history.

"Thank you, both. I am Marina." She then looks at Ruben. "You have met my father."

Ruben nods. "And I must admit that I am not fond of him. Does he treat your mother the same way?" He realizes before her response that he should have asked more sensitively.

"He did. He treated her even worse. He would hit her like he did me. Harder, and more often. He insisted she owed him her life. She died a bruised woman, but an angel."

You are an angel.

Together they walk to Ruben and Sancia's home.

While Ruben collects some food for them, Sancia prepares a bath. She gives Marina a skirt and shirt to wear while she washes her clothes.

Ruben appreciates how much Marina's presence has rejuvenated them. In just a few days, his mother is younger than when she arrived on the island, eight years ago.

Tonight's dinner will be different than the other three that they've already shared together. Sancia steps away to get the only non-clothing items that she brought with her from the Old World. She places the candlestick holders on the table and inserts candles made from the honeycomb of island bees. Ruben watches Marina for a reaction as his mother lights the wicks. And then he joins her in closing his eyes as she recites the prayer to HaShem, who has commanded them to light the candles of the Sabbath. Ruben feels the stare of the Spanish beauty with long dark-brown curls and dark-brown eyes to match. "Amen," he says before opening his eyes. He sees that, sure enough, Marina has been watching him. Ruben can tell that Marina is kind, but he wonders whether she'll tolerate them as Jews. He braces himself for her reaction.

Her expression is unreadable. "You are Jewish."

Suddenly insecure, Ruben whispers, "Yes."

Sancia asks, "Does that bother you?"

Marina shakes her head. "No. I mean, I have never met a Jew before. I have only heard stories from my father and mother. My father detested you. I mean he detested Jews. My mother felt otherwise. Both, her mother and father, were Jewish."

Your mother's mother and father were Jewish, but you never met Jews before? Ruben does not want to interrupt her to ask.

She continues, naturally addressing his curiosity. "My mother loved her mother and father, very much. They left her, and Spain, to keep her safe. When she was about fifteen years of age, she was convinced by some of her Christian friends, including the one she married, to become Christian.

She wanted to please them, but she also wanted the freedom she saw they enjoyed. Then the Inquisition came, and her mother and father watched as their neighbors, friends, and relatives, once-Jews, disappeared, to never be seen again. They became frightened that the Inquisitors would accuse their daughter, my mother, of being a secret Jew if they stayed with her, and that she would disappear, too.

Her heart broke the day they journeyed to Ottoman lands. My father accused them of being cowards who left their daughter, and sinners for not accepting Jesus. He made sure I understood that I am only 'something' because he saved my mother from sin, from the sin of turning from the son of God. He repeatedly reminded my mother and me how grateful we should be for his decision to marry her after her mother and father left her behind. But I know they gave her all they could. She told me that. She also told me about their traditions, their gentle ways, and their struggles. She remembered how at the end of every week there was a holy day, a day of rest — a gift from God. She told me about the prayers over candles. She told me she missed being a Jew." Tears glint in her eyes. "I think this is what she was talking about."

"Your grandmother was Jewish? Your mother's mother was Jewish?" Ruben hears his mother ask.

Marina nods affirmatively.

"My dear girl," Sancia says tentatively, "then you are also Jewish."

Marina shakes her head. "They baptized me as a baby. I am not."

Does Ruben detect disappointment in her voice?

Sancia seems to. "What is baptized? Some man sprinkled some water on you? That does not change your ancestry. It certainly did not change mine. I was baptized so that I may get my son back." Sancia explains a little more about their history in Seville and Lisbon.

Marina looks at the flames of the candles. "But I was also raised with Catholic tradition. And though I have wondered about my grandmother and grandfather, and traditions I shall never know, being Catholic is not bad. Sure, some of us are. My father brought a ship full of stolen men. He did it out of greed. Not religion. Just greed."

Sancia pours stew in a bowl and hands it to Marina. "Some Catholics do good things, and some do bad things. Some Jews do good things, and some do bad things."

Ruben thinks of the suffering his family had to endure under the Christians and wonders why his mother is defending them now. "They killed Grandfather before I was born, they killed Father, and they were responsible for the death of Grandmother."

Sancia's eyes betray an ache seeing her son angry. "Yes, but who took risks to save you and keep you safe for us?"

Ruben knows she is referring to Fernando and Beatriz, but he doesn't want to feel rational about this topic. The people bent on destroying his people aren't rational. And if he and his mother can convince Marina to accept her Jewish ancestry, that would be progress toward recovery for his people, for Marina's people, the ancestors of her mother.

"One of my dearest friends, Baltasar, the man who crafted these," Sancia motions to the candlestick holders, "is Catholic. He tried to convince me, that those who have brought hardship to the Jews, are not practicing his faith. I have my doubts. But no matter, we must make distinctions between good and evil and between coercion and free will. We must always try to see clearly." Then Sancia looks at Marina. "You have Jewish ancestry. Your mother was coerced into Catholicism. You can choose to observe either Judaism or Christianity. There is no need to rush to a decision."

Ruben hopes that Marina chooses Judaism, but fears that if she believes in Jesus, like he believes in HaShem, she might conclude that Judaism is not right for her. Would she leave them? Where would she go?

Ruben does not sleep until the Sabbath flames go out.

Ruben wonders if he's still asleep, dreaming, when he hears Marina say that she wants to be Jewish. He's overwhelmed but also skeptical that she is making a decision she believes is right for her. He thinks it is. But that might not be enough.

"What do I need to do to become Jewish?" Marina asks.

Sancia answers. "You are Jewish already. If you would like, at the end of this week, you could say the prayers and light the candles like your grandmother once did for her family."

Maybe she still does. Ruben dare not ask Marina if she knows of the wellbeing of her grandparents. He wonders if they are alive and if they know that their daughter is not. *Do they know they have a beautiful granddaughter?* Ruben feels overjoyed when Marina accepts his mother's invitation to lead the welcoming of the next Sabbath.

Friday night, Ruben and Sancia gather by Marina's side as she closes her eyes and says the prayer in Hebrew. Ruben senses she feels insecure regarding accuracy, but just right in her sense of belonging.

A refreshing autumn breeze signals the end of the harsh summer when Ruben, Sancia and Marina welcome the Jewish New Year. They light candles and eat sweet fruits dipped in honey. There is no synagogue on the island, yet. Though Ruben suspects there might be, one day, in Santiago in the areas of Santa Gloria and New Seville, where some Jews have been making their homes and practicing their faith.

After the festive dinner of the first evening of the holy days, Ruben and Marina take a walk by the water. He explains to her that Rosh Hashanah is a happy time, an opportunity for Jews to make amends before the Day of Atonement, Yom Kippur, which will approach in ten days' time. He warns that Yom Kippur is a difficult day, but one in which HaShem gives the Jewish people an opportunity to forgive and to be forgiven.

"Will this be difficult for you? There is no rabbi here to whom you can confess your sins." Marina has transitioned so naturally to Judaism that her question takes Ruben by surprise. Her innocence is endearing.

Ruben answers, "Rabbis serve a great purpose, but none is to forgive sins of one man against another. Even G-d will not do that. We will ask Him to forgive us for sins against ourselves and against Him, but any bad actions between humans must only be resolved between those humans. On Yom Kippur, we will ask G-d to unbind us from promises we make and break to Him."

Marina stops walking, turns to Ruben and lifts the palms of her hands to shoulder height. "What promises does one make to G-d?"

"I am sure you have made them. Like when you were on the ship." Ruben scrunches his face as he recalls feeling sick. "I did. I made promises such as 'HaShem, get me to land and off of this wobbly thing, and I will say the Shema every day and every night.' Of course G-d got me safely to this land, and I do say the Shema when I can, but some nights I am too tired, and some days I get too distracted and busy. So, I will make a special note to G-d, on Yom Kippur, to please forgive me for my broken promise and for any I might make in the future."

"So, G-d can forgive a sin against Him or yourself but cannot against another man." Marina states her question.

Ruben nods. "True. Though maybe I would reword 'cannot' to 'chooses not to.'"

Marina looks down and makes a line in the sand with her foot. "What if we knew we were to commit a sin? Would G-d forgive us in advance?"

"What are you talking about? Is there a sin you plan to commit?" Ruben asks before he realizes she was just being funny. He becomes flustered as he fumbles for words. This young woman makes him smile and brings him joy. Her laughter is music. He cannot recall the last time he heard music. He points to the stars. "The sky is amazing when the moon's light does not interfere with theirs."

"Where is the moon?" Marina asks.

Ruben then explains the phases of the moon to her and how, unlike the stars, it does not emit the light they see. "Rosh Hashanah begins during the phase of the moon when we cannot see it." He tells her about Admiral Cristoforo Colombo's trick with the Arawaks, and about the timing of the eclipse and how the admiral's knowledge saved his life. He tells her what he knows about celestial bodies and about his respect for the universe. He confesses about his struggle to reconcile the fact that he benefited from a man whose heroism was matched by his barbarity.

Marina walks to where the water recedes. "Maybe that is the type of man who is attracted to the idea of taming or mastering the ocean — one who insists they ought to tame people. This admiral sounds like my father. I feel guilty that my father went home alone. And I feel guilty that I do not miss him at all."

She is being too hard on herself. "I am not sure your father ever showed a kind side. The admiral, on the other hand, was a loving father and brother. He was kind to Fernando's mother. I could not imagine him harming her the way your father harmed your mother. All the people in his life who were family or friends loved and respected him and received that in turn. He was very kind to me."

"It is too bad that he did not extend that part of himself to everyone."

Ruben agrees. "I hope that his son, Diego, the charge of this island who appointed the governor, is a good man like his younger brother, my friend, Fernando." Saying his name, Ruben realizes he misses Fernando terribly. He wonders how much he ever learned about his father. He wonders how he is doing. He wonders if he'll ever see him again.

Marina and Ruben sit under the stars. They talk about their childhood, their adulthood, their dreams, and their fears. Several hours before the sun is to rise, they stand up and sweep the sand from their clothing and walk back home. Their hands gently brush against each other's. Ruben wonders whether it was intentional. Did her hand touch his, or did his touch hers? And then their hands clasp. They exchange no more words on the walk back home.

Yom Kippur comes quickly. Sancia, Ruben, and Marina create their own small ceremony. They fast the entire period of the holy day, and then they feast after sunset. Even though Ruben's body still aches from indulging on an empty stomach, he walks outside and hammers a piece of wood into the ground.

"Why did you just do that?" Marina asks.

Ruben gives the hammer a twirl before holding it upright. "This is for the start of another holiday. Alone, on this island, I felt no reason to celebrate. I was grateful for the harvest. Gratitude for the harvest was the only way I acknowledged Sukkot. That is how it was —" Ruben turns to his mother, "even after you arrived. But tomorrow we will start putting together the pieces I have prepared for a sukkah. It will be where we will eat each meal for the week."

Marina walks toward the wood in the ground to get a closer look. "What is a sukkah?"

Ruben motions with his hands what it will look like. "Well, it is somewhat of a shack."

Marina laughs. "Do we not already eat each meal in a shack?"

And then they all laugh. Ruben is smitten by the beautiful sound. The almost full moon shines on his mother's smile while the darkness washes away her wrinkles. She looks young. She looks happy — which makes him happy in turn.

Four nights have passed since the end of Yom Kippur. Ruben stands in the sukkah he built with Marina and his mother. Sancia lights the candles and recites the prayer thanking HaShem for bringing them to the season—in this case, the season of the harvest, the season of Sukkot. Ruben pulls out a surprise from under the table. Wine.

Sancia clasps her hands together with joy. "Where did you get that?"

He removes the top from the bottle. "I bought it from one of the ships that stopped on its way going further south."

Marina slides her cup toward him. Ruben pours for everyone, and then he looks to his mother and asks if she could help him with the prayer.

After Sancia says the blesssing over the wine, she lowers her eyes. "But I'm afraid I do not remember the prayer for the sukkah."

Marina smiles and points to the open roof of the structure. "I think He will understand." She then says the HaMotzi, the prayer over the bread.

Enclosed between the temporary walls and the roof they built together, under the stars, Ruben enjoys the dinner with these women he loves.

"I like eating in this little shack." Marina then tells them about the days when she would eat in an occasional fancy inn. "Only this is better."

Sancia finishes her glass of wine and then pours more. "Some people actually spend all of their time in the sukkah during the entire holiday. It becomes their home for the week."

"They sleep in it?" Marina asks.

Sancia nods.

Marina then stretches her arms and yawns. "I am sorry. The suggestion of sleeping is making me tired. Building this was a lot of work. Have you ever slept in a sukkah?"

Ruben shakes his head.

"I also have not, but I can sleep now. I am also tired." Sancia starts to clear the table, and the others help before going back into their home.

Ruben wakes in the middle of the night, startled. He sits up on his cot with a fast-beating heart. He is alarmed, but he doesn't know why. He gets up to look in the room his mother shares with Marina. *She is gone!* He calls for Marina in a hushed tone so as not to wake his mother. He runs outside and sees a vast darkness before he looks at the sukkah and sees her silhouette. He exhales a sigh of relief and stands still to allow his heart rate to return to normal. He looks through the entrance to see more clearly. She is lying on the ground, fast asleep. He is struck by her beauty, her curiosity, and her strong will. He sits guard outside of the structure until she wakes.

Moments after the sun rises, she walks out of the sukkah toward the door of their home.

She has no idea how much she worried me. "Good morning."

She turns back. "Oh, good morning. I am sorry — I didn't see you there. You frightened me."

You frightened me! This is the first time he is irritated with her. "I was worried about you! You cannot just leave without telling us. It is not safe to sleep in the sukkah alone."

She tilts her head, seeming a little taken aback by his tone. She folds her arms across her chest and looks at him. "Then next time sleep out here with me."

Ruben's heartbeat comes to a sudden halt. He can't do that. It would mean something different to him than it might mean to her. He is speechless as he watches her turn to go into their home. He remains sitting, keeping guard by the entrance of the sukkah, as if he is still protecting her.

Once their work routine resumes, they harvest food and bring some to the surviving Arawaks. Marina and Sancia tend to the orange trees that Ruben received in a trade from a ship that arrived years before.

Sukkot is about to end, Ruben is unable to sleep. He looks in on his mother and Marina and sees that they are sleeping soundly. *Then next time sleep out here with me,* he recalls Marina's words. He cannot fall asleep, so he walks into the sukkah. He needs to think. He sits down. He then looks at the night sky and he imagines having this moment with the young woman he is in love with.

His dream is interrupted by the breeze from a blanket that has been fanned out next to him. *Marina.* She lies on it and stares at the sky.

He looks at her and then he looks up.

"It is much more comfortable to enjoy the view on the blanket." She then motions for him to lie next to her. "Your neck will not hurt that way."

Once he settles, she points up and tells him a story using the stars and the moon as characters. "I used to see stories in the sky when I was a child. But I only did so during the daylight hours and with clouds, not stars."

Tonight, Ruben sees a cloudless sky twinkling with a canvas of sparkle and story. They each take turns connecting the dots — to make a horse, an archer, a pot.

"And there is an orange tree," Marina says.

"Where?" Ruben asks.

She points up. He takes hold of her hand and brings her fingers to his lips. She doesn't withdraw. Instead, she returns his affections.

The lovers do not have the luxury of falling asleep without the risk of losing their privacy. They hold on to each other until the moon sets and the stars fade.

WHAT'S IN A DATE?
I MEAN, A DAY

On my way to work, I lean my head against the window of the bus. I haven't heard from Ari since our lunch with Ben — almost a week. I suppress feelings of disappointment, trying to convince myself there's nothing to suppress.

I hop off the bus and stop at a café. When I get to work, I scramble to open the door with two hot coffees in hand. Ben gently kicks a soccer ball toward me when I pass over the threshold.

My spirit lifts at the site of the familiar orb. "Another invitation?"

He shrugs his shoulders. "I found it right outside the door as I was unlocking it."

I put down the cups and pick up the ball. "It has today's date. This afternoon."

"That barely gives us enough time."

"Gives *us* enough time?"

Ben holds up his phone. He just got a text. "I've arranged for the ship to come to us. I'll be right back." And then he leaves.

He returns with a young man and a young woman, both in their mid-twenties. As soon as they enter, Ben invites them to set up their equipment in a semi-uncluttered area of our workspace. "Abi, this is Moshe and Zahava. They've been working with *El Carrillo*."

The students. I wonder which one of them is going to find my candlestick holder. And when? I touch my locket. And then I imagine.

Zahava fiddles with equipment. "The ship is not too deep. Divers have been able to access it relatively easily. Have you seen all of the images that we've uploaded?"

I shake my head. "Still images only. I haven't seen any videos yet. But thank you. Everything so far has been great! But you seem disappointed."

"Oh, I'm not really." Zahava struggles with the leg of a tripod before finally getting it to snap in place. "I'm grateful, actually. I love being able to touch the ship. It's just that I've wanted to experience operating an ROV—you know, a remotely operated vehicle. *El Carrillo* is easily accessed, so an ROV won't be necessary. They're very expensive and they're only used to go to depths that are beyond what is safe for divers. I've learned that they can do incredible things in the water."

"We can too." Moshe plugs a cord into the outlet.

The students treat us to a surprisingly clear video of the ship.

Ben points to the plaque with the ship's name. "Look. There it is!"

El Carrillo. Amazing, really. This never gets old. Every ancient item gives birth to new understanding. "Is that you two guiding the lift bag?"

Zahava shakes her head.

I point to the object being pulled up. "Do either of you know what it is?"

"I don't," Zahava answers. "But I'm guessing it'll show up here soon."

Hopefully. Patience is a virtue imposed, not possessed. I have less than two weeks before I return home — until I come back again. I fiddle with my locket and remain glued to the screen. I know I've felt close to my treasure three times before, just to be disappointed. But there is something different about this time. Or is there? The video ends.

Moshe holds out a palm-sized clump of wood. "Here, look at this. You can hold it."

"Fantastic!" I balance it on my open palm. "I cannot adequately express the thrill I feel holding a piece of decomposing wood." Of course I know the significance of this artifact.

"You might express yourself differently when you realize that it's from the ship you're working to demystify, *and* it might have been harvested during a day that didn't exist."

"Come on, Moshe, you know I'm thrilled to hold decomposing w—" I want to continue jousting, but then my brain processes the rest of his statement, *it might have been harvested during a day that didn't exist.* "Really?" I ask.

Ben rubs the palms of his hands back and forth. "Oh, I do love riddles."

Zahava seems less amused. "Well, I'm ready to hear the punchline now."

Moshe doesn't seem ready to reveal anything before describing the process that fueled his conclusion. Referencing dendrochronology, he describes the sophisticated process of tree-ring analyzation he used to date the wood, and how he had to compensate for the poor condition of the small sample. He explains how he concluded that the wood originated in Spain and was harvested during autumn. "That quite possibly puts the wood fragment to 1582. For dramatic effect, I'd like to think that it was harvested in the week of October 6th of 1582."

"The week that didn't exist." I smile and then I hand the wood back to him.

"Precisely." Moshe holds it up.

Ben takes it and brings it close to his eyes. "Okay, you two, what happened then, on, what did you say? October 6th of 1582?"

"Nothing, Ben. Nothing happened on that day, in Spain. It really didn't exist." I smile. And I stare at him. I know he'll figure it out.

Ben hands the wood back to Moshe and then places his thumb and forefinger at his chin. "Oh, now I see. It didn't exist on the Gregorian calendar, the one we use today."

"That's right, Professor Irelander." Moshe carefully wraps the wood back up and places it in his bag. "But it also didn't exist in the Julian calendar. That week, in Spain, didn't exist in any calendar."

I reach for an outdated paper-calendar of the museum that happens to be collecting dust on a shelf. I brush it off and open it to October. I section the applicable days with my index finger and thumb so that the others have a visual. "In the Catholic regions of the world, October 6th of 1582 did not exist. Neither did the 7th, 8th, all the way through the 14th. Because of a moving Easter that gravitated further away from spring, the pope at the time, Pope Gregory, insisted that a calendar be created to make sure that Easter would always be observed in the spring. So that year the calendar changed from the Julian calendar, named for Julius Caesar, to what we use now, the Gregorian calendar, after the pope who insisted on the change. Among other tweaking, astronomers realized that the change required a deletion of ten days. So, people of that region went to sleep on October 4th of 1582 to wake up the next day, on October 15th. The days in the middle simply didn't exist in either calendar."

Moshe's eyebrows furrow. "The adjustment of calendars, which took effect in different countries during different years, has made research a little tricky, because many historians don't account for the switch."

I'm so excited to be in the company of a fellow amateur horologist. "Exactly. For example, historians agree that Jews were expelled from Spain in the year 1492, during Tisha B'Av, the 9th day of the month of Av."

"The solemnest day of the year," Zahava says.

I nod. "The Alhambra Decree, the edict of expulsion, was originally to be executed July 31st of 1492. But, Tomás de Torquemada, the Grand Inquisitor, pushed for a change of date, likely so the exile of the Jews from Spain would coincide with Tisha B'Av, the anniversary of the exile of the Jews from England in 1290 and from France more than a hundred years before that. And the anniversary of the destruction of our First and Second Temple in Jerusalem."

"You'd think people would stop imposing injustice on us already." Zahava's comment reminds me of Ari.

I nod. "History books regarding the final expulsion of the Jews from Spain place the 9th of Av, of the Hebrew year 5252, as August 2nd and August 11th of 1492. Certainly a singular event couldn't be both days."

"Unraveling the discrepancy forced you to understand the formula of the calendar change." Zahava guesses correctly.

I put the calendar back on the shelf. "Because the expulsion predates the Gregorian calendar, the correct corresponding date would indeed be the one belonging to the Julian calendar, August 2nd, 1492, the day before Columbus and his crew set sail." I look at Zahava. "Now you know more than many historians— too many of whom overlook that distinction."

"That's confusing." Zahava smiles, seemingly satisfied. "But I get it."

"There's more. Leap Year is not simply every four years like it was before the switch, and like we're taught in school. There's a formula for that too."

Zahava stops me. "What is the formula you used to process the items in that tank?"

Enough of the horology.

Ari picks me up from work for the soccer match. The kids practice English and I revive my soccer skills. The game is close. And, being on the winning team, again, makes the afternoon all that much sweeter. Ari congratulates me and suggests we get a bite to eat.

Great idea. I'm so hungry. "I burned a lot of calories with my fast-paced fumbling. So, dinner *and* dessert!"

We go to Greg's at HaTachana, where Ben first took me. I open the menu. I love it here. A perfect place to be hungry. I could make a meal out of their warm bread and sauces alone. "I'm really in the mood for a salad. This sabich salad sounds good. I think I'll get that."

Ari laughs.

I can feel my face redden. "What's so funny?"

"You said that you want the 'sa beach' salad."

"That's funny?"

"It is sabich salad." He corrects my pronunciation. The last syllable is a letter that is unique to Hebrew. It's elegant when spoken by him but sounds like purging phlegm when I try. When the waiter takes our order, like a coward, I just point to what I want.

Ari recognizes him and asks about a small line of stitches that stretches from his brow to the side of his right eye. "Tough week, Dvir?" He points to his own face.

I imagine that if Dvir wanted to smile, it'd be painful for him to do so. His soft expression reveals large dark eyes. He looks to be in his mid-twenties. I wonder how Ari knows him. A soccer alum? A family member? A neighbor? It's not important now — maybe I'll ask after he steps away.

Dvir touches his wound. "I have relatives visiting who want to explore *all* of Israel. Last week, when I took them to the Temple Mount, a Palestinian hit me above my eye with a rock while I was waiting for them. I was just talking, very quietly, on my cell phone."

I gasp. "That's horrible!"

Ari just stares up at him. "Did you get arrested?"

Why would he ask him such a stupid question? "Someone hit *him* with a rock!"

He looks at me. "I heard." Then he looks back up at Dvir to wait for the answer.

No, you didn't hear. "You asked him if *he* got arrested."

Ari looks at me and leans forward. "It's illegal for us to pray on the Temple Mount because we are not Muslims. It doesn't matter that we reclaimed our holiest site in 1967 from Jordan's illegitimate occupation of it. And, to keep the Middle East from totally exploding, after we reclaimed it, we allowed the Islamic Waqf to be guardians of it." He then sits back and folds his arms across his chest. "Well, not *we*. I wouldn't have done that. But our leaders did."

Dvir's face remains expressionless, yet I can hear the sarcasm in his voice. "The Islamic Waqf, as a courtesy to the world, decided to allow only Muslims to pray there. They will not allow anyone else to pray there. They even forbid Christians from praying where Jesus worshipped, as a Jew, half a millennium before the man who dreamed up Islam was even born."

"But you said you were talking on your phone. Not praying." Not that such an attack would even be okay if he were just praying, I suppose. What do I mean *I suppose?* Of course it wouldn't be okay. But who knows what he might have really done to provoke getting hit.

Dvir's expression, still frozen, seemingly to keep his stitches from tugging, shakes his head. "It does not matter. If they see any non-Muslim speaking on a phone, on the Temple Mount, the Islamic Waqf will accuse us of praying — using the phone as a prop. To maintain peace, the Israeli police enforce the Muslims' discriminatory orders. They will usher away Jews, or Christians, for that matter, suspected of praying — even if that means arresting us, to keep the Muslims from bringing more violence against us. It is preposterous, no?"

Sounds like a preposterous exaggeration, actually. Now this guy sounds like an Islamaphobe, too.

"In the warped world we live in, the victim often gets blamed." Ari looks up at Dvir. "You should have put the phone away."

Was he even really a completely innocent victim? I watch Dvir walk away in unmistakable frustration as soon as he finishes taking our order. "I think you irritated him." *Or rather . . . pissed him off.*

"We are all irritated. We are all frustrated. We have mean-spirited people constantly attacking us, and good-natured, but under-informed people, fortifying the strength of their attacks."

I know that last part was directed toward me. I would

understand if nothing they said was an exaggeration, but –

"We are all fighting for our lives, and we do not want to be fighters. We are too busy to be fighters." He looks sincere.

"Aren't you exaggerating, even just a little bit? Will a Jewish visitor really be arrested by Israeli police, or assaulted by a Muslim, for *thinking* a certain way in a certain place?"

He looks down and puts his napkin on his lap. For the first time, it seems like he is letting silence answer the question for him.

Maybe I need to investigate further to see how much of this is true and to what extent. I think of him playing soccer with Arab and Jewish boys. I think of our conversation with Ben. Maybe I've been misjudging him. I cringe thinking of my overreaction when he joined us at Café Suzana. He's not a racist. He's not a fighter. *I bet he's an outstanding lover.* Where the hell did that come from? Am I turning red? I can't let him suspect what I just thought. *Anger.* That'll deflect my crush. No, not a crush. Quick – speak – push back. "Maybe the Palestinians would be less violent if *they* weren't so frustrated. Checkpoints must be terrible — the long lines waiting to get into Israel, the settlements being built on land that they'd hoped would be theirs during a peace agreement. I know that you have to deal with some enormous challenges, but you are in the stronger position to offer more."

Ari seems surprised by my sudden gust. "We are in a strong position because we work hard and learn from the past, and not just *our* past. When you start investigating *above* the surface of this planet, you might stop making such ridiculous suggestions."

That wasn't ridiculous! "The Palestinians have legitimate grievances against Israel!"

"Palestinians have a lot of legitimate grievances. But against Israel?" He shakes his head. "Only in the way Israel needs to respond due to the violent actions of so many of them who have been cruelly conditioned into believing it is their religious duty to kill us. They are not imprisoned by us, but by the hatred forced upon them from their political and religious leaders. We did not build the security wall until the 90s, in response to Palestinians killing people by bombing pizza parlors, discotheques, and buses. The wall has saved many lives. Are Palestinians upset that Jews are building in Judea? Yes. Islamists are upset when Jews build anywhere."

"I admit that I haven't studied the modern political history of Israel and there is much I don't know, but I just wonder if there would be peace if Israel would just give up a little land." I hold up my index finger and thumb a quarter of an inch apart from one another.

"On most maps, Abi, the finger width you are holding is larger than the entire width of our country. Come on — would there be peace if Islam spreads more and there is no Israel, then no Jews?"

"I'm not saying anything about 'no Jews.'"

"Well, you should be, because that is what would happen. That is what has been happening. After Muhammad abandoned peaceful persuasion to promote the religion he was forming, he and his followers banished, belittled and decimated Jews who lived in the Middle East many generations before he was even born."

"Christians did that too, and not just against Jews."

"Sure, there was a lot of violent invasions during the Middle Ages, but the laws established by Muhammad fortified misery into code and brought it into the twenty-first century." He sighs. "You were wrong, Abi. I am not against Muslims. I see them as the most intimate victims of Islam, many who've barely been acquainted with the cultures stolen from their defeated ancestors — whether Buddhists, Hindus, Zoroastrians, Christians or Jews." He motions his hands suggesting that even more than those cultures have fallen victim to Islam. "In fact, there is an interesting and credible theory that some people who identify as Palestinian are likely descendants of ancient Jews. Think about it — almost every Muslim has an ancestor who was defeated by Islam – just to have their descendants carry on the identity of those who took away their happiness, their freedom and often the lives of their loved ones. And people globally are angry at us — the remaining Jewish people — authentic resisters."

I haven't thought about it that way before. "But, so many people say it's a religion of peace and that when terrorists kill innocent people, they are perverting Islam. But what you are saying is that what Muhammad did then is very much like what the Islamic State is doing now and Boko Haram, the Taliban, Al-Queda, al-Shabaab . . ." I motion my hands indicating an unspoken, extensive list of Islamic terror groups that have been in the news. "The organized murders, maiming, enslavement and rapes. It's so awful. However they originated, and whoever they copy, I don't think the world is doing enough to stop the carnage."

"The world is too focused on Israel and what we are doing wrong, whether real or fabricated, to even understand why that particular brand of carnage exists. The fact is that the youngest monotheistic faith, appears a lot older than it is because its most dedicated soldiers have been colonizing lands, homogenizing people, destroying cultures, and subjugating its victims at alarming rates. It erases the histories of more ancient customs, leaving the illusion Islam was always there. We know what we are up against. We are not only up against those seeking to turn this country into another human rights pit, but against the kind-hearted folks who think it's the right thing to do."

Was that line aimed at me? I don't know enough to counter. What Ari is telling me is so different than anything I've heard before regarding Israel, Palestinians, and Islam.

This salad is awesome! I love this restaurant.

Ari seems to be enjoying his meal too. "If we do not protect ourselves, we certainly will not be in a position to protect anyone else. Coexistence is great. I'm a fan. It works well, even if imperfectly here, in Israel, and in the United States. But there is so much suffering in Muslim-majority lands. I have yet to see an example of equitable coexistence flourishing in any of them. They demand if of us, yet it is not there. Can you name one?"

"Name one Muslim-majority country that practices

healthy coexistence?" Fuck. I can do this. *Name one Muslim-majority country that practices healthy co-existence.* Think. Think. Yes! I've got this! I was in one just last year. "Bosnia!"

Ari places his hand under his chin. Good. He's thinking. "Bosnia has had an extremely troublesome history regarding coexistence, and I do not think that it is one of the 56 nations of the OIC—you know, the Organization of Islamic Cooperation. I'm not sure if it is half-Muslim or close to half-Muslim."

"You can look those things up. I successfully answered. You didn't give me any caveats." I hope I don't look too smug. Eh, I can look smug. I deserve this victory.

He rips off a piece of bread and dips it into the green sauce. "Fair enough. You win this round. But my point still stands. An exception does not invalidate a rule. Look at those in the OIC. Look at the pattern. Take note of the rule." He then points to the sauce and gives a nod of approval.

"Agreed. An exception does not invalidate a rule. But, it might not be the only exception."

"Maybe not." He smiles with a twinkle in his eyes. "Even I don't know everything." He can get away with his arrogance because he is so darn cute. But he can't get away with finishing the sauce.

I dip my bread into it. "Let me ask you a question. When a Palestinian commits an act of terror, why does Israel often destroy the home of his family, even if they were not involved? And why does Israel not do the same to the homes of Jewish criminals?"

He holds up two fingers. "That is two questions."

"Stumped?"

He takes a deep breath and lets out a sigh. "No. I'm not stumped – but saddened. The Palestinian Authority sets aside millions of dollars of foreign aid to invest in what they call their 'Martyrs Fund' – their financial account that monetarily rewards terrorists and their families. If a Palestinian is imprisoned or killed for trying to murder Jews, the PA promises substantial financial security to his family as a result."

"Wait a minute. You are saying that the government of the Palestinians actually pays their citizens to murder people?" Come on. Is that really what they do with their foreign aid? I know I need to look this up later – mental note – word search *Palestinian Martyrs Fund.*

"'Pay to Slay,'" Ari sighs. "Look, the Israeli government needs to disincentivize this sick scheme. Answer one: When Israel destroys the home of a terrorist, it is to counter the Palestinian monetary system that rewards murder and maiming people. Answer two: Israel does not apply that same deterrent of house destruction against Jews because there is no incentive given to Jews to murder. Any who do are swiftly punished by the Israeli judicial system – as they should be."

"Is that justice?"

"It's survival. Look. I want mutually respectful peaceful coexistence. That is one reason I volunteer with Arab and Jewish Israeli teens at the Peres Center for Peace. I want them to get to know each other. I want all citizens of my country to prosper, Jew, Arab, Muslim, Christian, Druze, anyone. The problem is that too many Palestinians have been conditioned by the PA and Hamas—and, quite frankly, the books they call holy—to believe that their lives are worth less than the Jews' death. And the United Nations, which is supposed to be secular, has perpetuated the suffering of the Palestinians and intensified their resentment toward us and has helped them to solidify that sentiment."

"Let me guess — UNESCO?"

Ari shakes his head. "The UNHCR."

"You mean the UNH*RC*. Right? We already discussed that."

Ari shakes his head again. "No. Well, yes, that too. But I mean the UNH*CR*. The High Commissioner for Refugees. It was created to settle *all* refugees throughout the world fleeing violence and conflict — all refugee populations but one. Want to guess which one it doesn't help?"

"The Palestinians?" *That's too ridiculous to be true.*

"Yes. The Palestinians do not get settled through the UNHCR like *all* other refugees the UN assists. They've even given Palestinians a unique definition of refugee and their own branch, UNWRA, which perpetuates their dismal living conditions. This is toxic to them and to us."

"Maybe they have their own branch because their land is in dispute."

"Their land? Do you have any idea how many land disputes there are in this world? About a hundred. There is no UN branch for the peaceful Cypriots who've been overrun by the Turks, nor for the Kurds, who are very deserving of sovereignty. The Tibetans—"

"Are you saying there should be no peace agreement?"

He shakes his head. "'Peace agreement'—semantics. I'd like there to be a two-state solution, but I don't know exactly how it could work. Jordan is marginally older than Israel and it attacked us as soon as we became a country. In doing so, it annexed East Jerusalem and expelled all the Jews from Judea and Samaria. They wouldn't even let us approach our holiest sites. But they also did not set aside East Jerusalem to be any part of a Palestinian state. They just kept it, destroyed about 50 synagogues and kicked us out. If Israel didn't reclaim it in a defensive war, it would still be part of Jordan. Gaza would still be part of Egypt. Only now do people demand those places become territory to form a previously nonexistent country called Palestine. You must see that the bad guys use smoke screens to mask their crimes. Hamas in Gaza creates smoke screens by burning tires, while *Hamas on Campus* uses college students as smoke screens to manipulate truth."

I cringe at his mention of students on college campuses. As a visiting lecturer of archaeology at several universities, I've felt shame walking by displays disparaging Israel. I would see them all the time. The ugly pictures, the scattered bodies of people acting dead, the fake blood, the staged wall, the chanting and shouting. It never occurred to me that they were grossly distorting the truth. I just hoped they wouldn't link me to Israel just because I'm Jewish. Now I feel shame for feeling that shame.

"How are you enjoying your sa-*beach* salad?" Ari

smiles as he emphasizes the last syllable, mimicking the way I first said it.

I can't help but smile. And then I motion behind his shoulder. I think I recognize Bassam, his friend and co-coach from our soccer match. He's standing at the bar.

Ari briefly looks back. "That's Bassam and his wife, Rayhana. She's such a lovely person. You have to meet her." He waves for them to join us. The couple brings their drinks from the bar and sits at our table. Ari introduces Rayhana to me.

"Nice to see you again, Abi," Bassam says as he scoots in his chair. He then looks at Ari. "Did I tell you about our upcoming trip to Istanbul?"

"Turkey!" Ari's face brightens. "Will you be seeing Burak?"

Bassam nods. "He agreed to meet us in Istanbul for a couple of days."

"That is fantastic! I need to send a note to him. It's been too long." Then Ari looks at me. "Burak is not just any friend. He is incredible. Bassam and I met him when we were sent to Turkey as part of a search and rescue team to recover victims from the powerful earthquake that damaged much of the northwestern region in 1999. That disaster was horrible." Ari looks at Bassam, who solemnly nods.

"Israel sent people to Turkey to help?" I break their moment of silence. "I thought Israel and Turkey were enemies."

"Not then." Rayhana is elegant, even in jeans and a plain shirt. She's not overly made up, yet is impeccably manicured, except for her eyebrows, lending a more exotic nature to her appearance.

Ari enthusiastically returns to his friend. "Burak is a journalist. Bassam and I met him when he was covering the events of the earthquake."

I look at Bassam. "Are you a doctor too?"

He nods.

"We all are. Only I wasn't on that trip. I'm not that old." Rayhana has sass. I like that.

"My gosh. That was about twenty years ago." Ari looks at Bassam. "We are old."

"Oh, stop that. I was only kidding." Rayhana tenderly reaches for Bassam's hand. Then she looks at Ari. "In any case, I can't wait to visit Turkey. I've never been there before. And, I am really excited to meet your friend. Bassam has told me so much about him, and I started following his writing. I have to say, he is quite courageous and very intelligent."

"The smartest. The bravest. I love him! And he is so much fun." Ari orders a bottle of wine for the table so that we can toast to his Turkish friend.

"How do I look him up?"

Ari spells his last name and says his first. "Burak Bekdil. He writes for American outlets that don't censor him. Look at the *Middle East Forum* and *Gatestone Institute*. And now there is a new site called *Sigma Insight Turkey*. It's the only Turkish site that will print him uncensored."

I enjoy listening to everything, including their concerns over the decline of Turkey and the couple's vacation itinerary. Maybe next time I'm back, I'll be able to hear how it went.

Ari and I decide to burn off some of the meal before heading home. The night is beautiful. Warm and clear. We leave Greg's and walk the nearby cobblestone streets of Jaffa.

"So, your family comes from Spain?" I recall from our lunch with Ben.

"On my father's side. His ancestors came here after the expulsion. They eventually established roots in Hebron, where my mother's side is from, from as far back as anyone can trace. My saba and savta survived the Hebron Massacre."

"Hebron Massacre?"

"Yes. Have you not heard of it? In 1929, Muslims brutally attacked Jews in our ancient villages of Hebron. But, an Arab couple risked their own lives to save my saba and savta. There were several brave Arabs who were noble like that. Yet, my saba and savta lost so many friends to the murderers. And they lost their home to the attackers. Hebron became Jew-free for the first time in thousands of years."

I had no idea. I press my locket. "I'm sorry about the suffering your grandparents endured. 1929. That was long before the Holocaust."

Ari shakes his head. "Before the Shoah, we were regularly attacked here. I assume you have not heard of the Looting of Safed. If you have not heard of the Hebron Massacre, you would not have heard of the Looting of Safed in 1834."

I haven't. But — I point out reason for hope. "I see your

friendship with Bassam and Rayhana. I see it's genuine. They're remarkable people. I want to be friends with them. And they are Israeli Arabs who are Muslim and you are an Israeli Jew."

"We are relatively secular. It isn't our religion that unites us, but our free-thinking ideologies that does. Back to my friends, did you know that the first known Rayhana was a young Jewish woman?"

I shake my head. What's his point?

"Years after he started forming what would be known as Islam, Muhammad had Rayhana's father and husband killed along with all the men of her peaceful tribe of Banu Qurayza. They lived in what's now Saudi Arabia."

"He killed *all* the men?"

Ari nods. "Every one. About 800 peaceful men. And he enslaved all the women and children and distributed them as booty, along with the tribe's hard-earned wealth, among his followers."

"I had no idea. Until tonight, I thought Muhammad was peaceful . . . like Jesus."

"Hmm. Well, when adherents to Christianity aim to emulate Jesus, we have remarkably different results than when adherents to Islam aim to emulate Muhammad. Understanding the origins of any faith is relevant to understanding its modern-day outcomes. Banu Qurayza is only one victimized tribe. There were so many others before and after them. Muhammad took Rayhana captive after killing the men she loved and selling the women and children she was close to. There seems to be dispute as to whether or not she eventually 'accepted Islam,' and then marriage to the murderer of her husband, but under the circumstances, she was a victim ripe for coercive control."

"Coercive control?"

"Yes—domestic abuse in which an abuser controls the behavior of those close to them — usually with psychological manipulation. There are laws against it in the UK now." He then stops walking and turns to me. "I just realized, those laws seem to conflict, in some instances, with 'freedom of religion.' Such sticky distinctions."

"What?" I lost my focus thinking about a woman I never heard of until tonight. Rayhana, her heartache and despair – a survivor of mass horror – condemned to live with those responsible for the death and captivity of her loved ones.

"Never mind. He didn't take just her. He took another Jewish woman, too. And then there was the daughter of an Arab chief whose tribe he conquered. Her name was Burrah, until he changed it to Juwayriyah."

"He changed the name of a woman he took captive?"

Ari nods. "That was an effective way to fortify ownership and erase authentic identity, carried on by his most devout followers. Burrah to Juwayriyah, Constantinople to Istanbul, Kever Rachel to Bilal bin Rabah Mosque —"

"Rachel? What! The matriarch of Judaism's tomb – a mosque?"

"—for a couple of decades now. How could you not know this?"

That's creepy. "Why doesn't anyone do anything?"

"Oh, they do! UNESCO endorses that change and issues criticism against Israel for clinging to its original identity. Rewriting or whitewashing historical facts in the hopes to ward off attacks or to protect people's feelings is more harmful to all in the long run. It'll only encourage more of the same. Does anyone really believe that replacing the one Jewish state on this planet with a newly created 57th Islamic state will make the world safer? Do they think jihadists would then stop ambushing innocent people in Fort Lauderdale, Orlando, New York, Boston, Nice, Paris, Barcelona, London, Manchester, Toronto, and so on because there would no longer be an Israel?"

"Some do think that." I probably wasn't too far from thinking that myself.

He points his finger up. "The ambushing would increase! Even worse. What do those people think will happen if the Iranians, through Hezbollah, or the Islamic State gets access to our weapons? They call for the destruction of the United States too. If Israel carelessly gives up more of our tiny bit of land, it will be an existential threat to the *world*, including for those robotically fighting against us."

"Do your views put tension between you and Bassam?"

How could they not?

Ari shakes his head. "Bassam keeps his faith private. He mentioned researching an organization in the United States — Ex-Muslims of North America."

"Ex-Muslims? Does he reject the faith?"

"He hasn't gone as far as saying that. For him, like for me, it might be enough to keep practicing 'religious light.'

We do talk a lot about religion. He is the one who told me about Rayhana."

"That she was one of Muhammad's wives?"

He shakes his head and corrects me as I'm about to correct myself. "Though he had about 15 wives too."

I drop my jaw.

He lifts my chin and brings his face close to mine. His breath caresses my face. "But not at the same time."

My heart pauses and my knees weaken. "Is that even allowed?"

"When a man can effectively convince people that he gets messages from a god, *anything* he wants becomes allowed. Who knows. Maybe he did. Maybe I'm just not a fan of his messages because accordingly, I'd be a vilest of creatures."

"Because you are Jewish?"

He shakes his head. "Because I'm not a 'believer.'"

Wait a minute! I'm not a believer either! I need to investigate later to see how much this guy is exaggerating or taking out of context. I'm just not informed enough now to know. It's time to transition from serious to playful. "Well then, if you'd become a believer, you'd no longer be considered a 'vile beast.' Problem solved. No?"

"Hm. You do have a point."

"It is something to consider." I take a step closer and hold his gaze. "You are a little bit hideous."

He takes my hands by my side and gently touches his forehead against mine. "Did you just call me hideous?"

Yes, and I want you. Do I tilt my lips upward? *Oh my*

gosh, I am such a bad person. I step back. *Why is it so difficult for me to step away from him?* I try to play it cool, as if illicit thoughts are not running through my mind. I use a mental broom to sweep them away. *I'm married. I love Daniel, Harry, Sandy and Maya.* I wouldn't dream of damaging my family. *Just say something. Be natural. Say something.* "I wonder if Rihanna, the singer, knows the history to her name. I like her a lot. Do you know her?"

"Oh my gosh!" Ari bounces with excitement. "I love her! She came here in 2013 despite pressure from the BDS movement."

"Did you see her?"

"I couldn't. I was in Haiti, working at the clinic." He points to his nose to remind me of his inability to smell. "But, my friends sent me a clip of her performance." He then says something about having my heart.

My heart skips a beat. *Why does it keep doing that?* Then I hear him mumble something about being worlds apart. And then what sounds like the hook to "Umbrella." Wait a minute! Is he singing? Then a bit louder with more confidence. He *is* singing. How charming, awkward, and adorable. I wish he would stop. I wish he wouldn't stop. "Are you serenading me?"

Instead of answering, he holds an imaginary microphone to my mouth. I push his hand away. We both smile and continue our walk, through cobblestone alleys, down narrow staircases and between closed shops. We peer into the windows of a couple of stores to see artwork on display, housed in beautiful ancient buildings.

He turns to me. "Tell me about your candlestick holder, the one whose match you are looking for."

I touch the locket from my parents. "My mother gave it to me right before I became a Bat Mitzvah, the same year my parents gave this necklace to me."

He shines the light from his phone on it. "That is beautiful."

"Thank you. It's the last gift my father gave to me before he passed."

Ari lowers his eyes. "I'm sorry."

"Me too. I still miss him."

"What is inside of your locket?"

"It's personal." *I haven't told anyone.*

"Ah. And where have I heard that before?" He turns away with a smile in his voice. I'm glad he is going to let it go.

I playfully swat his arm. It's just an excuse to make contact. "The locket was a gift from both of my parents. The candlestick holder was from my mom, a family heirloom passed down to her from her grandmother. She never used it. I didn't even know it existed until I unwrapped it."

"What makes you think there is an identical piece? You seem so sure."

"A Jewish family traveling with just one candlestick holder at that time would have been cause for suspicion. But no one would question the need for a Jewish family to have a pair."

"Suspicion?"

That was a slip. I don't want to reveal that it has a hidden compartment. Not because I don't want to put the focus on the treasure inside, but because a part of me does buy into the whole 'don't tell and it might come true' possibility. I don't want to jinx finding my candlestick holder. "Jews had to pack lightly so why would they pack something so heavy that had no spiritual value? I believe that there is another one. I care deeply about every artifact that comes my way and I give each piece the same care I would should I suspect I'm holding its match."

"And you think that its match will be on the ship that you are currently working on?"

"I do. I just have a strong feeling. This is the fourth assignment in which I've had reason to hope. But I feel something different about this one." Though I've thought that before.

"So, you knew that you'd be an archaeologist when you turned twelve?"

"No. However, I became interested in archaeology a couple of years before. I think that's why my mother gave the candlestick holder to me instead of my older sister when she was finally ready to pass it down." I hear a voice coming through the outdoor speakers. At first it sounds pretty, soft, and musical. But then it becomes so loud, it literally hurts my ears. I feel ridiculous having to cover them with my hands, but I fear that if I don't protect my eardrums, they'll rupture. I lose my train of thought. It stops. Finally.

"Where were we?" Ari asks, rather unfazed.

"Holy cow, what was that?!"

"The *adhan*, the Islamic call to prayer. You've lived here and have not heard it before?"

"I guess I haven't been in this neighborhood when it's happened. Does it happen every night?"

Ari looks at me funny, clearly surprised this is new to me. "Yes — every night. And every day. Daily. Five times — from before sunrise, up to midnight."

"That is so loud! Before sunrise? What if people want to sleep?"

"One part of the *adhan* instructs that prayer is better than sleep."

"Are you serious?"

He nods. "If people in this neighborhood want to sleep during the Islamic call to prayer, they better have functioning air-conditioners and closed windows. The Israeli government has tried to enforce a decibel limit, but then they face opposition insisting that enforcing a lower volume interferes with the rights of Muslims."

"Rights of Muslims to have their ears damaged and thoughts disrupted? Isn't there a phone app for that call? I can't imagine that Bassam and Rayhana want to be disturbed by this imposing volume. Doesn't this outrageously loud call interfere with their rights?"

Ari shrugs. "It's one reason they live in Tel Aviv."

Now I'm beginning to see what he meant during dinner. Being against Islam isn't about being against Muslims. It's about being against intrusive orders that pierce through a peaceful night. It's about being against the glorification of conquest and being against a phenomenon that seeks to destroy this wonderful country and ruin the lives of the people who work so hard to make it great.

We continue walking along the sidewalk that connects Jaffa to Tel Aviv and borders tonight's moonlit Mediterranean. The soothing laps of water wash away the disturbance of the *adhan*. Ari's hand brushes against mine. *Was that by accident?*

He doesn't give a hint as to whether or not it was. "Where were we? So, you knew that you wanted to be an archaeologist even before you were twelve years old?"

"I didn't necessarily know that I was going to be an archaeologist before I was twelve. But I knew, since I was ten years old, that the story behind an item is often more precious than the item itself. That's when I went on a family trip to Las Vegas. Needless to say, my parents wanted to spend time in the casinos. My older sister, Alicia, and I were too young to gamble, but not too young to shop. So, we spent a few hours one day wandering through stores before meeting up with my parents for dinner and a show. One store, a pawn shop, had a memorable name for its location. Las Vegas is a valley surrounded by mountains. The store's name was La Montagne dans la Vallée, meaning 'mountain in the valley.' My sister and I lingered in that store, eating the complimentary cookies, enjoying the air-conditioning and browsing. As we reached for a second snack, the owner approached us. I was afraid he was going to reprimand us for taking seconds. But that wasn't the case at all. He was Mr. Lamontagne, proud of the store that incorporated his family name. We were his only customers. So, he spent time telling us more about his inventory while likely hoping to convince us to convince our parents to spend their winnings there." I remember how much I enjoyed seeing Alicia twirl in front of the full-length mirror while holding up dresses. And there was that one dress that seemed made for her. Gorgeous! When Mr. Lamontagne suggested she try it on, I was so disappointed she didn't. I wonder if it really was worn to a royal ball. "He told us stories behind the gowns, watches, rings, bracelets, and guitars that made up his inventory. I was not so much impressed with the actual fancy jewelry and fame-touched instruments. But I was enchanted by the stories that fueled them. I was captivated by some of the agonizing decisions people had to make as to whether or not to abandon them in an exchange for cash. I knew then that whenever I'd see certain items, I would want to decode their messages."

"I hope you find your other Shabbat candlestick holder."

"Thank you." My phone rings. It's Harry. "It's my daughter. Please excuse me."

"Is everything okay?"

I lift my shoulders. "I'm not sure. She doesn't typically call me. She just texts. You can go. I know my way home from here."

"I'll wait over there." Ari politely walks out of earshot but remains within view.

He returns to me after I hang up. I'm embarrassed to tell him what's wrong, "Everyone is okay. Just Harry is having a tough time with some of her friends. They've been taunting her."

"About? — or is that private, too?" He's being playful.

I'm not feeling playful. "About here. Her friends have been hearing the news about the IDF killing protesters along the Gaza border. Like I once did, she is allowing the misinformed to chip away at her conscience — a conscience that is golden. She is such an awesome kid." I barely got her to stop crying before we hung up.

"Have you been paying attention to what's been going on at the Gaza border?"

I shake my head. I need to really start paying attention. "She said that her friends said that Israeli soldiers killed peaceful protesters. Look, I know they must have had a good reason—"

"Not peaceful. And the IDF doesn't kill unless it is to save more lives than will be ended. Not to say that there are never rogue soldiers or tragic mistakes. The majority of people killed at the Gaza border weren't peaceful at all. They were rioters with gangs formed to cut through our security fence, burn tires, and kidnap civilians and soldiers. They were equipped with maps of Israeli villages. The IDF warned they would use live gunfire. It is more precise. Rubber bullets can still kill. They certainly injure and they are less precise. Have Harry ask her friends how they think the Egyptians would respond to Palestinians bringing wire cutters to their border at

Gaza while they light tires on fire and send rockets and flaming kites into their country."

I never think of these things. How can this guy not hate me? "Americans are not known for geographic precision. People probably don't even realize that Egypt borders Gaza—"

"Or that Egypt keeps a blockade to protect their people from the Palestinians like Israel does." He takes out his phone and pulls up a map of the United States. "Look at this little state." He points to Rhode Island. "Let's suppose the people of both Massachusetts and Connecticut do not want the people of Rhode Island attacking their states. Would it make sense for the world to only be angry with Massachusetts for protecting its border from violence, and not Connecticut?"

"No. Of course not."

"Of course not. No other region would be condemned for protecting its borders from a population who boasts wanting to destroy it. Only Israel." He puts his phone back into his pocket. "The unfettered hatred people have against us and this country is going to lead to the destruction of much more than the Jews and Israel. Look at all the energy people put into destroying our borders and reputation. Israel is less than a tenth of one percent of the Middle East. Put that in context of its size in the world."

"I'll discuss all this with Harry." I'm disgusted with the way I've been. I was so ignorant and even a little mean. "After dinner with Yoni, did you not hate me?"

"You think I've been spending so much time with you,

showing you the country that I love, the country that you've been hiding from on these digs of yours — do you think that I led us by the ocean, just to catch a glimpse of your silhouette in the moonlight, despite that I might hate you? Does that make any sense?"

"Why have you been trying to spend so much time with me?" I search his eyes for an answer.

I can read them: *Sometimes silence is the most precise answer I've got.*

Can he read mine? *You aren't allowed to rely on that. That's my line.*

"Do you want to grab dinner later this week?" Ari breaks his silence.

Let's just talk all night long. I look at my building and back at him. "I can't." *I can't because I'm getting too close to you.* "The pace of the divers has picked up. I really need to spend more time at work and a bit of time with Annette. I don't think I'll get a chance to go out again before I leave." I need to pull away from his grip before he irreversibly takes hold of me. Why do I feel that's happening? "But I'll text you when I find my other candlestick holder."

"I want to see you again."

I want to see you again, too. But, I can't. I'm married. Happily married. "I had a lot of fun. You've challenged my views. Do you know how exciting it is to entertain new views at my age?"

"You've also helped me grow. Abi, you represent a world of hope. When I'm with you, I feel like I matter. Sure, I repair hearts—but you've been repairing mine. I know you are married. I don't want to bring harm to your family. I just really like being with you."

Why does your heart need repairing in the first place? I really like being with you, too. I can barely hold back my tears. "You are amazing, Ari. You use your hands to heal the sick and your legs and feet to bring hope and friendship to a soccer field of kids. And you dispense knowledge in a compassionate and non-judgemental way." *Well, an obnoxious, but quite sexy way.* I pause. Giggle. "Well, that very last part is debatable. You are a little judgemental." I smile and hold up my thumb and forefinger to show an inch. Deep breath. *Eyes, please stay dry.* "You do so much to help this world. I'm really glad I met you. But I'm leaving here soon. Really soon. It's best that I say goodbye now." I squeeze his hand and thank him and then I turn to walk toward the building. I feel his presence lingering. *Go. Please just go. Don't make this more difficult.* I walk through the lobby door. I can't go up to the apartment yet. I'm not ready to talk to Annette about my day or to avoid talking to her about my day. I wait out of view. *Ari, just leave.* When I suspect he is gone, I walk back outside. I sit on the bench in the courtyard and cry.

Annette pounces on me as soon as I walk through the door.

"Is that your evening wear?" She laughs.

Oh right. I'm in soccer gear. I need to give it back to Ari. I'll wash it and leave it at the center. "I'm going to jump into the shower." I avoid her gaze.

"Wait a minute. Let's talk. You've been staying with me

for over two weeks, and I barely get to see you. I miss you, Abi. I miss spending time with you. Are you full from dinner?"

"Yes." One-syllable answer. I feel my strength waning and the tears pushing their way to the surface again. I don't want to arouse suspicion. I don't want questions. I don't want her to analyze my feelings for Ari and say aloud that which I already know. "Give me a few minutes to jump into the shower. Then if you're up for it, I'll let you do my hair." As kids, we would often play beauty shop.

"Deal!"

I turn on the shower. I cry. There's no difference between the tears streaming down my face and the water pouring out of the spout. My emotions are simply jumbled because I'm exhausted. *Okay, so maybe I have a crush. I bet Harry has a crush that's more intense than mine.* I'm also physically drained from work and the soccer match. I miss my kids. Maybe I drank a little too much tonight and maybe I'm still getting adjusted to the different time zones.

I know this exercise is in vain. And I know Ari is not just a crush. But why? What has he taken from me that is making my heart ache and my soul search? I move my hand to support my heart. My tears halt. My breath stops. *My locket is gone!* Overcome by panic, I hop out of the shower before I even soap up. I wrap the towel around me and run to Annette. She is sitting on the couch reading. "My locket! It's gone!"

She closes the book. "What happened?!"

"I don't know. The clasp must have broken. I was wearing it when I was walking home from dinner with Ari after the game." The tears I cry for my necklace mask the tears I cry for Ari. They shield me from questions.

Annette hugs me. "We'll call in the posse. I know how much it means to you. We're going to find it."

"It was the last gift I got from my mom and dad right before . . ." And the photo on the inside means so much to me.

"I know." Annette dries my cheeks with her hands. "Maybe Ari can search for it on his way back home. He might still be walking. Text him."

"I can't."

"Why not? I thought you had his number."

"I do, but I said goodbye to him."

"Why? You're not leaving for almost two weeks."

"Never mind. I'll text him." I squeeze her hand in thanks, text Ari and walk back into the shower to wash up. Then I get into pajamas. Annette still wants to brush my hair. No fancy designs, just a calming motion.

Ari returns my text. He assures me he'll look out for it.

I turn in for the night feeling numb. I have a hard time falling asleep. Everything about that locket is important to me—the inscription, places I've worn it, its gifters. The picture inside. Maybe my loss is symbolic. Maybe I was getting too close to a new friend who could disrupt my routine at home and my closeness with my children. Am I supposed to see that message? Or maybe the message is that I shouldn't be pushing away a new friend like I did tonight. Maybe the loss is prophetic and symbolizes what will be my lack of success in finding the other candlestick holder. Or maybe the necklace simply broke; maybe there's no Divine message at all.

But then I realize that I have to warn Ari . . .

I find his building. I have to get off on the 8ᵗʰ floor. The elevator opens. It closes before I can get off. It moves up a level. I'm trapped in this small moving box. The door opens and I see my necklace floating in the threshold, as if the chain is spider silk and the locket is a spider. I reach for it, and the elevator door closes before my fingers clasp it. The walls are a dull gray. I have to warn Ari and tell him about the falafel. He needs chips. The elevator brings me up a level and the doors open. A soccer ball rolls in. The elevator doors close. It goes up a level and opens. Ari's floor. It closes before I can get out and warn him. I press the button. A mouth emerges from the button I touch on the panel. It bites me. The buttons have teeth and talk and buzz in different tones. The elevator moves up to the next level, past Ari's floor. I start to walk out. One foot over the threshold. The soccer ball rolls past me. There is no floor. I fall. I wake up. I manage an hour more of sleep. Annette and I get out of bed at the same time to go to work.

She needs to go in a little early today. "I'm rushing out the door, but let's plan on dinner together tonight. Just the two of us. Out. We'll walk to Greg's and keep on the lookout for your locket the entire way." She then suggests that we will need some drinks. She's right.

Not Another Exodus

1530

Pedro, Ruben's closest friend, approaches him with a sense of urgency that takes him by surprise. He closes his eyes to wipe sweat from his forehead, tense with concern. And then he opens them, revealing a blue several shades darker than the sea. "Ruben, I need to talk to you about a plan. The Inquisition is not so far away. It seeks us."

Ruben pauses to look up from the chair he is building. He waves his hands in a calming motion. "I wish you told me sooner that this was on your mind so that I could have put your mind at ease. I've been here for twenty-seven years and there is no sign that the Inquisition will be coming here. A church was built about four years ago, and still no one bothers my family. There is no king here. This island belongs to Diego Columbus, and he will not allow it."

Pedro doesn't look any calmer. "Who is to say what may

change his mind, and if not his mind, then the power he has? I see word of New Spain has not reached you yet."

Ruben shakes his head. "We have not received news in some time." *And certainly not of a place as far as New Spain, in the large continent north of the Isthmus of Panama.*

Pedro opens a coconut, takes a sip, and hands the rest to Ruben. "The Inquisition has struck this New World. Many Jews, like us, have helped to establish so many new places, like New Spain and Recife, making them more livable for people from back home. Yet the Inquisition burned their first victim in New Spain two years ago —Hernando Alfonso. May his memory be a blessing. I cannot believe we have not discussed this before. Maybe I was too focused on making a life here. We need to talk about it now. They lust for more of our ashes. We might need more options. Between the two of us and some of the others, we can buy or build a ship, and sail it to our homeland."

Until this news from Pedro, Ruben didn't know that the Crown and the Church had driven their murderers so close to him. "I do not know how to sail." Ruben hopes that's enough to convince Pedro that he is not a good candidate for this expedition.

Pedro points to the chair that Ruben has been building outside of his home. "But you know how to build, and you know how to maintain the ship's structure in the face of storms or sea worms. Every man will do his part."

Ruben picks up a hammer and pounds a nail into the wood. "I cannot leave my family. I do not want to leave my family!"

Pedro puts his hand on Ruben's elbow, urging him to stop working and to pay attention. "If we do not protect ourselves and look for another place, the Christians might destroy our families, here! Look, the Ottomans have overpowered the Mamluks in our homeland some time ago. Now is the time to head to Jerusalem and at least connect with our brethren there. They will allow us."

Ruben shakes his head. "It is not safe. You said yourself the Ottomans overtook the Mamluks. — That they hold the same beliefs in the same god didn't matter. In Hebron, the Ottomans were as bad as the Mamluks were to our people, they killed Jews and plundered businesses. That news I have heard."

"They got more aggressive so they could replace the Mamluks. That was over a decade ago — in 1517. Now the Ottomans rule the land without threat from the Mamluks."

"So that makes them less cruel?"

"The sultan allows Jews on the lands conquered by his army. That includes our homeland. Look, we do not have to commit to making our home there. We can decide after we return. We will simply explore the land and the people and see if that is where we could bring our families. This journey will just be for a few months. We could bring goods to Jerusalem for trade and even bring goods back here. Maybe this island, where you now have roots, will remain our best option. We can decide after we return. But we need to have options. We need to make connections in other lands, especially in the land of our ancestors."

Ruben checks on his sleeping children, and then joins his mother and wife at the table. "Pedro approached me today with concerns about our security on this island."

Marina pours hibiscus tea in a cup for each of them. "The women are worried about the same thing. They are convinced that the Inquisition will come here."

Ruben takes a sip of tea. "Pedro suggests that he and I, along with some other men, travel toward Jerusalem to see what other options we might have. I told him that is not necessary, that the first church was built here four years ago, and those Christians have not brought us harm."

"Yet there is a church," Sancia says.

"We could build a synagogue." Ruben thinks of the many *conversos* who came on the last ship. "We could strengthen our presence and form our own army."

"Build an army?" His mother shakes her head. "Better to build a boat."

"No!" Marina stands abruptly. "We are happy here. We are safe here. There is no need for you to go."

Sancia stands near Marina and takes her hands. "Do you not agree that the Inquisition is coming too close? New Spain is still far from here. That is true. But it is also quite a distance from the Inquisition's origin. Death is traveling, seeking our belongings, seeking to destroy our lives. You heard the same stories I heard, the same stories Pedro told Ruben."

"I do agree." Marina pulls her hands away and then folds her arms across her chest. "But Pedro and the others can look at Jerusalem and report back to us, and then we can decide if we all will go. But we will not be apart." She looks at Ruben. "You can help them build the boat, but you do not go."

Ruben thinks back to twenty-eight years ago, when he was a fourteen-year-old boy having such a talk with his mother, trying to convince her to let him journey across the world.

Sancia glances at her son and then back at Marina. "He will come back. I will be here to help you with the children. But I think Pedro is right. A group of men must go. Ruben is smart and strong. Their chance of success increases if he joins them on the journey. He is a master with wood and familiar with the damage done at sea. Look at what he has built on this island. The boat might not have a chance of staying afloat if he will not be there to repair damage that happens along the way. We do want all these men to return."

Ruben does not want to go but knows he must. "Marina, do you not know how much it aches my heart to leave you for so long? I love you. Our children. Mother. But we must do what we need to do to stay ahead of those who seek to destroy us, to bring harm to our children, to take our belongings and impose their awful way of life on us. It may never happen. But there are signs that show it might. We need to protect ourselves. We need to be prepared to fight or leave."

Marina's silence makes him nervous. And then she answers. "Okay. You can go, but for no longer than two months."

"I'll try. I just do not know if that is possible." He knows full well it isn't.

"Make it possible!"

Ruben shrugs his shoulders. "I do not even know when we are going to leave or what we are going to leave on. This is the early stages of planning. All of us together do not have much money. Without money, we cannot buy or build a ship. I can build more small pieces of furniture to trade, but —."

"Just one moment." Sancia leaves the room. She returns and then opens the palm of her hand to reveal a small cylindrical piece of gold. "You can sell this. It will help."

Ruben is in awe. "Mother, where did you get this?" A trade would allow him to buy substantial material for a ship.

Sancia explains everything. Ruben already knew about the man who made the candlestick holders, but he did not know of the secret they held.

Sancia continues, "Until now we had no use on this island for gold. I almost forgot that we had it. When I took Baltasar's gift from Spain, I did not even know I had the gold with me. He wrote a message for me to take into exile. He did not know how to write, yet he managed to think of a clever way to get his message to me after I would pass through the border and would not be in danger." She then goes into her room and returns with the paper Baltasar gave to her all those years ago. It's worn and faded. But its illustrations are still visible. She hands it to Ruben so that he and Marina can look at it together.

Then Marina holds it with both hands. "The gold was in the candlestick holders all this time?"

Sancia nods. She then picks up one of the candlestick holders and twists the top. She opens it. "He crafted them himself out of bronze, a metal that the king and queen did not

prohibit us from taking. He hallowed out a secret compartment. This is the other bit of melted jewelry." Sancia holds
out the gold with the small emerald melded to it. "It is from
your grandmother's brooch and wedding band. Save it until
you need it, until you know it is right. That one piece of gold
should be enough to contribute to the buying of a ship sturdy
enough for your journey." Sancia gently takes the paper from
Marina. "When I roll this up, it fits inside the space the gold
once occupied." His mother is suggesting they use that space
and the paper for a message. He knew she would find a way
to comfort Marina. And him. Ruben watches as she hands
the candlestick holders and the gold to the mother of her
grandchildren and kisses her on the cheek.

Marina unravels the paper with its illustrations, turns
it over, and writes on it a message to her beloved.

Ruben and Pedro put together a crew of sixteen others.

The two men approach the nearly completed ship.
Pedro stops before they get closer. "The ship needs a name."

"It already has a name." Ruben holds out the folded
final sail.

Pedro glides his hand along the fabric. "I am grateful
that your mother helped so much with these."

Ruben brings the sail to his chest. "She seemed happy
to make them, especially this last one."

He and Pedro ask for help from the others to hoist the
mainsail. Once they attach it, the men climb down and distance themselves just enough to be able to see the ship in

its entirety. It's beautiful and sturdy. But, it's the final sail, with deep-indigo lettering, that fills Ruben's spirit with a sense of security.

Pedro reads, "Baltasar?"

Ruben continues staring ahead at the sail. "Yes. That's our ship. The *Baltasar*."

The small boat that will ferry Ruben to the *Baltasar* is at the edge of the shore. His heart aches as he bids farewell to his family. He kneels to his children. "I cannot wait to tell you stories about my adventures when I return. Come closer my loves." And he holds them all. *I do not know how I will be able to be away from you for so long.*

He then puts his arms around his mother. At the end of their embrace, she moves the children away, leaving Marina and Ruben to a private farewell.

Ruben takes Marina's hand. "You know that Pedro got word to his relatives in Morocco to look out for us. We will be safe. I am going to be back."

Marina's eyes water. "I know. And I'll be waiting for your return. Go find our people in Morocco and then our people in Jerusalem. Tell them about us. And then tell me about them, especially those who have sustained our unbreakable bond to Jerusalem."

"We have all done that – sustained our unbreakable bond to Jerusalem. Some of us just did it from there. We have done it from here."

Marina smiles through her tears. She then hands a

pouch to Ruben. "You must be careful lighting the candles on the ship."

Ruben looks inside and sees the candlestick holder and enough wax for a lighting once a week for eighteen weeks. "I only plan to be gone for sixteen weeks."

"I know. It's *chai*. Life. We will light the rest together. After you return." She then removes the top of his candlestick holder and tilts it to let a rolled piece of paper slide out.

Ruben gently unravels it. "You wrote this in Hebrew."

She smiles and nods. "It is our language. Your mother taught me well."

He reads aloud. *"Wherever you are in the world, you will be with me and you will bring in the Sabbath with our family. When the sun sets on Santiago, we will light together, you there and I here. When you return, we will stop running and stop searching, for once we are together again we will be home. Our flame will be bright when the candlesticks unite."*

Ruben does not want to leave. He brings his wife close and holds her tightly. "I love you." He then rolls the paper and returns it to the compartment in his candlestick holder. He picks up the small bag he packed and takes the pouch that Marina gave to him. "Everything else is on board."

"I know. You have been working so hard these past few days. I have missed you before you have even left."

He kisses her as he did the first time under the see-through roof of their first sukkah. He squeezes her hand with just enough restraint to hold back tears, and then makes his way toward the *Baltasar*.

Ruben uses Abraham Zacuto's almanac to know when it is sunset in Santiago every Friday. Each week he retreats to a quiet spot below deck, away from the wind, and he lights the candle while knowing his wife is saying the same prayer at the same time. Because of the danger of letting the candle burn on a wooden ship, he blows it out after a couple of minutes. Nonetheless, he lights it dutifully and lovingly.

In Morocco, Pedro's cousin, along with some men he gathered for the journey, boards the *Baltasar*. As soon as they all set sail, the newcomers explain that the weight of living under the oppressive rule of Muhammadans who conquered the native Berbers and ancient Jews of Morocco centuries ago, makes them more concerned about the idea of living under the Ottomans and the lands those Muhammadans conquered. Yet, after contemplating the Inquisition and the destruction by the Christians, the men maintain course. Maybe they will find more strength with more Jews in the land developed by their ancestors. On the way to the Holy Land, the men exchange stories of family well-being. Pedro's cousin tells of how thousands of their brethren escaping persecution from Spain, fared. He tells them about the gangs waiting to attack the Jewish exiles on their way to Fez. "With a look at the past, it makes sense we would have had such difficulties. The Muhammadans, who conquered Morocco, killed more Jews in Fez during the Massacre of 1033 than the Muhammadans killed Jews near where you are from, in Granada, three decades later. Yet, as a young boy, I had no idea how lucky I was when we got to Morocco in 1492. We already had family we could live with. Of course, we were confined to the mellah, or would have to face violence. But we were not exposed to the harsh climate, wild animals, and lack of food like too many of our brethren. So many have perished soon after the expulsion. There is still endless heartache. That is why we are joining you."

Ruben is grateful that their journey is smooth and the sky is clear. He tells stories about the Spanish colony of Santiago, where he now lives, the Admiral Cristoforo Colombo, Fernando, and Diego. He talks about his family and the new Jewish settlers who arrived the year before on the ship that brought Pedro. Ruben finds a new strength in these men, strength he will need when, in the vast ocean, where there is plenty of room for travel, he spots another ship aggressively getting too close to them.

He panics as he becomes certain they're being pursued by pirates. How could they not have been prepared to fight? They have sailors, a physician, navigators, interpreters, blacksmiths, woodsmen, and traders. But no soldiers.

While Ruben and the others focus on the large ship speeding alongside them, men climb aboard from a previously unnoticed small boat. Four pirates aim weapons at the crew — three with muskets and one with a rapier. Ruben says something in Hebrew so that just his crew will understand.

The pirate holding the rapier speaks Hebrew. "Where are you from and what is your destination?"

Ruben is surprised. "You are Jewish?"

"No. But I often ride the sea with Sinan Reis whose Hebrew name is Ciphut Sinan." He lowers the rapier. "Have you not heard of him? He is the Jewish pirate who fought alongside Hayreddin Barbarossa, the famed Ottoman admiral."

"Are you saying that you are an Ottoman pirate who works with a Jewish pirate?" Ruben's fear turns into confusion. *Why am I focusing on clarification when I should be focusing on escaping?*

The pirate keeps his weapon lowered. "Why not? He and I also served in Suleiman the Magnificent's navy against your worst enemies of Spain and Portugal. Sinan has enjoyed a good life with us." And then he smiles. "Would you like to give it a try?"

"To be pirates?" Ruben asks.

The pirate finally tucks his rapier into a sheath. "Why not?"

Us be pirates? He cannot be serious. "We have families waiting for us. We want to return to them after we make it to the Holy Land."

The Hebrew-speaking pirate looks at his crew watching this interaction from his ship. Then he says something in an unfamiliar language that causes the other three pirates, standing on the *Baltasar*, to burst into laughter. Ruben soon realizes they have other plans.

Marina sits on the shore during low tide. She knows something is wrong. Has she been losing her mind? *No.* She knows what she felt. She knows that each Sabbath, while her beloved was at sea, she lit one wick, but felt the heat from two flames. She tested her senses midweek when she placed a candle inside of the candlestick holder, and lit the wick. *I know I only felt the heat of one flame that day, midweek, but every time I lit one candle on the Sabbath, when Ruben would be lighting, I would feel the heat of two flames. His and mine. I know I did. Until I didn't.* The realization fills her with dread.

The lapping of the waves lulls her to sleep until the tide comes in and rouses her. But Marina isn't sure whether she is awake or dreaming. She stands and backs away from the waterline. Something catches her eyes, on the horizon, in the moonlight. The silhouette in the distance looks like the *Baltasar. But they are not due back for a couple of months.* There must be hundreds of ships that look the same from that far away. Perhaps there is no ship and she really is losing her mind.

Her eyes lock on the vessel as it approaches the island.

Just before dawn, the ship anchors. As the sun rises, she sees the mainsail. It's the *Baltasar.* They're here! Why are they here now? Why didn't she feel the extra warmth? What if Ruben isn't on the ship? Her mind becomes a spinning mess of questions, speculation, and worry.

She is overwhelmed with relief as Ruben steps onto the shore. She crashes into his arms. They collapse into tears. Then Marina wipes her tears away. "You are back early. What happened?"

Ruben tells her of his voyage.

"So you never made it?"

He shakes his head. He goes into detail about their encounter with pirates. "There is war brewing on the waters from the Kingdom of Spain to the Holy Land. Even if Jerusalem is safe for us, getting there will not be. We were fortunate to be intercepted by pirates who only stole from us. One spoke Hebrew and he let us go. It could have been worse."

Marina looks at her hands, making sense of the varying heat sensation. She looks at Ruben. "They took the candlestick holder – almost three weeks ago?"

He nods sorrowfully. "Until they stole it, I lit it every Sabbath. It kept me with you even when it was not lit."

Marina exhales a sigh of relief. "They did not take you. You are safely here. That is all that matters to me."

Marina and Ruben go home, where he tells his family about his ordeal. "And there are even Jewish pirates. They attack Spanish ships to try to redistribute the treasures that were stolen from the Jews, back to the Jews. There are some important changes about to take place, but for now, we will do what we can to keep this island safe, to keep this island home."

Prior to Departure

———⟨◆⟩———

Out of habit, I reach for the spot on my neck where the locket once rested. It's still not there. The days go by and work goes on. Each day, newly excavated material is brought into the museum. Each day, I prepare them for additional steps. Each day, I still hope my candlestick holder will be among them.

Ben walks in with his husband. I haven't seen Guy since he and Ben got married in New York about four years ago. He washed out his charming gray for an equally charming brown. I jump up to hug him. "I'm so happy to see you."

"Hm. I don't recall you being that excited to see *me*." Ben makes a face at me.

"Oh knock it off Ben. You know this girl adores you." Guy then steps back and adjusts his glasses. "Abi, I'm so happy to see you too."

I can't wait to tell them what I've uncovered. "Gentlemen, we struck gold! Well, silver actually, with the discovery of some *reales*, *maravedís*, and *pesos de ocho*, the famous pieces of eight, otherwise known as Spanish dollars." These are not only impressive artifacts in and of themselves, they help tremendously with homing in on the location and date that the ship likely left its last port, and they offer hints about the people who were on it. "Despite the corrosion, we can see enough detail for proper identification." I explain where the *reales* and the *maravedís* were discovered on the ship as I point to the corresponding location on the grid hanging by my work space. "I'm still waiting to learn what other items were found in the area to piece together some answers, or some questions for that matter. My first guess is that they came from the pocket of a passenger or crew member. Unlike those *maravedís* and *reales*, however, these Spanish dollars weren't randomly scattered on an area primarily occupied by the passengers. They were found in a pile among the cargo. There would have been a cloth bag holding each pile together, until they disintegrated and got washed away with the current, leaving behind some of their contents, buried under the weight of sea growth."

Guy closely looks at the Spanish dollar I handed to him. "Money is a talker."

It is. "The ship may have been built in Spain and originated in Spain, as the wood would indicate, though the room for error in dating decomposed wood is somewhat large. In any case, the cargo gives a hint to the time period, which may not be totally different from Moshe's guess— though, of course, may not quite be within his poetic guess, either." I remind Ben of the week that didn't exist during the calendar change. "Spanish dollars were often manufactured in the New World and then transported to Spain. A large amount found together indicates that this money was likely intended for first circulation elsewhere, probably after being produced in a New World factory. The first factories of that kind started with the Mexican Mint, established in 1535, so the ship's last voyage began at least after that date. It's likely that people on the ship were either responsible for getting that currency to Spain, or they stole it and intended to keep it — hiding it with the cargo. Pirates often targeted ships that transported coins. It's possible that the ship became a pirate ship after being commandeered by them."

"Excellent, Abi." Ben holds up a coin and then hands it back to me. "Don't stay too late. It's Shabbat. Guy and I are going to enjoy the rest of the day, and you should too."

I deserve to enjoy the evening with Annette. I've accomplished a lot at work. I've impressed Guy and pleased Ben. I'm getting closer to answers about the ship.

I head back to the apartment, stopping at a store along the way to pick up groceries. As soon as I get home, I begin making dinner. I get satisfaction seeing Annette admiring the aroma of minestrone. I look over at the table where I laid out salad, fresh challah, and seasoned olive oil. What else could we need? *Wine of course.* "White or red?"

"White. And with a tall glass of water." Annette answers as she heads into her room to change out of her work clothes. She reappears with pajamas.

She looks so comfortable. I should've changed too. Too late. Too hungry.

"How are you doing?" She walks up to me and gives me a hug.

"Not bad."

"Not bad is not good, either."

Since when are you a pessimist?

She sits at the table. "I'm so glad that you're with me tonight and that we're able to spend a little more time together. I've been looking forward to catching up with you, even though I know you probably wish you were with your friend."

"Ari?" I question with the nonchalance I'm trying to sell to her. "Naw. I think I haven't even talked to him in over a week."

"Abi, today is Friday. You saw him Sunday when you lost your necklace. It hasn't even been a week."

I try to mask that disappointment with my other disappointment. "No leads on my necklace." I ladle soup into two bowls and muster up an optimistic tone to tell her a little about the developments at work. "Spanish dollars—"

"Oh, Abi, stop the pretense! It's so obvious you miss him."

I place the bowls on the table. "Excuse me?"

"You know exactly what I'm talking about!"

"Annette, I'm married!"

She sits back in her chair, extends her arm and points at me with an obnoxious smile. "Ha. So, you do know what I'm talking about!"

I snarl. "Bravo." *What a bitch.* "So how does that change anything? I'm *happily* married." And I want to keep it that way!

She holds my gaze. "But you're in love with another guy."

The rules of love are the opposite the rules of the birth-day wish. Love can be denied until it's announced — even an uninvited announcement by an observer. I just stare at her in disbelief. I have nothing to say.

"You didn't do anything wrong. I'm hungry." She then casually rips a piece of challah from the loaf. "Do you mind if I start eating before prayers?"

"I didn't do anything wrong because I didn't do *any-thing*!" And now I'm not in the mood to eat.

"I know." She takes a bite while I silently stare at her. "I also know that you were crying before you realized that you lost your necklace."

I lean back in my chair and fold my arms across my chest. "Do you want a trophy?"

"I love you, Abi. Your happiness is my reward. I want you to be happy."

I pick up a spoon and start playing with my soup. "I am happy. I love my family and my marriage of fifteen years."

"Yoni was married for fifteen years, mostly happily, when we started dating."

"He just got divorced?"

She shakes her head. "He isn't divorced." Then she casually takes a sip of soup. "Hm. This is delicious Abi." She continues eating like this is a normal conversation. "He's married."

"Yoni is married?"

She nods with her mouth full. And then she says, "Yes. Happily."

"To someone else?" Of course, to someone else. I know Annette is not married.

"Yes." Her eyes light up. "It's a brilliant setup actually—one that saved his marriage."

So, this is what I get when I examine life above the surface instead of trying to decode artifacts. And now I'm more confused than ever. "Dating people outside his marriage, saved his marriage?"

"I certainly don't think it's a good way to start a marriage. But I think it's something to think about when trying to save one." Marriage was never for Annette — always a free spirit. "Who knows. There is no right answer in navigating relationships. There are lots of laws and rules, but no singular right answer. Monogamy can become suffocating. Cheating is cheating. Open marriage is a settlement between the two, and even that can get messy."

Evan that? "So, Yoni has an open marriage? He is dating other people? Are you also dating someone else?"

"We don't talk about other romantic relationships. I don't think he is seeing anyone else. He spends a lot of time with me, and he does have a family that he is dedicated to. Like you, he has been married for fifteen years. I think this has been a thing with him and his wife for a little over two years. I don't see anyone else, because no one else has interested me." She takes a sip of wine and smiles. "Although, if Hillel Neuer weren't so geographically undesirable . . ."

"How could you not have mentioned this to me before?"

She tilts her head as if she is confused by my question. "What? My crush on Hillel?"

My eyes pierce her.

She places her elbows on the table and leans toward me. "Because I knew this would be your reaction. I didn't want to deal with your judgement, Abi. But now I realize that I don't want to deal with your sadness caused by restrictions that might not be right for you and Daniel anymore." She pauses in thought. "Look, different people appeal to a different part of who we are. If it were easy to ignore that, there wouldn't be so many rules and restrictions enforcing monogamy. Think about how many marriages could maybe be saved if partners could recognize that when they find an interest in someone else, it isn't because they made some wrong choice decades or even just years before, it's because their interest has been piqued by someone new. We're designed to be interested in more than one person. How else could our species survive? Societies have expectations as to how people should behave within relationships to keep a sense of order. The sense of order doesn't have to entirely collapse because we are wired in ways that contradict expectations."

She has a point, but the idea makes me squeamish. "Do you really think someone can be devoted to another while nourishing multiple relationships?"

She lifts her shoulders. "I'm guessing for quality there has to be some kind of limit. But otherwise, I think so. I don't doubt Yoni's devotion to his wife nor to me. You can love more than one person. You and Daniel do go way back. Haven't you ever thought of anyone else?"

"In my imagination, not for consideration. I couldn't be

with more than one person at once. I don't know if I could really be with anyone but Daniel. I don't think it's for me. And really, Ari is not for me. I don't know enough about him."

"What you know, you like."

"But there's so much I don't know."

"So, get to. You already know Daniel. He already knows you. Discover someone new. Be discovered by someone new. I see you've already been doing that, and you've been glowing. I want you to keep your marriage strong and your spirit alive."

"And you think the answer is an open marriage?"

"Technically it's referred to as consensual non-monogamy . . ."

I shrug off the label. "It's not right."

"It is if you say it is. You can see what Daniel has to say. He might like the idea."

I can feel my face tighten. "He would hate it."

"How do you know?"

"Ari might hate it."

"He knows you are married. You show no signs of eroding your family." She is right about that.

"Until you decided to flush all this out." I'm so irritated with her.

"When structures are too rigid, whether they are buildings, belief systems or emotions, they break. When they're built with flexibility, they become sustainable. I want what you and Daniel have to be sustainable. I also want you to be honest with yourself, if not with me, that you like Ari."

"I like him. That doesn't mean I need to act on anything.

I'm fine. I'm practical. My priorities are with my kids and my husband." I stand up out of my chair and walk to the cabinet to get another bottle. It's Friday. No work tomorrow. I start with my own glass and then offer to pour a glass for Annette. "Port?"

Ben asks if I got a note from Zahava.

I just walked in — give me a moment for heaven's sake. "I didn't check my messages over the weekend. Let me start my computer."

Apparently, he can't wait. "Well, she says they detected new objects below the seafloor using a metal detector. Very exciting. They tried to dig for them, but the sediment created too much of a cloud. They're hoping that next week there will be a current more conducive to clearing away the disturbed debris."

They'll find my candlestick holder! How exciting — and how agonizing. "Ben, next week is my last week." I can't believe a month is almost gone. I'm tempted to extend my stay. I want to be here when they bring my ancestors' candlestick holder up. But, I would feel too guilty extending my stay, knowing it's really just to nurture my dream. Plus, I really miss home.

"You'll be back, Abi. I need you here."

Do you? "Thanks, Ben. I'm so grateful to you. You have no idea."

My phone signals it received a text. *Must be Zahava to give me the exciting and disappointing news.* I fish it out of my purse. "It's Ari. He is in the lobby and wants me to meet him." *Don't make me say goodbye to you again.*

Ben makes a scooting motion with his hands.

"My computer just turned on."

"Go!"

I meet Ari in the lobby of the museum.

"Hi." His tone is urgent. "Let's go."

"Go where? I'm leaving in a week, Ari."

"Just come with me."

I walk out with him and he then opens the passenger-side door of his car and closes it once I'm inside. He then runs around to get into the driver's seat.

I buckle up. "What is this all about?"

"I'll explain when we get there."

"Get where?"

He shrugs and shifts into drive. Neither of us talk. No tension, just quiet.

He parks. "It is about a block away."

I don't bother asking *what is about a block away.*

We walk until we reach a shop with a sign indicating that it specializes in custom-designed jewelry—*creation and repair.* Oh my gosh. He is so thoughtful. I realize immediately what he is up to. "Ari, this is so sweet. But the locket can't be duplicated no matter how gifted this jeweler. It was just so unique. I don't have a picture of it. I couldn't even describe it. No amount of consulting will. The detail of the design, the touch from my parents . . ."

He opens the door to the shop. "Just come in with me, please."

A man with a white beard, yarmulke and a thick Hebrew accent, greets us. "Ari, it is so nice to see you." He then reaches to shake my hand. "And you must be Abi. I've been looking forward to meeting you."

Ari finishes the introduction. "And Abi, this is Tomer."

Tomer walks behind the jewelry counter and sinks below the display case. "Abi, I have something that is yours, and I believe that you have something that is mine."

Well, this is cryptic.

He re-emerges to hand Ari a small brown envelope and places a mirror on the counter within my reach. Ari then motions for me to look into the mirror. I don't. Instead, I watch as he pours the contents of the envelope into his hand. He quickly hides from view what he is holding and again motions for me to look into the mirror. I do. He then reaches around my neck. I see it before he finishes the clasp. I touch . . . my locket!

How can I thank him, them, without bursting into tears? I keep my mouth closed so that the floodgates remain locked. I feel my eyes glisten. *Please understand my gratitude.* I continue looking in the mirror, not to look at the locket I've so longed to see and thought was gone forever, but simply to avoid letting my eyes meet Ari's.

A brief attempt. He peers into the mirror to speak to me with his eyes.

Tomer breaks the silence. "The original chain was worn too thin. It wasn't reparable. I had to replace it." And then he hands an envelope to me. "This is what is left of it."

I place my hand on Tomer's as a gesture of thanks. I then move my hand to take the envelope that he holds out to me.

Ari turns me toward him. He takes both of my hands into his. "There is something else."

"How did you find it?" I manage to ask, before saying *thank you.*

Ari lets go of my hands so that he can talk with his. "The morning after you lost it, I put out a call to all of the kids to help."

I touch my locket. "But it wasn't on the soccer field. I had it on after dinner. Remember, I showed it to you during the walk home."

He nods. "I remember. I had the kids scour the city. I gave them the parameters."

"You're kidding. And they did? They scoured the city for me?"

Ari nods and smiles. "They like you a lot. Well, and I promised them a pizza party after the search party."

I laugh a little. "And one of those kids found it?"

"Mazen. Do you remember him?"

I nod. I do remember the bright soccer star with the warm grin.

Ari points to the envelope. "The chain was broken, and so I brought it to Tomer to replace and to see if he could repair your locket, which was broken too. Someone might have stepped on it. It was twisted and wouldn't clasp quite right."

"Did you look inside of it?" I don't know why I still care. The question was a little rude.

He shakes his head. "I wanted to honor your wish to keep it a secret. I brought it to Tomer without looking inside of it."

"Until I asked him to." Tomer seems giddy at a potential clash. "It looks a little different now. When you open it, you'll see. It looks better now."

I liked it the way it was. It was perfect as it was. A photo of my heirloom, the bronze candlestick holder posed on a black velvet cloth. That's all I want in there—well, until I find its match and take a picture of that to slip into the empty space.

Ari unclasps the new chain from around my neck and places my necklace on a felt pad. He instructs me to open the locket.

I do. How odd. They duplicated the photo and placed its identical counterpart on the other side. It must have been obvious to Ari what I would have wanted to put in there. That's somewhat of a clever joke. I'm not thrilled. But at least they didn't damage the original photo. They just duplicated it. I have to applaud their efforts. "This is good. I'm impressed. How did you manage to make such a flawless copy of my tiny old photo?"

Ari clasps my hands. He turns me to face him. "Well, we didn't."

"Yes you did! I see it right here. It's an impressive duplicate."

He shakes his head.

I conduct a mental replay of our exchange:

Me: "How did you manage to make such a flawless copy of my tiny old photo?"

Him: "Well, we didn't."

Of course they made a copy. It's the same exact picture.

I look at it again. *Wait! It can't be! This isn't a copy.* "This isn't a copy?"

Ari shakes his head.

"Impossible."

Ari reaches for the magnifying glass sitting on the counter and holds it a couple of inches over my open locket. I see it — the slightly different coloration in the bronze and the tear in the black fabric supporting the candlestick holder where mine had none.

I look at Ari and state what he has known all along. "It's not a duplicate."

His lashes flutter and his eyes glisten. "It's the match."

I can't breathe—but it's a good *can't breathe.* The men take turns telling me the series of events: How Ari came to bring the necklace into the shop, and how Tomer fiddled with the locket and saw the picture. How he stopped in his tracks and then turned to his jewelry archives to find the candlestick holder that looked like the one in the locket. He took a photo of it for an apples-to-apples comparison, and then he reported back to Ari. "Well, that's my story," Tomer says. "It seems to me that you might also have an interesting story to share."

How did the other candlestick holder end up in Tel Aviv – so far away from its match? "How did you get it?"

"After you," Tomer insists.

Fair enough. I fill him in on the parts I already told Ari about my ancestry, and about how I received the candlestick holder as a gift before my bat mitzvah ceremony. I point to the hidden seam at the top of the piece. "It separates here. Mine has a hidden compartment that holds a stick of gold and an emerald. It seems it was smuggled out of Spain with the candlestick holders."

"That is remarkable." Tomer then points to framed photographs on the wall behind him. "I come from a family of goldsmiths, jewelers, and merchants. I cannot hold on to too much over sentimental value, or I'll have no business. I need to try to sell everything. So, I fix, or I buy, or I make and then I sell. I inherited many items from my parents, who owned this store, and from my father's parents and his grandparents, who owned a variation of this store in Jerusalem. Most everything sells quickly, but this candlestick holder didn't sell. My parents tried to sell it, their parents tried to sell it, and by the time it was my turn to take over the family business, it was the only piece I choose to keep."

"Is it because of what's inside of it?" I ask.

Tomer shakes his head. "No. I actually did not know of the compartment until you pointed it out. And I cannot tell you enough how much I've valued the artistry of this piece. How did I miss that seam?" He continues with his story. "My grandfather told me that it was retrieved from a damaged Ottoman pirate ship before it sank. His grandfather told him. Someone from our family, generations ago, bought it from the salvagers. It's a memorable story because legend has it that one of the pirates spoke Hebrew. Imagine, a Hebrew-speaking pirate. Fishermen on a boat nearby allowed the passengers of the sinking ship to climb on board their vessel. I'm not sure if they realized they were pirates when they invited them, but they did soon enough. The pirates were saved, and the salvagers sold their goods. My ancestors paid a single price in exchange for a large bag of items, only to sort through them later. The candlestick holder seems to have been the only item that didn't sell."

Was I a descendent of pirates? "So, you are not a descendent of the man who . . .?"

Tomer shakes his head. "You and I are not related, though clearly we are connected. You, Abi, are the descendant of the people who had this before the ship got in trouble. This does leave the question of ownership to be a rather sticky one. Abi, until you told me about your story, I didn't even notice that the design was as complex as it is. I pride myself at being a skilled jeweler, but I missed that." He bends below the counter. I brace myself for the event I've been anticipating for my entire adult life. He resurfaces with the item I've never seen before yet whose image has been embossed into my memory for almost a quarter of a century. "Will you do the honor of opening it?"

Oh my gosh! Yes! Yes! Yes! Why am I crying again? I nod and motion for him to wait a moment. He places the candlestick holder on a felt pad on the counter. I pick it up. "Thank you, Tomer. Just looking at it, just holding it, just knowing that it really exists means so much to me." I pick up the cloth and the solution that he placed next to the candlestick holder. And then I lubricate the seam in the metal. Something is not quite right. "Are you sure no one opened this?"

He tilts his head and lifts his shoulders. "Most certainly. If they did, no one ever told me about it."

I hold it out on my palm. "I can tell you right now that it weighs slightly less than the one I have at home, with the gold inside of it."

Ari looks surprised. "You can remember the feel of that small a difference?"

"I'm a trained archaeologist, and this has been my focal point."

I twist off the top of the candlestick holder and look inside. As I suspected, there is no gold. But, it's not empty, either. I tilt it in Tomer's direction and then I ask him for permission to remove a tiny rolled scroll of paper. He nods. He then hands me a pair of cotton gloves. I pull out the scroll and unravel it. "I can see writing." I lay it on the felt cloth on the counter. I let it curl into its natural position. That scroll holds a message from my ancestors. I'm eavesdropping on their correspondence. My eyes water. With the back of my cotton gloves, I wipe away my tears.

Ari places his arm over my shoulder.

I nuzzle against him. "Help me do this."

He gives my shoulders a squeeze and smiles. "Don't get the note wet. You won't be able to read it." He makes me smile.

Tomer hands him a pair of cotton gloves. He puts them on and then he carefully unfurls the scroll. "It's in Hebrew."

The writing is light brown from ink that has faded with time and is blended with images from illustrations on the back of the paper, also faded. The words are difficult to read but intact and legible.

Ari reads aloud in Hebrew and then translates:

"'Wherever you are in the world, you will be with me and you will bring in the Sabbath with our family. When the sun sets on Santiago, we will light together, you there and I here. When you return, we will stop running and stop searching, for once we are together again we will be home. Our flame will be bright when the candlesticks unite.'"

"So much love and so much pain." I again use the back of my cotton gloves to wipe my eyes — and my nose. *A little gross and embarrassing.*

Ari points to the last word.

"It is signed 'Marina.'" I sniffle again. I know Hebrew well enough to read her name. "That's such a beautiful name."

Tomer hands a tissue to me. "Where is Santiago?"

That's a good question. "I'm not exactly sure. Chile, maybe?"

Tomer suggests I take a picture of the note. Then he puts on a pair of cotton gloves and proceeds to roll the scroll up and place it back inside the hollowed-out space in the candlestick holder. And then, with what appears to be a change of heart, he insists I take the piece for the week. His trust and generosity are unbelievable.

I'm deeply touched. "Thank you."

"And now, not to forget what brought you here." Tomer

then picks up my necklace from the felt pad and motions for me to turn around so that he can clasp it around my neck. "It truly is a beautiful piece."

I turn back overwhelmed by my instant kinship with this stranger. "Thank you, Tomer, for everything."

"Yes," he says aloud to himself. He then looks at Ari. "No charge."

"Are you sure?" Ari asks.

"I would be insulted if you suggest otherwise."

I lean up over the counter to give Tomer a kiss on the cheek. Ari shakes his hand and then we walk back to the car. At this hour, it makes little sense for me to return to work, so I ask him to take me back home. Annette will not be home yet. I want to invite him into the apartment but know that would not be a good idea. Always practical. But it's okay. Ari's friendship is significant. Maybe fateful. And of course, it all comes together. He was born on December 16th of 1968, the day Spain officially stopped criminalizing Judaism. I certainly won't forget his birthday.

He stops the car by my building. After I close the car door, I thank him through the open window.

He looks at me from the driver's seat. "I hope to see you before you go back home."

I can't leave Israel without seeing him again — maybe a drink, maybe coffee in the next couple of days. Otherwise, it just wouldn't feel right. I tell him I'm going to research the details of the note and update him on any new information. I walk around to the driver's side. His window is open. I lean and kiss him on the cheek before saying goodbye.

Nunu approaches me in the courtyard. I scoop her up and carry her inside. I give her a treat and prepare dinner.

Annette walks into the kitchen just as I'm about to take out a casserole to cool. I haven't called to tell her about what happened today. I've been wanting to tell her in person.

She inhales pleasurably. "It smells great in here!"

I turn to her and smile a big smile.

"And you're in a good mood," She says.

"I am." I suppress my impulse to explode—the happiest of explosions. "I had a really good day today." *Oh, come on, Annette! My locket is staring you straight in the eyes. I can feel it.* I know she can, too, and I'm not fooled for a minute when she says, "You found it! A new hair style just right for you! I noticed right away there was something different."

I take off one of my oven mitts and throw it at her.

She catches it and gives me a hug. "How in the world . . . ?"

I tell her everything, even the mundane details, so that I can relive it all.

"So, that's what has been in your locket all this time." She seems almost sad. "Your candlestick holder is not reunited with its match. You are, but it belongs to someone else." She actually seems more disappointed than I am.

I think about the lovely man who it does belong to. "It's okay." It really is.

After we finish eating, I start to clear the table and clean the kitchen.

She stops me. "I'm going to do this. You have research to do. Go!"

I kiss her on the cheek before running off to dig

through some old PDFs that I've saved from the relevant time period. I browse different internet sites. Alas, the emotion of the day gets to me. I call my mother and tell her everything.

All this time I was right. I knew this was a set. I had doubt, but I knew. Here, I found it, or it found me, thousands of miles from home. Staring at it doesn't tell me enough. How do I feel about holding my family heirloom knowing it belongs to someone else? My thoughts stray. How do I feel about Ari? I do have feelings for him. He is remarkable. And the chemistry between us. How can I not? I can't focus. I have to turn in for the night.

I wake up feeling refreshed. I can't wait to go to work to tell Ben the whole story and relive it again. I sit at my desk and Ben sits at his.

He looks up at me while leaning back in his chair and fidgeting with a pencil. "I wonder if *El Carrillo* is the ship that your ancestor was on before finding safety in Israel. Zahava did say that most of the items were found in the storage compartment, not where the bunks were. The bunks were mostly empty. That could be because items on the higher levels were tossed about when the ship was going down —"

I know where he is going with this. "Or they were carried off by survivors and salvagers who grabbed whatever they could before escaping the sinking ship."

Ben nods, confirming I followed his train of thought.

I'm not sure if either of those are right, though. "Maybe. My ancestor might have been on this ship."

"Thank goodness!" Ben says emphatically with playfulness in his voice. "Or you would have lost interest in your job."

"Never, Ben. I'm sad that my first phase with it is coming to an end."

He picks up his briefcase. "I'm not staying today. I just wanted to stop in to see how you were doing. You left so quickly yesterday. I'm going to get ready for Shabbat. Guy has invited some friends over for dinner tonight." He kisses my forehead and orders me not to stay too long.

"Shabbat Shalom, Ben."

"You too, dear."

After I finish up for the day, I walk to the store and buy some food, including challah, for tonight's Shabbat dinner. Yoni is going to join us. This will be the first time I'll see him since learning about his marriage. I thought it would be awkward, but now I'm not sure. Nothing has changed except my new knowledge.

We cook this Shabbat meal together. We talk, we laugh, we eat, and the evening blurs. Several evenings blur. I have what I've been searching for all these years. Despite the statistical unlikelihood that I would find it, I found it. Or it found me. Now I'm left thinking over the note, the story, and the bits of history that might have driven the two lovers apart.

My last day of work. My last day, for now, of puzzling over the artifacts of *El Carrillo*. And puzzling over this empty feeling that's been plaguing me. I pick up my family heirloom, on loan. I marvel at it. I trace its lines and details with my fingers. It represents ingenuity, perseverance, and love.

The magic from this wondrous reality doesn't allow me to escape a painfully deep ache, an ache that intensifies the more I try to occupy my thoughts with my curiosities.

My family is a blessing. My cousin, my boss, my job, my life experiences . . . I'm so blessed. But blessings are not without their responsibilities. They are bestowed upon us, and they often come with caveats. I laugh to myself because I realize that no one knows this more than the Israelis do. *Blessings are loaded.*

I can no longer fight the blessing that is Ari. I'm leaving in two days and I cannot leave without him.

My heart races as I think I might have thrown the envelope away. No, I'm certain I didn't. I dig through my purse and find what I'm looking for: the envelope that held my locket. It's in Hebrew, but I can still make out his address.

I leave work and take the bus to my usual stop. But I don't walk toward Annette's. I walk toward Ari's. I've been too distant from him—grateful but distant. And now I need to just be in his presence. I walk past the end of Rothschild Boulevard, and past the very non-vegetarian restaurant, A Place for Meat. I walk by Cafe Suzana, where we first had dinner. I glance at the top of the majestic tree that stands over the diners on the porch below. I walk further down the street. I stop to look at the map on my smartphone. I continue walking until I come to Ari's building. I knock. *I can't believe I just knocked. What if he opens the door?*

He opens the door.

I wave. "Hello."

"Hello." He opens the door a little wider. "And what have I done to deserve this visit? —Other than finding, with ease and speed, an object you've been combing the world for, for years and years. Did I mention with ease and speed?"

What have *I* done to deserve this visit? "Don't go tooting your own horn, Ari. I already thanked you for what you've done. I'm not here for that."

"Oh?"

I'm here because I'm in love with you. "I'm here because you lost."

He looks at me with his hand gripping around the edge of the opened door. He is blocking the entrance. "What?" He then motions for me to step inside.

"When we played soccer the first time — you lost. Badly. You took a risk and agreed to a bet. You placed your bet and you lost the game. You lost your shirt."

He closes the door behind me. "Abi, I treated you for dinner that night. It was my pleasure, but it was also my payment."

I purse my lips and furrow my eyebrows. I fold my arms across my chest. "Dinner was lovely, and as much as I appreciated it, we didn't gamble on dinner that afternoon. A bet is a bet, and you lost your shirt. That is what we gambled, and that is what I want."

"How sweet. I'm so touched. You want a token of me to

take home with you. Okay . . . you want that football jersey? It's dirty. I played earlier this week, and I didn't get around to washing it. It's still in the basket. It might smell bad, but I wouldn't know." He smiles and then points to his nose to remind me of his sensory disorder. He is so cute. "I'll go and dig out that artifact. I'll be right back."

I pull on his partially untucked shirt as he starts to walk away. I stop him. I muster up all the courage I have. I take a step closer, completely closing the space between us. "This shirt." I hold his stare and tug on the overlap hanging out haphazardly from the front of his jeans. I whisper, "I want this one."

His face softens. My fingers reverse his shirt button right above his waistline. He brings his hand up to support my chin as he draws himself even closer to me. His lips press against mine. I finish working my way through the rest of the buttons of his shirt. We move to his room.

He pauses to ask me if I'm sure. I nod. He was a part of me before I became aware of his existence. The sun offers just enough light through the closed window shades. I'm unaware of the outside world. I'm lost in him. We linger. And it all feels so right. I would love to stay and fall asleep, but I know I need to go. Ari gives me a ride back home. We agree to meet the next day, at the jeweler's, to return the candlestick holder.

I spend the early morning of my last full day in a cafe and make use of their WiFi. I sip coffee and savor the moment. I enjoy being alone—well, surrounded by people who speak a language that I haven't mastered. I don't feel lonely because there's too much chatter, and yet I don't feel distracted, as I can't understand conversations at the speed that they go. The background becomes soft noise, quiet music, created by people who are engaged with each other. It's my own private concerto.

Time to go. Armed with all of the relevant clues I've collected, I meet up with Annette, and we walk to the jeweler's together. Ari is already waiting outside. He holds the door open after greeting each of us with a hug.

"Hi, Tomer." I introduce him to Annette. "I finished doing my research on this piece just in time. I'm leaving tomorrow." I don't like the way that sounds. I place the candlestick holder on top of the counter in front of him. I unfurl the note from inside. "Santiago must be referring to the Spanish settlement of the island we know of today as Jamaica. It was the only one of Christopher Columbus's discoveries that his family retained control of for some time. And it was the only government that successfully prevented the Inquisition from hunting down our people in the New World. Even today there are Jewish families who live on that island who can trace their roots to medieval Iberia. My family must have, at one time, been among them." I think of the flight I need to take tomorrow, grateful I have Meclizine to rely on, not even wanting to imagine what a day on an ancient ship would have felt like, never mind weeks on one. Spain to Jamaica to the United States, and who knows where in between. My ancestors' perseverance in maintaining their identity, and their strength to survive, gave me the freedom I so value, the love of life I embrace. I can best thank them by making sure the trend continues with their descendants, my descendants. "Though artists would often stamp their work, the creator of our holders seems to have deliberately withheld his identity. I couldn't find any form of insignia on your piece, and there isn't one on mine. Jews didn't have the opportunity to be skilled metalworkers at that time in Spain, so it's likely that these pieces were created by someone who was Catholic and most certainly a highly valued practitioner of his craft. I'm guessing there was gold in both of the candlestick holders and that this Catholic man accepted a personal risk to make them, and give them, so that the recipients would have something of value as they were forced into exile."

"Righteous among nations — even then," Tomer says.

I nod. "I'm guessing that one piece of gold was sold to buy something. Marina filled the empty space with her words of hope and love. She is likely a great-, great- —" I move my hand in a rolling motion to indicate repetition "— great-grandmother of mine."

I thank Ari for the translation of the note. "Marina penned the note to a lover, probably her husband, full of hope and sadness, a note that detailed their planned meeting of the heart, soul, and mind at exactly the same time, although they were to be time zones apart, hence her reference point of sunset in Santiago, Jamaica. Her note suggests that together they would sing to HaShem and welcome the Sabbath, clinging to each other and to their Judaism in the face of adversity. The waxy residue in both candlestick hold-ers indicates that the lovers did as planned." I draw their attention to the actual note and point to the upper-right corner. "See the faded number? 5291. That's the Hebrew year that correlates with 1531. The Inquisition started murdering people in the New World as early as 1528, in the part of New Spain we call Mexico. It must've been the Inquisition's close presence, even in the relative safety of their Jamaican island, that prompted the separation of the couple. It's likely that Marina's husband was going on a ship to find safe land in case they would need to escape again, should the Columbus government no longer be able to hold off the Inquisition. Since Jews knew that Spain, Portugal, France, England, and other nations already exiled them, they were naturally drawn to the promise of the Holy Land, which the Ottomans were ruling then. They were horrible, but not totally horrible to our people at that time. I strongly suspect that Marina was parting ways with her husband, who intended to come here."

"You are trying to connect *El Carrillo* to the story, aren't you?" Annette asks.

"I briefly thought so." I shake my head. "But no. *El Carrillo* is not the ship that brought the candlestick holder. Marina wrote the note in 1531. That was four years before the first coins were ever manufactured in the New World. We have New World coins excavated from *El Carrillo*. Her husband was on an earlier ship." I sigh. "I wish she wrote his name. I wonder if he made it back to her."

Ari waves his hands in repetition. "Your great-, great-,

great-, great- . . . grandfather carried the message from Jamaica to Israel, from the 1530s to today. I imagine that as certainly as he was able to transcend time and give his love to you, he transcended challenges and returned to Marina."

I love that. "That's beautiful."

Tomer looks at me. His tone is deliberate. "This is yours. It no longer has a place in my shop." He then picks up the candlestick holder and he hands it to me.

I shake my head as he nods. I can't even thank him, as I know that opening my mouth will release too many tears. Oh my gosh, I have to get past this. I hug him tightly so there will be no doubt of my gratitude. I wipe my eyes dry with the back of my hand. Annette also has to wipe her eyes dry. That makes me laugh. Which makes me able to speak. "What can I do to repay you, Tomer?"

"Friends don't keep score, my dear Abi. Just remember that you have another friend in Israel."

Saying goodbye to everyone is difficult. Yet I know that I'll be back soon to continue working on *El Carrillo*.

Daniel brings the kids to pick me up at the airport. I hold him and each child before walking to the car. We eat on the way home. We exchange stories and fill the meal with love. None of my feelings for any of them have changed. I love them all so much. Yet, my heart is achy.

Nonetheless, the days fly by.

It's Friday, the first one since I've been home, and it's almost sunset. It's almost Shabbat. Daniel had to leave for California the day after I came home, and the kids are each sleeping at friends' houses. I need the weekend to myself to recover from jet lag, and to tend to everything in the home that has been neglected for a month.

I pick up my original candlestick holder, the one I've had for 25 years, and I place a candle inside of it for the very first time. I then imagine how Marina would have done the same thing five centuries ago while her love lit the other.

Then I open my laptop and dial Ari.

He answers cheerfully. "Shalom."

"You don't sound like you are talking at almost 3:00 in the morning. You don't sound at all sleepy."

"I need to be alert. I have an assignment."

I can hear his smile. "You are sitting in the dark. I can't see you. I miss you."

"What?! It's almost 3:00 in the morning — you don't want to see me." He's still smiling.

"I love you. I do want to see you. And I want to see more than you just sitting there — get to it."

"We can do this the old-fashioned way. Before there were cameras, people relied on the dark mystery of romance."

"Pleeeease . . . There is plenty of time for the mystery-of-romance mumbo jumbo in the future. Come on, please. It's almost Shabbat here, so we shouldn't be talking for long anyway."

"You aren't that religious."

"Well, you need to get back to sleep—"

"Where it has been Shabbat for hours." Ari is a good sport.

I move Marina's Sabbath candlestick holder into view and watch him do the same with her husband's. We each light our respective candles on their identical holders, the same ones that accompanied my ancestors during their challenging times. And we speak words in an eternal language that too many have tried to destroy.

Grateful for the strength of my ancestors, who fought to keep me free, I close my eyes and wave my hands above the flame as together, Ari there and I here, say the Sabbath blessing over the candles:

בָּרוּךְ אַתָּה יְיָ, אֱלֹהֵינוּ מֶלֶךְ הָעוֹלָם, אֲשֶׁר קִדְּשָׁנוּ בְּמִצְוֹתָיו וְצִוָּנוּ לְהַדְלִיק נֵר שֶׁל שַׁבָּת.

APPENDIX:
FACTS WITHIN THE FICTION

I was inspired by real and serious issues to write this novel. I revised it several times with the goal of keeping it entertaining while conveying a message in the most honest, effective and meaningful way possible. I didn't expand on every detail, but for those in which I did, I address them here. And though I decided in later revisions, to remove some scenes, I've left the elaboration on them in this section. I include some resources that I used and encourage further exploration of those and beyond.

Chapter Title — First Page of Chapter
A Lie Encoded Into Law — Page 3
The pre-chapter quote that launches the historical portion of *Loaded Blessings* is a translation of an actual law mentioned in the book *Medieval Iberia: Readings from Christian, Muslim, and Jewish Sources* Second Edition, Edited by Olivia Remie Constable, (Pennsylvania: University of Pennsylvania Press, 2012) page 400.

"Blood libels," which began hundreds of years ago, have today morphed into variations in which Jews—specifically but not limited to Israelis—are erroneously and dangerously accused of consuming or thirsting for human blood—literally and figuratively. One of the great ironies to this accusation is that kosher dietary laws prohibit Jews from consuming any blood at all. Kosher meat is heavily salted to remove any excess blood. The false notion that Jews kidnapped non-Jewish children to use their blood in ceremonial foods, as believed by the antagonists in this chapter, have set the foundation for riots and massacres against Jews across the ages and throughout many lands. Crimes of libel and slander against the Jewish people have been prominent in the Christian world of the Middle Ages and in the Muslim world today.

Somewhere over the Atlantic — Page 12

The Israel Ministry of Foreign Affairs (MASHAV) sent a group of Israelis to set up a field hospital to help the Haitian citizens recover from the devastating earthquake of January 12, 2010. IsraAID went as well and remained in Haiti, providing quality support up through 2017. They've since been working in Puerto Rico and Dominica to help the locals recover from Hurricane Maria, 2017, and have more recently responded to the disasters in the Philippines, Indonesia and North Carolina, USA.

The cholera outbreak in Haiti happened after that earthquake and is linked to UN peacekeepers who inadvertently brought it with them after being exposed to the disease in Nepal. Fortunately, Israel already had field hospitals to help those who fell ill.

The underwater oil and gas fields are real, and shipwrecks have been discovered off the coast of Israel. The shipwreck featured in this story is fictional.

The Eretz Israel Museum, in Tel Aviv, is a real and lovely museum with gorgeous landscaping. The characters associated with it are fictional.

Warning From the Late Bereaved — Page 22

Though Jews, the originators of monotheism, have always faced challenges, it was with the advents of the two other monotheistic spin-off faiths—Christianity, established around 1,800 years after the life of Abraham, and Islam, established about 2,300 years after the life of Abraham—when life became even more difficult for the descendants of Abraham and his son, Isaac.

Muslim rulers, then later Christian rulers, forced Jews to wear identifying markings as part of a system of segregation and demoralization, long before the Nazis forced the Jews to. Every oppressor using that tactic demanded that Jews be marked for isolation and ridicule through visible discs, belts, or patches with varying shapes of a donkeys, discs or Stars of David. The red discs of Spain are mentioned in the introduction to the book by Joseph Pérez, *The Spanish Inquisition*, (Connecticut: Yale University Press, 2005). And, the United States Holocaust Memorial Museum has an online segment, "Jewish Badge: Origins." The article, "History of the Yellow Jewish Star," in the website *Jewish Magazine,* addresses specifically how the Muslims of Granada forced Jews to wear humiliating badges, mentioned in this chapter.

The *Jewish Virtual Library's* section, "Virtual Jewish World: Granada, Spain," and the *Haaretz* article "This Day in Jewish History//1066: Massacre in Granada, Spain," Dec 30, 2012, report how Muslims massacred the Jews of that region in 1066, during the era some refer to as the Islamic Golden Age. Mohammad Ballan wrote a compelling article, "Beyond 'Tolerance' and 'Intolerance': Deconstructing the Myth of the Islamic Golden Age," April 3, 2014 in *Jadaliyya.*

More can be found about the Christian plight under Muslim rule in *Medieval Iberia: Readings from Christian, Muslim, and Jewish Sources* Second Edition, Edited by Olivia Remie Constable, (PA: University of Pennsylvania Press, 2012) pages 61–66, as can a variety of laws and practices the Christians initiated against Muslims or Jews of that era.

The desecration of the Host is another erroneous accusation that has been wielded against Jews for centuries. Volume one of *Letters of Jews Through the Ages,* edited by Franz Kobler (New York: Horovitz Publishing Company, 1952), is a particularly touching compilation of written messages from Jews to Jews. Page 289 references a real woman, Pelain, imprisoned in Germany in 1478 for allegedly torturing a consecrated wafer. The character, Jacinto, reads a portion of an actual letter which I excerpted from Rabbi Hasdai Crescas's account of the 1391 massacre, on pages 272 to 273 of that book.

Approaching Tel Aviv — Page 31

The Air Sickness Bag Virtual Museum is real, and this author is indeed a "Patron of Puke."

Cafe Suzana and any other restaurant I refer to by name, exists (though Buddha Burgers closed in the summer of 2018), as does the Israeli Football League (IFL), the American-style tackle football league.

What's In A Name? — Page 37

Ben and Abi discuss genuine historical figures—Christopher Columbus, Luis de Santangel, and Tomás de Torquemada, and theories as to why those figures might have behaved the way they did.

Archaeological procedures throughout the story have been incorporated with literary license.

Though the ship, *El Carrillo,* is fictional, its namesake, Archbishop Alfonso Carrillo of Toledo, was a real man who refused to allow the Inquisition in his diocese.

Anusim — Page 45

Anusim means "forced ones," specifically Jews compelled to leave their faith due to extreme political or physical pressure, such as in Inquisition-era Iberia and beyond. More can be found at the *Jewish Virtual Library*, "Encyclopedia Judaica: Anusim."

The *Jewish Virtual Library's* section "Jewish Concepts: The Name of God," addresses the mention of HaShem, meaning "the Name," referring to God, who is known by many names. Jews typically do not spell the name of God on anything that can be destroyed.

Every Friday night, before sunset, observant Jews regularly light candles to bring in the Sabbath. Secular Jews might too, with as much or less consistency. Ritual candles used for the Sabbath and Chanukah do not get blown out or in any other way extinguished, and Jewish days are observed from sunset to sunset.

Friar Hernando de Talavera is a real historical figure who was a convert from Judaism and was Queen Isabella's confessor. He did warn *conversos* that they would be persecuted if they did not change their ways. He aimed to deepen their understanding of their new faith and to avert more extreme measures against them, with little success. Joseph Pérez touches upon him lightly in his book *The Spanish Inquisition (Connecticut: Yale University Press, 2005)*.

Distorting Faith — Page 53

Teofilo F. Ruiz details religious events and processions in his book *Spanish Society, 1400–1600* (Pearson Education Limited, 2001), as does Joseph Pérez in his. The first *auto de fé* in the region took place in Seville on February 6, 1481, when the first men and women were murdered by fire by order of the [Catholic] Holy Office. People charged with heresy who confessed to the so-called crime, who publicly repented or kissed a cross, would be "awarded" a quicker death of strangulation before having their bodies burned.

Horrifically, bringing harm to people who don't think the prescribed notions of a nation or religious identity, have not been done away with. And in some cases, governments who subject their more enlightened citizens to punishments such as fines, imprisonments, whippings and death, are rewarded in the global arena—today. Pew Research Center's "Which Countries Still Outlaw Apostasy and Blasphemy?" by Angelina E. Theodorou addresses heinous punishments imposed by governments, some that serve high positions in today's United Nations, for thoughts or actions that democracies do not categorize as a crime. Theodorou writes, "We found that laws restricting apostasy and blasphemy are most common in the Middle East and North Africa, where eighteen of the region's twenty countries (90%) criminalize blasphemy and fourteen (70%) criminalize apostasy." Israel, though erroneously singled out for the harshest condemnation globally and in the United Nations, is not one of those Middle Eastern countries, and, on the contrary, is a country where freedom of religion and thought are valued and protected.

Even the Leaves Can Hear — Page 62
United Nations Watch, a human rights NGO currently led by its executive director, Hillel Neuer, functions to fight for human security, dignity and freedom globally.

The United Nations Educational, Scientific and Cultural Organization (UNESCO) has recognized Tel Aviv for its Bauhaus architecture while funding an academic chair in Gaza to support studies that would destroy it. More can be found in the Canadian paper, *The National Post's* article,

"UNESCO Establishes Chair at Gaza University Accused of Housing Hamas Bomb Labs."

The United Nations Human Rights Council (UNHRC) is comprised of some of the world's worst human rights abusers. Saudi Arabia (which also serves on the UN Commission on the Status of Women alongside Iran who arrests women for not wearing a scarf that covers their hair), since 2017, has allegedly been allowing women to visit a doctor without permission of a male guardian and to drive and at the same time, the government created an app that allows men to track and restrict women. "Apple and Google accused of helping 'enforce gender apartheid' by hosting Saudi government app that tracks women and stops them leaving the country," by Bill Bostock Feb. 8, 2019, in *Business Insider,* touches upon this. In Saudi Arabia, women are prohibited from walking without being covered head to toe and it is a punishable crime to be gay. Every citizen of Saudi Arabi is required to be Muslim. In 2015, Saudi Arabia was the head of a panel of the UNHRC, and it still has a seat in 2018. Human rights abusers continue comprising much of the UNHRC. Qatar, which exploits millions of migrant workers and funds terror groups, Venezuela which intimidates journalists and locks up opposition leaders, Afghanistan, which has routine violence against women and girls, join their colleagues from Saudi Arabia to set expectations for the treatment of people internationally. Iran, Iraq and Saudi Arabia are current (2018) member states of the UN Commission on the Status of Women.

Some higher institutions (universities and colleges) employ faculty deeply hateful towards Jews. They use techniques that would pit Jewish people against one another. "I think separating Jewish identity from Israel as a state is very important." Abi, channeled that quote from the talkbacks, from a UCCM minister, to a student columnist, on an online magazine published by an elite university. The number of professors and university officials given legitimate platforms at some of our finest institutions, to chip away at the only democracy in the Middle East, is chilling.

I recommend checking UN Watch's website and Twitter account regularly. View and circulate video clips like, "Shocked UN Delegates as PLO Abuses Exposed by Palestinian Hero," speech by Mosab Hassan Yousef, and "Banned Speech: Hillel Neuer Takes On UN Human Rights Council."

Before I edited it out, this chapter included information about how Israel withdrew from Gaza in 2005, forcibly removing Jewish citizens, who left most businesses intact. *Christian Science Monitor*'s, "Troubled Season for Gaza's Greenhouses," (October 25, 2005) touches upon this. Islamic militants looted the businesses, preventing Gazans from using them to produce fruit and vegetables, and then shot rockets from their ruins into Israel immediately following the withdrawal. See website IDF article, "Updates: Rocket Fire From Gaza On Israel in Past Week," (June 19, 2012). To protect its citizens, Israel needed to implement a blockade in response to the terror Hamas was unleashing on its citizens. Egypt implemented a security blockade as well, but that is little known. See *The Jewish Virtual Library's* "Fact Sheets: Israel's 'Blockade' of Gaza." If Islamist money was put toward peace and development instead of combat and destruction, the Palestinians and so many others would be much better off.

Committing to Live, Being Torn Apart — Page 78 and Options of Mortals — Page 88

Doorframes of many homes of Jewish families display mezuzahs, decorative cases that contain kosher parchment with a prayer. Some people will touch the mezuzah upon entering the home or room and then kiss their fingers that made contact. *Jewish Virtual Library* covers this in "Jewish Practices & Rituals: The Mezuzah."

Throughout Christendom, synagogues were destroyed or converted to churches. What became Iglesias de San Bartolomé, as mentioned in the novel, was one of them. The article, "The Incredible History of the Jewish Quarter of Seville" on the website, Shavei Israel, touches upon them in greater detail.

"Bar/Bat Mitzvah & Confirmation" (*Jewish Virtual Library*) describes how, when Jewish children reach the age of 12 for a girl and 13 for a boy, they become a Bat (daughter) or Bar (son) Mitzvah (of the commandments or law). They are then expected to follow Jewish law as an adult. This milestone in modern times is often marked with a celebration after the Bar or Bat Mitzvah first reads aloud from the Torah during services.

Ferrand Martínez was a prominent Friar in Andalusia when he provoked Christians to massacre the Jewish community of Seville in 1391, forcing surviving Jews to flee or convert. In Perez's book, his name is spelled Fernand, but in most online documents I came across, it is Ferrand.

Diego de Suson is a real victim of the Inquisition. According to Meyer Kayserling's *Christopher Columbus and the Participation of the Jews in the Spanish and Portuguese Discoveries,* translated by Charles Gross, (New York: Longmans, Green, and Co., 1894), "Several of the richest and most respected men of Seville were soon consigned to the flames—Diego de Suson, who possessed a fortune of ten million sueldos, and who had some repute as a Talmudist; Juan Abolafia, who had been for several years farmer of the royal customs; Manuel Sauli and others. Several thousand persons, mainly rich Marranos, perished at the stake in Seville and Cadiz in 1481. Even the bones of those who had died long before, were exhumed and burned by the Holy Office, and the property of their heirs was ruthlessly confiscated by the state." (Page 34).

The Inquisition was not to draw blood from their victims, so they implemented excruciating methods of torture that avoided doing so. They assigned the killing of alleged apostates or blasphemers (thoughts and actions that should not even constitute a crime) to the kingdom's secular authorities.

Forced Festivities — Page 99
Jews were forced to attend Christian festivities, including the annual Corpus Christi, or face arrests or fines. Though

the parades and celebrations were different in different cities, the description in this chapter includes information that could be applied to describe the basic elements of many.

Marrano, meaning "pig," was said to belittle New Christians (once Jews).

Inquisitors were accompanied by bodyguards. The Grand Inquisitor, Tomás Torquemada, was flanked by hundreds. Names of victims in this chapter are real, as is the name of the Inquisitor who was assassinated. Juan de Esperandeu was a rich tanner who was forced to watch his father burn before having his own hands chopped off and being drawn and quartered and burned as a punishment for killing the Inquisitor Pedro de Arbués, documented in *Christopher Columbus and the Participation of the Jews in the Spanish and Portuguese Discoveries*, by Meyer Kayserling, translated by Charles Gross (New York: Longmans, Green, and Co., 1894).

A Soccer Ball Is Not an Artifact — Page 109
The Peres Center for Peace was founded by former Israeli president Shimon Peres and offers a variety of peace-building programs.

Searching for Life — Page 125
The order of the procession was relatively consistent throughout each *auto de fé*. Teofilo F. Ruiz offers a reliable account in *Spanish Society, 1400–1600 (Pearson Education Limited, 2001)*.

The Last Day of Abraham — Page 136

Luis de Santángel is a genuine historical figure—a Jewish man who became a *converso* and continued serving Queen Isabella. He was instrumental in financing the first voyage of Christopher Columbus.

Many names, including Columbus's (Colombo, Colón), had different spellings and pronunciations in different lands, time periods, and languages. This made finding the balance between authenticity and modern understanding tricky— even for places like Jamaica which was Xaymaca by way of the Arawak native tongue. Columbus called it Santiago.

Churches would decorate their walls with the sanbenitos worn by the Inquisition's victims. Different colors and emblems had different meanings that correlated with the crime and punishment imposed by the Church against innocent men and women. Those to be murdered by fire were forced to wear black sanbenitos during the *auto de fé*. Kriah continues to be an expression of grief today. Often, however, instead of tearing clothing, a mourner would wear a black cloth pin or ribbon.

A Trusted Catholic — Page 145

The Alhambra Decree required all Jews to convert, leave the kingdom, or face death. The Spanish monarchy sent Jews into exile in 1492, and Muslims in 1609. Jewish exiles were prohibited from taking valuables out of the kingdom, most specifically gold and silver. They could sell property, but because buyers knew the Jews were forced to sell, they bought at a pittance.

Jews continue to use Haggadahs today as an accompaniment to the Passover Seder and retell the same account of freedom from slavery from the ancient Egyptians. Removing wine from the glass drip by drip, to acknowledge the sadness in life lost among enemies, is still practiced at each Seder.

In *The Spanish Inquisition*, Jospeh Pérez touches upon how Archbishop Carrillo of Toledo kept the Inquisition away until his successor, Cardinal Mendoza, allowed it.

More about Jewish dietary laws can be found in the *Jewish Virtual Library's* "Jewish Dietary Laws (Kashrut): Overview of Laws & Regulations."

A Frayed People — Page 159

King João II (King John II), the king who did receive the Spanish Jews upon restrictive conditions, did kill his brother-in-law, Duke Diogo of Viseu.

The 1066 massacre of the Jews by rioting Muslims of Granada was previously covered. "The Islamic Trade in European Slaves," by Emmet Scott, in the *New English Review*, (December 2016) succinctly describes the vast Islamic slave trade. An excerpt: "Under sharia law the position of Christians was never secure, and Christian girls were regularly kidnapped by Muslim raiders and sold into the harems of Constantinople and Anatolia. In addition to this, Ottoman policy was to recruit Christian boys into the army and these youths formed the elite core of Janissaries. But they were 'recruited' by force, essentially kidnapped from their families and never again seen by them." "British

Slaves on the Barbary Coast," by Robert Davis (BBC 2/17/11) touches upon the impact of such slavery on the later end of the medieval period.

Salonika is now Thessaloniki, a part of Greece that has a rich Jewish past. Romaniotes are ancient ethnic Jews in Greece, distinct from the Sephardic Jews who settled there after the expulsion from Spain. Some of those Jews converted to Islam following a rabbi they believed to be a Jewish prophet, Sabbatai Zevi, a descendant of the Romaniotes, who chose conversion to Islam over execution, by order of the sultan. The descendants of the Jews who clung to their faith were later subjected to the Nazis who tortured, deported, and killed almost the entire population of well over fifty thousand. For more information on this once-cosmopolitan city, see Yad Vashem's online educational material under the heading, "Traces of History—The Jewish Community in Salonika."

Ruben says, "Next year in Jerusalem." This is a phrase of old said after each Passover Seder.

Fernando Columbus, Christopher Columbus's son, left Spain to stay in Portugal at his Uncle Bartolomeo Colombo's house (Bartholomew Columbus). That his mother took in any of the Jewish children is fictional, though the king ordering the kidnappings was not. (Chapter: New King, Old Horrors).

The Gift — Page 168

Jews were prohibited from bringing gold and silver out of the kingdom, but they were allowed to bring other metals. They got a pittance for the property they were forced to sell.

Three Is Definitely a Crowd — Page 171

IsraAID, MASHAV, and A Wider Bridge are organizations that focus on helping or connecting people. Check out their sites. There are so many great organizations in Israel—I couldn't highlight them all. But I include some in the resource list at the end of this book.

The Spectator's Benjamin Weinthal addresses the horror of Iran hanging innocent people to death from cranes in his article, "Just because European companies can trade with Iran doesn't mean they should." An excerpt from that piece: "A Wikileaks British dispatch from 2008 revealed that Iran had executed 4,000 to 6,000 gays and lesbians in the three decades since the 1979 Islamic revolution." Dan Littauer addresses the horror associated with pressure to undergo gender reassignment surgery in his piece, "Iran performed over 1,000 gender reassignment operations in four years," in *Gay Star News*.

And MEMRI uncovered an especially concerning phenomenon in Texas in which American Muslim children are being taught to revere the Islamic leader, Khamenei, despite his calls for death to the United States. A video of these children is on the *WDN* article, "Houston: Muslim Schoolkids Sing 'Khamenei is our Leader' 'Allahu Akbar . . . We Are Your Soldiers." (March 25, 2019).

Martin Luther King Jr.'s connection to the Jewish people and to Israel is evident in his talk and actions. Few people have so creatively gathered quotes and images that support this than musical artist, Ari Lesser. I'm a big fan. After listening to and watching his video "Ari Lesser—Martin

Luther King Jr.," I suggest looking at his other work that touches upon a variety of topics, including the hypocrisy of the BDS movement, the evil of erroneously accusing Israel of apartheid (and not just because it is a huge injustice to those who've really had to suffer under it), and on and on. He is clever, talented, reflective and fun. His song, "Life," is simply beautiful.

Stratfor's online article, "Israel Confronts Its Changing Demographics" (April 23, 2018) provides a sober analysis of Israel's demographics.

"Christianity Crackdown: Crisis in Nigeria as THOUSANDS killed in 'pure GENOCIDE,'" by Joey Millar (June 30, 2018), in the *Express,* touches upon Islam's threat against Nigeria's Christian community as does the article, "'A Living Hell': Some 3,000 Displaced Nigerian Christians in Agony Amid Slaughter," by Stoyan Zaimov, *The Christian Post,* (Jul 6, 2018).

The Forward addresses the toxicity of distorted intersectionality in, "By Rejecting Jews, Intersectionality Betrays Itself," by Sharon Nazarian, (January 25, 2018). The satirical Mossad Twitter account illustrates the irrationality of this beautifully. Because no one does anti-Israel humor quite like they do, I'll just have to leave it at this: https://twitter.com/TheMossadIL/status/948981791758614528

The Mosaic Magazine's June 2018 article, "Black Lives Matter Has an Israel Problem," highlights the absurdity of The Black Lives Matter movement's policy against Israel. Israelis are simply trying to survive attacks from people who harbor the same dysfunctional ideology as those who are mercilessly attacking the Christian Nigerians, Yazidis, Kurds, etc.

The Alhambra Decree, the comprehensive law against the Jews of Spain, was an official law of the Spanish government from 1492 until it was annulled, almost 500 years later, on December 16, 1968. Descendants of the Jews forced into exile were invited to apply for Spanish citizenship in 2015, and Portuguese citizenship a year later.

Old Family, New Life, More Horrors — Page 184

Jews who escaped to Portugal were soon trapped and abused by discriminatory laws and evil acts. They had to pay to enter and pay to leave. Most had to live in unsanitary conditions on the outskirts and were subjected to disease.

King João did kidnap Jewish children, and he sent them to die on an island and enslaved the adults. The woman pleading to King João, witnessed by the fictional Sancia to spare her children, is documented in *Popular History of the Jews*, Volume 4 by Heinrich Graetz and Max Raisin, (New York: Hebrew Publishing Company, 1919) page 235. For more information about the lost children of São Tomé, I recommend the article "Signs, Sugar, and Slaves: What Happened to the Children of São Tomé?" (2003) by Libi Astaire, author of The Jewish Regency Mysteries. The woman who Sancia encounters right after she sees the woman whose children were stolen, and the conversation that transpired, is fictional.

The hope that King Manuel would be kinder, especially since he freed the Jewish people whom his predecessor enslaved, quickly faded when he took actions to satisfy his prospective wife, the daughter of Queen Isabella. She insisted that he rid his kingdom of Jews, like her mother did. King Manuel didn't want to rid his kingdom of productive, law-abiding people, so he kidnapped Jewish children and force converted them, hoping their parents would follow. Though he gave the option of exile for Jews, he made it extraordinarily difficult for them to leave, with heavy taxes to do so. And few ship captains were approved for transporting them away.

Cork is beneficial for the environment. Laws protecting it in Portugal existed for hundreds of years. The Amorim Group's website on its page, "A hotspot of life," says, "It is estimated that every year cork oak forests retain up to 14 million tons of CO2, a sizeable contribution for reducing greenhouse gas emissions, the main cause of climate change."

I took the liberty of bringing the fictional Ruben into the home of the real Beatriz Enríquez and her son, Fernando, who is also Christopher Columbus's son.

New King, Old Horrors — Page 200
In 1497, King Manuel ordered Jewish children to be kidnapped to force them, and consequently, their parents, to convert and to remain in the kingdom as Christians.

An Unjust Trade: One's Faith for One's Child — Page 212
Jews who converted to Christianity removed mezuzahs and etched over the indentation to form a cross on the doorpost. Though Fernando Columbus and his mother,

Beatriz Enríquez de Arana did live in the home of his Uncle
Bartholomew during this time period, that they took in a sto-
len child is fictional (but that Jewish children were stolen by
order of the Portuguese King—is true). King Manuel misled
Jews, resisting conversion, to gather into the courtyard where
they were assured they'd have access to leave the kingdom.
Instead, tens of thousands were trapped and force converted.
Many died, and none were able to flee. Despite the ongoing
horrors against the Jews of Portugal, a formal Portuguese
Inquisition wasn't established until years later, in 1536.

New Land and Native People — Page 223
Fernando Columbus did journey with his father on his
fourth voyage. And there were converso cabin boys who
were dedicated to Christopher Columbus, on that voyage.
I took the liberty of having Ruben join Fernando as one of
those cabin boys. The ages of the real and fictional boys and
timeline are in sync.

The spelling and pronunciation of names of people and
places often varies throughout history and geography. In
Italian, Christopher Columbus was Cristoforo Colombo
while the Spanish called him, Cristóbal Colón.

Christopher Columbus did use his sophisticated
knowledge of astronomy to trick Chief Huero into believing that the eclipse was a Divine event. Chief Huero's tribe
responded by gathering food to bring to Columbus and his
crew so they would be nourished enough after that.

A ship did arrive in Jamaica in 1509 with the first
Spanish colonists, three years after the Lisbon Massacre.

The Columbus family did fight for ownership of (Santiago) Jamaica and it was given to them by Spain. They kept the Inquisition, which aggressively attacked conversos in the New World, away from Jamaica.

Jamaica — Page 240

The first ship of stolen men from Africa forced to be slaves in Jamaica arrived in 1517. I took the liberty of placing Marina on that ship.

What's in a Date? I Mean, a Day — Page 258

In my attempt to understand how the Gregorian calendar lined up with the Jewish calendar, I noticed how some historical sources said that the Jews were forced into exile from Spain on August 2, 1492, while other historical sources said August 11th. Certainly, both couldn't be correct. Pushing through my stubborn discomfort with math, I aimed to make sense of the discrepancy. Whereas the Julian calendar was still in use in 1492, the correct date of the expulsion of the Jews was August 2nd. That is also the 9th of Av in the Jewish calendar of that year.

In Spain, the calendars switched from the Julian to the Gregorian in 1582 (other countries switched in other years). So, in October of 1582, long after the historical portion of this novel ends, the people of Spain went to sleep on Thursday, October 4th, and woke up the next day to Friday, October 15th. The days in the middle simply did not exist in either the Julian or the Gregorian calendars.

Tisha B'Av is the 9th day of the Hebrew month Av. The

Babylonians destroyed the First Temple on the 9th of Av, 586 BCE. The Romans destroyed the Second Temple, rebuilt in the same location, on the 9th of Av of the year 70 CE. The Jewish people faced injustices and humanitarian disasters on that date throughout history, such as being exiled from their homes in the Diaspora from France, 1182, and England, 1290, and Spain, 1492. Though the date for the Spanish expulsion was initially set for July 31st, it got moved to align with Tisha B'Av, likely not a coincidence.

Throughout history, Jews have faced expulsion from Jerusalem and the areas that make up today's Israel, from various conquerors, including Christian and Muslim; the latter built a mosque on top of the holiest Jewish site and to this day cause trouble for any Jew who dares try to pray on it. No other peoples, except for the Jews, chose to make Jerusalem a capital under their own rule, in ancient and modern times.

The Virtual Jewish Library has a brief History of Jerusalem: Jordan's Desecration of Jerusalem (1948–1967) as does CAMERA 1948-1967: Jordanian Occupation of Eastern Jerusalem. For quick clarity, I recommend a four-minute video produced by Stand With Us titled, "Origins of the Word Palestine." (January 4, 2017)

After the Jews reclaimed the holy sites from the Jordanians following the war of '67, the Six-Day War, which was a defensive war based on legitimate and immediate threats, the Israelis allowed the Islamic Waqf to be guardians of the Temple Mount (where Muslims built a mosque on the ruins of the holiest site of the Jews). This was a pragmatic decision to prevent the Middle East from being consumed by flames. The Islamic Waqf forbids any form of prayer, except for Islamic prayer, on that Jewish site, which UNESCO calls Haram esh-Sharif, in reverence to the Islamic name given to erase the original and lasting Jewish identity of the structure. By ignoring history, UNESCO actively erodes truth, history and justice.

Historian, Tsvi Jekhorin Misinai's, *Engagement* project explores and supports the theory that many Palestinians are descendants of Jews who succumbed to conquest by Christians and Muslims. His website is http://the-engagement.org. The Shavei Israel site has a page, "Do the Palestinians Have Jewish Roots?"

On September 16, 2015, Mahmoud Abbas, the president of the Palestinian Authority, said to his people, broadcasted through government television and posted on his website, "The Al-Aqsa [the mosque built on Temple Mount ruins] is ours . . . and they [Jewish people] have no right to defile it with their filthy feet. We will not allow them to, and we will do everything in our power to protect Jerusalem . . . We bless every drop of blood that has been spilled for Jerusalem, which is clean and pure blood, blood spilled for Allah, Allah willing. Every Martyr will reach Paradise, and everyone wounded will be rewarded by Allah." (Palestinian Media Watch, "Abbas: We won't allow Jews' 'filthy feet'"). Since then, Islamists in Israel sought aggressively to stab Jewish people and ram them with cars as newer techniques of jihad, techniques that have since been exported to lands outside of Israel and against both Jewish and non-Jewish people.

Hamas on Campus is a term that refers to multiple Islamist networks that seek Israel's destruction by using students, most notably the erroneously named Students for Justice in Palestine (SJP), co-founded by Hatem Bazian, a professor at UC Berkeley who also co-founded Zaytuna College, the first Muslim liberal arts college, to distort truths in the Middle East. On April 10, 2004, during a rally in San Francisco, Bazian spoke, "We're sitting here and watching the world pass by, people being bombed, and it's about time that we have an intifada in this country [USA] that change fundamentally the political dynamics in here. . . . They're gonna say, 'some Palestinian being too radical'—well, you haven't seen radicalism yet!" In 2018, with no change to his language or attitude, he was invited by the "Berkeley Peace and Justice Commission" to be a standby officer. Clarion Project describes this in the article, "Berkeley Peace and Justice Commission Appoints Anti-Semitic Terrorist Sympathizer," by Alex Vanness, September 28, 2018. This is a brief video about some Hamas on Campus groups and activities. https://www.youtube.com/watch?v=00PODH73ylo

Palestinian Media Watch archives dangerous and hateful propaganda against the Jewish people, produced and shown by Islamists to Palestinian citizens of all ages. For example, "Hamas to kids: Shoot all the Jews," (May 5, 2014) shows the brainwashing and child abuse the Islamic militants inflict on their own children.

The Taylor Force Act, named after a young American man killed in Israel by a Palestinian terrorist, ends aid to the Palestinian Authority until they do away with using the funds as a reward for their citizens to murder people. The act seeks to have the PA do away with their "Martyr's Fund," the insidious "Pay to Slay," system.

The Quran, chapter 98 verse 6 reads, "Verily, those who disbelieve (in Islam) from among the people of the Scripture and Al-Mushrikun will abide in the Fire of Hell. They are the worst of creatures." It's this real sentiment that the fictional Ari refers to.

In this chapter, I mention the singer Rihanna. But here, I'd like to give another nod to Ari Lesser a talented musician with compassionate and truthful political messages. And a nod to Matisyahu, singer of the beautiful song, "One Day," who stood his ground when he was bullied by the organizers of a Spanish music festival who caved under pressure from the BDS movement to disinvite him—an action linked to him being Jewish. (The Spanish government and Jewish groups pressured the festival organizers, successfully, to let him perform).

WikiIslam, a scholarly resource maintained by ex-Muslims, supplies a description of, "A list of Muhammad's Wives and Concubines." Muhammad had a policy of changing people's names. According to *The Ideal Muslimah* in the segment, "JUWAYRIYAH BINT AL-HARITH," "Changing the names of his [Muhammad's] companions was a known habit of the Prophet (peace be upon him), whether male or female. He did this so that his Companions would shun anything which was related to the time of ignorance."

There were other ancient Jewish tribes conquered by the adherents to Muhammad's newly emerging faith that institutionalized seizure and theft. Modern day jihadists too often have chanted, around the world, for Jews to remember Khaybar, the battle in which Muhammad and those who were loyal to him, attacked an ancient peaceful Jewish tribe in what is today's Saudi Arabia (years after annihilating the Banu Qurayza) and forced the survivors to give the Muslims half the fruit of their labor. The descendants of those Jews were expelled by the caliph that ruled after Muhammad's death. While most Muslims today don't chant, "Khaybar, Khaybar, O Jews, Muhammad's army will return," the influence that inspires the chant is the influence that brings erroneous hatred to the Jews from across the Muslim world and undermines the only country Jews have sovereignty over. *The American Thinker* offers a more detailed description of the attack in, "Muhammad's Attack On Kaybar," by F. W. Burleigh, April, 12, 2015. https://www.americanthinker.com/articles/2015/04/muhammads_attack_on_khaybar.html

Coercive control is now a crime in the UK.

https://www.gov.uk/government/news/coercive-or-controlling-behaviour-now-a-crime

Examples of religiously sanctioned coercive control can be found in the video series Undercover Mosque.

The Bridges for Peace site has an important article that addresses outright lies that are given a boost of credibility by outlets, such as UNESCO, to replace truth. It also addresses the issue around Rachel's Tomb. It's written by Rev. Cheryl Hauer, and titled, "The Battle for Israel's History." (February 2011)

Though there was always a Jewish presence in what is now Israel, it increased through immigration in the late 1800s under permission from the Ottomans. The Jews then improved the economy and land. That attracted many Arabs from nearby regions to move and to settle in what is now parts of Israel, including the disputed territories. There was coexistence, but not entirely without problems. Jews formed Haganah (1920), a military defense unit, to protect farms and kibbutzim from attacks by the local Arabs/Muslims. The Irgun (1931-1948), was a Zionist paramilitary offshoot of the Haganah, that fought to minimize the damage from the Muslim/Arab attacks on Jews. The Irgun did not preemptively fight back until after the Hebron Massacre of 1929 in which Islamic attacks made Hebron Jew free for the first time in thousands of years. The Haganah evolved into the Israeli Defense Forces (IDF).

Upon Israel's independence, when Arab nations joined forces to attack the Jews and drive them into the sea, the Jewish people survived and stood ground. Yet, hundreds of thousands of Jews living in the lands of the Middle East, long before they were conquered and then occupied by Islamic warriors, were forced from their ancient homes. Those Jews escaped to the modern state of Israel, which took care of them. The Arabs who lost their homes in 1948 in the war their brethren started, have been kept in a perpetual state of victimhood and homelessness by Arab/Muslim nations, some who took them in, but who never allowed them to assimilate, even today. To better understand this devastation, deepened by the international community,

I recommend exploring articles written by Khaled Abu Toameh, specifically Gatestone Institute's, "Arab Apartheid Targets Palestinians," (December 27, 2017) and "Palestinian Children: Victims of Arab Apartheid," (December 20, 2018) and Word Press's, "What About the Arab Apartheid?" (March 21, 2010). Documentaries produced by The Center for Near East Policy Research, specifically about UNWRA, can be reached by going to their website and clicking on "documentary films". The *Stop Child Abuse: UNRWA Prepares Child Soldiers for War* video is a succinct, three minute, start.

While Israelis were defending citizens from another attack at the outset of the Six-Day War, they captured Gaza from Egypt (Note: Gaza was once part of the country "Egypt"; never before was it part of a country called "Palestine"). In 2005, the IDF forcibly removed the entire population of Jews who lived in Gaza and withdrew its military presence, leaving behind valuable greenhouses to help the Palestinians of Gaza flourish. Islamic militants in Gaza immediately destroyed the businesses and used the region as a rocket-launching pad against Israel. The world was quiet until Israel implemented a security blockade a couple of years later in response to the constant attacks. Egypt also implements a blockade on Gaza, but that is seldom addressed in the news. *Bridges for Peace* contributor, Joshua Spurlock, addresses that and more in his article, "Did You Know? Surprising Facts about Israel and the Middle East." (August 30, 2018)

I give my dear friend, Burak Bekdil, a nod in this section. He is one of the most courageous, intelligent, and honest writers in a world desperately in need of brave, intelligent, and honest reporters. He hails from Turkey, a country that is becoming less and less friendly to people with those virtues. Though he was the bureau chief of CNBC, and though Israelis did help the people of Turkey during the earthquake of '99, Burak didn't cover that story. I simply combined those events to place him with the characters discussing him. He has, however, written many pieces on subjects that only he covered in Turkey, and he was censored, and then fired, from the Turkish paper the *Hürriyet Daily News*, where he worked for 29 years (which was recently bought out by a pro-government businessman). I learned about *Gatestone Institute* and discovered other wonderful writers, like Khaled Abu Toameh, Bassam Tawil, Fred Maroun, Douglas Murray, Denis MacEoin, Uzay Bulut, and more when I followed Burak there. He is one of the founding members of the online Turkish news outlet *Sigma Insight Turkey*.

Israelis—and now also people from other ideological Western countries—have grappled with the extraordinarily loud and untimely Islamic calls to prayer on outside speakers. The Israelis had to face another public relations nightmare when they tried proposing ways to enforce lowering the, at times painful, volume, especially before sunrise. Though Muslim, Christian, and Jewish Israelis complained about the oppressive noise from the loudspeakers, those who wanted to inflict the Muslim call on the loud speakers five times a day on everyone, accused anyone who wanted to moderate it, as intolerant—at best.

The website, Canary Mission, mentions professors and others who are publicly hostile to Israel and to its supporters, with at-a-glance items documenting publicly accessible activity. Canary Mission cites the accusations they post. AMCHA Initiative is also a good reference for college-bound students who are looking into school selection. Universities have become hotbeds of anti-Israel (and too often, anti-American or anti-Western), hatred based on erroneous or incomplete information. I recommend viewing the documentaries produced by Raphael Shore, *Crossing the Line UK* and *Crossing the Line 2 (US)* to better understand the atmosphere. Behind the Smoke Screen episodes 1 and 2 by Pierre Rehov documents what really goes on in Gaza and who really harms the Palestinian people who live there. (See "Resource" page for links).

Ex-Muslims of North America is a critical organization with an intelligent website full of mini documentaries, articles, opinion pieces and other information to support anyone on a quest for knowledge. It's powered by some of the most remarkable people.

Not Another Exodus — Page 295

A ship full of *conversos* from Spain and Portugal did arrive in Jamaica in 1530. I took the liberty of putting Pedro on this ship.

Hernando Alonso, who served with Cortés and gained wealth in land, was the first *converso* to be killed by the Spanish Inquisition in Mexico, in 1528. More can be found in Edward Kritzler's *Jewish Pirates of the Caribbean (New York: Anchor Books, 2008)*, on page 41. It was that book that influenced the direction mine would go.

The complexity of Ottoman rule is addressed in the novel through the travel considerations of the characters. Though Ottomans (Turks) did treat Jews better than others in the region, they too committed heinous crimes against people, including Jews (when they ransacked Hebron in 1517). Toward the end of the Armenian Genocide, the Turks also deported thousands of Jews from their homes in Tel Aviv (April 1917), homes the Jewish people built on the foundation of sand dunes. Many died from the brutal conditions of the deportation before survivors were able to return to their homes under British rule.

To learn more about the Barbary slave trade (the later name for the era in which Muslim pirates kidnapped and brought much harm to European and African men and women), I again refer you to "The Islamic Trade in European Slaves," by Emmet Scott, in the *New English Review* (December 2016). Raymond Ibrahim's, March 26, 2019 piece in the *American Thinker* titled, "America's 233-Year-Old Shock at Jihad," also addresses this.

It's necessary to challenge the often-mentioned platitude that minorities lived well under Islamic rule before the creation of Israel. Many Muslims don't live well under Islamic rule, much less non-Muslim minorities. Anti-Americanism, romanticizing barbaric times and attitudes inflicted by an oppressive ideology, is becoming too trendy, leading to distorted scholarship. Take for example the 2018 Thomson Reuters Foundation list of the most dangerous countries in the world for women. They listed the United States in the top ten, leaving no room for Iran, which has arrested and tortured many women simply fighting to stop the compulsory hijab, and leaving no room for Turkey, where many innocent women sit in prison under trumped-up charges of terrorism for disagreeing with their authoritarian government. Anti-Zionism and anti-Americanism often go hand in hand. The dangers and quantity of attacking imperfect democracies while overlooking authoritarian regimes are too great to address here, in this novel and appendix, but it is worthy of further and critical exploration.

Rabbi Abraham Zacuto was an astronomer who worked for King João's (Portugal's King John II) court. He is featured in the novel, *The Broken Bracelet*, by Gershon Kranzler.

Jews faced extreme difficulties getting to and being in Morocco as a result of the Spanish expulsion (though not exclusively). There were many riots against the Jews in Morocco. The 1033 Fez Massacre that the fictional Pedro referenced was one of them.

More information about Ciphut Sinan, "the Great Jewish Pirate," and Hayreddin Barbarossa, can be found in Edward Kritzler's, *Jewish Pirates of the Caribbean*.

Prior to Departure — Page 309
Despite the efforts of too many people to destroy the spirit of the Jews, along with their culture and language, they continue to recite blessings in Hebrew with a spirit of optimism, agency, kindness and love of life. The last words of this novel form the prayer Jews have used from ancient times, and of today, to bring in the Sabbath.

RESOURCES

When it comes to the Middle East in general, and specifically, Israel, Western academics and outlets have an agenda. Almost none are completely unbiased – and too few aim to represent truth. Quite often, the loudest and most intimidating voices, the most theatrical settings on college campuses, are designed to block truth. This is a partial list of sources that have proven themselves committed to investigative honesty, courage, justice and liberty.

News and opinion sites that are pro-Israel, pro-coexistence and have much journalist and academic integrity.

Gatestone Institute
https://www.gatestoneinstitute.org/

Middle East Forum (MEF)
http://www.meforum.org/

Begin-Sadat Center for Strategic Studies
https://besacenter.org/

The Center for Near East Policy Research
http://www.cfnepr.com/site/index.asp?depart_
id=205640&lat=en

Mosaic
https://mosaicmagazine.com/

Tablet
http://www.tabletmag.com/

The Algemeiner
https://www.algemeiner.com/

The Tower Magazine
http://www.thetower.org/magazine/

Blogs with fun and flair:

Elder of Ziyon
http://elderofziyon.blogspot.com/

Israellycool
http://www.israellycool.com/

Boycott Israeli Goods (Satire/serious- pro-Israel)
https://boycottisraeligoods.wordpress.com/

The Mideast Beast (satire)
http://www.themideastbeast.com/

Twitter with Fun and Flair:

The Zioness Movement
https://twitter.com/zionessmovement?lang=en

The Mossad
https://twitter.com/themossadil?lang=en

News Sources from Israel:

United with Israel
https://unitedwithisrael.org/

World Israel News
https://worldisraelnews.com/

The Times of Israel
http://www.timesofisrael.com/

The Jerusalem Post
http://www.jpost.com/

Arutz Sheva - Israel National News (more conservative)

http://www.israelnationalnews.com/

About Jews and Israel:

Jewish Virtual Library
http://www.jewishvirtuallibrary.org/

Jewish Wikipedia
http://www.jewishwikipedia.info/index.html

Shavei Israel
https://shavei.org/

College Cautionary sites:

Hamas on Campus
http://www.hamasoncampus.org/

Canary Mission
https://canarymission.org/

Amcha Initiative
http://www.amchainitiative.org/

Campus Watch (founded by Daniel Pipes of MEF)
http://www.campus-watch.org/

CAMERA on Campus
http://www.cameraoncampus.org/

Stand With Us
http://www.standwithus.com/

Organizations that improve Israel and/or the world and bring support and comfort to those in need:

Peres Center for Peace
http://www.peres-center.org/

Ex-Muslims of North America
https://www.exmna.org/

Free Hearts, Free Minds
https://www.freeheartsfreeminds.com/

IsraAID
http://www.israaid.org/

Save a Child's Heart (SACH)
https://www.saveachildsheart.com/

MASHAV
http://mfa.gov.il/MFA/mashav/What_We_Do/Pages/default.aspx

UN Watch
https://www.unwatch.org/en/

Hillel Neuer, the director, is featured speaking out in many short clips - here is one: https://www.youtube.com/watch?v=35eEljsSQfc

Ayaan Hirsi Ali's
https://www.theahafoundation.org/

The Jewish National Fund
https://www.jnf.org/

Footsteps
https://www.footstepsorg.org/about-us/

A Wider Bridge
http://awiderbridge.org/

United Hatzalah
https://israelrescue.org/

Magen David Adom
https://afmda.org/about-us/

Media Monitoring Sites, translations, links analyses:

Committee for Accuracy in Middle East Reporting in
America (CAMERA)
http://www.camera.org/?x_context=24

NGO Monitor
http://www.ngo-monitor.org/

Americans for Peace and Tolerance
http://www.peaceandtolerance.org/

WikiIslam (Endorsed by ex-Muslims of North America)
https://wikiislam.net/wiki/List_of_Muhammads_Wives_
and_Concubines

The Middle East Media Research Institute (MEMRI)
https://www.memri.org/

Palestinian Media Watch
https://www.palwatch.org/

The Clarion Project
https://clarionproject.org/

Honest Reporting
https://honestreporting.com/

Organizations that support Israel politically:

American Israel Public Affairs Committee (AIPAC)
https://www.aipac.org/

Christians United for Israel (CUFI)
https://www.foi.org/vision/

Documentaries:

Above and Beyond produced by Nancy Spielberg

The J Street Challenge produced by Charles Jacobs (For those who support J Street and those who don't, because it is really important to understand what you are fighting for):
https://www.youtube.com/watch?v=9zDZ-BjEisc

Stop Child Abuse: UNRWA Prepares Child Soldiers for War (three minutes) produced by David Bedein
https://www.youtube.com/watch?v=PjrxpxDIAks

Or look at any documentaries published by the Center for Near East Policy Research site:
http://www.cfnepr.com/205640/Movies

Crossing the Line 2: The New Face of Anti-Semitism on Campus Official Full Film, produced by Raphael Shore :
https://www.youtube.com/watch?v=tNDCcsH_wgU

Crossing The Line (UK):
https://www.youtube.com/watch?v=uGtrvAv1Nr4

Behind the Smoke Screen directed by Pierre Rehov, Parts I and II:
https://www.youtube.com/watch?v=c7OoPiNBlJI
https://www.youtube.com/watch?v=YoqhjKjuQac

A brief 4.5 minute tutorial on the "Origins of the Word Palestine":
https://www.youtube.com/watch?v=BHsqVB9nxFY

And for facts and fun:
68 Facts You Probably Didn't Know About Israel:
https://www.youtube.com/watch?v=i3wmT2wH690

Acknowledgements

―――――◆◇◆◇◆◇◆―――――

If it were not for the support of my husband, Steve, I wouldn't have been able to complete, nor even start, writing this book. In 1989, when I was a homebody in college contemplating a study abroad program in Israel, Steve, my boyfriend at the time, well versed in the Middle East, encouraged me to go.

Steve, I can't thank you enough for your confidence and support and for challenging me to stay tempered with a subject that makes me so emotional. Thank you for always being there as a sounding board, a cheerleader, a critic, an editor and a quasi tech specialist. Thank you for encouraging me to study in Israel while we were in college, and for being my best friend for 30 years and counting. I love you!

As I do my most wonderful "distractions." I'm grateful to Samara for opening my notebook, when I wasn't looking, to sneak in encouraging messages among my scribble. I smiled when I saw her name in the list of names I collected for the ancient characters. That inspired me to use the Hebrew names of my children as characters for the modern setting. Samara's Hebrew name is Zahava which means unrefined gold. Mason's is Moshe. Both made appearances as graduate students of archaeology. I thank Mason for being a patient sounding board and brainstormer when I started developing this story. His soft spot prevented me from killing off more characters than necessary to demonstrate the times. (Spoiler alert) - Mason is the reason Ruben safely escapes his confrontation with the pirates.

Virginia and Michal are remarkable teens who became part of my family as soon as they entered our home.

I'm grateful, with love, to my late dad, Morton Shapiro and my mom, Sandy for providing me with an early foundation in Jewish formal education, even though it was a financial struggle for them to put me through Hebrew School.

A nod to my cousin Annette and her family. They all bring me so much joy! And so glad Natie is back in my life – looking forward to moments with Ben and Jordan, too.

As a student in college, my friend, Paula (Berkun) Binyamin, asked me to go to Israel for a semester with her before I ever considered studying abroad. That nudge opened a world for me. My friend, Barbara Lamontagne, prepared me to speak through the dreaded agent pitch slams and made suggestions regarding various portions of the book. Cielo Ramirez cheered my first draft more than it deserved and insisted that there was a great story there. I worked in several of her suggestions. Rosie Segil also gave me several suggestions to improve the story, as did her mother-in-law, Debby. She also checked out books from her university library. My friend Idan also allowed me to borrow books from his Jewish library and has given me immeasurable support. And Arik believed that

I could effectively relay a message he expressed needed to be told. I have so many friends I'm grateful for, who've listened to me vent about not having enough time to write - I won't be naming all. Some mentions – Cori, thank you for spontaneous long walks in which I could release steam, and Eileen, Grace, Kristin, and Franny - for coffee breaks, and Jodie - for being there in pixels after you moved across the country.

I'm grateful to the Lappin Foundation and to BBYO, organizations whose good works have directly impacted my family.

I wish I could thank the late historian Edward Kritzler, whose book, *Jewish Pirates of the Caribbean*, inspired my novel to take the shape I gave it. By extension, I thank those he thanked for helping him to complete his book. I'm grateful to the people behind the sources I used and cited in my appendix (facts within the fiction). I am incredibly grateful to my country, the United States of America, with all her freedoms, including speech. I fear lies a lot less when truth is not a punishable crime (as it is or is becoming in lands that are less free).

I'm honored to be among the first to employ the young and talented artist, Sophia Smith. Her customized art for this novel inspired the idea for the cover. A copy is on the page following the story. I thank her mother, my friend, Jodi, who is always generous with advice and support.

I thank Tania Helhoski for creating my publishing company logo. My first editor, Joanne Gledhill, gave me substantial guidance on my earliest draft, which I soon recognized to be just a very detailed and long outline. She was a springboard for a better version. I'm grateful to my developmental editor, Ronit Wagman, who was both sensitive and to the point. She offered insight that strengthened the characters and trimmed the story to keep each moment relevant. I've grown tremendously as a writer under her tutelage. And I also learned a lot from my copy editor, Marcus Trower, who fit my project into a tight schedule so that I could hope to publish this novel before the 50th anniversary of the annulment of the Alhambra Decree, December 16th, 2018. I have been my own worst enemy in time.

Thank you to Alan Dino Hebel and Ian Koviak of The Book Designers for their brilliance and patience in designing the cover and formatting the pages. Sometimes it takes a second look before noticing the two silhouettes that face each other on either side of the candlestick, but that first miss adds to the satisfaction.

A special thank you to my dear friend, esteemed journalist, Burak Bekdil. When he was first censored from the Turkish paper he contributed to for decades, I followed his writing to the outlets who would publish his work. By doing so, I was introduced to reliable sources like the *Gatestone Institute*, *Middle East Forum*, the *Begin-Sadat Center for Strategic Studies* (BESA) and *Sigma Insight Turkey*. I've been inspired by his intelligence, compassion and bravery. My gratitude extends to his ideologically similar colleagues who I learn from tremendously.

And of course, I'm grateful for the imperfectly wonderful country, Israel.

About the Author

Loaded Blessings is my first novel. I graduated from Emerson College, earning a BS in Mass Communication and then from Harvard University, earning an M.Ed., focusing on human development and psychology. I attended a semester at Tel Aviv University in Israel and worked as a volunteer on a banana plantation in Kibbutz Magal.

I wish for all people to have an opportunity to be free from any unjust shackles that bind them, be they physical, spiritual or intellectual. I wish for a peaceful world for all – with many blessings, loaded or otherwise.